BLEEDING
HEART
SQUARE

BLEEDING HEART SQUARE

ANDREW TAYLOR

HYPERION
·····
NEW YORK

ISBN: 978-1-4013-0286-3

Hyperion books are available for special promotions, premiums, or corporate training. For details contact Michael Rentas, Proprietary Markets, Hyperion, 77 West 66th Street, 12th floor, New York, New York 10023, or call 212-456-0133.

Book design by Ralph Fowler / rlf design

FIRST EDITION

10 9 8 7 6 5 4 3 2 1

For Ann and Christopher

. . . *don't go of a night into Bleeding Heart Square,*

It's a dark, little, dirty, black, ill-looking yard,

With queer people about . . .

—Extracted with modest modifications from
"The Housewarming!!: A Legend of Bleedingheart
Yard" (The Rev'd Richard Harris Barham: *The Ingoldsby
Legends, or Mirth and Marvels*, Third Series, 1847)

BLEEDING
HEART
SQUARE

SOMETIMES you frighten yourself. So what is it, exactly? A punishment? A distraction? A relief? You're not sure. You tell yourself that it happened more than four years ago, that it doesn't matter anymore and nothing you can do can change a thing. But you don't listen, do you? All you do is go back to that nasty little green book.

Thursday, 2 January 1930

Tomorrow I shall go to Bleeding Heart Square for the first time. It was young Mr. Orburn's idea. I always think of him as young Mr. Orburn, though he must be 35 or 40 if he's a day. He is young compared with his father, who used to call at my aunt's, and she would give him Madeira and seed cake. All those years ago—how time flies.

This is my first entry in the diary, and I feel rather awkward as though I were talking to someone I had only just met. My niece gave me the diary when I spent Christmas Day with my brother and his family. I suppose it was kind of them to ask me, and it was certainly better than having to eat my Christmas dinner at the Rushmere Hotel with the other residents who don't have a family to ask them elsewhere. All the same, it was a little awkward.

Anyway, this is the beginning of a new year and I'm going to put my best foot forward. I have made several resolutions—I shall be cheerful, I shall think of others less fortunate than myself and try to help them, I shall reread every book in the New Testament and make notes as I go. I shall keep this diary. I shall record in it interesting impressions, conversations, thoughts, etc. that come my way. I need to keep active because we all know who finds work for idle hands!

So—back to Bleeding Heart Square. It's such a strange name. I asked Mr. Orburn where it came from but he didn't know.

Memo to myself: find out what the name means.

It's as if you hear her talking, as if she's standing at your shoulder. When it's really bad, you imagine you smell her perfume. You think her thoughts, you dream her dreams.

Now there's a thought: Miss Philippa May Penhow is not dead, only sleeping.

At ten past three on Tuesday, 6 November 1934, Lydia Langstone fumbled in her handbag for the latchkey. The house loomed over her like a dirty wedding cake. A cold wind, flecked with rain, nipped at her ankles. In her haste, she dropped the key and found herself laughing with a sort of idiot joy as she stooped to pick it up.

Leaves shuffled along the pavement. The taxi pulled away from the curb and she glanced over her shoulder at the sound of its engine. The front door was several feet above the level of the pavement and framed by a pair of white pillars.

But this, she thought, will make everything all right. Now. At last.

The key turned in the lock. She pushed open the door. The house was silent, wrapped in the calm that descended on it between lunch and tea when for an hour or two the servants became invisible, wrapped in the mystery of their own lives.

Marcus's hat lay on the polished chest at the foot of the stairs. For once she was pleased to see it. He had been lunching at his club and had said nothing about when he would return. She registered the presence of a second hat, one she did not recognize, but failed in her absorption to draw the obvious conclusion that its owner must be in the house too.

Marcus would be upstairs in his study or the drawing room. Still in her hat and coat, Lydia went in search of him. She ran up the stairs, which were far too large and imposing for the hall below and the landing above. It was that sort of house—it strove to impress and succeeded in sacrificing comfort and convenience.

On the landing, she hesitated a moment and then tried the drawing-room door. The room was empty, the fire unlit. She darted across to the study and opened the door without knocking. Marcus was sitting in one of the armchairs in front of the fire with a cigar in his hand and a glass of whisky at his elbow. He looked up at her and she stopped in the doorway. He stared at her, his face flushed and his eyes wide open.

The visitor stood up and turned toward her. He was slim and dark, with a small moustache and a face like a determined seal's. Marcus, too, rose to his feet, though without enthusiasm, as if reluctantly obeying the dictates of a higher power.

"Ah, Lydia, my dear," he said, articulating his words with the precision of the almost drunk. "I don't think you know Rex Fisher." He turned to his guest. "Rex, this is my wife."

Fisher limped toward her, holding out his hand and smiling. "Indeed, we have met, Mrs. Langstone."

"Of course we have, Sir Rex," Lydia said. "You came down to Monkshill for a weekend. It must have been just after the war."

They shook hands. Fisher had a trick of looking very keenly at you as if you were, for the moment, the most interesting thing in the world. It was at once flattering and alarming.

"And how are Lord and Lady Cassington?" he asked.

"Very well, thank you." She smiled at him. "I know it must sound awfully rude, but would you mind if I took Marcus away for a moment? There's something I need to tell him."

Fisher stood back, the smile still in place. "Of course not, Mrs. Langstone."

Marcus made an inarticulate sound that might have been a murmur of protest. But she gave him no time to think. She left the room and crossed the landing to the drawing room. She heard her husband apologizing to his guest, the closing of the study door and his footsteps behind her.

Once they were both in the drawing room, he shut the door. Irritation made him puff out his lips in what was almost a pout, and his eyes looked larger than ever. When they were children she had thought of it as his angry frog face, though of course she had never told him that. She realized with dismay that he was drunker than she had thought.

"You bloody little fool," he said. "What the hell do you think you're playing at?"

"Marcus, there's something I—"

"Do you realize what you've done?" he interrupted in a low voice. "You've probably scuppered my political career before it's even begun."

"That's nonsense, you know—"

"Rex has got Mosley's ear. But he's prickly as hell, always ready to take offense. And he was about to offer me—"

She took a step toward him, her hands outstretched. "You don't understand," she began. "I—"

"I understand only too well," he snapped. "Marrying you was the worst thing I ever did in my life."

It was as if her mind was seized by a sudden frost. She felt nothing but cold. She could not think, let alone move. She stared blankly at her husband. Something about her passivity seemed to enrage him further. He lunged forward and slapped her cheek with the palm of his right hand. It was a relatively light blow that made her head jerk to one side. She gasped and lifted her left hand to cover the spot where his blow had fallen.

"Dear Christ," he said. "You're such a silly little bitch."

As he was speaking, she knew he was going to hit her again. It was in a sense a continuation of the first blow. Having slapped her cheek with the palm of his right hand, he reversed the thrust of his arm and increased the impetus of the swing. The back of his hand smashed into her cheekbone. The force of the blow was enough to drive her against a chair. The top of its seat caught her just below the knee. She lost her balance and fell inelegantly so her body sprawled partly on the floor and partly on the chair. A jolt ran through her. She cried out with the snaking pain it brought in its wake. She was dimly aware of Marcus standing over her.

"I hope I don't have to remind you again," he said, speaking slowly and clearly as if to a slow-witted servant. "You must not interrupt me when I'm in the study. Never. Understand?"

She shut her eyes and listened to the roaring in her ears. She heard his footsteps receding, the door opening and closing. She rested her head in her arm. Her body was a dark continent like Africa, she thought, full of strange peoples and unexplored places, a source of plunder for greedy men. She tried to make her mind empty, like the Sahara Desert, a perfect vacancy.

Time passed. On the mantel, the horrible French clock that Marcus's parents had inherited from some dusty Langstone great-aunt ticked like a metronome. The pains in her cheek throbbed obediently in time with it. The Langstones controlled even her pain. She thought her cheek might be bleeding but did not want to find out.

At one point the men went downstairs. Fisher was saying something. He had been plain Mr. Fisher when Lydia had met him at Monkshill. Just out of the army. His father had done rather well out of the war, she remembered, and Lloyd George had given him a baronetcy—or more probably sold him one. The old man had died a couple of years ago and Fisher had come into the title. Prickly, Marcus said, and he might be right. The *nouveaux riches* always looked for slights where none existed.

Left to herself, she might have stayed there forever with her eyes fast shut. It was only the thought of the servants that made her move. Sooner or later the maid would come in to draw the curtains and light the fire, and the kettle would go on the range downstairs in the basement, ready for someone to ring for tea. She couldn't face the servants. She couldn't face anyone. She stood up, swaying, and opened her eyes. The light was already fading out of the short November afternoon. She went upstairs to her bedroom.

Of all the rooms in this horrible house, this was the one that seemed the least unwelcoming. She locked the door. Most of the furniture had come with the house—in other words the pieces were grim, ugly and built to last, like almost everything else the Langstones owned. But she had brought a few things of her own from Monkshill and these at least connected her with her former self. And she had her own bathroom.

She went into it and sat down. After a while, she looked at her face in the mirror over the washbasin. Her left cheek was unmarked. But there were signs of a bruise and a faint reddening where Marcus's knuckles had hit her right cheekbone. His signet ring had broken the skin, leaving a smudge of blood, now dried. She squeezed the flesh between finger and thumb. No more blood. *All gone now.* But she still felt the pain.

It struck her as curious that her reflection looked so normal,

so completely unaware that it belonged to somebody quite different now.

When her maid knocked on the door, Lydia sent the girl away, saying that she had a sick headache and did not want any tea. By this
time, she had the smallest of her suitcases open on the bed.

Packing was not something she usually did, and she was surprised to find it so difficult. At first she put in all her jewelry, but
then she took it out and sorted through it, piece by piece, discard-
ing anything that had come from the Langstones. She kept her
wedding ring, because it was a statement of fact, but decided to
leave behind her engagement ring, a diamond solitaire that had
once belonged to Marcus's grandmother. She took her Post Office
savings book, which was still in the name of Lydia Ingleby-Lewis,
but left her checkbook and bank deposit book, which belonged to
Mrs. L. M. Langstone.

She did not know which clothes to take because she had no idea
which clothes she would need. After a while, she lost patience with
herself and filled the case with whatever came to hand. At the last
moment she dropped a snapshot of her sister Pamela inside. Her
pulse seemed to be accelerating. Delay was dangerous. Sometimes it
was better not to think. One should act instinctively, like an animal.

When the suitcase was full, Lydia put on her hat, coat and gloves
and picked up her handbag. She carried the suitcase downstairs. It
was surprisingly heavy. The study door was shut. She glimpsed the
glow of the fire in the drawing room. She heard voices and the clatter of crockery from the basement. The two hats were no longer on
the chest. Lydia opened the front door, went outside and closed it
softly behind her.

The cold air caught her throat. She wished she had brought a
warmer scarf. She walked carefully down the steps and on to the
pavement. The road was empty. There was still light in the sky but
it was the gray, dispirited kind that was worse than darkness. She
walked along the pavement, slightly lopsided because of the

suitcase, and told herself that she was free. She had assumed that freedom would have at least an element of euphoria about it. Instead it seemed to be characterized by a dull sense of misery, a certain amount of physical discomfort and a worrying lack of certainty about anything whatsoever.

She reached the Bayswater Road, a river of hooting, grinding, rattling traffic. On the other side, beyond the railings, was the park where the dusk was further advanced than elsewhere. She saw a taxi approaching and raised her arm. The driver's thin little face was almost invisible beneath an enormous cap. She wanted to say, "It's as if you've got a mushroom on your shoulders." That would have been foolish. She wondered whether she were feverish.

"Where to, miss?"

Until he asked the question, it had not occurred to Lydia that she would have to tell the man where to take her. The problem was, there was nowhere she wanted to go. But the suitcase was heavy and seemed to be growing heavier. She couldn't walk the streets of London forever. She couldn't go to family or friends, either, because they belonged to Marcus as much as to her. She could have asked the man to recommend a hotel, but she wasn't sure how much that would cost or how a respectable establishment would react to the unannounced arrival of an unattached woman with a small suitcase and a bruised face. There was, now she came to think of it, only one possibility open to her, and it had a pleasing sense of finality to recommend it.

"Bleeding Heart Square," she said.

As they traveled east in fits and starts, the driver drummed his gloved fingers on the steering wheel. Outside Selfridges, a woman in an enormous fur coat was buying a red balloon from a man with only one leg. Lydia had been up and down Oxford Street hundreds of times in her life. Now, for the first time since childhood, it was strange to her. She had changed, and Oxford Street had changed with her.

The taxi moved slowly eastward. Holborn was a different country from Oxford Street. It was darker here, too, as though the sun rarely penetrated. The taxi inched its way into the traffic around Holborn Circus and turned left into Hatton Garden. They swung right, and the driver swore at a man weaving his way across the road with the ramshackle absorption of the truly drunk. He pulled up at the curb opposite the opening of a cobbled alley on the right-hand side. The entrance was partly obscured by a brewer's dray.

The cabby slid back the partition. "Here we are. Too tight to drive in, but it's just in there."

Lydia opened her handbag and found her purse. There was a pub called the Crozier on the corner of the alley, its lower windows still shuttered. It was painted a curious shade of red, so dark it was almost purple, that reminded her of a joint of beef in a butcher's window.

The taxi driver made no move to help her as she got out. He hadn't driven into the square or offered to carry the suitcase. Not that it mattered. It was simply that it meant something. She was no longer the mistress of a house in Frogmore Place and another house in Gloucestershire. She was a woman in a plain coat and hat, carrying a small suitcase, who had asked to be taken to Bleeding Heart Square.

She paid the cabby, giving him a smaller tip than she would usually have done. He grunted, peering impertinently into her face, and drove off. Lydia crossed the road, trying to walk like someone who knew where she was going, and marched up the entry. It led to an ill-lit open space, much darker than the street she had left behind. A man passed her, walking quickly, his face no more than a white blur above his upturned collar.

Lydia glanced from side to side, fighting panic. Smudges of smoke drifted across a gray sky. Buildings reared up on every side, some with lighted windows, none matching its neighbor. In front and to the right was the jagged outline of what might have been a small church. From somewhere on the left came the sound of hammering. There were too many shadows for comfort and it was all too easy to imagine the presence of invisible watchers.

Her eyes adjusted slowly to the lack of light. No one seemed to be about. The so-called square was an irregular quadrilateral, with the pub and the church on the two longer sides. She picked her way across greasy cobbles toward an uneven row of houses on the right. The houses were built of smoke-blackened brick, and the ground-floor windows, a mixture of modern and Georgian sashes, were protected with vertical bars. At the far end of the row was a short flight of steps leading up to a paneled door with a grimy fanlight above and a tarnished brass 7 above the letter box. There was a card in the window on the right of the door, bisected by one of the bars.

A/W1

At least the address really existed. Lydia rang the bell and waited. Nobody answered the door. She tried again, ringing the bell and giving a double rap with the knocker.

Almost immediately the door opened, as though someone had been standing just inside waiting for her to use the knocker. A small, plump man stared at her with intense curiosity. He had fair, curly hair and wore gold-rimmed pince-nez attached to his lapel with a black ribbon. His tweed suit looked as if he had slept in it. He smiled at Lydia and rubbed his right hand up and down his trouser leg.

"Yes?" he said.

"Good afternoon," Lydia said. "I'm looking for Captain Ingleby-Lewis."

"First floor," the man said, standing back and holding the door open with an expansive gesture. "Second door on the left."

He stood back to allow her to pass. But the hall was not wide and his arm brushed hers as she passed. She caught a whiff of his sweat, too, overlaying other smells which had something to do with old cooking and inadequate drains and rotten fish. Breathing through her mouth, she walked upstairs, her shoes tapping on the bare boards. She knew he was watching her.

On the landing she paused. The smell was really rather beastly, even up here. She tapped on the second door on the left. The plump man was now climbing the stairs.

"He may be dozing," he called up to her. "Try the door. It won't be locked."

Lydia knocked again. She waited a few seconds, turned the handle and went in, partly to escape the man behind her.

The room beyond was at the front of the house. There were two tall windows. At one end was an unlit gas fire. At the other stood a heavy dining table, its top scarred with cloudy rings and dark burns. An old man in a shabby black overcoat slumbered in an armchair near the fireplace.

Lydia glanced from side to side, taking in unwashed plates, empty bottles, a pile of broken glass beside a table leg, a patched hearthrug and a pair of shoes, lying on their side at the old man's feet. The uppers were well polished but the heels were worn down and there was a hole in one of the soles. She touched the top of the table with her gloved finger. It felt tacky, like drying paint, and left a gray oval smudge on her glove.

A change in the man's breathing alerted her. She glanced at his face, which was dominated by a blunt, swollen nose and a neatly trimmed moustache. His eyes were open.

"Who on earth are you?" he asked, and yawned.

"I'm Lydia," she said. "Your daughter."

Herbert Narton slipped back into Bleeding Heart Square. He was just in time to see the girl who had passed him by the Crozier going into number seven. That fat little man Fimberry had let her in, so she probably knew him or someone else in the house.

The door closed. He glanced around the square. No one was about, though the mechanics at the other end were making one hell of a din in their workshop by the row of garages. He stood back, sheltering in the shallow recess in front of a gate on the other side of the alley from the pub. It wasn't dark but it was such a gloomy afternoon that there was little risk of his being seen unless someone passed close to where he was standing.

At number seven, they had already turned on the electric light in several of the rooms—in Mrs. Renton's on one side of the front door, and Fimberry's on the other. There were also lights in the two windows on the first floor that belonged to the old drunk. Narton had seen him an hour or so earlier, weaving across the square from the saloon bar of the Crozier.

He waited. His feet and hands were freezing. His left wrist was itching again and he scratched it under the glove. In the end his patience was rewarded by a glimpse of the girl on the first floor. He watched her drawing the curtains across the windows. He was too far away to get a good look at her face. But she wasn't wearing her coat anymore. So her connection was almost certainly with old Ingleby-Lewis.

Now that was interesting because, of all the people in that house, Ingleby-Lewis was the closest to Serridge. Perhaps the girl was one of his, and he'd sent her here with a message. She looked a bit old for Serridge but the bastard had been known to stretch a point when there was money to be had.

The doors of the workshop opened, and light and noise spilled onto the cobbles. There were signs of life in the Crozier—it wouldn't be long before they opened up for the evening. Better to call it a day, Narton thought, get out while the going was good.

He walked to Liverpool Street to save the bus fare. The exercise warmed him, and so did the sense that the day had not been entirely wasted. At the station he had time before his train to buy a cup of tea at a stall. While the tea cooled at his elbow, he took out his notebook and jotted down the afternoon's movements.

Not a bad day, taken all in all. No sign of Serridge, of course, but at least he was building up a detailed picture of the house and its occupants. Also, at three o'clock he had seen the young man again, the one Narton suspected might also be watching the house. The chap didn't fit the picture, and he had looked shifty in the unpracticed way that people had when they were generally honest.

Finally, just before he had gone off duty, there had been that girl. He had a hunch about her, and he had learned to trust his hunches. She meant something. She was going to be important.

Around him swirled the crowds hurrying home through the glare, the din and the racket of the station. He didn't want to go home. There was nothing he wanted there, not now. He wanted to go back to Bleeding Heart Square and wait for Serridge.

2

YOU WAKE to another day, another entry in the little green
book. Enter the devil.

Monday, 6 January 1930

*Mr. Orburn arrived promptly at 10:30 in his motor car
and drove me off at great speed to Holborn. On the way he
explained that he felt the time had come to modernize the
house, and that it would be an investment for the future. In
particular, he says we should bite the bullet and install
electricity and overhaul the plumbing arrangements. The
roof needs work as well. I expect he is right, though I
always think electric light is rather harsh and unbecoming
and really gas lighting is perfectly adequate.*

*I must confess that at first sight Bleeding Heart
Square came as rather a disappointment. I suppose the
word "square" had made me expect something rather
grander, and so had the way my aunt used to speak about
the house. In fact the "square" turns out to be a funny
little yard. As you go in, you pass a low-looking public
house with an old pump (rather picturesque) on the corner.*

On the left are what look like workshops and garages, and on the right are some higgledy-piggledy houses, one of which is number seven. At the back of the yard is a high blank wall with a big gate and what looks like part of an old chapel.

Number seven is a gloomy, soot-stained little house at the end of the row. Mr. Orburn showed me over some of it and made suggestions about the improvements he thinks necessary. He believes the cost would not be more than £100, and that we should easily recoup this in the long run.

I met one of my tenants as we were leaving—a Major Serridge. He struck me as rather a rough diamond, like so many military men, but perhaps one of nature's gentlemen underneath. Mr. Orburn introduced us and we had quite a little conversation about the house and Bleeding Heart Square. Major Serridge said it was a very interesting area and he believed it had a great deal of history. I said I should like to find out more about it, and he said that, in that case, he would see what he could do. There was quite a twinkle in his eye, I thought.

Unfortunately, Mr. Orburn had another appointment so we had to leave.

If Philippa Penhow hadn't gone to Bleeding Heart Square on that January day, you and perhaps everyone else might have lived happily ever after, forever and ever amen. Even Joe Serridge.

The air was cold and damp and the horsehair mattress on the truckle bed was filled with lumps of what felt like rock. In the early part of the night there had been a good deal of shouting and, a little after midnight, what had sounded like an inconclusive fight. Lorries rumbled in the distance, their engines mingling with the ebb and flow of the snores next door. In the early hours came the rattling of the early trams, barrows jolting across the cobbles, the whistling of the milkman and the chink of his bottles.

Lydia's room was next to her father's bedroom and at one time perhaps had been used as a dressing room or a closet. It was furnished with a bed, a chest of drawers covered with chipped green paint, and a rickety washstand with a cracked marble top. There were two hooks on the back of the door and also a chair with a broken wicker seat, which she had wedged under the door handle when she went to bed. The fireplace was choked with soot. The only gas fire in her father's flat was in the sitting room.

"You're lucky the room is empty," he had told her. "The last lodger left the week before last."

She left the warmth of the bed a little before eight o'clock and washed unsatisfactorily in the handbasin of the freezing little lavatory at the end of the landing. One of the first of her jobs today would be to rectify the inadequacies of her packing. She had brought Virginia Woolf's *A Room of One's Own* but had forgotten her toothbrush.

The house was still quiet around her, apart from the faint rasp of her father's snoring. The smell on the landing was worse than it had been the previous evening. A piece of fish that had gone off? A rat under a floorboard? Someone really should investigate.

She went into the kitchen opposite the sitting room. Little more than a cupboard, it contained a gas ring, a sink, an Ascot water heater, a meat safe and, below the sink and draining board, a cutlery drawer and a dank cupboard. The only window was a small, cracked skylight. An unwashed saucepan and two mismatched bowls were standing in the sink; they had dined last night on powdered soup, which she had made with her father's guidance. She rummaged in the cupboard but found no sign of tea or milk.

Her mind filled with a vision of the dining room at Frogmore Place with the kidneys and the bacon sizzling on the hotplate, the coffee pot and the teapot on the table. Her mouth watered. Hunger clawed at her stomach. There was nothing for it. She would have to venture into the strange world outside this house.

Her father had given her a latchkey last night when he went out for what he referred to as a business meeting. Lydia left a penciled note for him on his sitting-room mantelpiece. She met no one on her way out of the house.

Outside, the cold, raw air made her gasp. It had a strange, almost metallic tang to it. Two men in brown overalls were looking under the bonnet of a motor car at the other end of the square. They looked up and whistled at her. She ignored them and hurried past a decaying pump on the corner by the Crozier and into the alley to Charleston Street. Opposite the pub was a public library, with a queue of bedraggled people waiting patiently outside the doors. The pavements on both sides of the road were crammed with hurrying men and women in cheap clothes. Clerks, Lydia supposed, or people like that, on their way to work.

She allowed herself to be swept like a twig in a current into Hatton Garden. A flock of young women, chattering as incomprehensibly as starlings, carried her across the road and into the street on the other side. More by luck than good judgment, she found herself in a curving lane called Fetter Passage. Among the row of shops it contained was a small café called the Blue Dahlia. The windows were steamed up but the smell of fried food drew her inside.

Nobody took any notice of her. An enormously fat woman in a stained apron was standing behind a counter. After a quick glance at what other people were eating, she joined the huddle waiting to be served. When her turn came, she ordered tea and a bacon roll. The woman was surly to the point of rudeness with her, though she seemed happy to talk to her other customers, sometimes breaking out into cackles of laughter. The tea came in a chipped white mug. It was milky and sweet. The bacon tasted strong and was mainly fat and rind. Afterward, she wondered whether one left a tip. She wasn't sure how these things were managed, if they were managed at all, in an establishment like this. In the end she pushed a penny under the rim of her plate and hurried out of the café.

One of the neighboring shops sold her a toothbrush, toothpaste, a face flannel and soap. She had at least remembered to pack a towel. The food and exercise had warmed her. She walked south down Fetter Passage into Holborn, where she turned left by the vast Prudential building. She crossed the southern end of Hatton Garden and immediately came to the mouth of a cul-de-sac.

She paused to get her bearings. The cul-de-sac was guarded by two sets of railings separated by a tiny lodge with a disproportionately tall chimney sprouting from its roof. A man in a brown top hat and frock coat was standing by the railings with a pipe in his mouth. His mouth was almost entirely concealed by a nicotine-stained moustache in need of a trim. He saw Lydia and touched his hat.

A small white dog pattered round the corner of the lodge and sniffed Lydia's ankles. She bent down to scratch his head.

"Nipper! Come here!" the man said. "Sorry about that, Miss. He's got an eye for the ladies."

"That's all right—I don't mind."

"The trouble is, you have to watch him. He can be a bit funny with strangers. And his bite's worse than his bark."

The dog sat down and scratched his ear with a hind leg. Lydia looked through the railings at the terraced street beyond. Though still respectable, the houses were clearly past their best. At the end was a chapel or small church. The line of its roof looked familiar.

"Is Bleeding Heart Square over there?" she asked. "On the other side of the church?"

"Yes, Miss. All part of my beat."

"Your beat?"

He waved his hand at the cul-de-sac behind him. "I'm the Beadle for what they call the Rosington Liberty. Chief of police and head porter all rolled into one, at your service."

A car pulled up at the lodge, and the man hurried to swing open one of the roadway gates. Lydia walked on toward a busy crossroads with Smithfield market on the far side. The dark, sour smell of blood and raw meat mingled with the fumes of the gasoline. That, she realized, was the source of the tang in the air as she had come out of the house that morning. Bleeding Heart Square smelled, quite literally, of blood.

Quickening her pace, she turned left into Farringdon Road. A little later she turned left again and discovered that she was back in Charleston Street. A few hundred yards ahead was the sign of the Crozier, the public house guarding the approach to Bleeding Heart Square.

Hugging herself against the cold, she walked back to number seven. The mechanics whistled at her again. As she was unlocking the front door, she heard footsteps behind her. She glanced back. An old woman in a gray overcoat was walking rapidly toward her. The key turned and Lydia opened the door. The woman was now on the steps behind her. Wispy hair escaped from under the brim of a hat like a squashed currant.

"Hello. Are you looking for somebody here?"

"I live here," the woman mumbled. "What are you doing?"

"My name's Lydia Langstone. My father's Captain Ingleby-Lewis."

"Didn't know he had a daughter."

Lydia had no reply to that so she went into the house. The smell in the hall was even worse. She swallowed, trying not to retch.

"Dead cat?" the woman said, making it sound like an accusation.

"I don't know what it is."

She pushed past Lydia and sniffed the air. "It's over there."

She nodded toward the back of the hall, where a table stood near the foot of the stairs. Lydia walked toward it. On the table was a dusty brass gong, in front of which was a tray holding what looked like circulars and a small parcel wrapped in brown paper and tied neatly with string.

She bent down and sniffed in her turn. She pulled back sharply, putting her hand over her mouth and nose. "It's foul. It—it couldn't be something in the parcel that's gone off?"

The woman came to stand beside her. She screwed up her face. "Looks like blood," she said.

"What does?"

"On that parcel."

Lydia stared at it. It was true that there were rusty stains on one side of the brown paper. But surely only a lurid imagination would identify it as blood? To her relief, she heard footsteps above them. Captain Ingleby-Lewis slowly descended the stairs, holding tightly but warily on to the banister rail as though grateful for its support but afraid that it might at any moment give him an electric shock. He was wearing his overcoat but neither collar nor tie. When he reached the safety of the hall, he stared at the two women and rubbed the stubble on his chin.

"Ah—Mrs. Renton. You've met my daughter, I see."

"Is she having the attic?"

"No. What were you talking about? I heard somebody say something about blood."

Mrs. Renton indicated the parcel. "There's blood on it. See? And it stinks, too. It was smelling yesterday, but it's much worse today."

Ingleby-Lewis propped himself against the newel post and frowned. "Who's it for? I haven't got my glasses."

"Mr. Serridge. Postman brought it on Friday."

"Well, he's not here, is he? Heaven knows when he'll be back."

"We can't leave that parcel there," Mrs. Renton pointed out.

"Then you'd better open it," Ingleby-Lewis said.

"Mr. Serridge wouldn't like it. He's most particular about his post."

"Nonsense, Mrs. Renton. I take full responsibility." He glared at her. "Open that parcel."

She shrugged. "If you say so."

Mrs. Renton pulled the knot apart and coiled the string into a roll. She unwrapped the parcel gingerly. The smell grew steadily worse. Finally she drew back the last fold of brown paper, exposing an object like a misshapen egg about four inches long and two inches high. Most of it was a dark, mottled red, but there were streaks of a pale yellow embedded into its texture, and minute white specks milled about almost invisibly on its surface.

"Meat," Mrs. Renton said.

"But it's rotten," Lydia said, shocked.

"I can see that," Ingleby-Lewis barked. Holding his nose, he came nearer. "Damn it, those are maggots. What the blazes is it doing here?"

Mrs. Renton looked at Lydia. "Nothing to do with me."

"What is it, anyway?" he asked in a quieter voice.

"It's a heart, sir," Mrs. Renton said. "A rotten heart."

At half past eleven, Captain Ingleby-Lewis went out, saying that he had an appointment and that he would not be back for luncheon. Lydia wasn't sure what lunch would have consisted of if he had come back because she had found nothing to eat except a small tin of sardines.

Not that it mattered. A trace of the decaying meat that she and Mrs. Renton had found lingered in the air, even here, upstairs and with the door closed. It wasn't so much a smell as a pallid, unlovely ghost that probably had more to do with memory or imagination than actuality. But it was enough to stifle hunger.

Why would somebody take the trouble to send a piece of offal in the post? She tried to think about it as an anthropologist might think about the practices of a primitive tribe. After all, she was in a strange place, among strangers, and no doubt they did things differently here.

She remembered, quite irrelevantly it seemed, how Marcus had shown her a dead rabbit at Monkshill Park when they were children. He had shot it in the head with his .22 rifle. She had known what the outside of a rabbit was like, the fur, the white tail, the long ears. Now, for the first time, she saw what lay beneath the fur: the blood and bone and sinew, and the gray matter of the brain. The discovery made her sick. "Just like a girl," Marcus had said, and laughed.

She went into her room and unpacked her suitcase, marveling at the curious assortment of clothes that she had brought with her. Apart from the hooks on the back of the door, there was nowhere to hang them so she had to put most of them back in the case. She washed the bowls and saucepan in the little kitchen but could not find a tea towel to dry them with. She returned to the sitting room and tidied it as best she could. At least it was warmer here than elsewhere in the flat because she had fed the gas meter with a couple of shillings.

By the time she had finished, the room looked almost as bad as before. She sat close to the gas fire and tried to fill the emptiness by reading *A Room of One's Own*. "One cannot think well, love well, sleep well, if one has not dined well." She wondered whether Mrs. Woolf had ever had to live somewhere like Bleeding Heart Square and lunch on thin air, with the prospect of dining on a small tin of sardines. Her attention strayed to her bookmark, the snapshot of her sister. The photograph had been taken on the Riviera that summer: Pamela looking mischievous in a bathing costume, with a cluster of young men around her. Looking at it made Lydia want to cry.

Her father returned a little after three o'clock. She heard his footsteps on the stairs and his coughing on the landing. He pushed open the door so violently that it banged against one of the chairs at the table. Lydia looked up, closing the book, shutting Pamela and Mrs. Woolf away.

"There you are," Captain Ingleby-Lewis said, sounding mildly surprised.

Swaying slightly and bringing with him a strong smell of beer, he advanced slowly into the room. He pulled off his overcoat and draped it over one of the chairs at the table. He sat down heavily in the armchair opposite hers. His waistcoat was smeared with ash but the suit had once been a good one, and the trousers were neatly creased. Perhaps he put his trousers under the mattress of his bed while he slept.

For a moment they stared at each other. The usual social niceties—"Have you had lunch?" "I see it's stopped raining"— seemed irrelevant here. They were separated by five feet of threadbare carpet and an enormous gulf of mutual ignorance.

"This can't go on, you know," he said abruptly, patting the pockets of his jacket. He took out a packet of cigarettes. "You can see for yourself. It's—ah—it's not suitable."

"My being here?"

"Exactly. You've got a perfectly good home of your own. And a husband."

"I'd rather stay here, Father." The word *Father* felt awkward in her mouth, as though it belonged somewhere else, but it was also a weapon.

"But why do you want to come *here*?" He struck a match with a trembling hand and squinted at her through the flame. "You've got along perfectly well without me for nearly thirty years. To all intents and purposes, that fellow Cassington is your father, not me. Anyway, you're married now. You're Langstone's responsibility. He can give you everything you need."

"I've had enough of all that," Lydia said.

"A wife belongs with her husband, you know."

"This one doesn't."

"And your mother? What does she say?"

"She doesn't know I'm here. No one does. She won't even know that I've left home unless Marcus has told her."

He smoked in silence. A cylinder of ash fell from the tip of the cigarette to the carpet. Somewhere outside a woman was shouting, "So where's it gone then, you bastard? I want it back." She repeated the same words over and over again: "I want it back, I want it back."

Ingleby-Lewis cleared his throat. "I don't mind telling you, my dear, I've had a few ups and downs lately. Shares not doing as well as they might. Taxation. This damned government of ours. It's all changed since the war. If you want to live like a gentleman these days, you have to be as rich as Croesus. The long and short of it is, I can't afford to keep you."

"I needn't be a burden on you."

"But how are you going to live? Have you got any money of your own?"

"A little. And I have a bit of jewelry. I thought perhaps I could sell some of it and that would tide me over until I could get a job."

"But you've got nothing coming in on a regular basis?"

She shook her head.

He sighed gustily. "A job, eh? And what sort of job could you do?"

"I don't know. Anything."

"Can you use a typewriter?"

"No, but I'm sure I could—"

"Have you had any sort of job in your life? A real job, I mean?"

"Well, not as such."

"Not as such," he echoed. "Lydia, have you ever done anything useful? Do you *know* anything useful? There are millions of unemployed out there. Go into that library in Charleston Street any day of the week, and it's packed with the blighters. Why should anyone want to give you a job?"

Lydia glared at him. "I'm sure somebody would. I—I know how things are done, for example. That could be useful."

"How things are done," he echoed, and this time he didn't try to disguise the sarcasm. "You mean, whether the wife of a peer goes into dinner in front of the wife of an ambassador, eh? Which flowers are best for the drawing room in September? I don't think you'll find there's much call for all that. Not around here."

"I'm sure someone must—"

"Perhaps one of your mother's friends might take you on as a companion? Though I'm not sure your mother would be very happy about that. She'd put a stop to it if she could."

"Then I shall advertise. It may take a while but—"

"But if you're lucky you might find a position with the wife of some jumped-up tradesman in Turnham Green." He flicked the cigarette end into the fireplace. "On the other hand you almost certainly wouldn't last five minutes because as soon as you open your mouth you'd remind them what ghastly little snobs they were."

"Father," Lydia said. "I know it may not be easy, but could I at least stay with you for a few weeks? I can pay my own way. And I could help with—with the housework, perhaps."

"Have you ever done any housework in your life?"

"I'm sure I could learn. Perhaps your housekeeper would be able to show me."

Ingleby-Lewis threw back his head and laughed. "I don't have a housekeeper. I don't have anyone."

She frowned. "Surely someone comes in and—"

"No. There's nobody, Lydia, it's as simple as that. Sometimes Serridge's charwoman takes pity on an old buffer and tidies me up a bit but that's out of the kindness of her heart." He leaned toward her. "All right," he said in a gentler voice. "You can stay for a week or two. But I'm telling you now, you won't enjoy it. You're not used to this sort of life."

"Thank you."

"Mind you, I'll have to square it with Serridge."

"Who's he?"

"My landlord, among other things. That parcel downstairs was for him." Ingleby-Lewis smiled at her, exposing brown jagged teeth. "You had better let me have a few pounds for him. He won't let you have the room for nothing."

Lydia opened her handbag and found her purse. "Would five pounds do for a start?"

Her father nodded. He took the money and put it in his wallet. He stood up slowly. "I have to go out for a while. I'll leave you to it, shall I?"

"I wonder . . . what about food?"

"What about it? If you want to buy some, you'll find shops in Charleston Street. Or go across to Fetter Passage." He nodded to her and said, with a ghostly geniality that seemed to belong to a much younger, happier man, "Must dash. Au revoir, my dear."

Lydia listened to him on the stairs. The door banged. She went to stand by the window. Captain Ingleby-Lewis walked slowly and carefully across the square and into the doorway of the Crozier. She waited a moment. From the windows of her father's room you could see the length of Bleeding Heart Square and, on the corner by the old pump, the alley leading past the pub to Charleston Street. On the right was the bulk of the chapel with its pinnacles dark against a sky the color of dirty cotton wool. If she craned her neck she had a glimpse of Rosington Place beyond, where the long, shabby terraces faced each other, cut off from the rest of London by the railings at the end and the lodge where the Beadle stood guard with his little dog. She shivered with a mixture of cold, fear and excitement.

As she was about to turn back into the room she caught sight of the figure of a man standing in the alley near the Crozier. She expected him to go into the pub. But instead he stood looking from one end of Bleeding Heart Square to the other with leisurely attention, as though he were a sightseer. Automatically she stepped back so he would not be able to glimpse her face against the glass.

She wondered idly who he was. Just a young man in a brown raincoat with a flat cap and a muffler round his neck. Perhaps a clerk of some sort or somebody who worked in a shop. One of the army of little people, as Marcus used to say, one of those who needed other people like Marcus to tell them what to do.

The young man hurried out of the square and into Charleston Street, where he glanced up and down as if wary of pursuit. Half a dozen schoolgirls from St. Tumwulf's threaded their way around him. He began to walk rapidly east. Narton, who had been sheltering from the wind on the steps of the public library, crossed the road and followed. He calculated that he had nothing to lose and perhaps everything to gain.

He caught up with his quarry in Farringdon Road. Maybe he was heading for the Tube station. Narton touched his shoulder, and the man swung round, alarm flaring in his eyes. He had a long bony face and the tip of his nose was red with cold.

"Excuse me, sir. Can I have a word?"

"What about? Who are you?"

"My name's Narton, sir. Detective Sergeant Narton." He took out his warrant card and allowed the man a glimpse of it. "And you are?"

"Me—oh, my name's . . ." He paused, and Narton wondered whether he was nerving himself to come up with a false name. "Wentwood. Roderick Wentwood."

"You've got proof of that, have you, sir?"

"Of course I have. Look, what is this about?"

"Perhaps you could show me."

Wentwood muttered something under his breath. He unbuttoned his overcoat and produced a worn brown wallet. Inside was a letter, addressed by hand to R. Wentwood, Esq., c/o Mrs. V. Rutter, 43 Plessey Street, Kentish Town, with a Hereford postmark.

"All right?" Wentwood said. "Satisfied?"

"No call for sarcasm," Narton said mildly. "Why don't we get out of this wind? I could do with a cup of something, and I dare say you could too."

Wentwood's eyes darted to and fro. Maybe he wanted to make a break for it. Surely he wouldn't be so stupid?

"I've done nothing wrong, you know."

"I'm glad to hear it. Let's go and have that cup of tea, shall we?"

The café was opposite the Dead Meat Market at Smithfield. Most of the other customers were men with bloodstained overalls. Narton ordered two teas, trying not to begrudge the expense. They stood side by side, leaning on a shelf sticky with spilled sugar and speckled with ash. Wentwood rubbed a circle in the steamy haze on the plate-glass window and looked out at the lorries and vans in Charterhouse Street. The rank smell of raw meat hung in the smoky air.

"You've been hanging around Bleeding Heart Square," Narton said.

"Not really. I've strolled past once or twice, I suppose. Is there a law against it?"

"Depends why you're doing it. Not somewhere you stroll past by accident. It's a cul-de-sac, Mr. Wentwood. You have to make up your mind to go there."

"I told you: there's nothing suspicious about it."

"But you do have a reason."

"It's a private matter."

"In my job nothing's private." Narton paused. "On the other hand, I've no interest in things that don't concern me. But sometimes I need to know something that's private. Just so I know it don't matter. So I can rule it out. See?"

Wentwood nodded.

"You're interested in number seven, aren't you?"

He nodded again.

"Why?"

"There's a man there. A friend of a friend."

"Why don't you knock on the door and ask for him?"

"Because he's not there at present. Anyway, he doesn't know me. I'm waiting for him to come back."

"Ah." Narton swallowed a mouthful of tea. "And who might that be?"

"His name's Serridge."

Narton felt a glow that had nothing to do with the warmth of the tea. "Now that's interesting."

"What is?"

Narton didn't reply. He produced a packet of cigarettes and, feeling reckless, offered one to Wentwood. "So," he said, bending toward the match that Wentwood held out to him. "Tell me about you and Serridge."

The other man sighed, which made his long face look even more melancholy than it naturally did. "I—I just want to see him. To get an idea of what he's like. He used to know the aunt of a friend of mine."

"Miss Philippa Penhow," Narton said.

"Yes, as a matter of fact."

"And what's your connection with the lady? Do you know her?"

"No. But I know her niece."

Narton fished out his notebook. "Miss Fenella Kensley. Lives with her parents in Belsize Park."

"Her parents have died."

"I'm sorry to hear that, I'm sure," Narton said mechanically, and made a note. "You must be very friendly with her."

Wentwood flushed. "As a matter of fact we're engaged."

"Congratulations."

"It's not official yet. We are waiting until we can afford to marry. That's why I'm here, in a way."

"Looking for Serridge?"

Wentwood shook his head. "In this part of London, I mean. I'm looking for a job, and also for somewhere to live. Somewhere central. And while I was in the neighborhood I thought I'd look at Bleeding Heart Square. Just—just in case."

"In case what, Mr. Wentwood?"

"In case I saw Serridge . . . or even Miss Penhow. Or perhaps he might tell me where to find her."

"You say Serridge doesn't know what you look like?"

"No—I've been in India since '29." Wentwood grinned, which made him look much younger. "The idea was, I was going to make my fortune and then send for Miss Kensley. But it didn't work out so I came back."

"Money," Narton said. "It always crops up somewhere. So maybe that's why you and Miss Kensley are interested in Miss Penhow. In case a little of hers comes your way."

"No, of course not. Though it still seems odd, her just vanishing like that. Anyway, I thought you chaps had decided there was nothing suspicious about the business. Does this mean you think something's happened to her?"

"What do you mean, Mr. Wentwood? Are you asking if she's dead? Murdered, even? Is that what you're saying?"

"I'm not saying anything, Sergeant. Miss Kensley says Miss Penhow's abroad."

"Just suppose she ain't, what then? All we know for certain is that she was last seen in April 1930. So where might she be? And what about her money?"

"I've no idea where she is. And I keep trying to tell you, Sergeant —we're not interested in her money."

"Oh." Narton smiled. "Really?"

"Yes, really. The money comes from the Penhow side of the family, nothing to do with the Kensleys."

"Of course. Though you'd be surprised how many people are concerned about money, wherever it comes from."

3

WHEN YOU READ these early entries, you can't help feeling it was Miss Penhow's fault too. Why didn't she realize that he was flattering her? That he could want only one thing she had to give?

Wednesday, 8 January 1930

This morning there was a letter from Mr. Orburn waiting beside my place at breakfast. He enclosed a memorandum itemizing the works he considers necessary at 7 Bleeding Heart Square. It comes in all to a little over £105, and he recommends rounding it up to £110 in order to allow for contingencies. It seems a great deal of money but I suppose I should go ahead. No doubt Mr. Orburn has a better idea of what is necessary than I do.

He also enclosed a letter from Major Serridge, the gentleman I met on Monday. It struck me as very much like the man himself: gruff and to the point, written in a clear, plain hand; but there was no mistaking the kindly intention behind it. I think it worth copying out here in full:

My dear Miss Penhow,

When I had the pleasure of meeting you on Monday, you asked whether I knew where the name of Bleeding Heart Square came from. I wasn't able to satisfy your curiosity then, but this morning I came across a piece of information I thought might be of interest to you.

According to a man who lodges in the house and has made something of a study of these matters, there is an old legend relating to Bleeding Heart Square and Rosington Place next door. It seems that it was once the site of a palace, of which the only remaining sign is the chapel. Many years ago, there was a ball at which a devil appeared, dressed as a gentleman. He danced a great deal with the lady of the house, who was much taken with him. They danced out of the palace together, and vanished. In the morning, the only sign of her was a human heart, still warm—left in the middle of what is now Bleeding Heart Square!

I'm afraid this is rather a sinister story for a lady's ears, but I thought you would be interested in such a quaint old legend.

Yours very sincerely,
J. S. Serridge

The Major is quite right—it is a sinister tale. It was most sensitive of him to take account of my feelings, though. Of course it is only one of those funny old stories that *abound in these old places. Still, it's not without interest so I record it here.*

Memo: write and thank him for his kindness.

On her second morning at Bleeding Heart Square, Lydia went out for breakfast again. She bought a copy of *The Times* from a newsagent's in Charleston Street, partly to give her something to do while she was at the café and partly because reading *The Times* was an activity that seemed to connect her to the person she had been before she left Frogmore Place.

The same woman was behind the counter of the Blue Dahlia but she showed no sign of recognition. After ordering tea and a fried egg, Lydia worked her way through the pages of the newspaper with a growing sense of unreality. She scanned the Situations Vacant columns and wished she were a man. A stretch of the Thames in its upper reaches had turned a rusty color and thousands of fish had been found dead. The Women's Appeal Fund for German Jewish Women and Children had held a luncheon at the Savoy Hotel yesterday. The Welsh coalfields were in crisis again, and the Prince of Wales had made a gramophone record in aid of Poppy Day. According to the weather forecast London would have local morning fog and probably occasional rain later, though in Fetter Passage there was no later about it.

Her breakfast arrived. Lydia folded the newspaper open at the crossword. "Not shown by game birds (two words) (5, 7)." She ate quickly, alert to her surroundings like a cat in a strange place.

Two men came in and took a table near the door. One was in his fifties, a skinny fellow who threw off his shabby tweed overcoat to reveal a greasy suit. He wore a hard collar but no tie. All his clothes were a little too large for him, as though he had recently shrunk. He hadn't shaved, and his hair needed cutting.

His companion was much younger. His suit was obviously off the peg and his flat cap was frankly awful, the sort of thing a chauffeur might have worn on his day off. But she liked his long face, which seemed crowded with overlarge and irregularly distributed features. It looked unfinished, as though its maker had been tempted away by a more interesting job, which gave it a sort of vulnerability. For an instant he glanced in her direction. His eyes were striking, a vivid blue that was out of place among the muddy browns and shades of gray around him. He looked away.

It was the flat cap that jogged her memory. She was almost sure this was the man she had seen yesterday afternoon, standing outside the Crozier and staring at Bleeding Heart Square.

The door closed behind the elegant young woman who had been sitting by herself with *The Times*. Rory Wentwood watched her walking along the pavement in the direction of Hatton Garden.

"That girl you've been staring at," Sergeant Narton said. "You'll know her again, eh?"

"What? Oh—that one? The one who just left?"

"You've been looking at her all the time we've been in here."

"Not really," Rory said stiffly. "It's just that she—she stood out. One noticed her in here, somehow. Not like the other customers. I was naturally curious."

"Have you seen her before?"

"No."

"Sure?"

"Of course I am. I'd remember."

"She knows someone at number seven. I think she spent the night there."

Rory shrugged. "That's nothing to do with me, Sergeant."

"All right." Narton leaned forward and lowered his voice. "First, I'm grateful you agreed to meet me this morning."

"I don't understand why—"

"Now look here, sir, from what you said yesterday, you've never met Mr. Serridge?"

"That's correct."

"So he's never met you?"

"He doesn't even know I exist."

"Well there's a thing. I've thought it over and discussed it with my superiors. And now I've got a little proposition for you. Could kill two birds with one stone. But it's confidential. Police business, see? You mustn't mention it to a soul, even your young lady."

Lydia unlocked the front door of 7 Bleeding Heart Square with her father's spare latchkey. The hall no longer smelled of rotten meat, only of old cabbage and the bedroom slops. As she was closing the door behind her, she heard footsteps at the back of the hall. It was the plump man who had let her in when she had first arrived at the house.

"Hello, hello," he said, smiling broadly. "It's Miss Ingleby-Lewis, isn't it?" He had a high-pitched, breathless voice, cockney with a veneer of education spread thinly over the vowels. "I hear you're staying with us for a few days."

"It's Mrs. Langstone, actually."

"Beg pardon?"

"My name," Lydia said, and tried to slip past him.

But the man had contrived to pin her into the angle between the table and the wall. He smiled at her and his face twitched. "I don't think we've been properly introduced. I'm Malcolm Fimberry."

"How do you do," Lydia said without enthusiasm. "Now I must really—"

"I'm so glad to have run into you. Seeing as we're going to be neighbors, I understand, in a manner of speaking. It's a friendly house, and that's good because it's much nicer if everyone gets on well together, I always think." He gave her arm a little squeeze for emphasis. "Anything you want to know, you can always come and ask me. I'm on the ground floor, that door there."

Lydia tried to push past him but his arm, surprisingly solid, was suddenly in the way.

"Will you please let me pass?" she said. "I'm going upstairs."

At that moment the door opened behind her.

"Mr. Fimberry?"

The plump man jumped away from Lydia as though she had poked him with a stick. Mrs. Renton was standing in the doorway of the room to the right of the front door. She had a needle in one hand and what looked like a woman's blouse in the other. "If you want your sheets mended, Mr. Fimberry, you'll have to pay in advance this time, if you please."

"Of course, Mrs. Renton. Can't make bricks without straw, can we?" He produced a leather purse and shook a handful of change into the palm of his hand.

"Three shillings will cover it."

He handed her a florin and a couple of sixpences. "Much obliged, I'm sure. Now I really must be off." He aimed a smile midway between the two women. "Father Bertram will be wondering where I've got to. No peace for the wicked, eh?"

As the front door closed behind him, Mrs. Renton stared calmly at Lydia. "You have to watch that one," she said. "Mind you, his bark's worse than his bite."

"Unlike Nipper," Lydia said.

"What?"

"A dog I met the other day."

"Oh, that one." Mrs. Renton peered at Lydia. "Nasty little thing. So you're having the little room next to the Captain's for the time being?"

"Yes. My father thinks it will be all right. But I—I'm not quite sure how things are managed here. In all sorts of ways."

"I dare say the Captain isn't much help on that front."

"I don't know how things are run, you see." Lydia felt absurdly foolish, like a child again. "How the cooking and cleaning are done. That sort of thing."

"A char comes in to do the stairs and the hall and so on," Mrs. Renton said. "And the bathroom and the WCs. It's meant to be once a week. All the flats and rooms share the same bathroom—you know that? She obliges some of the tenants too, including Mr. Fimberry, but not your father. He manages for himself, most of the time."

"What about cooking?"

"There's a kitchen on each floor except the attic. The flats share. But I don't think the Captain has much use for kitchens. Well, that's natural. Nor does Mr. Serridge, come to that. Mr. Serridge has got the other two rooms on your landing."

"I wonder if you would be able to advise me about what to do," Lydia said. "I haven't done much of . . . of this sort of thing. And I'm afraid my father's rather an old bachelor."

Mrs. Renton looked up at her and pursed her lips. Lydia thought how unnatural it was, that someone like herself should be practically begging this old woman for help.

There was a knock on the front door. Mrs. Renton marched in an unhurried way down the hall and opened it. A tall young man was standing on the step. He whipped off his hat, a flat cap, and at that moment Lydia recognized him as the younger of the two men from the café at breakfast.

"Good morning," he said to Mrs. Renton. "I saw the sign in the window—apartments to let. As it happens, I'm looking for somewhere myself."

"Single gentleman?"

"Yes." The bright blue eyes looked over Mrs. Renton's shoulders and stared at Lydia. "What exactly is available?"

"There's the attic flat," Mrs. Renton said. "Bedroom and a sitting room. Share kitchen and bathroom. No meals or laundry."

"I see. May I see the rooms?"

"The landlord likes to show people round himself."

"And when's he due back?"

"Not sure. Maybe tomorrow or Saturday."

"Thank you. Then I'll call back tomorrow afternoon. My name's Wentwood, by the way. Can you tell me what the rent is?"

"You'll have to discuss that with Mr. Serridge. He does all that side of things."

"Righto. Well, thank you for your help." Once again his eyes sought Lydia's. "I'll say goodbye then."

As he turned to go, a postman mounted the steps behind him. Mr. Wentwood stood to one side to allow the man to approach Mrs. Renton. The postman groped inside his bag and produced a small parcel wrapped in brown paper and string. He handed it to Mrs. Renton, who closed the door on the two men and put the parcel on the hall table.

"Who's it for?" Lydia asked.

"Mr. Serridge."

"It looks like that other one."

"None of our business." Mrs. Renton bent down and sniffed it. "Unless it begins to smell."

Lydia was reading *A Room of One's Own* and feeling increasingly envious of Mrs. Woolf:

> *My aunt . . . died by a fall from her horse while she was riding out to take the air in Bombay. The news of my legacy reached me one night about the same time that the act was passed that gave votes to women. A solicitor's letter fell into the post-box and when I opened it I found that she had left me five hundred pounds a year for ever. Of the two—the vote and the money—the money, I own, seemed infinitely the more important.*

Five hundred a year? The money shone like a mirage, a glittering pile of gold, in Lydia's mind. If a woman had that, she could do almost anything she wanted. She dropped the book on the table, dislodging puffs of dust and tobacco ash.

Her father had gone out, and she had the flat to herself. She wandered from the sitting room to her father's bedroom, which was larger than her own and looked out on a gloomy little yard surrounded on all sides by high walls of blackened brick. It was sparsely equipped with the sort of furniture Lydia would have considered inadequate for a servant's bedroom. The air smelled of stale cigar smoke, and there were two empty brandy bottles in the wastepaper basket. She resisted the temptation to look inside the chest of drawers and the wardrobe, partly because she felt it beneath her to pry, but more because she was afraid of what she might find. She pitied her father but pity was perilously close to disgust.

In the sitting room, kitchen and bedrooms, every surface seemed covered with a fine layer of sooty grime, slightly oily. Lydia found a moderately clean dishcloth under the kitchen sink and wiped the woodwork around the sitting-room windows. It was much harder work than she had expected, and much dirtier. Before moving to the mantelpiece, she tied up her hair with a silk headscarf. How did people manage without servants, she wondered for the first time in her life, and indeed how did servants themselves manage?

There were footsteps on the landing and she looked round. The door was open, and Mrs. Renton was staring at Lydia kneeling by the hearth. The old woman sniffed and moved away without speaking. But a few minutes later, she returned with an enamel bucket in her hand and a pinafore over her arm. In the bucket were dusters and rags. She put down the bucket in the doorway and draped the pinafore over the back of the nearest chair.

"The dustbins are out the back in the yard," Mrs. Renton said. "There's a door at the end of the hall."

She nodded at Lydia and marched away. The work seemed a little easier after that, and not just because she was better equipped for it. When she had finished the dusting, she filled the bucket and washed the windows. Even that was harder than it looked because one tended to smear the dirt on the glass rather than remove it.

Lydia worked on until her stomach told her it was lunchtime. There was still no sign of Captain Ingleby-Lewis—she suspected she might find him in the Crozier but she didn't want to put the theory to the test—and nothing to eat in the flat, except those wretched sardines. She would have to go out again. As she made herself ready, she noticed that there was a sooty line on her skirt. She tried to remove it without success. As for her hands, they looked red and wrinkled, like a washerwoman's. She had another vivid mental image of Frogmore Place, this time of her bedroom: the dressing table, with its array of silver-backed brushes and pots and jars; her clothes laid out for her, with her stockings rolled ready for her to put on; and Susan, her maid, hovering near the door, hands clasped, eyes down.

She found a shopping basket in the kitchen and went outside. The fog had lifted but the rain had grown heavier, and her feet slithered on the cobbles. She heard singing, faint but dreary, and guessed it came from the chapel. She walked to the Blue Dahlia in Fetter Passage again. Going there had almost become a habit, and a habit of any sort was reassuring in a world where almost everything was strange.

The café was crowded and full of noise and smoke. She found a place at a table laid for two. She was surprised to find herself much hungrier than usual and ordered cutlets and peas, with plum pie and custard to follow. It would cost her half a crown, plus perhaps a tip. In the last forty-eight hours, she had become conscious about money in a way she had never been before. Soon she would have to sell some jewelry.

While she was waiting for her cutlets, she returned to the crossword in *The Times*. Instead of attempting the clues, however, she jotted down items on a shopping list. Tea. Milk. Bread. As she was wondering whether she should economize and buy margarine rather than butter, somebody brushed her arm.

"Excuse me," a man said. "Do you mind if I join you? All the other tables are full."

She looked up and saw the young man who had come to inquire about the vacant flat. She had seen him in the café before, of course, so perhaps he worked nearby. She nodded and went back to her shopping list. He sat down and ordered the cutlets as well. After a moment, he cleared his throat.

"I say, I don't mean to interrupt, but didn't I see you earlier today at that house in Bleeding Heart Square?"

She looked up. His face was long and bony, with strongly marked eyebrows arching over the unexpectedly blue eyes. There was a small red scab on his jawbone, as if he had nicked himself while shaving that morning. No one could call him handsome but it was a face you could look at more than once. Should you wish to do so, of course.

"Yes—you came to ask about the flat upstairs."

He nodded. "What's it like? Have you seen it?"

"No." She crumbled her roll and allowed her eyes to drift back to *The Times*.

"Curious name, isn't it?"

"Bleeding Heart Square?"

"Yes—do you know where it comes from?"

She shook her head.

"That's what I like about London," he went on, showing no sign of discouragement. "These old corners with layers of history attached to them. They seem to exist in more dimensions than most places do."

"What do you mean?"

"I'm not quite sure I know. I suppose I mean it exists in time as well as space. So there's always more to it than there seems. Only you don't quite know what."

She burst out laughing, not so much at what he said, though that was ridiculous enough, but at his face, whose features had realigned themselves into an expression of mock horror. Rather to her relief, the waitress arrived with her cutlets, which gave her the opportunity to break off the conversation. She ate a few mouthfuls and returned to the crossword.

"Not shown by game birds (two words) (5, 7)." The answer came to her in a pleasing flash. "White feather." She penciled the words into the grid and wondered how the man made his living. His own lunch arrived and for a few minutes they ate in silence. He could be worse, Lydia conceded—at least his table manners were reasonable.

His hands were clean but his arms were too long for his sleeves, and the cuffs of his shirt were frayed and slightly grubby.

He coughed. "I don't know if I should mention this, but six down is 'hostile.'"

Startled, she looked up.

"Sorry," he said, and his face became a clown-like mask of unhappiness. "It's a bad habit. I can't help reading things upside down. Actually, it's one of the more useful things I learned at school."

"I was looking at the clues across first, actually." Nevertheless she filled in the solution to six down.

"It's very trusting of you," he said. "May I see it the right way up? Just to make sure."

There was no help for it. Lydia pushed the newspaper toward him. He would see her embryonic shopping list in the margin of the newspaper. The forced intimacy suddenly jarred on her. It was as though she were a silly little shopgirl, and he were trying to pick her up. Why the hell had she found the man interesting? Perfectly pleasant in his way, no doubt, but—well, not to mince one's words—rather common.

"Yes," he said. "'An exclamation at a crossing place is not friendly.' 'Ho' and 'stile,' you see. It can't be anything else."

Her pudding arrived. She ate it quickly and decided against coffee. When she pushed back her chair to leave, he put down his fork and rose politely to his feet. He handed her the newspaper.

"I hope I haven't spoiled your crossword," he said.

Lydia shook her head but avoided looking at him. She picked up her basket and said goodbye. As she left the café, she was sure that many eyes were watching her. The clerks and lady typists knew she didn't belong here, and so did the man who had shared her table.

The next forty-five minutes were devoted to shopping, which was on the whole an unsatisfactory experience, by turns mystifying and mortifying. How much bread should she buy? How did you tell whether a loaf was stale merely by looking at it? Was the milk fresh? It seemed to her that the shopkeepers treated her with a mixture of surliness and disdain.

With the basket on her arm growing steadily heavier, she walked through the rain to Bleeding Heart Square. The wind was stronger, and the umbrella swayed and bucked in her hand. A taxi had parked in the lee of the chapel, opposite the door of number seven. She put the shopping on the doorstep and opened her handbag, looking for the latchkey. There were footsteps behind her.

"Lydia!"

Panic surged through her. She wanted to scream. Marcus came up beside her and clumsily embraced her. She edged away from his arm.

"Lydia, darling. I didn't realize."

The smell of him turned her stomach. "Realize what?"

He stared down at her, his big pink face alive with concern, hope and even perhaps a form of love. "Oh darling. I didn't realize. It's wonderful news."

Cornwallis Grove lay north of Primrose Hill and south of Hampstead. It was a quiet street of detached red-brick houses, thirty or forty years old, set back from the road in small gardens full of trees. The Kensleys lived at number fifty-one, and so had Rory when he had studied with neither enthusiasm nor success for an MA degree in French literature at University College London.

The four-story house was divided into two maisonettes, the lower of which was leased to the Kensleys. Rory had rented a bedroom on the first floor from Fenella's parents. Mr. Kensley, who had once aspired to be a barrister, felt with some justification that he had come down in the world. With less justification he blamed this partly on his choice of wife, the daughter of a prosperous grocer in Lewisham, though he had lived for much of his adult life on an annuity purchased with the grocer's money. A heart attack had carried off Mr. Kensley in 1932, while Rory was in India. Then, in July 1934, Mrs. Kensley herself had died and the annuity had died with her. That was one reason Rory had decided to come home to England.

He walked from the Underground station at Swiss Cottage. It was already dusk, and housemaids were drawing curtains across windows in Eton Avenue. Leaves clogged the gullies and lay in swaths across the pavement. The first time Fenella touched him, they had been walking down to the station at this time of year; she had slipped on a drift of sodden leaves and seized his arm to steady herself; and somehow by the time they reached the station they had been arm in arm and, if not a couple, aware of the possibility that they might become one.

Fenella was five years younger than he was. When he lived in Cornwallis Grove, she had been only seventeen. She attended a secretarial college for young ladies in Portland Place where you learned about flower arranging and table placements as much as typing and shorthand. Not that she had learned very much. Until her father died, she used to harbor vague ambitions of being an artist.

She was small and slight and looked younger than she was. But what you noticed most of all—or at least Rory had—was how pretty she was. He had tried to write a description of her one evening but was unable to get much beyond a list of clichés. Hair waving like corn in the sunlight. Eyes of cornflower blue. Even, God help him, elfin grace and wayward charm. A pocket Venus.

Of course marriage had been out of the question. He didn't have a job. He could expect nothing from his family, and nor could she. They would need at least four or five hundred a year to set up home together, and jobs like that for someone without experience didn't grow on trees. Which was why he had listened to Cousin Gordon's suggestion. Cousin Gordon had a pal on the *South Madras Times*, a pal who was on the lookout for bright young men. There was an opening in the advertising department. In a year or two, Rory had thought, he would be established enough to send for Fenella, who promised she would come when the time was right.

He hesitated at the gate of number fifty-one. The garden looked untended and desolate. Pushing open the gate, he skirted the patch of oil that marked where Mr. Kensley's car had once stood and struck off toward the side of the house—the former front door was reserved for the occupants of the upper maisonette on the second and third floors.

He rang the bell. When Fenella let him into the house, she led the way into the sitting room, where there was a very small fire.

"How are things?" he asked.

"Pretty grim. I never thought I'd say this but I wish Miss Marr was still here. Or rather, I wish her rent was."

Miss Marr had replaced Rory as the Kensleys' lodger until an encounter in October with a dead mouse under her bed had resulted in a bitter parting of the ways, accompanied by dark threats of a private action against Fenella under the Public Health Act.

"Let's not talk about her. You look tired. Do you want some tea?"

He shook his head. "Listen, I went to Bleeding Heart Square yesterday."

Fenella sat down abruptly and stared up at him. "Why?"

"I know you don't like the idea. But there's no harm in it, surely?"

"It makes me feel like a vulture."

"But darling, that's absurd. Miss Penhow is your nearest relative. Of course you want to find out where she is. She may not even know your father's died."

"I don't think she wants to get in touch with us. I think my father was so rude the last time she saw us that she's decided she's better off without us. I can't say I blame her."

"But your father was her half-brother. That must count for something." Rory sat down opposite her. "Anyway, things have changed since you saw her last. Your mother's died. Quite apart from anything else, you've lost the income from the annuity. And now Miss Marr's gone, too."

"I'll find another lodger. It has to be the right sort of person, that's all."

"And what's going to happen when the lease comes up for renewal next year? You haven't a hope in hell of finding the money. Not as things are."

She turned her head toward the fire. "I'll manage. Perhaps I can sell something."

"What have you got left to sell?" he asked. "You've already sold the car, and that was the only big asset you could dispose of. I thought I'd have a word with that chap Serridge. He must have some idea where she is."

"I don't want you talking to him."

"But if your aunt—"

"And I don't want to think about Aunt Philippa. All right?"

Her voice had risen, and so had her color.

"Two can live cheaper than one," he said, changing his line of attack. "We could get married now rather than wait."

"No. It wouldn't be fair to you."

"Let me be the judge of that." He offered her a cigarette.

She leaned toward him, cupping her hands around the flame of the match. "Rory—it's not just that it wouldn't be fair to you. It's also that—well, you know, we need time to get to know each other again. You've been away for so long. All we've had are letters."

He felt numb. "You want to break the engagement?"

"No. Yes. Look, I don't know what I want—that's the point, can't you see? And then there's Mother. I—I have to grow used to the fact that she isn't here. It was easier with Dad, somehow. But Mother . . . I don't know, her dying came as rather a shock."

"I can wait," Rory said desperately. "Have as long as you need."

"You'd go mad. So should I. Look here, it's not as if we've ever been officially engaged. I just want us to have a breathing space. It doesn't change anything, not really."

Rory thought it changed everything. A moment before he had been engaged. Now he wasn't.

They smoked in silence. Embers rustled in the grate. The only light came from the standard lamp. He wanted to make love to Fenella more than ever. She might even let him if he kept on asking, he thought, but would she say yes out of pity? As a way of saying sorry? Or—and this thought shocked him—because she didn't much care one way or the other?

He threw the cigarette end into the heart of the fire. "I'm definitely not going back to India. I posted the letter yesterday morning. I'll find something here."

"Still in journalism?"

"Or advertising. I've got a few leads."

"Will your father help until you get a job?"

He shook his head. "He couldn't, even if he wanted to. He's got my sisters to think of. Anyway, he's only got his salary." He paused. "I'm looking for new digs. Somewhere more central."

"Will you be able to manage?"

"For the time being."

He had saved a little from his salary in India. His grandmother had left him a hundred pounds when she died last year. He had enough for a few months in London, if not enough to marry on.

"But I can't stay where I am. It's not convenient, and anyway Mrs. Rutter's idea of a square meal is tinned tongue and green slime. I don't suppose you'd consider . . . ?"

Fenella stood up abruptly. "No. I'm sorry. It wouldn't be decent for you to come and live here, and you know it."

"I could pay rent. I could—" He broke off and ran his fingers through his hair. "Sorry. It just seems so damned stupid. These conventions."

"You wouldn't say that if you were a woman, Rory. Can you even begin to imagine what people would say?" She looked at the clock on the mantel.

"I'd better go." He cleared his throat. He wanted to tell her about Narton and the flat in Bleeding Heart Square, despite what the Sergeant had said. He should also mention the improbably smart young lady who had been at both the house and the café.

But she was already on her feet and moving toward the door. Rory felt light-headed when he stood up, as if unhappiness made one dizzy.

"Are you all right for tomorrow evening still?" she said.

"Yes. I suppose so."

"I've got tickets."

"I'm surprised anyone's willing to pay."

"It's a good cause. And the speaker's jolly good. I've heard him several times before."

"I'll call for you about a quarter past seven, shall I?"

The smell of cooking in the hall reminded him of Smithfield market yesterday afternoon, of meeting Sergeant Narton, of raw meat and blood.

Fenella touched his arm. As he turned back to her, she stood on tiptoe and her lips brushed his cheek.

He wound his scarf around his neck. I'm imagining things, he thought. I'm imagining the smell of unhappiness.

4

You see now Serridge was desperate for money. But it was more complicated than that.

Tuesday, 14 January 1930

Major Serridge came to tea this afternoon to show me his engraving. The presence of a bluff military man caused quite a stir among the old tabbies in the dining room, especially the six of them at the table in the bay window, which they treat as their personal property. I thought Miss Beale stared in really quite a rude manner. I know for a fact that she has been here for nearly 20 years. She celebrated her 75th birthday in September. So she must have been about my age when she came to live at the Rushmere. It quite chills the blood to think about it.

But to return to Major Serridge. We had a most interesting conversation. He has served all over the Empire. He was even in China—he spoke very feelingly about the famine they are having at present, and said it was the children he felt most sorry for. He left the Army for a few years but he was soon back in uniform for the Great War.

But when I asked him if he had been on the Western Front, he winked at me and said that he wasn't allowed to talk about it, even now. I suspect he was in military intelligence.

After tea the Major showed me the engraving. It's not his, in fact, but belongs to a man who also lives in my house—some sort of scholar, I understand. It had the date 1778 at the bottom. It showed the splendid palace of the bishops of Rosington which once covered all the land now occupied by Bleeding Heart Square, Rosington Place and several of the surrounding streets. It was a great Gothic building with cloisters, a great hall and a private chapel. Only the chapel now remains, and it's just beside my house!

There was a grand gatehouse, too, which Major Serridge believes must have stood roughly where the Beadle's Lodge now stands at the bottom of Rosington Place. The whole area is still part of the See of Rosington and is known (rather quaintly) as the Rosington Liberty.

Something else happened today. I don't want to make too much of it, but it brightened my day. The Major paid me a compliment, which meant all the more because it was so obviously unforced and unplanned. He asked me why "a young lady like yourself" was living among all the old pussies at the Rushmere—and then he looked quite embarrassed and apologized, saying that he hadn't meant to seem impertinent. I said I wasn't offended at all (!), and indeed I wasn't, though not for the reason he thought!! Several residents are rather younger than I am (in chronological terms, at any rate!!), including Mrs. Pargeter, *who claims she's not yet forty (!!!). I find that very hard to believe, and I'm sure she dyes her hair—no one can convince me that that brassy color is natural. I happened to mention her to Major Serridge, in fact, and he said, "Who? The one sitting by herself? I don't want to seem rude, but she reminded me of something my dear old mother used to say, mutton dressed up as lamb."*

Isn't it strange? Exactly the same words had passed through my mind, just before he spoke them!

The Major also complimented me on my dress—I wore my new afternoon frock, the one with the charming floral pattern. He said what a pleasure it was to meet a lady who dressed as a lady! Then he apologized again! Partly to ease his embarrassment, I said how hard it was to find a good seamstress for repairs, etc., since the war—someone who had an eye for things, too, who knew how things should be done, and who didn't charge the earth—and he said that, as it happened, one of my tenants, a Mrs. Renton, was reckoned a very superior needlewoman and had worked in Bond Street in her time. . . .

Now you realize it was more complicated than you had thought. It wasn't just that Philippa Penhow wanted Joe Serridge. It wasn't just that she wanted a man, any man. It was also that she was terrified of staying where she was with all the aging women, of growing older and dying at the Rushmere Hotel.

The first time Lydia encountered Marcus Langstone, he had been with his family, but she had only the vaguest recollection of his parents and his older brother. Marcus she remembered very clearly because of what he had done.

She had been five years old, which meant he had been eleven, almost twelve, and his brother practically grown-up. It must have been quite soon after Lord Cassington had taken the lease on Monkshill Park. Lydia remembered how big everything had seemed that first summer, not just the house but the gardens and the park. To a five-year-old, it was a place without limits, more like an entire country than a home.

The Langstones arrived in the afternoon. Lydia did not meet them until teatime. Nurse scrubbed her face and hands and brushed her hair so hard it hurt. She was introduced to the visitors and sat by her mother. Adult conversation crashed and roared above her head. She drank her milk, ate her bread and butter and wanted to escape. She avoided looking at anyone so there was less chance of their noticing her. Once or twice, though, she glanced up and caught Marcus looking at her. He was a tall, handsome boy, with blond hair and regular features. He reminded her of a picture of the young Hereward the Wake which Lydia had seen in the *Book of Epic Heroes* in the nursery bookcase. She thought him very handsome.

Her mother said to her, "I'm sure Marcus would like to see the gardens and the park. Why don't you show him round, darling?"

The prospect of being alone with a strange boy filled her with fear. There was nothing to be done about it, however, and a few minutes later the two of them were walking along the path that led from the house toward the monument and the lake. On their right was the high, sun-warmed wall of the kitchen gardens, pierced at intervals by doors. They walked in silence, with Marcus in the lead. At the far end, where the wall ended, there was a belt of trees. Marcus stopped, so suddenly that Lydia almost cannoned into him. Hands on hips, he stared down at her.

"What's that?"

He nodded at a small shed that leaned against the outer wall of the kitchen garden at right angles to the main path. It was almost completely shrouded in trees.

"I don't know," Lydia said.

Marcus thrust his hands into his pockets. "I'm going to find out."

He swaggered into the trees without looking back to see if she was following. She padded after him, feeling that, as his hostess, she had a duty to look after him. There were nettles here and they reached her bare legs. She ran into a spider's web hanging from a branch of a tree and screamed. Marcus glanced back.

"Don't be such a baby," he said, and carried on.

At the end of the path, the tiled roof of the shed sagged and rippled. It was muddy underfoot, and the air felt damp, which was strange because it was a sunny afternoon. In memory, at least, it seemed to Lydia that the little spinney tucked against the north wall of the kitchen gardens had its own climate, its own atmosphere.

Marcus kicked over a fragment of rotten plank lying across the path. Woodlice scurried frantically. There were gray, slimy things, too. Lydia assumed they were leaves, or roots, or even a special sort of stone. Marcus picked up a twig and prodded one of them. To Lydia's horror, the shiny object slowly curled itself around the tip of the stick. The thing was alive. Lydia opened her mouth to scream but no sound came out.

"Slugs," Marcus said, and trod on it. "Do you know what they like to eat?"

She stared wide-eyed at him and shook her head.

"Human flesh," he whispered. "Children for choice. The younger the better, because they taste nicer."

Lydia screamed. She couldn't help herself. She couldn't move. Her mind had no room for anything except a terrifying image of her own naked body covered with those gray, shiny things, browsing on her, nibbling at her, just as the sheep and the Highland cattle browsed and nibbled at the grass of the park. One of the slugs was moving toward her, and another, and soon they would be climbing up her legs and—

Marcus snatched her up, lifting her under the armpits. In an instant she was high in the air and her face was level with his. He held her for a moment at arm's length.

"They'll eat me," she whispered. "The slugs will eat me."

He stared at her, neither agreeing nor disagreeing. Then he hefted her over his shoulder as if she were a sack of potatoes and walked toward the shed. He kicked open the door. Lydia could see down the back of his Norfolk jacket and the line of his long legs to his boots. It was such a long way to the ground. She was safe up here. The slugs couldn't get her.

Marcus lifted her from his shoulders. She shrieked with joy and fear as her head turned through 180 degrees. He set her down on a broad and dusty shelf fixed to the brick wall at the back of the shed. There was a sieve on one side of her and a pile of flowerpots on the other. In the gloom below, Lydia made out the outlines of the machines the gardeners used for mowing the grass. There were wheelbarrows, too, and rusting machinery whose purpose she did not know.

"Don't move," Marcus told her. His face was level with her chest now. "I won't be a moment."

She couldn't have moved even if she had wanted to. She was far too high above the floor. If she jumped off, she knew she'd break every bone in her body, and probably kill herself, and get her dress filthy as well so that Nurse would smack her too.

Marcus returned, his body almost filling the low doorway. He held out his hands to her, the fingers curled into fists.

"Look," he said gently.

Lydia stared at his big handsome face. He was smiling at her. He turned his hands over and uncurled the fingers. On each palm was a glistening slug. They looked even larger than the others, and they were moving.

"I can feel their mouths," he said. "I think they're hungry."

She began to cry.

"It's all right. Don't worry." One by one, he flicked the slugs onto the caked mud floor of the shed. He wiped his palms on his trousers and showed them, pink and empty, to her. "I'm going to make sure you're all right," he said as gently as before. "I'll look after you."

His kindness made her cry even harder.

"We have to make sure that none of them climbed up you while we weren't looking."

At the time, the logic of this had seemed impeccable. She screwed her eyes shut. She felt his hands on her legs. He gripped her knees and held them apart. She whimpered as he pushed up her skirt.

"We have to look very carefully," he said in a voice that was suddenly hoarse, and almost a whisper. "They like it especially here, you see, that's where they really like to eat. So we'd better see if they've got underneath."

It was sheer bad luck that Malcolm Fimberry chose that moment to open the door. Lydia was standing on the doorstep, a latchkey in her hand, and in another moment she might have escaped from Marcus. Her husband was standing there, bareheaded in the rain, and he looked all wrong in Bleeding Heart Square, like an elephant at the North Pole or a racehorse pulling a plough. Nothing in his life had prepared him for this situation and he didn't know what to do.

Fimberry didn't see Marcus at first. "Mrs. Langstone!" he cried. "Been shopping, I see. Let me help you with that basket."

Marcus lost his paralysis. Here at last was something he understood. "No need for that, thank you." His arm shot out and he scooped up the shopping basket. "After you, my dear."

Lydia allowed herself to be herded into the house. Fimberry flattened himself against the wall to allow them to pass. He was wearing a raincoat and carrying his hat and umbrella so he had obviously been on the verge of going out. Nevertheless he shut the door and pretended to be examining the circulars on the hall table. Marcus towered over him—indeed he towered over everything—and the hall shrank because he was inside it. He sniffed, and Lydia wondered whether there was still a trace of Mr. Serridge's rotten heart in the air.

She climbed the stairs, conscious that Fimberry was watching and listening and that Marcus's heavy footsteps were ascending behind her. She led the way into the sitting room. He put the basket on the table and pushed the door shut with his foot.

"You can't live here," he said in a voice that sounded more surprised than anything else. "It's no better than a slum."

"There's nothing wrong with it," Lydia said. "This is where my father lives. How did you find me?"

He dropped his hat on the table and peeled off his gloves. "You've no idea how worried we've been. How could you, Lydia?"

"We?"

"Your mother and I. No one else knows about this . . . this escapade of yours. We've told the servants you were suddenly called away. That a friend was very ill and had summoned you."

Lydia burst out laughing. "It sounds like something out of a penny novelette. Anyway, the servants won't believe you. Servants always know. I don't know how, but they do."

Marcus took out his cigarette case. "I don't find this very amusing."

"Nor do I."

"And then there's Pamela—she tried to phone you and was quite put out when I said you were away."

"You should tell her the truth." She paused but Marcus said nothing. "You still haven't said how you knew."

"About your news, or about where you were?" He held out the cigarette case to her, and she shook her head. "There was a letter from that chap in Harley Street. Enclosing his bill, of course."

"You opened my letters?"

"What else could I do? I was worried. Your quack wanted to recommend some diet or other that is good for pregnant women, so it was damned obvious what was in the wind. I just wish you'd told me."

"I tried. But you wouldn't let me. You remember?"

Marcus turned away to light a cigarette. "All right—I'm sorry. It's just that you came in at an awkward time, and I didn't want to queer my pitch with Rex Fisher." His face reddened. "But let's forget that now. The important thing is the baby. It changes everything."

"Everything?" she said quietly.

He waved his cigarette. "Of course. The main thing is, of course, it will mean an heir. Even these days, that's important."

"An heir to what?" she snapped. "Nine hundred acres in darkest Gloucestershire? A house you can't afford to live in that leaks like a sieve when there is the slightest drop of rain? And the lease on Frogmore Place only has another twenty years to run, and you'll probably have to let it in any case because you've already spent all my money trying to hang on to everything. What's it all *for*, Marcus? I wish you'd tell me."

For a moment she thought he was going to hit her again. "I happen to believe that some things are worth hanging on to," he said. "People like us, we've a duty to maintain standards. If we don't, nobody else will. The landed classes are the backbone of this country, any fool can see that. This socialist rot is all very well—I know some of those chaps are well-meaning enough—but it's leading this country down the road to ruin. Ramsay MacDonald couldn't run a butcher's shop. He's completely out of his depth."

"And my having a baby would somehow drag the country back from the brink?"

"Don't be stupid," he said coldly. "The point is, families like ours stand for continuity. You should listen to Sir Oswald on the subject."

"I don't want to, thank you. Anyway, I'm not having a baby."

"What? But your quack said—"

"You've added two and two and made five. The gynecologist said he could see no reason why I shouldn't conceive. He promised he'd send me details of a diet that's meant to be good for women's fertility and when you're pregnant. That was my good news. I was happy, Marcus, because it means I'm probably not infertile after all. Except I no longer want to get pregnant. But I do want to know how you found out where I am."

Marcus sighed. "I went through your bureau."

"It was locked."

"I had to force it."

"First you open my letters, then you break into my bureau."

He ignored this. "I found a letter from your father, written from this address. I thought he was in America."

"He came back last year."

Marcus raised his eyebrows. "And you didn't see fit to mention it?"

"I didn't think it would interest you. You hadn't shown any signs of interest in him before. Or I thought you'd get angry. Just as you are now."

"Have you been seeing him all this time behind my back?"

Suddenly she felt weary. "Until two days ago I hadn't seen him since I was a toddler."

"But you wrote to him?"

"Yes. I sent him a little money." She hesitated. "That was what he wanted. If you've read the letter, you'll know that. Does my mother know?"

"I told her everything. It was she who advised me to come here. She is as shocked as I am. You must understand—you must come home. Lydia, I—"

Marcus broke off. There were footsteps on the stairs and on the landing. The door opened, and Captain Ingleby-Lewis came in.

He stared at Marcus. "Who's this?" he demanded.

"My husband," Lydia said. "Marcus Langstone. Marcus, this is my father."

Marcus held out his hand. "How do you do, sir."

Ingleby-Lewis shook his son-in-law's hand vigorously. "Delighted to meet you, dear boy." His bloodshot eyes slid from Marcus to Lydia and then back again. "Not quite sure why we haven't managed it before. Still, better late than never, eh?"

"Marcus was just leaving," Lydia said.

"The thing is, sir, there's been a bit of a misunderstanding," Marcus said. "I came here to smooth things over and take Lydia back home."

"Splendid," Ingleby-Lewis said.

"I've a taxi waiting outside."

"I don't want to go back with you," Lydia said. "I'm staying here."

"Darling, be reasonable. You can't stay here. It's not fair to anyone."

"I want to stay here."

Marcus took a step toward her. "Now look here, Lydia—you must see sense."

Ingleby-Lewis cleared his throat.

Marcus turned to him. "I'm sure you agree, sir. A woman's place is with her husband, and all that."

"I must admit, it's not something I've noticed from personal experience."

"Father, please. I'd prefer to stay here. Anyway, I'm not going with Marcus."

For a moment, no one spoke. Ingleby-Lewis shuffled over to the sofa, sat down heavily and closed his eyes. He sighed and said slowly, "If Lydia wants to stay here for a few days, it's up to her."

Marcus glared at her. "This is ridiculous."

"Go away," she said. "Just go away. Please."

"We'll discuss this later. You're making a great mistake."

Her temper flared. "Has it occurred to you that if it's not me who's infertile, then perhaps it's you who should see a doctor?"

His lips were bloodless. He turned on his heel and left the room, leaving the door open. She listened to his footsteps on the stairs. The front door banged. Her father's eyes were still closed and he was breathing heavily. The air smelled of whisky and tobacco.

She went to the window and looked down on Bleeding Heart Square. It was quite absurd, so Victorian. Her fate had apparently been in the hands of two men, her husband and her father, a young bully and an old drunk. Marcus was walking across the cobbles to the taxi. From this angle he looked like a dwarf.

The following day, Friday, Lydia sold the first piece of jewelry. Captain Ingleby-Lewis said that it made sense to sell outright rather than to pawn: you received more money, and of course you didn't have the bother of redeeming it. She chose a small brooch, a ruby set round with diamonds which had once belonged to a great-aunt. The setting was too ornate for modern taste but she thought the stones were good.

Her father took her to a poky little shop in Hatton Garden and negotiated on her behalf with a tall, hunched man who would not offer them more than twenty-three pounds.

Ingleby-Lewis lit a cigarette. "Dash it all, Goldman, you strike a hard bargain. Still, I don't choose to haggle over it. But you'll do the business at once, eh? I don't want to be kept hanging around."

Mr. Goldman inclined his head. "Is that agreeable to you, madam?"

Lydia nodded. She had not expected to feel so humiliated.

"One moment, sir." Goldman opened a door behind the counter and retired into a room beyond.

"We'll not get a better price elsewhere," Ingleby-Lewis confided in a hoarse whisper. "Goldman knows he can't pull the wool over my eyes. And he's not going to keep us waiting either. That's what some of these sheenies do—they give you a price and then take their time paying it. But Goldman's all right as these people go. Serridge uses him a good deal."

"Mr. Serridge sells jewelry for a living?"

Her father glanced sharply at her. "No, no. But he occasionally has pieces he wants to dispose of."

Lydia wondered whether she had imagined a furtive expression on his face. "What does Mr. Serridge do? Is there a Mrs. Serridge?"

"Ah—no. I believe not." He turned aside to blow his nose. Then he rapped the counter with his knuckles and called out, "Come along, Goldman. We haven't got all day."

Afterwards, outside in the chilly bustle of Hatton Garden, Ingleby-Lewis laid his hand on Lydia's arm.

"Ah . . . perhaps you would like me to look after the money for you. It's a lot for a girl to carry around in her handbag."

"I think I'll keep it, Father. There are things I need to buy." She glimpsed the gloom descending on his face like mist. "But I ought to give you something. I ought to pay my way."

He beamed at her. "I won't pretend that money isn't a little tight at present. A temporary embarrassment, as they say." He watched her open her handbag and find her purse. She took out a five-pound note, which he almost snatched from her gloved fingers. "I have a business appointment a little later this morning," he went on. "First, though, I'll introduce you to Howlett."

"Who?"

"The Beadle chap in Rosington Place. He's a bit of an ally of mine."

"I think I met him the day after I arrived."

"He ought to know you're my daughter. Have you got half a crown, by any chance?"

"Why?" she said, thinking of the five-pound note.

"I haven't any change on me. I like to give Howlett something now and again. It's an investment, in a way."

They set off toward Holborn Circus. Smoke drifted up from the chimney of the lodge at the foot of Rosington Place. He rapped on the shuttered window facing the roadway with the head of his stick.

Instantly the dog began to bark. The shutter flew up with a crash, revealing Howlett's head and shoulders. "Shut up," he said and the barking stopped abruptly, as if the dog had been kicked. "Morning, Captain."

"Morning, Howlett. This is my daughter, Mrs. Langstone. Mind you keep an eye out for her."

Howlett touched the brim of his hat. "Yes, sir. We met the other day, didn't we, ma'am?"

Lydia nodded. The dog began to bark again.

"I suppose Mrs. Langstone might find it convenient to use the back gate occasionally," Ingleby-Lewis went on.

Howlett grunted. The dog began to yap again.

Her father turned to Lydia. "There's a gate up there in the corner by the chapel—you can get directly into Bleeding Heart Square from there."

"We don't like all and sundry using it," Howlett said firmly.

"No, indeed. Only the favored few, eh?"

"The little tyke," Howlett observed. "I'm going to have to let him out."

His face vanished from the window. The door opened. The dog ran round the lodge and sniffed Lydia's shoes.

"Beg pardon, ma'am." Howlett edged the dog away from her with the toe of his boot. "Get out of it, Nipper."

"Plucky little brute," Ingleby-Lewis said.

"He's got a terrible way with rats."

"Well. Mustn't stand here chatting all day. Work to be done, eh, Howlett? Here, something to keep out the cold."

The half-crown changed hands. Howlett touched his hat again. Lydia and her father walked up Rosington Place toward the chapel at the far end. The two terraces on either side were drab but primly respectable. Judging by the nameplates on the doors, they consisted almost entirely of offices.

"Must be a living death, working in one of these places," Ingleby-Lewis observed, quickening his pace because the Crozier would now be open. "Just imagine it, eh?"

Lydia stared up at the chapel. Now they were closer, she saw it was much larger than she had first thought. From the other end of Rosington Place, it was dwarfed by the perspective: the height of the terraces created the impression that you were looking at it from the wrong end of a telescope.

"Belongs to the Romans now," Ingleby-Lewis said. "That chap Fimberry is always in and out—knows all about it. Odd place, really. Still, that's London for you, I suppose: full of queer nooks and crannies. And queer people, come to that."

The chapel was set back into the terrace on the left-hand side. A door on the left gave access to the house that abutted on the chapel; there was no other sign of an entrance. Immediately in front of them was a gate, painted murky brown, that sealed the northern end of Rosington Place. It was wide enough for a carriage, and it had a wicket inset in one leaf. Ingleby-Lewis raised the latch.

"Old Howlett's got the only key," he said. "Sometimes he keeps the door locked just to show who's top dog."

"You don't like him much, do you?" Lydia said.

Her father held open the wicket for her. "It's not a question of liking or not liking. Howlett's a fact of life. You want to keep on his right side. Rosington Place and Bleeding Heart Square count as a private jurisdiction, you see. It's a sort of legal oddity—Fimberry knows all about it. In theory even the police can't come in unless they're invited."

The door beside the chapel opened. They glanced toward the sound. A tall young man came out. Lydia caught her breath. He smiled and touched his hat to her before walking rapidly down Rosington Place toward the lodge.

"Who's that fellow?"

"I think his name's Wentwood, Father. He's interested in the attic flat. Mrs. Renton told him to come back today when Mr. Serridge is here."

She stepped through the wicket. In Bleeding Heart Square, a man was standing at the entrance to the public bar of the Crozier and shouting at somebody inside. A mechanic working at the garage at the far end whistled at Lydia. There was a little pile of excrement, possibly human, in the angle between the gate and the pillar supporting it.

Ingleby-Lewis followed her through the wicket and closed it carefully behind him, shutting out the seedy respectability of Rosington Place. "Serridge," he said thoughtfully. "Yes, he'll have to talk to him. And you haven't met Serridge, either, have you?"

Later that morning, while she was tidying the shelves on the left of the fireplace in the sitting room, Lydia came across an old writing box. It was a portable writing desk, a solid mahogany affair, its corners reinforced with brass. When she lifted it onto the table to dust it, however, she discovered that it was less robust than it looked. The lid slid off and fell to the floor with a crash. At some point in the box's history, the hinges had been broken. The fittings inside had vanished as well.

But the box wasn't empty. It held a jumble of pens, paper, pencils, envelopes and inks. The paper was no longer white but turning yellow and brittle with age. Some of the nibs were spotted with rust. Lydia's eyes rested on a small sheet of paper, blank apart from seven words at the top: *I expect you are surprised to hear—*

She pushed aside the sheet. Underneath it was a sheet of foolscap with more writing on it, a long column of names—all of them the same: *P. M. Penhow.*

There was a knock on the door. Lydia dropped the lid clumsily on top of the box. When she opened the door, she found Malcolm Fimberry standing very close to it on the other side. He stared at her through his pince-nez and smiled. His lips were moist and very brightly colored, almost red. He was trembling slightly.

"Mrs. Langstone. I do hope I'm not disturbing you."

"What is it?" Lydia said, knowing that she must sound rude. Mr. Fimberry was the sort of person to whom you found yourself being rude without meaning to be.

"I heard the noise upstairs—I'm just beneath, you see—so I knew somebody was in. I thought perhaps Captain Ingleby-Lewis was here."

"He's not, I'm afraid." Lydia realized that she was still carrying the cloth she had been using for dusting. "May I take a message?"

"Yes—no—you see, it's rather delicate. I lent him ten shillings some time ago, and I wondered whether it was convenient for him to pay me back now. He . . . he said he would pay me at the end of the week—that was last month—but he must have forgotten, and after that when I happened to mention it, it wasn't convenient, but perhaps if you were to have a word with him . . ."

He broke off and lowered his eyes. He seemed to be staring at her chest. She registered the fact that he hadn't shaved and that the stubble on his chin was more ginger than the hair on his head. She also saw that the breast pocket of his tweed jacket was in need of repair and that he hadn't changed his collar for some time.

"It must have slipped my father's mind," she said. "I'll give you the money now."

"Thank you, Mrs. Langstone, you are very kind. I think I saw you and your father near the chapel this morning, didn't I?"

"Yes."

"It's a very interesting building, of course. Did you know that I work there, by the way? In an honorary capacity, that is."

She found her purse and counted out ten shillings in silver. His fingers touched hers as the money changed hands.

"Father Bertram calls me his assistant sexton." He gave a little laugh that was unexpectedly high and girlish. "Perhaps you would allow me to give you a guided tour. There are so many interesting stories associated with the old place."

"That's very kind. Actually at present I'm rather busy and—"

"It needn't take up much of your time, Mrs. Langstone. You see, because it's on the doorstep, one can pop in for ten minutes here and ten minutes there. Oh, you would enjoy it, I promise you. Such a lot of history, so many strange yarns."

There were footsteps on the stairs, and the small, shapeless figure of Mrs. Renton appeared.

"You left your kettle boiling, Mr. Fimberry," she announced. "Must be almost dry by now."

"Oh—yes, thank you. Goodbye, Mrs. Langstone." At the head of the stairs, he turned back. "Thank you, Mrs. Langstone," he murmured.

"Has the Captain heard when Mr. Serridge will be back?" Mrs. Renton asked Lydia.

"Today at some point. That's all I know. By the way, I saw that young man this morning, Mr. Wentwood—the one who came about the flat. He seemed to have been looking round the chapel."

"Then him and Mr. Fimberry should have something to talk about," Mrs. Renton said. "I'd best be getting on. At least it's not smelling yet."

Lydia blinked. "What isn't?"

"The parcel in the hall," Mrs. Renton said. "Mr. Serridge's new heart."

JOE SERRIDGE plays Philippa Penhow like a fish. He knows just what to say, and how, and when. But the fish makes it easy for him. The fish wants to be caught.

Wednesday, 29 January 1930

Major Serridge called again this morning—he wanted my advice about the choice of wallpaper for his room. "It needs a lady's eye," he told me. He added that of course it had to be an artistic lady! I offered to pay for it, but he was quite obstinate—he didn't want to put me out, it was for his benefit, etc., and he insists on bearing the whole cost himself.

He wasn't able to stay long. When I went with him to the door, there was a beggar outside with a poor, half-starved mongrel, and the Major said he would go after the man and make sure he gave the dog something to eat. How typical of his warm heart! I told him about Aunt's dog Susie, and he told me about a dog he had when he was a little lad.

Then he said, "Long before you were born, I'll be bound!"

ℭℭℭ

That afternoon there were Fascists on the streets. In twos and threes, they patrolled Holborn and Clerkenwell, handing out leaflets and selling copies of the *Blackshirt*. They were very smart, like athletic chauffeurs, and attracted a good deal of interest from young women and even from St. Tumwulf's schoolgirls. Some were young, little more than boys, but others looked as if they might have fought in the war. All of them were very polite. Lydia found it hard to distinguish one from the other. One noticed the uniforms, not the faces, just as one did with members of the Salvation Army.

Marcus had been interested in the movement since Mosley had founded the New Party, the predecessor of the British Union of Fascists, in 1931. It wouldn't have been difficult for Sir Rex Fisher to recruit him. Fisher wasn't just a party member—he was said to be one of the Leader's closest advisers, and a personal friend. He was also a war hero, with a Military Cross or something, which must give him additional glamour in Marcus's eyes. Marcus was almost grovellingly keen to impress people who had had a good war because he himself had done nothing much except step into the shoes of his dead brother.

A hint of fog hung in the air and it caught the back of the throat, the promise of worse to come. But even the weather failed to dent the enthusiasm of the Blackshirts, though some of them were pink-nosed and peaky in the cold. On her way back to the flat, Lydia accepted a pamphlet advertising a meeting to discuss "Fascism and Empire" to stop them pestering her.

She loitered outside the window of a Lyon's Corner House. Two shopgirls came out, and with them came a waft of warm, sweet and smoky air. A cup of tea would be a penny. Two buns would cost another penny. She could afford it easily at present, but she forced herself to turn away and walk back to the flat. A cup of tea and a slice of toast at the flat would cost even less. She must learn to be economical. She no longer had money for luxuries. She had nothing more than she had received from Mr. Goldman that morning, together with two more pieces of jewelry and a Post Office savings book containing seventeen pounds and a few odd pence.

In Bleeding Heart Square, Lydia found her father in front of the sitting-room gas fire with an unlit pipe clenched between his teeth. "That husband of yours. I happened to be in the Crozier at lunchtime, and he looked in to have a word."

Lydia felt weary, cold and footsore. She sat down opposite her father.

"He says there was a misunderstanding and you rushed off. Bit impulsive, wasn't it? Throw away a whole marriage for that?"

"Marcus had just knocked me over, which may have had something to do with it."

Ingleby-Lewis looked away from her. "He didn't mention that. I—ah—I'm sure he regrets it."

"So do I."

Her father peered into the bowl of his pipe as though hoping against hope to find a marriage counselor inside. "Ah. Still. Hmm. All the same, you must keep it in proportion, my dear. We men are rough brutes occasionally, you know, and we can lose our tempers. Regrettable, of course, but there it is."

"Is that what you did to Mother?" Lydia said, finding comfort in a vicarious anger against the only male available. "Hit her? Is that why you had to leave her?"

Ingleby-Lewis turned the pipe round and round in his hands. "No. I'm not proud of my record in that department but not that. No, the long and the short of it was, we weren't getting along very well. But that's nothing to do with this. Point is, you've got a perfectly decent husband and a very comfortable home of your own. I'm sorry about the—ah—unpleasantness, but these things do happen, you know."

Only if you let them, Lydia thought.

"You take my advice: go back to Marcus, and the next thing you know you'll have a baby on the way."

"But I'm not sure I want a baby. And certainly not with him."

Lydia picked up her hat, turned and left the room. She went into her bedroom. She removed her shoes and climbed into bed fully clothed. She lay there, staring at the ceiling. She shivered.

Somebody came into the house. There were footsteps on the stairs. Her father had a visitor. She heard men's voices, rising and falling, one of them much deeper than her father's.

She couldn't stay in bed all day. It was a coward's way out. In a moment, she would get up and go back to the sitting room.

Her fingers played with the hem of the sheet, feeling its chilly roughness on her skin. It was made of old linen, she thought at the same time in a remote part of her mind, quite good quality, though much worn. She registered the fact that there were unexpected ridges of stitching underneath her fingertips and automatically glanced down to see what they were.

Exactly what one would expect: a laundry mark. Crazy capitals in faded red thread. Suddenly the letters assembled themselves into a name. PENHOW.

Mr. Serridge was a big, broad man with sloping shoulders, a tangled beard and a deep voice that was almost a growl. He looked ten years younger than Captain Ingleby-Lewis and was probably about the same age. He was also three inches taller. His hand enveloped Lydia's.

"Hello, Mrs. Langstone." He stared down at her. "Pleased to meet you. You don't look much like your dad, do you?" He smiled. "Take after your mother, I suppose. Ha! I bet you're glad about that."

"My daughter's staying here for a few days," Ingleby-Lewis said warily. "In the little room next to mine. That's all right, isn't it?"

Serridge was still staring at her, making no effort to disguise his curiosity. His manners were offensive, Lydia thought, but it was clearly pointless to take offense. Serridge seemed not to care what anyone thought of him. He was carelessly dressed and his dark hair, streaked with gray, needed cutting. He must have been handsome once, but time and hard living had taken their toll.

"Your father tells me you've left your husband, Mrs. Langstone."

She nodded, knowing her color was rising.

"None of my business, but you've never been to see the Captain before, have you?"

Lydia raised her face. "You are perfectly right on both counts, Mr. Serridge. He ran away from his family responsibilities when I was two years old."

He grinned at her, and sucked his teeth. For the first time she felt the man's charm sweeping out from him, an invisible fog to cloud the emotions. Beneath the charm was an unsettling hint of calculation.

"I'm sure she'll only be here for a day or two," Ingleby-Lewis said. "Not a problem, is it?"

Serridge frowned and glanced at Lydia. "As far as I'm concerned, she can stay for as long as she likes."

"What?" Ingleby-Lewis said. "Eh?"

"You heard, William." He grinned at Lydia again. "The place could do with a woman's touch. Do you think you could make me a cup of tea, Mrs. Langstone?"

Lydia said warily that she would see what she could do. As she was crossing the landing, she heard the doorbell. In the kitchen, she filled the kettle and put it on the gas ring. Mrs. Renton was talking below, and a man was replying. Lydia recognized Mr. Wentwood's voice. Through the open door of the kitchen she glimpsed his tall, bony figure coming up the stairs. He gave her a smile and a wave.

Mr. Serridge came out onto the landing. He had a small, pink bald patch on the back of his head, and he was so large that he blocked her view of Mr. Wentwood entirely.

Mr. Wentwood. How odd to think that a man who could live anywhere in the world would want to live in Bleeding Heart Square.

The attic flat cost twenty-five shillings a week, unfurnished, and for an extra five shillings Mr. Serridge agreed to bring up some furniture from the cellar. All the necessities would be there, he assured Mr. Wentwood. Shared kitchen, shared bathroom on the floor below, both with water heater. The electricity had recently been installed, at considerable expense. That was metered, naturally, as was the gas supply.

"I was rather hoping I could move in within a day or two," Mr. Wentwood said as they came down the stairs to the first floor and paused on the landing. "I'm out in Kentish Town and it's not very convenient."

"Convenient for what?" Mr. Serridge said.

"Looking for jobs."

"Oh—so you're out of work, are you?"

"I'm just back from India," Mr. Wentwood said. "I've a number of irons in the fire."

"But no regular income, eh?"

"Not at present. But I do have savings. There won't be a problem."

"There'd better not be, Mr. Wentwood. I tell you what. You pay me a month's rent in advance as a returnable deposit, and you can move in on Monday. I'll need references, naturally. All right?"

"Absolutely, Mr. Serridge."

"Rent day is Saturday."

"I'll write you a check now, shall I?"

"I'd prefer cash, if you have it. You know where you are with cash, I always say."

Mr. Wentwood looked embarrassed. "Of course." He took out his wallet.

"Four weeks at twenty-five bob a week," Serridge said cheerfully. "A five-pound note will do nicely." He turned to Lydia, who was assembling cups and saucers in the kitchen. "And now,

Mrs. Langstone. All the talking's made me parched. What about that tea?"

The speaker addressed his audience as comrades. His name was Julian Dawlish, and he wore very wide flannel bags, a gray pull-over and muddy brown shoes. Horn-rimmed glasses gave the only touch of stern angularity to a round, smooth-skinned face.

The international situation was very bad indeed, he told them in a high-pitched, well-bred voice, because of Herr Hitler and Signor Mussolini, who were now revealing themselves in their true colors. Even in England's green and pleasant land, Fascism was on the march, grinding the poor and the vulnerable beneath its jackboots. But all was not lost. There were gleams of hope in Spain and a positive beacon of light in Russia. If the workers of the world united, there was nothing they could not achieve.

Mr. Dawlish's talk was followed by questions from the floor which had a habit of turning into lengthy statements. The meeting trailed away a little after nine o'clock. Afterward, tea, orange squash and stale biscuits were served. The audience stood about smoking, chatting and relishing the fact that they were no longer sitting on chairs designed for children.

"Shall we go?" Rory said. "I'm dead beat."

"All right." Fenella glanced toward the knot of people around the speaker. "I was going to ask the time of the next meeting, but they'll put up a notice."

They joined the trickle of comrades slipping out of the church hall. In Albion Lane, the pavements shone with rain.

She took his arm. "It was interesting, wasn't it?"

"It was a lot of hot air. I don't believe that chap's done a day's work in his life. Silly ass."

"I think what Mr. Dawlish says makes a lot of sense. He can't help his background. In a way that makes what he does for the cause all the better."

"You know him, do you?"

"I've met him once or twice."

"How old is he?"

"I don't know. Early thirties? Why?"

He grunted. "Old enough to know better."

They walked in silence.

"You're angry with me, aren't you?" she said after a moment. "About not being engaged."

"Of course I'm not angry."

"Of course you are. But it's better this way, truly."

"Better for who?"

"For both of us. We've talked about this."

Rory let the silence lengthen. Then he said, "I've found a flat."

"That's wonderful. Where?"

"In Bleeding Heart Square."

Fenella snatched her arm away. "In Aunt Philippa's house?"

"Yes."

"I thought we agreed to leave all that."

"We agreed nothing. Listen, it's a perfectly good flat in exactly the right place for me. I can walk into the City, I can walk into the West End. They know nothing about us, nothing about my connection with your aunt. There's no harm in it. Besides, I'm fed up with Mrs. Rutter's."

All this was perfectly true. There was also a small malicious pleasure in going against Fenella's wishes, something Rory did not choose to examine too closely. If she had given him any encouragement, he might also have told her about Sergeant Narton. But she didn't. They turned into Cornwallis Grove.

"Did you hear anything about Aunt Philippa while you were there?" Fenella asked.

"No."

"Who did you meet?"

"Some of the lodgers. There's a dressmaker, and an old chap and his daughter. Perhaps other people. And the landlord keeps a room on, but I gather he's not always in residence."

"So you saw him too? Mr. Serridge?"

"Yes. How often did you meet him?"

"Once or twice. Mother didn't take to him, and Father was awfully rude. Aunt Philippa was furious. She wanted us to like him." Fenella walked on in silence for a moment. Staring straight ahead, she said, "What did you think of him?"

They paused at the gate of number fifty-one. He sensed that she didn't intend to ask him in.

"Bit of a brute, probably, but quite straightforward in his way," Rory said. "I shouldn't have thought he'd have much in common with your aunt, or she with him."

Fenella lifted the latch. "Aunt thought he was wonderful." She pushed open the gate with such violence that it clattered against the retaining wall of the lawn. "Aunt thought he was God."

There was a time very early in their acquaintance when Lydia had considered Marcus to be a god. Not God himself, whom they visited every Sunday in church, and who was supposed to be uncomfortably omnipresent, seeing everything one did or failed to do; Marcus's divinity was of a different kind.

When Lydia was nine, she had had a governess who told her stories from Greek and Roman mythology. Marcus was the sort of god who appeared in classical legends. There was something anarchic and capricious about him. Though enormously powerful in some areas, he was weak, even powerless, in others. He could be cruel and he could be kind, switching from one to the other with bewildering rapidity. But he was always impersonal, for gods are like that. It was she who interpreted his actions as cruel or kind, whereas for him such labels were meaningless.

His standing as a god was further supported by the fact that he was six years older than she, and by the brief and unpredictable incursions he made into her life. Also, she later came to realize, if she came to see him as a god it was partly because she wanted a god and he was the only realistic candidate available.

Even at the time, she bore him no malice for the episode of the child-eating slugs at Monkshill Park. Later, she looked back on what had happened in the shed at the end of the kitchen garden almost with pleasure. After all, it had been the first time she had met Marcus. Moreover, she had never been in any real danger, either from the allegedly man-eating slugs or from the less obvious but more serious risk of falling off the shelf from sheer terror. Nor had he actually put the slugs on her legs. And there had been, at least in retrospect, something almost pleasurable in being so utterly powerless and so utterly terrified.

It was true that Marcus had examined what Nanny used to call her "front bottom." Lydia had known for as long as she had known anything that this part of her anatomy was something to be ashamed of, which it was best to cover up and pretend did not exist. But Marcus clearly thought it was not something to be ashamed of: on the contrary, it was something he found profoundly fascinating. That was rather flattering, if anything. He examined it for what seemed like hours and probably was at least a couple of minutes, moving her legs this way and that, so he could get a better view. Finally he touched her, very gently, at the point where the crack was, the very epicenter of all that shame.

When he had finished his inspection, he had lifted her down and they had walked on, hand in hand, as far as the lake. He said in a casual voice on the way back that what she had shown him in the shed was of course a secret. She had to promise that she would tell no one. Otherwise he would not be able to stop the slugs tracking her down and eating her. She had sucked the first two fingers of her right hand and nodded vigorously.

During the war, Lydia had had a recurring nightmare that Marcus had become a soldier and been killed. She never told anybody about this, even Marcus when the war was over, but she prayed every night that the fighting would end before he was old enough to join up. Her prayers were answered but, as is so often the case, there was a catch. Marcus lied about his age and tried to join up in 1916 but he was rejected as unfit because of flat feet. Marcus's elder brother was not so lucky.

The Cassingtons were staying in Upper Mount Street when they heard the news. Her stepfather saw it in *The Times*, in the list of fallen officers near the Court Circular.

"Poor Wilfred Langstone," he said heavily, setting down his coffee cup.

"Oh dear," Lady Cassington said.

Lydia's stepsister Pamela, who was spoiled by everyone including Lydia and allowed to get away with murder, continued banging the top of her boiled egg with a spoon.

"Died of wounds, poor chap. I didn't know he'd transferred to the Royal Flying Corps."

"I must write to his mother. Poor Maud."

Lydia stared at her plate. Pamela continued to hit her egg. The saucer around her egg cup was now a mass of shell fragments.

"This frightful slaughter." Lord Cassington put his elbows on the table, leaned forward and turned down the corners of his mouth; he looked like a gnome with indigestion. "We can't carry on like this. There will be a revolution. You mark my words."

Lady Cassington was pursuing a different line of thought. "At least she has another son. That must be some consolation. Thank heavens they wouldn't take him."

Pamela dug the tip of the spoon violently into the top of her egg. Yolk spurted out and a few drops fell on the tablecloth.

"Marcus?" Lord Cassington said. "Yes. What's he doing now?"

"According to Maud, he's running errands for Charlie Verschoyle at the War Office. Pammy darling, don't do that. Either eat it or leave it. Fin, could you cut off Pammy's crusts?"

Lord Cassington obeyed. He was called Fin within the family because of a long-standing joke so old that its origins were lost in the mists of time: it was believed to have had something to do with the shape of his hands. He removed the crusts from his daughter's toast and cut what was left into soldiers.

But his mind was still running on the Langstones. "It's a shame Jack died in the spring," he said, wiping his fingers on his napkin.

"Isn't it better for them? It must be awful if your son dies before you."

"The point is, it means two lots of death duties within a year. One has to be practical."

"Perhaps we should ask Marcus to dinner. Or even down to Monkshill for a weekend. It might help him take his mind off things."

"If you like."

Lord Cassington's eyes returned to the casualties. The egg cup toppled over and fragments of ruined egg sprayed across the tablecloth.

Lady Cassington smiled. "He's much better-looking than Wilfred," she said. "And really quite grown-up."

On Friday evening, Captain Ingleby-Lewis returned from the Crozier humming the opening bars of Offenbach's Barcarolle over and over again. He let himself into the house and, still humming, zigzagged from side to side of the hall in the general direction of the stairs. At this moment, Mrs. Renton came out of her room carrying a pair of sheets. He collided with her, and the sheets fell to the floor.

"Madam," said Captain Ingleby-Lewis, wrapping an affectionate arm around the newel post. "I can only apologize. The fault is entirely mine."

Alerted by the noise, Lydia appeared at the head of the stairs. "Is everything all right?"

Mrs. Renton stared up at her, and said nothing. The Captain began to hum again and hauled himself steadily up the stairs. Mrs. Renton picked up the sheets.

Lydia came down to help her fold them. "Mr. Fimberry's?"

"Yes," Mrs. Renton said shortly. "No, no, Mrs. Langstone—you take the corners, all right, and then bring them toward my corners."

Above their heads, the Captain and his Barcarolle moved across the landing and finally came to harbor in the sitting room.

Lydia said, "Does the name Penhow mean anything to you?"

"Why?"

"The sheets reminded me. I found a laundry mark on my sheet that said Penhow."

The folding of the sheet had brought the faces of Mrs. Renton and Lydia only a few inches apart. The dark little eyes examined her.

"Now we fold it this way," Mrs. Renton said. "This house used to belong to Miss Penhow."

"What happened to her?"

"She went away." Mrs. Renton stepped back and put the folded sheet outside Mr. Fimberry's door. "Shall we do the other one?"

6

PHILIPPA PENHOW liked music. You had forgotten that. She considered that a taste for good music was doubly refined, both spiritual and genteel. Serridge played on that. He was good at finding out exactly what people wanted and then giving it to them.

Thursday, 13 February 1930

Yesterday evening I met Major Serridge at the Tube station at Oxford Circus. We had an early dinner at a very nice Italian restaurant in Soho whose name I forget. I had a glass and a half of wine and my head began to swim! Afterward he was all for getting a taxi, but I said I should prefer to walk.

We reached the Wigmore Hall at a quarter past eight. Major Serridge had bought the expensive seats, at 12 shillings each. He refused to allow me to pay for mine. The recital began at half-past. Moiseiwitsch played divinely. I have never heard Chopin played with such feeling. The Prelude in A-flat major was particularly moving. I distinctly saw Major Serridge touch his eyes with his handkerchief.

When it was over we stood for a moment outside the hall. It was a dank, foggy evening but I felt as if I was floating on air. He said, "After music like that, we should by rights have moonlight and roses." The more I get to know him, the more I realize how sensitive he is. I was quite happy to catch a bus home but this time he positively insisted on hailing a taxi. At the Rushmere, he took me up to the door and thanked me for a wonderful evening. As we said goodnight, I fancy he gave my hand a little extra pressure.

This morning, imagine my surprise when I found an envelope waiting at my breakfast table. A Valentine!! A day early, but never mind! Of course I don't know who it was from, but I can't help wondering.

Who else could it be?

On Saturday afternoon, Mr. Howlett came to Bleeding Heart Square with a young assistant, a hungry-looking man who stared at Lydia as though he would have liked to devour her. Mr. Serridge had arranged for them to move the furniture from the cellar into Mr. Wentwood's flat.

Mr. Howlett was out of uniform. His brown canvas coat deflated him and made him ordinary. Nipper followed the men into the house. He sniffed Lydia's ankles and would only leave her alone when Mr. Howlett kicked him aside. Afterward, he tried to make friends with Mrs. Renton but she pushed him away.

"I don't like dogs," she said. "Stupid animals. Watch he doesn't bring mud in the house or scratch the paint."

Howlett and his assistant tramped up and down the stairs between the cellar and the attic flat. Nipper followed them from floor to floor, his claws scratching and rattling on the linoleum and the bare boards.

The furniture was old, dark and heavy. The men swore at the weight of it. They rammed a chest of drawers against the newel post on the first-floor landing and left a dent in the wood nearly half an inch deep. It was quite good furniture too, Lydia noticed, old-fashioned and gloomy but rather better than the pieces in her father's flat. Perhaps it was a sign that Mr. Serridge valued Mr. Wentwood more than Captain Ingleby-Lewis.

Mr. Serridge supervised the work. Pipe in mouth, he wandered from attic to cellar. Lydia, as she passed to and fro between the kitchen, her bedroom and the sitting room, found him staring at her on several occasions. It was unsettling, but not in the usual way when men stared at her. It seemed to her that there was nothing lustful in his face, at most a look of curiosity and concentration, as if he were trying to work out a mathematical problem in his head.

Once or twice, he nodded to her and said, "All serene, Mrs. Langstone?"

Later that day, a smell of liver and onions spread through the hall and up the stairs.

"That smells good," Howlett said to Mrs. Renton as he came down the stairs for the last time with the dog at his heels. "I wish I had that waiting at home for my tea."

"If wishes were horses, then beggars would ride," Mrs. Renton said. "Good evening, Mr. Howlett."

He grunted. The front door banged behind him, the hungry-looking assistant and Nipper. Mrs. Renton glanced at Lydia, who was coming downstairs with the rubbish.

"Anyway," she said in a confidential whisper, "it's not liver I'm cooking. It's Mr. Serridge's heart. Shame to waste it."

Lydia disliked Sundays. She did not believe in God but she had endured for most of her life the necessity of paying her respects to him at least once a week. The Langstones, of course, were church-goers. When they were in Gloucestershire, they attended church with the same unthinking regularity with which they voted Conservative or complained about their servants. Marcus's mother said the Langstones were obliged to set an example. Privilege conferred its responsibilities.

But this Sunday was not like other Sundays. It was the eleventh day of the eleventh month—Armistice Day. It was an occasion that Marcus took seriously because the death of his brother Wilfred gave him a personal interest in commemorating the glorious dead. The houses where Marcus lived, the farms and investments that paid for the servants who looked after them, the club subscriptions, the bills from the tailor, the wine merchant and the butcher—all these should have been Wilfred's. A quirk of fate had given Marcus flat feet, and had allowed Wilfred to be killed. Marcus felt obscurely that he owed his brother something. The observance of Armistice Day was the tribute that Marcus paid to the glorious dead, and in particular to Wilfred.

After breakfast, which Lydia ate alone because her father was still asleep, she went out for a walk. It was a gray morning, but in places sunshine filtered through the mist. She went through the wicket gate into Rosington Place, where she found Mr. Fimberry, dressed in black and wearing his poppy, loitering near the notice-board by the entrance to the chapel. A steady trickle of churchgoers flowed up the cul-de-sac toward them.

"Good morning, Mrs. Langstone." Fimberry raised his hat. "Are you joining us today?"

"No, thank you," she said politely.

Lydia walked down to the lodge. Mr. Serridge was standing by the railings, smoking a pipe and idly watching a small crocodile of St. Tumwulf's girls, the school's Roman Catholic contingent, filing up to the chapel. He nodded to Lydia but did not speak.

She drifted south and west across London. The closer she came to Whitehall, the more crowded the pavements became, with the current of people flowing more and more strongly toward the white stone Cenotaph. She arrived shortly before eleven.

She could not even see the Cenotaph, let alone the King and the politicians and the generals. A gun boomed on Horse Guards Parade. The sound bounced to and fro among the buildings like an India rubber ball. Then came the tolling of Big Ben. After that, the silence ruled, heavy and stifling. Lydia listened to what noises there still were—the rustle of leaves, a crying baby, several coughs, one defiant sneeze. She thought it probable that Marcus was somewhere in the crowd. Her stepfather, too.

The two-minute silence ended with a shocking crash of gunfire and the roll of drums. The crowd stirred and shifted like trees in strong winds. Trumpeters sounded the Last Post. Suddenly everyone was singing "Oh God, our help in ages past."

Lydia turned and pushed her way through the singing figures and made her way to Trafalgar Square. All those hearts beating as one, she thought—Marcus loved this sort of thing. He liked it when crowds acted together like an enormous animal, united by a single purpose.

She noticed a couple about thirty yards away walking along the north side of the square in front of the National Gallery. The man was Mr. Wentwood and he was accompanying a young woman with a slight, elegant figure. Mr. Wentwood glanced back and caught Lydia's eye. He ducked his head in a sort of bow and half raised his arm, as though trying to acknowledge her, but wanting to do so as discreetly as he could.

But the girl had noticed. She too looked back. She had a pretty face and fair hair beneath the black hat. Then people flowed between them and the meeting, if it could be called that, was over almost as soon as it had begun. But it gave Lydia a glimpse of Mr. Wentwood's private life, of a hinterland that extended beyond Bleeding Heart Square and the Blue Dahlia café. The young woman had been very good-looking. A sister, Lydia wondered with an uncomfortable pang, or even a girlfriend?

"Here," Rory said. "Have my handkerchief."

Fenella took it without a word. Turning to face St. Martin-in-the-Fields, she blew her nose and wiped her eyes. Rory turned away from her and lit a cigarette. Lydia Langstone was no longer in sight.

"Sorry," Fenella said behind him. "I'm all right now."

"What was it? Thinking of your mother?"

She shook her head. "All this." She waved a gloved hand toward Whitehall, toward the ebbing crowds: men in uniform, men on crutches, men with medals, wives, mothers and daughters. "They say we're mourning the unforgotten dead, but of course they're forgotten. All we're mourning is our own beastly misery. We don't give a damn about the people who died."

"I say," Rory said. "Isn't that a bit bleak?"

"Anyway, it's pointless," Fenella went on. "Anyone can see it's all going to happen again, and this time it will probably be much worse."

"Another war?"

"Of course. You heard what Mr. Dawlish was saying at the meeting the other night. The Nazis are just waiting for the right moment. And it's not just them, either."

Rory ground out a cigarette beneath his heel. "You're exaggerating. People will never stand for another war. They remember too well what happened in the last one. It's only sixteen years ago."

"I wish you were right. Who was that woman?"

For a moment he was tempted to say, which woman? "Her name's Mrs. Langstone," he said. "I think I mentioned her the other day. Her father has a flat in the same house as mine, and she's staying with him."

"So she must know Mr. Serridge?"

"Yes. But I'm not sure how well. She struck me as a bit of a dark horse, actually."

"Why?"

"She doesn't really belong in a place like Bleeding Heart Square. I wouldn't be surprised if she and her father have come down in the world."

Fenella laughed, with one of those sudden changes of mood that had always amazed him. "You sound like your grandfather sometimes."

He grinned at her, relieved at the change of tone. "They probably lost their money in the slump or something. The new poor."

But Fenella was no longer smiling. "I think I'll go home now."

"I'll take you."

"No. If you don't mind, I'd rather go by myself." She looked up at him. "I just feel like my own company. It's nothing personal, you know."

"I know," Rory said. "That's rather the problem, isn't it?"

Lydia Langstone hadn't realized that being poor brought with it so many unpredictable humiliations. Being poor meant more than not being able to buy things. It changed the way that people looked at you. It changed how you looked at yourself.

After breakfast on Monday morning she went to the Blue Dahlia, where she ordered a cup of coffee and asked to speak to the manageress. The manageress turned out to be the fat woman behind the counter who took the orders.

"I wondered whether you had any vacancies," Lydia said.

"You what?" demanded the woman.

"A position." Lydia lowered her voice, aware that the other customers were probably listening avidly. "I'm looking for a job, you see."

The woman shook her head. "We ain't got anything going here, love." She leaned on the counter, bringing her face closer to Lydia's, and added in an unexpectedly gentle voice, "Anyway, our sort of job wouldn't suit you, and you wouldn't suit it."

Lydia left the café with her ears burning. It wasn't so much the rejection that embarrassed her. It was the way the woman had talked to her at the end, the way she had called her "love." On her way home, she went into the library in Charleston Street. Upstairs in the reference room, the Situations Vacant columns from the daily newspapers were pinned up on boards. She couldn't reach them because there was a crowd of unemployed, both men and women, heaving like a football scrum in front of her.

It was nearly lunchtime by the time she got back to Bleeding Heart Square. There were letters on the hall table—none for her or her father, but one of them was for Mr. Wentwood. She heard a sound behind her and turned to see Mr. Fimberry advancing down the hall, smiling broadly.

"Mrs. Langstone, I thought it must be you! You see—I recognize your footsteps already." He laid his hand on her arm. "I wondered whether this afternoon might be a good time for me to show you round the chapel in Rosington Place."

"No," Lydia said, pulling her arm away. "I'm afraid it wouldn't."

"You're back home for lunch? I was just about to warm up some soup for myself, and—"

To Lydia's relief, she heard footsteps on the stairs. Fimberry glanced past her.

"Good afternoon, Mr. Serridge," he said.

"Mrs. Langstone?" Serridge said, ignoring Fimberry. "Can I have a word?"

Fimberry slipped into his own room, closing the door.

Serridge towered over her. "He's not been pestering you, has he?"

"Not really."

"That means he has." Serridge scowled. "I'll have a word."

"Please don't. He's just trying to be friendly."

"It's up to you, Mrs. Langstone. How are you getting on?"

"Very well, thank you."

"I heard you were looking for a job."

Lydia nodded, wondering who had told him.

"Any luck so far?"

"Not yet. But it's early days, I suppose."

Serridge scratched his untidy beard. He was such a big man, Lydia thought, and not just in terms of physique. He took up too much space. She found him far more oppressive than she did Mr. Fimberry, though she was not sure why. There was the sound of hammering upstairs, perhaps from the attic flat. Mr. Wentwood must be making himself at home. At least Mr. Wentwood seemed relatively normal.

"If you want a job," Serridge said, "I might be able to help you."

A narrow flight of stairs rose up to the tiny attic landing. Doors to left and right led to the sitting room and to the bedroom respectively. Both rooms had dormer windows, steeply sloping ceilings and gently sloping floors of ill-fitting, creaking boards. The rooms made you feel as though you were living life at an angle and were slightly drunk as well. The furniture was plain and old-fashioned. Most of the pieces were dull with lack of polish but they had a solidity lacking in Mrs. Rutter's furniture in Kentish Town.

It took Rory nearly an hour to unpack. He set up his typewriter, a Royal Portable his parents had given him as a leaving present before he sailed to India, on the table in the sitting room. It squatted there, looking efficient and important. It was his badge of office, he thought, a visible sign that he was, or soon would be, a working journalist or copywriter.

Most of his clothes went into a big chest of drawers with tarnished brass handles. One of the two top drawers had jammed, and he returned to it last of all. He was obliged to take out the drawer below it before he was able to ease it out of the chest. The drawer itself was empty but removing it dislodged a folded sheet of paper that had wedged itself at some point in the past between the drawer and the side of the chest. Yellowed with age and spotted with damp, it was covered with sloping handwriting in faded ink.

> *. . . rather lax about making notes, as I had intended. Still, as I was rereading the Parable of the Prodigal Son this evening (Luke 15), I could not help be struck both by the beauty of the language and the spirituality of its message. We must rejoice when a sinner repents, Our Lord tells us, because Our Father which is in Heaven will . . .*

Someone's Bible study notes, Rory thought idly, and began to screw up the sheet. As he did so, he noticed something written in pencil on the other side.

> *Dear Mr Orburn*
>
> *Thank you for your letter of the 7th inst. I have considered what you say your proposals about re the house very carefully and decided to proceed as you suggest, so long as it doesn't cost more than the cost does not exceed your estimate of £110. Please let me know when you will require the money, and I will so that I may instruct my bank manager to withdraw it from the deposit account.*
>
> *Yours faithfully truly,*
> *P. M. Penhow*

Rory frowned. *P. M. Pehow.* Fenella's Aunt Philippa and Narton's Miss Penhow came together in the signature. For the first time, she was more than a couple of words in someone else's mouth. This piece of paper was independent proof of a living, breathing woman. It was a draft of a business letter, presumably—to a builder? No, more likely to her agent or her lawyer. Clearly she had not been used to writing this sort of letter. He touched the signature with the tip of his finger. Had she once owned this chest of drawers?

Footsteps were coming up the stairs from the landing below.

Rory dropped the paper into the drawer, closed it and turned toward the open door. Mrs. Renton appeared, carrying a tray.

"I brought you some tea," she announced.

"That's awfully kind."

"Not that I'm going to make a habit of it, Mr. Wentwood. And there's a letter come in the post. Mind you bring the cup down when you've finished, and don't forget the tray."

The Lamb in Lamb's Conduit Street was far enough away from Bleeding Heart Square for Narton to be able to relax. He ordered half a pint of mild-and-bitter and nursed it by the fire. He wondered whether Wentwood would turn up. That was the trouble with having to deal with amateurs. You couldn't rely on them. Five minutes later, however, the young man came bounding through the door. Christ, thought Narton sourly, the chap's like an overgrown puppy. But at least he was here.

"I had your letter," Wentwood said. "Everything all right?"

Narton nodded. "You needn't shout about it though."

To his relief, Wentwood didn't expect to have a drink bought for him. Indeed, he asked Narton if he wanted the other half of what he had in front of him. When the young man rejoined him at the table, Narton smiled at him with something approaching benevolence.

"Cheerio," Wentwood said, raising his glass. "We have to toast my new home."

Narton drank obediently, then sat back and wiped his mouth. "So you've moved in all right?"

"There wasn't a great deal to move. Still, it's a place of my own. I know I'll have to find my own meals but I can't tell you what a relief it is to get away from Mrs. Rutter and Kentish Town. Listen—I found something." He took a sheet of paper from his pocket and passed it across the table. "It was in a chest of drawers in my room."

Narton took his time examining it.

"Is it important?" Wentwood demanded. "It proves she was there, doesn't it? And who's this chap Orburn?"

"It proves nothing. It was her house, remember—she probably furnished it with her cast-offs. As for Orburn, he was her solicitor. He used to manage Bleeding Heart Square for her before Serridge took over." Narton put the letter on the table. "Have you seen Serridge?"

"He turned up to give me the keys and read me a lecture about keeping up with the rent." Wentwood searched his jacket pockets for cigarettes and matches. "He's a formidable character, isn't he? Do you know what Miss Kensley told me the other night? That Miss Penhow thought he was God. I'd the feeling that she might not have been speaking metaphorically."

Narton grunted. "You've talked to her about Serridge then?"

"I had to tell her where I was moving to."

"I asked you to keep all that under your hat."

"I know. But it wasn't that easy. Besides, I said nothing to her about looking into what happened to her aunt. I just said that I happened to be passing, and saw there was a flat vacant that would suit me. Is it a problem?"

Narton took the cigarette that Wentwood offered him and leaned across the table toward the match. "As it happens, no. I've changed my mind on that front, see? I've got a request for you, Mr. Wentwood. A suggestion, if you like. But we'll need her cooperation."

"I'm not sure how she'd feel about that."

"The thing is," Narton said quietly, "you could do me a favor, a big favor. There is an important piece of evidence in this case, and I think we need a second opinion on it. Either Miss Penhow was murdered or she wasn't. The official line is that she can't have been murdered because she went to the States instead with person or persons unknown. We know that because she wrote a letter from New York, which is why our investigation was officially closed. The thing is, some of us aren't convinced that letter was genuine."

"Surely the police can call on handwriting experts?"

"Oh we have, Mr. Wentwood. Our man says there's a better than fair chance that the letter was really written by Miss Penhow. But

I'd like another opinion. Now I bet that young lady of yours has got letters from her aunt, maybe other pieces of writing."

"Perhaps she has. Why don't you ask her?"

"Come to that, you've got your own sample, that piece of paper you found. The point is, the letter from New York is no longer in our hands. When the investigation was closed, it was returned to the recipient. If we go and ask for it back, it's as good as saying that we're still suspicious, that we're reopening the investigation."

"What's wrong with that?"

"Ever heard of softly softly, catchy monkey?"

Rory said, "Who did she write to?"

"The Vicar of Rawling. Man called Gladwyn."

"Rawling?"

Narton stubbed out the cigarette half-smoked and put the rest away for later. "It's a village in Essex on the Hertfordshire border, not far from Saffron Walden. It's where Serridge bought a farm with Miss Penhow's money, and it's the place where Miss Penhow was last seen alive, more than four years ago. I can't afford to upset Mr. Gladwyn. For one thing, he's rather a chum of Serridge's. For another, he's the godfather of my chief constable's daughter. Tricky business all round, see? If we make an official approach, it's going to get back to Serridge, and that could put the kibosh on everything. But if someone representing Miss Penhow's relatives comes along, that's another matter. You see that, don't you?"

Wentwood sat back. He had hardly touched his beer. "This is rather a lot to ask, isn't it?"

Narton screwed up his face and let out a sigh. "I'm not doing this for fun, sir, as I'm sure you'll appreciate. Our job depends on members of the public being willing to cooperate with us."

"This would be rather more than cooperation, wouldn't it?"

"Look at it from our point of view. You're the fiancé of Miss Penhow's niece. You're back from India, and you weren't on the scene when the old girl vanished. Of course Miss Kensley wants to find out what happened to her aunt. Of course you want to help her. So it's perfectly natural you might turn up on Mr. Gladwyn's doorstep and ask to see that letter. Don't write beforehand—don't give him a chance to say no. Just turn up. Even better, turn up with the girl in tow."

Wentwood opened his mouth and then closed it again. Then he said, "I can't see one good reason why I should do what you ask. I'm sorry, Sergeant, but there it is."

"You want a reason?" Narton said. "How about this? If Serridge gets away with this murder, then ten to one he'll commit another sooner or later. For a man like him, killing a woman is an easy way to make money. So that's the question, Mr. Wentwood: do you want to stop another murder?"

7

W AS SERRIDGE really married? Perhaps there are dozens of Mrs. Serridges scattered around the globe, some living, some dead, some with marriage certificates, some without. He must always have had a way with women.

Saturday, 15 February 1930

Today I had tea with Major Serridge. He insisted on taking me to a very pleasant establishment in Kensington Church Street. It looked frightfully expensive. He said he wanted to repay me for tea at the Rushmere the other week. I think I got by far the better part of the bargain!!

He looked very serious, rather sad in fact, this afternoon. He talked less too. He was very friendly, though, without saying much, and once or twice I caught him looking at me in what I can only call a meaningful way. Outwardly he's such a big, masterful man, but he can be as sensitive and gentle as a child, at least with me. In the end I asked him if there was anything wrong.

He smiled at me and in that simple way of his said that we all have to shoulder our burdens, and on some days they seem to weigh more heavily than others. I don't know how it was but somehow this led to an extraordinarily intimate conversation—truly, I can never remember speaking to anyone so frankly in my entire life. I even found myself telling him about Vernon, and how I so nearly married him when I was eighteen. Of course Aunt wouldn't let me, and I had no money in those days, and so it was out of the question, and Vernon went back to sea. Sometimes, even now, I find myself wondering what would have happened if I'd flung caution to the winds and agreed to marry him. All that was nearly forty years ago, though I must admit I did not mention the precise number of years to Major Serridge. A lady must have her secrets.

Afterward he honored me with an even greater confidence. Today was his wedding anniversary. At this, I was considerably surprised, even shocked, because I had no idea that he was married.

He was reluctant to tell me more. He said it was too shocking for a lady's ears. In the end, though, I coaxed it out of him. In a moment of madness, when he was a very young man on the verge of leaving with his Regiment on active service, he had married a woman who later proved unworthy of him—indeed, unworthy of any man. It was hard, he said, for a fellow to come home to a cold and unloving hearth. But that had been his lot.

And there had been much worse to come. His wife turned out to be a moral degenerate of the worst sort. She had left him and was now living in New Zealand with another woman in circumstances so shameful that I cannot bear to sully the page of my diary with them. To make *matters worse, she had once been a Catholic, so she refused to countenance the very idea of divorce. The hypocrisy makes my blood boil.*

He said, very simply, "It's my cross, my dear Miss Pen-how, and I must somehow learn to carry it on my lonely journey through life."

After lunch, if it could be called that, Lydia Langstone went to her first job interview, leaving Captain Ingleby-Lewis snoring in his armchair, his legs covered with a blanket. He looked old, frail and ill.

In her gloved hand was a page torn from Mr. Serridge's loose-leaf memorandum book. On it he had written in pencil: *Mr. Shires, 3rd floor, 48 Rosington Place, Tuesday, 2.30 p.m.*

Lydia found the house with no difficulty. It was almost imme-diately opposite the chapel. Like most of the houses in the cul-de-sac, it had a cluster of brass plates beside its front door. A notice invited her to walk inside without ringing the bell. She found herself in a drab hall with a high plastered ceiling whose discolored moldings were draped with dusty cobwebs. There was brown linoleum on the floor and the air was filled with the clack-ing of typewriters. She scanned the noticeboard on the wall. It listed the offices of at least ten firms, including two sets of lawyers as well as Shires and Trimble, a jewelry importer, a surveyor, a company manufacturing kitchen stoves and a furrier's.

She climbed the stairs. The house was much larger than it seemed from the street. On the second floor there was a door marked SHIRES AND TRIMBLE set in a partition made of wood and frosted glass. She knocked. After a moment she turned the handle and went in. Immediately in front of her was a narrow counter, beyond which was a general office containing four people. Two men were sitting at high desks, one talking on the telephone; a typist with very red fingernails was attacking the keyboard of her machine with noisily vicious efficiency; and a red-haired boy was licking stamps and putting them on envelopes. No one took any notice of her.

Lydia tapped the bell on the counter. The younger of the two men looked up, sighed theatrically, climbed down from his stool and sauntered over to her.

"Good afternoon," Lydia said. "My name is Langstone, and I've an appointment with Mr. Shires."

He conveyed her across the general office to the door of a private room, as if without his guidance she might be expected to lose her way. Mr. Shires' office was small, and most of it was filled with a large partners' desk. The gas fire was burning at full blast and the air smelled of peppermints.

Mr. Shires himself, a plump little man in a shiny black suit, was writing at the desk. He capped his fountain pen and rose to a crouching position, not quite standing. He extended a hand across the desk and said, "Good afternoon, Mrs. Langstone. Pleased to meet you. Do sit down," in a continuous rush of words that suggested he was in a terrible hurry. He sank back in his chair and popped a peppermint from a white paper bag into his mouth. His eyes drifted back to the pile of papers in front of him.

"I believe Mr. Serridge has talked to you about me," Lydia said.

"Yes." He sucked the peppermint and the tip of his nose twitched. "I understand you're looking for a position." He uncapped the pen, initialled the foot of one page and turned it over. "And that you have no experience of office work."

"That's correct."

"Married or widowed?"

"Separated," Lydia said firmly.

Shires stared at her with weak, watery eyes. "Are you living by yourself?"

"No. I'm staying with my father in his flat."

"Of course." There was a tinge of amusement in Mr. Shires' voice. "In Bleeding Heart Square. Yes, I see. Very convenient."

Lydia felt her temper slipping away from her. "I don't want to waste your time, Mr. Shires . . ."

"I don't want you to waste it either, young lady."

Lydia gave way to her feelings and glared at him. "I'm glad we understand one another. Though I've no experience of office work, I've run two large houses for several years. I'm a quick learner, I'm methodical, and I'm willing to learn."

"Splendid, Mrs. Langstone." Mr. Shires took off his glasses and sat back in his chair. "I'm looking for a girl to do some of the donkey work for Mr. Smethwick and Miss Tuffley. Mr. Smethwick is our junior clerk. Miss Tuffley is our typist. They spend far too much of their valuable time filing or answering the telephone or making cups of tea for our clients. I can make more use of them than that. So if you are willing to do that sort of thing, I can give you a month's trial on a part-time basis, and we'll see how we go. Are you interested?"

"What do you mean by part-time, Mr. Shires?"

"If you come to work for me, Mrs. Langstone, you will have to get used to addressing me as sir. Let's say three days a week. Our hours are eight thirty to five thirty. The precise days and hours may vary from week to week; you would have to fit in with us. Shall we say thirty shillings?"

"Thirty shillings a day?"

"No, no." Mr. Shires belched unhurriedly. "Thirty shillings a week."

"That's ten shillings a day."

"So it is. Will that suit, eh? Yes or no."

"Yes," Lydia said.

"Yes, what?" Mr. Shires said.

Lydia stared at him. "Yes, sir."

Finding a job was proving harder than Rory had anticipated. On Tuesday he had lunch with a friend from university who now worked at an advertising agency in the Strand. When Rory had been in India, the friend had written enthusiastically about the opportunities awaiting him back in London. But now Rory was actually here, those opportunities seemed to have vanished. "Everyone's tightening their belts, old chap," the friend said as they drank their coffee after lunch. "And people want chaps with the right experience. There's no getting round it, I'm afraid."

By the time Rory got back to Bleeding Heart Square, the Crozier had opened for the evening. It was a cold night, and he went into the paneled saloon bar and ordered whisky. The place was crowded with people having a drink on their way home. Lucky people, he thought, people with jobs.

Rory found a seat in an alcove almost entirely filled with a large table, around which sat four law clerks engaged in a slanderous conversation about their employer. He slumped behind his newspaper in a chair at the end of the table and turned to the Situations Vacant. He was aware of the ebb and flow of voices around him. His attention wandered from the newsprint. He tuned in and out of conversations in the alcove and the bar beyond, as though he were twirling the dial on a wireless set.

"No change then?" said an educated man's voice.

"Found herself a job, I understand. Extraordinary."

"Good God. I'd have thought she was unemployable. Where?"

"Some lawyers at Rosington Place. Perfectly respectable billet, you needn't worry about that."

Rory recognized the voice of the second speaker: Captain Ingleby-Lewis, his neighbor on the first floor. He knew he ought to make his presence known or at least stop listening but his curiosity was stronger than his sense of propriety.

"She's settled in much better than I thought she would," Ingleby-Lewis said. "I mean, she's not enjoying it, slumming it with her old father. But she's putting a brave face on it. Plucky girl."

"It can't go on."

"Of course not. But I can't just throw her out."

"Why not?"

"Because I can't," Ingleby-Lewis said, his voice suddenly sharp. "After all she is my daughter. Flesh and blood and all that. She is causing quite a stir in my place."

"What do you mean?"

"Serridge—my landlord—he's taken quite a shine to her. It's he who found her the job. Even Mrs. Renton downstairs, who disapproves of most of the human race—I wouldn't say she likes Lydia exactly, but she is being quite kind to her. As for that fellow Fimberry, he goes around with his tongue hanging out at the very thought of her."

"Who's this?" There was no mistaking the anger in the other man's voice.

"Fimberry. Nervy chap. He's got the room on the left of the front door, opposite Mrs. Renton's. He's meant to be writing a book. He's always hanging round the chapel in Rosington Place."

"He's dangling after Lydia? Making a nuisance of himself?"

"Let's say he's getting rather fresh. Don't worry, I'll give the fellow his marching orders."

"I must go. Would you give Lydia this for me?"

"Of course. You're sure you haven't time for another drink?"

The conversation continued but less audibly than before. Other voices drowned it out. When Rory left the Crozier ten minutes later, Ingleby-Lewis was no longer in the bar. He walked across the cobbles of Bleeding Heart Square and let himself into the house. Mrs. Renton was standing in the doorway of Fimberry's room.

"Good evening," he said.

"Settling in all right?"

"Yes, thanks."

"Could you do me a favor? I promised Mr. Fimberry I'd do his curtains. But he hasn't taken them down. I need a longer pair of arms."

Rory went into Fimberry's room. The electric light was burning brightly. It was almost as cold in here as it was outside. The room was sparsely furnished and anonymous. The only touch of individuality were the books that filled almost the entire wall opposite the window from floor to ceiling. They were housed in two bookcases around which had grown a precarious network of shelves consisting of unpainted planks resting on bricks. It looked as if the slightest vibration would bring the entire erection crashing down.

Rory stood on a chair and unhooked the curtains from their rail. Afterward, while Mrs Renton was folding them, his eyes drifted over the spines of the books. Most of them were historical or topographical; almost all of them were old. They made the room smell like the seediest sort of second-hand bookshop, full of dead and decaying words that no one in his right mind would ever want to read.

He turned away and looked out of the uncurtained window. There was enough light to see a tall man in a dark overcoat standing on the corner by the Crozier. A cigarette glowed briefly as he inhaled. For an instant the skin of his face was as red as the devil's.

When Lydia let herself into the house, Mr. Wentwood was climbing the stairs. He glanced back.

"Evening, Mrs. Langstone. You all right? You look as if you've seen a ghost."

"I'm fine, thank you," Lydia said, though in a sense she had seen a ghost: Marcus had been hovering in Bleeding Heart Square and had tried to speak to her. She had turned her face away and walked resolutely past him. She followed Mr. Wentwood up the stairs. "How's the job-hunting?"

"No luck yet." He paused on the landing, as if ready to talk. "Still, I'm having a day off tomorrow. I've got to run down to the country."

"Lucky you." Lydia nodded goodbye, wondering if he would be taking that girl with him tomorrow. She went into the flat's sitting room. Her father was dozing in the armchair in front of the fire.

Without opening his eyes he said, "There's something for you on the table. A parcel."

Lydia's stomach lurched. For a split second she glimpsed the possibility that someone might have sent her an uncooked heart. But this parcel looked very different from Serridge's—it was about the shape and size of a brick and it hadn't come in the post. She examined the superscription—only her name, no address—and recognized the large, square handwriting.

"Marcus," she said. "Has he been in the house again? I saw him outside."

"I happened to bump into him in the Crozier," Captain Ingleby-Lewis said, his eyes still closed. "He asked me to give it to you."

She stripped off her gloves and took off her hat. It was too cold to remove her coat. A car drew up outside the house.

The parcel had been professionally wrapped. Marcus could no more wrap a parcel than he could have performed an appendectomy. She undid the string and peeled back first the brown paper and then a second layer of tissue paper beneath. Finally she found what she was expecting, a box of chocolates from Charbonnel et Walker. Marcus was convinced that the road to a woman's heart was paved with expensive chocolates. There was also an envelope with her name on it. Inside was a sheet of paper with the address of his club at the top.

My dear Lydia,

I don't want to pester you but I do miss you frightfully. I do wish you'd come back. Everyone goes through these sticky patches. I'm awfully sorry about what happened, and swear it won't happen again. We ought to give it another try, don't you think?

I couldn't stand rattling around in Frogmore Place all by myself. So I've shut up the house for the time being and I'm living at the club.

The only other bit of news is that I had a long chat with Rex Fisher, and he arranged a private meeting with Mosley himself. Sir Oswald isn't at all what I'd expected—and, by the way, he says I have to call him Tom now; all his friends do—I've never met anyone like him, in fact. He's a real leader. The sort you feel you could follow to hell and back. Anyway, old thing, the long and the short of it is that I've decided to join the Party. I wanted you to be one of the first to know. I'm going to work directly with Rex. He's got a special role in mind. All rather hush-hush.

Do think about what I said. It's just not the same without you, old girl.

With my best love,
Marcus

A car door slammed in the square below. Lydia crumpled the letter and dropped it in the wastepaper basket. She threw the box of chocolates after it. The noise made her father stir in his chair but he kept his eyes resolutely closed.

Lydia went into her bedroom, where she hung up her coat and put away her hat. She stared at her pale, set face in the damp-stained mirror over the washstand.

"Damn it," she said aloud. "Damn, damn, damn."

She returned to the sitting room. Mr. Serridge was in the hall, shouting for Mrs. Renton. She retrieved the chocolates from the wastepaper basket, ripped off the pink ribbon that fastened the box and removed the lid. The smell of good chocolate rose to meet her. Her mouth watered. She began to eat.

8

U NTIL YOU READ Philippa Penhow's diary with the benefit
of more than four years' hindsight, you don't realize what a
methodical man Serridge was. He always gave the impression of
being impulsive, and somehow this impression was reinforced by
the untidiness of his appearance. He was the sort of man whose
hair always needs brushing. Who apparently needs mothering.

Sunday, 16 February 1930

*We walked in Kensington Gardens this afternoon. I
could not help watching the nurses and their charges. If I
had married Vernon all those years ago, one of those little
children might have been my grandchild. What an extraordinary thought! All that is impossible now, of course.
I have made my bed and I must lie on it.*

*It seemed surprisingly mild for the time of year and
Major Serridge was in high spirits. He protected me from
the attentions of an overenthusiastic Labrador in the
kindest way possible. I think he is particularly fond of animals, and they instinctively trust him.*

We watched the children sailing their boats on the

Round Pond and then walked over toward the statue of Peter Pan near the Long Water. He said the statue was charming, and that it made him wish that he could be a child again.

As we were strolling back, he told me something that rather disturbed me. He said he was a little concerned about Mr. Orburn, and how he was managing Bleeding Heart Square on my behalf. He thinks he may be overcharging me. "I don't say he's a crook, of course, that wouldn't be fair. But he's a lawyer, and he's always got his eye on his fee." (How like the dear Major: always bending over backward to be fair to everyone.)

I pointed out that Aunt and I had always used Mr. Orburn, and before him his father, for all our legal business. The Major said that perhaps that was the problem—that Mr. Orburn had become a little too used to my trusting him.

You may have read somewhere that that's how lions catch an elephant—they isolate it from the rest of its herd: they separate it from its natural protectors.

As the crow flew, the village of Rawling was hardly more than forty miles from Bleeding Heart Square. If you were an earth-bound mortal, however, the distance was longer, and seemed far longer still. The village was six or seven miles north of Bishop's Stortford in a bleak and sparsely populated area of country where lanes meandered from hamlet to hamlet.

The railway did not pass through Rawling itself so Rory was obliged to travel to the nearest station at Mavering. The journey took him the better part of the morning—the bus to Liverpool

Street Station, a train to Bishop's Stortford, another train on the branch line passing through Saffron Walden, where he changed again to a small, almost empty train that took him slowly to Mavering itself.

There was too much time to think. At Liverpool Street Rory found a window seat in a third-class smoker. As the scruffy suburbs gave way to the equally scruffy countryside, he found himself thinking not so much about what lay before him as about Fenella.

He had telephoned her the previous evening. She had been in too much of a hurry to talk for long—she was on the verge of going out to another of her political meetings. This one was going to be a smaller affair than the last but the same speaker, Julian Dawlish, would be there. There was talk of founding a committee, Fenella said, and Rory had heard the note of excitement in her voice without altogether understanding it. He had come back from India to find Fenella had grown into a familiar stranger.

He was glad to leave the last of the trains. Mavering turned out to be a thin, uncertain village, little more than a scattering of agricultural cottages linking two substantial farms. Only two other passengers joined him on the small platform. Both of them looked curiously at Rory, as did the solitary porter. Rory ignored them and strode away.

Narton had drawn a sketch map on the back of an envelope that showed the way to Rawling from Mavering. Fifty yards from the station was a squat little church. Rory swung onto the footpath running along the wall of its graveyard. It was muddy underfoot but Narton had prepared him for that as well so he was wearing stout boots.

Beyond the churchyard, the path dropped down between fields. It was lined with bushes and the casual trees of the hedgerow, and in the summer must have been a green tunnel. Now there were clear views of bare fields on either side and rows of feathery elms. Though it was a gray day, it wasn't raining and the air smelled clean and unused.

After a few hundred yards, Rory slipped into the rhythm of the walk and began to enjoy himself. Even if this was a wild-goose chase, at least he was out of London. He came to a junction, where he bore right as Narton had told him to. After another quarter of a mile, the path came to an end at a five-bar gate of rotten wood with a stile on one side. Beyond it was a metalled lane.

Rory paused on the stile to light a cigarette. To the right, on the brow of a low ridge, was a red-brick house of some size set in parkland. The wall that ran along this side of the lane was in poor repair and in places had been patched with barbed wire. He jumped down and turned left into the lane, following a long, lazy bend that passed a lodge cottage on the right. When the lane straightened out, he found himself within sight of the village.

Rawling had another small, squat church. Beyond it, half hidden by a pair of Douglas firs and a majestic cedar of Lebanon, was the Vicarage. It was an ill-proportioned building constructed mainly of dirty yellow bricks, with round-headed window and door openings picked out in red. Apart from the mansion on the ridge outside the village, it was the only residence of any substance.

Rory walked up the short drive. Parked on the gravel outside the front door was a Ford 8 painted black on top and white underneath, like a penguin. According to Narton, the Vicar was a creature of habit. He usually paid calls in the first half of the morning. The second half he devoted to working in his study. Then came lunch, followed by a lengthy period of recovery.

"You can set your watch by Mr. Gladwyn," Narton had said. "Silly old bugger."

Rory rang the bell. The door was answered by a middle-aged maid who looked Rory up and down. Her face was neither welcoming nor hostile. She just wasn't very interested in him.

"Good morning," Rory said. "Is the Vicar in?"

"I'll see if he's free. Who shall I say?"

"My name's Wentwood. I've got a card here somewhere."

He took out his wallet. He almost made the mistake of giving her one from the *South Madras Times*. He suspected Mr. Gladwyn wouldn't welcome a journalist, not in this connection. Fortunately he also had cards with his parents' address in Hereford on them. He gave one of these to the maid.

She glanced at it and then at his face. "You'd better come and wait in the hall, sir." The card seemed to have reassured her as to his potential respectability. "You can wipe your feet there. Shall I say what it's in connection with?"

"A lady who was once a neighbor," Rory said. "Miss Penhow."

The maid's face remained bland and unreadable. She knocked on one of the closed doors and went into the room beyond, leaving him, hat in hand, standing in the tiled hall. He heard the mutter of voices. He stared at an engraving on the wall above the umbrella stand. It was a view of the village, showing both the church and the house on the ridge. RAWLING HALL, read the inscription. THE SEAT OF CHARLES ALFORDE, ESQ. Both the church and the house looked considerably more impressive than they did in actuality. Then the maid returned, glanced once more at his boots, and said that the Vicar would see him now.

Mr. Gladwyn was a round-faced, cheerful-looking man with a high color. He greeted Rory with mechanical enthusiasm, pumping his hand up and down. "How d'you do, Mr. Wentwood, how d'you do?" He called sharply after the maid, who was leaving the room, "Tell Cook I have a fancy for Brussels sprouts, Rebecca, and we need more coal in here." He turned back to Rory, and his face once again became cordial. "Now do sit down. How can I help you?"

"It's about one of your former parishioners, sir. Miss Penhow of Morthams Farm."

"Yes, yes. Rebecca told me. May I ask what your interest is?"

"I'm here on behalf of Miss Penhow's niece Fenella Kensley." Rory adjusted the truth a little: "We're engaged to be married."

"I'm sure congratulations are in order," Mr. Gladwyn said automatically. "But—forgive me—I'm not sure how I can help you. I've not seen Miss Penhow for more than four years, and in fact she only lived in Rawling for a short time. I barely knew her. As I'm sure Miss Kensley knows, she moved abroad."

"Well that's it, you see." Rory hesitated, choosing his words with care. "Miss Kensley hasn't heard from her aunt for several years and naturally she's rather worried. Miss Penhow hasn't written since she moved down to Rawling."

"These things happen," Mr. Gladwyn pointed out. "Relations sometimes do drift apart from one another, especially if they move."

"There's also some sad news to pass on. Miss Penhow's brother died—almost certainly she won't have heard."

The Vicar had been standing with his back to the fire. But now he sat down at the desk in the window embrasure. He picked up a pipe and his tobacco pouch and swung round to face his visitor. "I know there was some concern about Miss Penhow's whereabouts. I talked to the police about it a few years ago. You see, I received a letter from Miss Penhow more than six months after she left Rawling."

"That must have been near the end of 1930. Mr. Kensley died in 1932."

Mr. Gladwyn nodded. "She felt embarrassed at writing directly to her relations—or to Mr. Serridge, her—her friend. You see there was an . . . an affair of the heart. It seems that she had met someone and decided on the spur of the moment to move abroad. The police examined the letter very carefully, and after that they were quite satisfied that there was nothing mysterious about Miss Penhow's departure."

Rory thought it depended on whether you wanted there to be a mystery. The police could not have had much to go on. A woman who had not lived long in the area was suddenly no longer there. There was no body. There were no anxious relatives pestering the authorities about their missing loved one. And presumably there had been no evidence of financial irregularity either.

Mr. Gladwyn lit his pipe. As he dropped the match into the ashtray on the desk he contrived to look at his wristwatch in a way that wasn't obviously rude but made its meaning quite clear.

"I wonder if I might see the letter, if you still have it?" Rory said.

The Vicar studied him through the smoke. "I suppose there's no harm in it. If it would clear the air, as it were. But it is a private letter. Though I've no objection myself to your seeing it, I have to think of others."

"Miss Kensley is now Miss Penhow's nearest relation, sir."

"I'm surprised the police have not told her that her aunt wrote to me."

"They did indeed. But I know she's still very concerned—increasingly, as time goes by without more news. I'm keen to relieve her mind, as I'm sure you understand. The point is, she has convinced herself that this letter is a forgery."

"That's nonsense."

"She may well be mistaken, sir, I quite agree. But if I could see the letter and compare it with a sample of Miss Penhow's handwriting which I have, it would allow me to set her mind at rest. Of course I would treat the contents as confidential. But perhaps you'd rather I didn't see it at all."

Rory allowed the implication, that the Vicar might have something to conceal, to hang in the smoke-filled air. Mr. Gladwyn struck another match and applied himself to relighting his pipe.

"I've nothing to hide, Mr. Wentwood," he said at last. "And naturally I don't want Miss Kensley to suffer unnecessary pain. Very well, I will let you see the letter here in this room for ten minutes on condition that you discuss it only with Miss Kensley, and even then only if you see fit. I must warn you the contents may be painful to her. It's not the sort of letter I should like a daughter of mine to read."

"I shall bear that in mind, sir," Rory said. "Thank you."

The Vicar opened the lowest drawer of the desk on the left-hand side and removed a buff folder. He took out an envelope and motioned to Rory to draw up a chair to the desk. He removed a letter from the envelope and held it out to Rory. It consisted of a single sheet closely written on both sides.

Grand Central Station
New York City
USA

December 3rd, 1930

My dear Mr. Gladwyn

I expect you are surprised to hear from me after all this time. I hope you won't mind my writing to you. This is a very difficult letter for me to write, the more so because I have a favor to ask. Perhaps I should have written to Joseph, rather than you. After all, it is he whom I have wronged. But I thought the truth would come better in person from you, a man of the cloth, than through a letter. I have hurt him enough without that. As I have cause to know, a tender heart beats beneath that rough exterior of his.

I am afraid you will have realized by now that Joseph and I are not married. We would have been if Joseph had not had a living wife who refused to divorce him. I must admit that my conscience was not easy with this, though I never doubted the sincerity of Joseph's love for me.

Out of the blue, just after we had moved into Morthams Farm, I received a letter from an old friend, a sailor I might have married many years ago had my aunt agreed. But he was poor and I was foolish. I made a mistake I have bitterly regretted ever since.

Everything happened very quickly. It did not take me long to discover that my friend's feelings hadn't changed, and nor had mine. He was free. So was I. At last I could right the wrong I had done so many years before.

Please tell Joseph that I am now married, and on the threshold of a new life with my husband. Ask him to forgive me. I know I

*have wronged him very deeply, but I know in the long run this will
be the best thing for both of us. I remember Joseph telling me once
that a clean break heals sooner. I hope this will be true in his case
too. I pray he will be able to forgive me.*

I send him my warmest good wishes—and to you, of course.

Yours sincerely,

P. M. Penhow

"May I see the envelope?" Rory asked.

Mr. Gladwyn passed it to him without comment. It was addressed
to him at the Vicarage; it had a franked American stamp and a New
York postmark.

"You see? All above board."

"Yes, sir."

Rory sat back in the chair and ran his fingers through his hair.
"May I compare the letter with a sample of handwriting I have
here?"

"By all means. Though the police have already done that. They
brought in one of their experts. They seemed perfectly satisfied."

Rory unfolded the sheet of paper that he had found in his chest of
drawers. He laid it side by side with the New York letter on the desk
and methodically compared individual characters. There was a
strong family resemblance between them, though there were small
differences in their formation, and the handwriting of the letter
from New York was smaller, squeezed to fit one sheet of paper. But
there were also minor but equally obvious variations between Miss
Penhow's hurried draft letter to Mr. Orburn and her more carefully
written commentary on the parable of the Prodigal Son.

"Well?" said Mr. Gladwyn. "What do you think?"

"That they could easily have been written by the same person."

"Precisely." Mr Gladwyn stood up, perhaps hoping to encourage his visitor to do likewise. "You've met Mr. Serridge, I take it?"

"Yes."

"I've seen something of him in the last few years. And what I've seen inclines me to give him the benefit of the doubt in a case like this. It is true that Miss Penhow left rather suddenly. But their relationship was unorthodox from the start, I'm afraid. We have a perfectly reasonable explanation of why she left."

"Isn't it strange that she's not been in touch with Miss Kensley or any of her friends?"

"I don't think so. You forget—this is a woman previously of good character who has been tempted into doing something of which she now feels greatly ashamed. She is trying to build a new life. The last thing she wants is reminders of the old." The Vicar looked at his watch again, and this time he made no attempt to conceal what he was doing. "I'm not naive, Mr. Wentwood—I fancy I can see as far into human nature as the next man. But remember your Bible, eh? Cast not the first stone."

Rory stood up. "Mr. Serridge still lives at Morthams Farm?"

"Yes, indeed. Though he spends a good deal of his time in town. These haven't been easy years for farmers, as I'm sure you know, but he's made quite a success of Morthams since he bought it from Captain Ingleby-Lewis." There was a tap on the door and the maid appeared with a coal scuttle. "Rebecca, would you show Mr. Wentwood out?"

During Lydia's first morning at Shires and Trimble, she learned how to place files in alphabetical order in drawers and how to moisten stamps and put them on envelopes. Her instructor, the junior clerk Mr. Smethwick, had pale, flaky skin and was very particular about how things should be done in the office. Stamps, for example, should be placed so their borders were as nearly aligned as possible with the edges of the envelope. Ideally the gap between the edge of the stamp and the border of the envelope should be about a sixth of an inch above and to the right of the stamp.

"These little details matter, Mrs. Langstone," he said. "It tells the client we are a firm that knows how to keep things straight, a firm he can trust with his business."

"But how can you be certain of that?" Lydia asked. "The client might not notice at all, or they might even think we were being rather too fussy."

"Nonsense. If you don't mind my saying so, Mrs. Langstone, you can tell that you've never worked in an office before."

The typist chipped in, "I bet there's not a lot you don't know about the secret workings of the mind, Mr. Smethwick."

Mr. Smethwick hesitated, visibly uncertain whether or not this should be taken as a compliment, and then smirked as his riposte came to him: "Then all I can say is you'd better watch what you're thinking."

Miss Tuffley gave a shriek of laughter, which won her a disapproving stare from Mr. Reynolds, the senior clerk.

Mr. Shires himself did not come into the office. Mr. Trimble did not appear to exist. Mr. Reynolds ruled supreme in Mr. Shires' absence. He was too wrapped up in his own work to talk to anyone unless it was absolutely necessary. But Miss Tuffley more than made up for his silence by chattering non-stop whenever her red nails were not dancing noisily on the typewriter keys, and sometimes even then. It soon became clear that she knew more about the cinema—the films, the actors, the gossip—than anyone else Lydia had ever met.

The office boy, who was usually entrusted with the envelopes and stamps, was ill. The work was tedious and oddly tiring. Lydia tried to avoid looking at the clock on the wall above Mr. Reynolds' high desk. She would not have believed it possible that time could move so slowly. At a little after eleven o'clock there was a variation in the monotony in the form of a stout woman in a pinafore who brought round a tray of tea, after which Mr. Smethwick taught Lydia how to answer the telephone. It was important to master the correct salutation: "Shires and Trimble. *Good* morning," with the emphasis firmly on the adjective, to create a mood of optimism and hope. According to Mr. Smethwick, one's intonation should create the impression that one was mentally in a state of high alert and also smiling in a welcoming way.

At one o'clock Lydia went to the cloakroom to fetch her hat and coat. There was a pause in the rattle of the typewriter keys in the general office. She heard Miss Tuffley's voice raised in argument with Mr. Smethwick: ". . . herself as Lady Muck. If you ask me she's . . ." Typing drowned the rest of the sentence and reduced Mr. Smethwick's reply to a low rumble. Lydia settled her hat on her head and went back to the general office. Mr. Smethwick asked her to post the letters she had so carefully stamped. "Think you can manage that, Mrs. Langstone?"

She went downstairs and opened the street door. She was so tired and angry she wanted to cry. Outside lay freedom, albeit for only an hour. She paused in the doorway to savor the gray pavement, a taxi, the east wall of the chapel and a gray sky. So that's what paradise looked like. An absence of Shires and Trimble.

As she stepped onto the pavement, the taxi's rear window slid down. A thin and very elegant woman stared at Lydia, who came to an abrupt halt.

"Hello, Lydia," said the woman, and the dream of freedom died a premature death.

"Hello, Mother," said Lydia.

Rawling's solitary pub was called the Alforde Arms. Rory ate bread and cheese by the fire in the saloon bar, and washed down his lunch with half a pint of bitter. In India, he would often daydream about this sort of day—a simple lunch in a village pub, logs smoldering on a hearth, a muddy walk under a gray, wintry sky swirling with rooks.

While he ate, he summarized to himself what he would report to Sergeant Narton when they met this evening. It wasn't a great deal: the Vicar had received a letter from New York which purported to be from Philippa Penhow; she could indeed have written it; and if it was genuine it offered a plausible explanation for her disappearance and her silence, particularly if one allowed for the shame she must have felt in allowing Serridge to seduce her in the first place. There was also the fact that Mr. Gladwyn seemed to like Mr. Serridge. Finally—and this was the only really disturbing piece of information he had acquired—Captain Ingleby-Lewis had sold Morthams Farm to Serridge. Lydia Langstone's father was somehow involved in this. He had a disturbing sense that the boundaries of the whole affair had shifted, and that even his own role in it might not be what he had assumed it was.

After lunch, he ordered a second half-pint. The landlord was ready to chat, though some of his attention remained with the farm laborers talking in the other bar.

"You on holiday or something?" the man inquired.

"Yes—just a day trip. I fancied stretching my legs and getting a bit of country air."

"I thought you were a townie. You can always tell. From London, maybe?"

Rory agreed that he was.

"Strange that," the landlord said, resting his elbows on the counter between them. "Your idea of a day out is coming down here. Our idea of a day out is going up to town."

"The grass is greener, eh?" Rory picked up his glass and began to turn away.

The landlord was not going to be deflected so easily. "What I say is, human beings are born dissatisfied. They always want something else, something they haven't got."

"That's very true." Rory glanced out of the window: the light was already fading and there were spots of rain on the glass. "Though at present I must admit I don't feel much enthusiasm for walking back to Mavering."

"You're making for the station?"

Rory nodded.

"That won't take you long," the landlord said. "Twenty minutes' brisk walk, if that."

"Took me rather longer on the way here."

"Which way did you come?"

Rory described it as best as he could.

"That's the long way round."

"Somebody gave me the directions."

"If you carry on down the road and take the field gate on the left, there's a much shorter route. Unless it's closed for some reason." The landlord turned his head and bellowed at the laborers in the public bar: "Jim? Nothing wrong with the footpath to Mavering, is there?"

"Which one?" came an answering bellow, and another roar of laughter.

"The one by Nartons', you daft fool."

"There weren't this morning. That's the way I came."

"Nartons'?" Rory said abruptly. "What's that?"

"Mr. and Mrs. Narton's place," the landlord said. "The path's on the left, just beyond it. Follow that, and you come out by Mavering church, same way you came but much sooner. That'll make life a bit easier for you, eh?"

"You're looking fearfully pale, dear," Lady Cassington said. "Are you sure you're eating properly?"

"Yes, thank you, Mother," Lydia said. "I haven't got long—I want to find something to eat and I need to post these letters."

Lady Cassington glanced down at the pile of neatly stamped envelopes that lay between them on the rear seat of the taxi. "You've actually got a job?" She made it sound like an unsightly skin condition.

"Yes."

"How odd. Marcus hasn't stopped your allowance, I know that for a fact—he told me himself. Think yourself lucky, my dear. Some men would have had no hesitation whatsoever."

"I don't want his money."

"Nonsense. Anyway, you should be at home. I simply don't know where you've found all these silly ideas. A woman's place is by her husband's side."

"You didn't stay by yours," Lydia pointed out.

Lady Cassington stared at her.

"My father's, I mean," Lydia said.

"That was quite different. Circumstances alter cases. You've seen what sort of man your father is."

Lydia stared out of the window at students carrying piles of library books and wearing brightly colored scarves. The taxi was driving north through the quiet squares of Bloomsbury. Lady Cassington screwed another cigarette into her tortoiseshell holder. When she next spoke, her voice was gentler.

"Marcus says he told you he's joining the Fascists."

Lydia nodded.

"They're obviously rather impressed with him—he's just the sort of recruit they're looking for. I saw Tom Mosley the other night, you know, and he told me that if they had more young men like Marcus they could be forming a government in eighteen months. Fin thinks Mosley's quite the coming man and it'll do us no harm as a family to have someone on the inside. Marcus will be working with Rex Fisher at first, I understand, so he's in safe hands."

"How is Fin?" Lydia asked, trying to deflect the conversation from Marcus to her stepfather.

"Very well, thank you. He sends his love, by the way. He's frightfully pleased about Marcus, of course."

Lydia listened to her mother's voice running on and watched the students. She wondered what it would have been like if she had been able to go to university. She could have had a proper job afterward. She could have earned £500 a year and had a room of her own. Her life would be full of people who led interesting and uncluttered lives, unencumbered with the routines, obligations and possessions that filled the existence of families like the Langstones and the Cassingtons.

"Talking of Rex Fisher, by the way," her mother went on, "I think he's rather interested in Pammy."

Lydia blinked. "But he's old enough to be her father."

"Nothing wrong in that. Fin's older than me, after all. I think it can make a marriage more stable if the man's older."

Lydia thought that stability was the last thing that her sister wanted from life. She said, "Do you think Pammy likes him?"

"I know what's in your mind. The Fishers are nobodies despite the title. One used to see old Fisher about occasionally but no one ever met the mother. But Rex himself is all right. Did you know he was at school with Wilfred Langstone? Apparently they were quite friendly. Anyway, Fin thinks he and Pammy would do very well together, and so do I. I mean, he's fearfully rich, you know. One can't argue with that."

Lydia stared at the back of the driver's head on the other side of the partition. The taxi chugged round another pigeon-streaked square of grimy London brick. She took a deep breath.

"The thing is, I don't want to go back to Marcus. I made a mistake in marrying him."

"Nonsense, dear. Many people feel that, especially if they've had a bad quarrel. It's enough to give anyone the hump. But you have to put all that behind you. You know, if Marcus goes in for politics, he's going to need a hostess. If he gets into the House eventually, and there's no reason why he shouldn't, he'll need you even more."

"Marcus in Parliament? I can't quite imagine it."

"Fin says that now it's only a matter of time before the Fascists acquire some seats. And if Marcus were to stand for Lydmouth, say, Fin could give him quite a lot of help."

Lydia looked at her wristwatch. "I'd better go back to the office. You could drop me off at Holborn Circus."

"You'll think about all this? You promise?"

"I promise."

"Marcus is being very patient. But he's a man, you know, and men have needs."

"So do women."

"Very true, dear. Though in my experience it's rather different for us. Which is rather my point. To be perfectly frank I doubt many women are able to satisfy their needs in Bleeding Heart Square."

9

YOU READ this entry over and over again. Was this just a way of making money? Or did Serridge actually enjoy it as well? Did he always enjoy it?

Wednesday, 19 February 1930

A red-letter day! I am so excited I can hardly hold my pen. We went to Hampstead Heath this afternoon for a stroll up Parliament Hill and afterward a cup of tea at the café at the bottom of Pond Street. Heaven knows, I was expecting nothing but a pleasant afternoon. But I have never been so surprised in my life—not just once, but twice!!

We walked up the hill, chatting of this and that. It was overcast with quite a chilly wind. I thought Major Serridge seemed rather distrait. At the top of the hill we paused to look down over the great smoky city below. Suddenly, as if by magic, the sun came out. He pointed out the Monument, the dome of St. Paul's, the river and even what he said were the North Downs far beyond, though I cannot be absolutely sure I saw them myself. Then he said, rather abruptly and apropos of nothing in particular, that he thought I was the sort of person who had a particular affinity with animals. I said I'd thought just the same about him. He went on in a very gruff voice that he hoped I wouldn't mind but he had a little present for me.

He looked away from me, toward a man standing farther down the hill so only his shoulders and his head were visible. The Major waved to him and the man gave a sort of salute and began to walk toward us. As he came nearer I saw that he was holding a lead, and at the end of the lead was the sweetest little dog in the world.

As soon as he saw me, the dog began to tug at the lead and bark. A moment later, it was sniffing my boots. Major Serridge took the lead from the man, who walked away from us at once. The dog was wagging its tail like anything. Its eyes sparkled with intelligence and mischief. Major Serridge asked me if I liked it. I said, of course I did. Who wouldn't? I asked what its name was. He said that was up to me. I said I didn't understand. And he said it was MY dog!

I said he mustn't make fun of me, that he knew they don't allow animals at the Rushmere Hotel, even a little darling like this one. He told me not to worry about that. He said he'd make sure the dog was looked after "until you've got a place of your own."

He pressed the lead into my hands. I could not help bending down and stroking the dear little dog, who turned out to be a little boy. He wanted to lick me, the darling.

Suddenly the Major said, rather gruffly, that he had "a plan that would remove every obstacle." I stood up and *said I couldn't understand what he meant. The doggy wound his lead round my legs.*

To my astonishment, Major Serridge went down on one knee, there and then on the summit of Parliament Hill! I remember almost exactly what he said next, his words are burned indelibly on my memory. "My dear—I may call you Philippa, may I not?—I know there are many obstacles between us. You are so far above me in every way. Even if you will consent to it, I know we cannot at present be married in the eyes of man. But would you at least consider whether we might be married in the eyes of God?"

Of course you can't know how reliable Philippa Penhow's account is. Her rosy spectacles were so thick that she was the next best thing to blind. Perhaps she saw and heard what she wanted to see and hear, just like everyone else does.

The Lamb was less crowded than it had been the previous evening, perhaps because it was later. Apart from a knot of noisy undergraduates from University College in the corner, there was little conversation. Most people nursed their drinks and read the evening paper.

Sergeant Narton was late so Rory took his beer over to the table they had used before. He stared morosely into the heart of the fire. On the way from Bleeding Heart Square, he had telephoned Fenella from a call box to ask whether he might drop in later in the evening. She had pleaded tiredness and said she was going to bed early.

"You can come tomorrow evening if you like," she had said, and it had seemed to him that she didn't much care one way or the other.

He glanced up as the door to the street opened. Narton came in, his eyes sweeping the room. He went to the bar, where he ordered half a pint of mild-and-bitter. He brought it across to Rory's table.

"You look as if you've lost a pound and found a farthing," he observed.

Rory shrugged, not caring how Narton thought he looked.

"Well?" Narton stared at Rory over the rim of his glass. "Did you get anywhere?"

"With the Vicar? Yes and no."

"What do you mean? Did he let you see the letter?"

"Oh yes. I compared it with the sample I found in the chest of drawers. I'm no expert but it looks as if the same person could have written both."

"Any address on it?"

"Grand Central Station."

"Fat lot of use," Narton said. "What about the envelope and the stamp?"

"They looked perfectly genuine to me."

"These things can be forged."

"I'm sure they can," Rory said wearily. "But it's not just me, is it? As the Vicar was at pains to tell me, the police found an expert to examine it and he couldn't find anything amiss either."

"The point is the so-called expert didn't necessarily want to," Narton said.

"I'm not sure I follow you."

The policeman scratched his wrist. "I don't think our investigation into the disappearance of Miss Penhow was as thorough as it might have been. This is between ourselves, you understand. I'm not saying there was anything going on that shouldn't have been, mind. All I'm saying is that some officers thought that looking for Miss Penhow was a waste of time and money. No body, you see. Nothing suspicious at all, not really, apart from the fact that she suddenly wasn't there. But that's not a crime. It's true that she sold a lot of shares in the month or so before she went. Some of it must have gone to buy the farm for Serridge. But not all of it. And realizing capital makes sense if you're planning to start a new life."

"Then why are you so convinced that something has happened to her?"

Narton planted his elbows on the table and leaned toward Rory. "Partly because there's evidence that suggests she had no intention of going away from Morthams Farm. It came to light after the investigation was finished. That's the reason we reopened the case."

"What evidence?"

"I can't tell you that. It's confidential."

Rory sat back in his chair. "Just as you didn't tell me you live in Rawling? Was that confidential too?"

"Don't take it the wrong way, Mr. Wentwood. It just wasn't relevant. No point in muddying the waters, eh? Did anything else come up?"

"There was one thing."

"Yes?" A spasm like pain passed over Narton's face. "What?"

"Something the Vicar said as I was leaving. He mentioned that Serridge and Miss Penhow had bought Morthams Farm from Captain Ingleby-Lewis. It must be the chap at Bleeding Heart Square."

"It is."

"You knew that too? Why didn't you say?"

Narton stared coldly at him. "Police officers try not to tell members of the public everything they know in the professional way, Mr. Wentwood. It wouldn't be very sensible, would it? It's perfectly true, though. The Rawling Hall estate used to belong to a family called Alforde. When the old man died a few years back, they had to sell up. The widow had a heart attack while they were sorting out the sale. They reckon the shock killed her. Most of what was left of the money went to Mr. Alforde's heir, his brother's son. But there was one farm, Morthams, that was outside the entail, because Mr. Alforde had bought it in the nineties to round off the estate. Mrs. Alforde had added a codicil to her will. She left Morthams to her own nephew."

"Ingleby-Lewis."

Narton nodded. "The place was heavily mortgaged, they say. He had a devil of a job trying to sell it. Then Serridge came along and suddenly the thing was done." Narton tapped the side of his nose. "I can guess whose money went to buy it. Ten to one Miss Penhow paid over the odds and Serridge and Ingleby-Lewis split the proceeds." He held up his hand like a traffic policeman. "Maybe. Who knows?"

"And now Ingleby-Lewis is living in Serridge's London house?"

"Which used to belong to Miss Penhow. Something fishy, eh? Serridge has got a tame lawyer, a man called Shires, and he handled the purchase of the farm and probably a lot of other business for Miss Penhow and Serridge. You can bet most of it was on a cash basis." Narton rubbed his eyes as though trying to erase his tiredness. "But proving it? That's another thing. And that's the trouble with this case. Nothing to get your teeth into. You can't point at anything and say, there's the body, there's the robbery, there's the crime."

"Can't you question Ingleby-Lewis?"

"Of course I bloody can't," Narton said.

"Why not?"

"It would give the game away. Besides, he may be on his uppers but he's not the sort of man whose arm you can easily twist. He's got friends."

"Serridge?" Rory thought that behind Serridge was Shires and the might and trickery of the law.

"Not just him. Do you know who Ingleby-Lewis's ex-wife is? That young lady's mother? She's Lady Cassington now. She's got a house in Mayfair and an estate somewhere in the West Country. Don't let anyone tell you we are all equal before the law, young man. Because we are not. And the gentry are the worst of all. Say the wrong thing to one of them, and you find the whole world comes down on you like a ton of bricks. They're all bloody related. They're all looking out for each other." He swallowed the rest of his beer and wiped his mouth with the back of his hand. "What this country needed was the guillotine. That's where we went wrong. Those Frenchies knew what was what."

Rory was conscious of a twinge of disappointment. Lydia Langstone wasn't just married—she was one of those upper-class women whose lives his sisters read about in magazines. She would have been presented at Court and had her wedding pictures in the *Tatler*. But what the devil was she doing in Bleeding Heart Square? Not that it mattered tuppence to him, of course. He was merely curious.

Narton coughed, hackingly, continuously. He took a cigarette from a packet and tapped it on the table. "If Ingleby-Lewis would talk, he could tell us a thing or two, I'm sure of that. But he won't talk to me, of course. He knows who I am."

"You've met him?"

"In the course of the investigation. He knows I'm a police officer and that I was concerned in the Penhow case. But who knows? Maybe he said something to his daughter. Maybe, if you and her get talking, you could slip in a question here or there, see if she knows anything about Morthams Farm or Miss Penhow."

"I don't know. It seems a bit unsporting."

Narton lit the cigarette and tossed the dead match into the ashtray. "Murder isn't a sport, Mr. Wentwood. It's a matter of life or death. You do understand that, don't you?"

Rory said nothing.

"Anyway, can't stay here chatting." Narton pushed back his chair and stood up. "Thank you for what you're doing, Mr. Wentwood. It's not gone unnoticed by the powers that be."

"There's the small matter of my expenses," Rory said, his uneasiness finding another outlet. "The train fare today, mainly. I don't know whether you'd run to lunch as well."

"Keep a record, Mr. Wentwood, and give me a list with receipts. It will be easier if I put in a single claim for you at the end of all this. But your money is as safe as houses, you can be sure of that. One advantage of dealing with the police."

"I don't want to carry on with this."

Narton wrapped his muffler carefully round his neck. "Let's have a chat in a day or two. I need to see one or two people, think about one or two things. Believe me, Mr. Wentwood, if I can find an alternative I will." He lowered his voice. "Now you can oblige me by keeping your eyes open. And don't do anything foolish. Serridge is dangerous. I don't want another death on my conscience."

"What do you mean? Who's died already?"

Narton looked blankly at him. Then his lips turned down at the corners. "Why, Miss Penhow, of course. You surely don't believe the poor lady can still be alive?"

He turned up the collar of his overcoat and pulled his hat down low so all that was visible of his face were his eyes and the bridge of his nose. He stubbed out the half-smoked cigarette and slipped out of the pub.

Rory stared at the broken cigarette in the ashtray, along with the other butts. He had watched how Narton smoked. The man either smoked his cigarettes until the ends grew so hot he could no longer hold them or kept what was left unsmoked for later.

So something had rattled him. There had been a false note in what he had been saying. Where, exactly? What if Narton hadn't meant Miss Penhow's death but someone else's? Who else had died?

Herbert Narton knew he had taken a terrible risk in encouraging young Wentwood to go to Rawling. True, the scheme had worked after a fashion, but there was no saying that it would not eventually backfire. Nor had the results been what he had hoped for. Still, Wentwood was living at Bleeding Heart Square and there was always the chance of progress in that direction.

At Liverpool Street he caught the train. He tried to doze during the journey. He knew he should eat but he found the consumption of food more and more of an effort. He seemed to be living on air. Perhaps because of that he felt literally less heavy and less substantial than usual, as though he were fading away. All that was left of substance was the hard, irreducible core of his anger.

Anger? Not quite the right word. Sorrow was almost as good. Fear was somewhere in the mixture, and even a form of love. But none of the words fit, and none of them ever would.

Nobody noticed him leaving the train at Mavering. It was a small station and the evening rush was long since over. Only one man was on duty and he was dealing with Hinks from the sorting office at the mail van. He walked down to the church and took the field path to Rawling. It was a clear night, and the moon was up, though slipping in and out of clouds. He had a torch in his pocket but did not use it. He had walked this way so often he could have followed the path blindfolded. When he came to the fork, he took the left-hand path. This was narrower than the one on the right that led to Rawling Hall before it reached the village. He walked more slowly, more cautiously. The going was muddier underfoot. The world seemed darker too, as though this tiny part of Essex had less light in it than the rest.

He came at last to where there was a gap in the hedgerow and he could look up the slope of the meadow to the house itself, with the huddle of farm buildings on the right. There was the soft glow of lamplight in two of the first-floor windows. Morthams Farm. He imagined he was an owl flying over Morthams toward Rawling, and his eyes scoured the fields between the farm and the village until they found the tiled roof of the little barn.

Scratch the itch.

Narton wondered why he had bothered to come. He scraped his nails into the soft skin of the underside of his wrist until he broke through to the flesh beneath—until, yet again, he made himself bleed. He scratched harder still and moaned with the pain. As he scratched, he allowed his eyes to sweep from side to side across the meadow. The grass was the darkest of grays.

Better now. He licked the blood, warm and salty. The moisture cooled on his skin.

It was all still there, he thought, beneath the field dappled with moonlight and shadows. Everything that had happened, layer upon layer, because nothing ever really went away. Bleeding Heart Square was full of layers too, layers of blood, and so was the barn. Especially the barn.

The meadow was full of shifting shapes. One of the shapes resolved itself into a girl wobbling on a bicycle as she followed the slope of the field toward the farmhouse. He heard her laughter, high and excited, and knew that her attention was not on him or the field or even the bicycle but on another shadow beside her.

"I'm a bloody fool to stand here," Narton said aloud. *All those layers of blood, you can never wash them away.*

His ears were unnaturally sharp. He heard the chink of harness from the farm buildings. A dog began to bark, though whether in the house or the yard he couldn't tell. The barn would be empty, though.

Empty of the living. Crowded with the dead.

At that moment an idea drifted into his mind, settled in the silt at the bottom, sprouted, put out roots and flowered. All that in an instant. Sometimes, he thought, all a man has is his folly. No wonder he clings to it.

Lydia cooked Welsh rarebit for supper, following the detailed instructions Mrs. Renton had provided. She had bought a bottle of pale ale to add to the cheese topping as it melted in the saucepan but Captain Ingleby-Lewis chanced to find it before she could use it. She cleared two thirds of the great scarred dining table and served the meal on matching plates, one slightly chipped.

It was the first time that she and her father had eaten in such a relatively formal way and in the soft light this end of the room looked almost like a normal room in a normal house. Her father complimented her on the rarebit. Though he had been drinking beer steadily since lunchtime, he appeared to have reached an equilibrium that left him, at least for the time being, amiable and reasonably alert.

"Well, this is cozy, eh?" he said, lining up fork and knife exactly at half past six on his plate. "You're full of unexpected talents, my dear."

"Thank you."

"How did you get on at that lawyer fellow's?"

"It's rather boring work."

"I can't imagine how those chaps manage it. Sitting in an office all day and shuffling bits of paper around. It'd drive me mad." He stroked his moustache approvingly. "Fact is, God didn't create me to be a desk wallah."

"Father, there's something I wanted to ask you." *Father* still sounded strange in her ears. "About those hearts."

"Eh? What?"

"The ones Mr. Serridge was sent in the post. There have been two since I've been here. Have there been others?"

"Perhaps," Captain Ingleby-Lewis admitted cautiously. "Can't really say."

"When did they start?"

"I don't know." He looked up at the ceiling. "A month or two ago?"

"But why should anyone do that sort of thing?"

Ingleby-Lewis gave way to a fit of coughing. When it had finished, he lit a cigarette. "Some crackpot, my dear. The world's full of them. Take my advice: best thing to do is put it out of your mind."

"But it's not that easy. Is there—is there something about Mr. Serridge I should know?"

"Perfectly decent fellow," said Ingleby-Lewis. "Known him for years. Not a gentleman, of course, but can't blame him for that. If you ask me, people talk a lot of rot about that sort of thing. Damn it, I shall have to pop out for some cigarettes."

At that moment there came a tap on the door.

"Come in," cried Ingleby-Lewis, and struggled to his feet.

The door opened, revealing Malcolm Fimberry on the threshold with a bottle of wine cradled in his arms.

"I say," he squeaked. "Sorry to disturb you. I—I thought I might open some wine and I wondered if I could borrow a corkscrew."

"Wine, eh?" Ingleby-Lewis sprang toward him. "Nothing simpler, old man. Come and sit down. Lydia, my dear, would you find Mr. Fimberry a corkscrew in the kitchen?"

"If you would like to join me in a glass," Fimberry suggested, "I'd be more than pleased."

"How very kind." Ingleby-Lewis patted him on the shoulder and removed the bottle from his grasp. "Three glasses as well then, please, Lydia. Ah, a Beaujolais, I see. How very wise. You're quite right of course—solitary drinking is not something one should encourage. Besides, life holds few finer pleasures than a glass of wine with friends."

When Lydia returned with three unmatched glasses and a corkscrew, she found her father and Mr. Fimberry sitting on either side of the fireplace and smoking Mr. Fimberry's cigarettes. Her father took the corkscrew and removed the cork with a skill born of long experience. He poured a stream of wine into the nearest glass.

"None for me, thank you," Lydia said.

"Nonsense," Ingleby-Lewis said. "Just a sip. Do you good. Warm you up." He turned to Fimberry. "My daughter feels the cold, you know. Especially at night." He measured a thimbleful into the smallest of the glasses and handed it ceremoniously to Lydia. He gave another glass to Fimberry and the largest one to himself. He raised his own glass to the light. "A fine color. Your good health." He swallowed a third of the contents.

"I hear you have a position at Shires and Trimble in Rosington Place, Mrs. Langstone," Fimberry said, leaning toward her. "That must be interesting. Working for a solicitor, I mean."

"It's early days yet," Lydia said grimly.

"You're just opposite the chapel, of course. In fact, as far as I can work out from an eighteenth-century plan of the palace, the house where Shires and Trimble are must be built over part of the Almoner's lodging. Remarkable to think of the people who must have walked about here in their time. Good Queen Bess, Sir

Thomas More, Richard the Third, John of Gaunt, all those splendid prelates of the Church. Why, we walk on history in this part of London. And that's why we need Mr. Howlett to guard our gates and keep order. In legal terms, Rosington Place, Bleeding Heart Square and their environs form the Rosington Liberty, and hence in many respects they still fall under the jurisdiction of the Bishop of Rosington."

"Very true," Ingleby-Lewis said. "A spot more? No?" He refilled his own glass. "You must know the place like the back of your hand."

Mr. Fimberry simpered, his eyes huge behind his pince-nez. "Oh, there are some fascinating stories associated with it, no doubt about that. After the Reformation, the Catholic dead were sometimes secretly interred beneath the chapel, in the days when the palace was rented to the Spanish ambassador. It is said that the bodies were brought here to Bleeding Heart Square, and then transferred to the chapel in Rosington Palace. They were secretly buried at midnight, to the accompaniment of solemn masses, beneath the undercroft floor."

"Extraordinary yarn," Ingleby-Lewis said, his eyes straying again toward the bottle.

"Nobody really knows if the story is true," Fimberry went on. "There are those who claim that the funeral processions still walk on certain nights of the year, with a line of recusants carrying the corpses from Bleeding Heart Square to Rosington Chapel. Others say they have heard singing from the chapel when it is empty. And some people believe that the bodies lie beneath the square itself. There are many ghosts, you know." He glanced sideways at Lydia and gave her a tight-lipped smile. "Though I can find no historical trace of the one that people claim to have seen most often."

"Ghosts, eh?" Ingleby-Lewis said. "Claptrap, if you ask me. If I ever come across a ghost I'm going to put my arm right through him."

"A little more wine, Mrs. Langstone?" Fimberry seized the bottle and gestured toward Lydia's untouched glass.

"No, thank you."

"Thank you, obliged to you," Ingleby-Lewis said, holding out his empty glass.

"Which ghost is that?" Lydia said quietly.

"The ghost of the lady who lost her heart." Fimberry swallowed the rest of his wine and gave himself another glass. His face was now pinker than ever and covered with a sheen of perspiration. He took off his pince-nez and rubbed the lenses on his handkerchief. "A tragic story. The legend goes that there was a dance, a great ball at the Spanish ambassador's. Royalty came. There was dancing and drinking and gambling far into the night."

"Good as a play, eh?" Ingleby-Lewis said contentedly, stretching out his legs in shiny, neatly creased trousers.

"There was one particularly beautiful lady there, Mrs. Langstone," Fimberry went on. "The story goes that she had married an old and wealthy husband, that she had been forced into the match by her parents. She did not love the man. Then, at the ball, which was a masked affair, I should have said, she met a charming stranger—tall and dark and everything a young woman could hope for in a lover. The husband was out of the way, playing cards in another room. The lady and the handsome stranger danced and drank and talked all night. As dawn was approaching, they were dancing so hard that they danced down the staircase, out of the doors and away from the rest of the party. There was so much excitement and so many people that no one realized the lady had gone until much later. Until it was too late."

He paused and sipped his wine. Lydia waited, drawn despite herself into the story.

"They found her the following morning in Bleeding Heart Square." Fimberry lowered his voice. "Lying dead beside the pump, still in all her finery. But her dress was—was disordered, and the body had been cut open. Her bleeding heart lay upon the cobbles."

"I say," Ingleby-Lewis said. "Rather strong meat, what?"

"Oh—yes. I'm frightfully sorry, Mrs. Langstone. I hope I—"

"What about the man who was with her?" Lydia asked.

"He was never seen again."

"But who was he?"

Fimberry smiled. "They say he was the devil."

10

Saturday, 22 February 1930

My hand is shaking so much I can hardly hold a pen.
Major Serridge—he says I must call him Joseph
now—called at two o'clock in a taxi. First he took me to
see dear little Jacko, who was so pleased to see his mistress.
He put his muddy paws all over my skirt, not that I
minded, and tried to jump up into my arms. I truly believe
he wanted me to carry him away.

I met Mr. Howlett, who is the Chief Beadle at Rosington Place. He is looking after Jacko for the time being. Jacko
seems quite at home in Mr. Howlett's little lodge. Joseph says
that he has taken care of everything, but I gave Mr. Howlett
an extra ten shillings just to make sure that Jacko has all he
needs. The little darling looked so sorrowful as we were leaving
him that I had to keep turning back to pat him.

Afterward, Joseph asked if I should like to see inside
the chapel in Rosington Place. We strolled up the
cul-de-sac, and it seemed deliciously natural for me to take
his arm. He gave my hand a tiny squeeze.

We went through a door and walked along part of the lovely old cloister. Joseph pointed out the remains of the staircase that must once have led up to other apartments in the Bishop's Palace. The chapel itself is on the first floor. It is surprisingly large, much bigger than it seems from the outside, with a great deal of interesting stained glass, old statues of saints, etc., etc. We had the place quite to ourselves.

After we had looked around the chapel, Joseph showed me the crypt. This runs the whole length of the building and is very plain and simple. A room to one side is called the Ossuary, but the door was locked. He said that he always thought this to be a particularly holy spot. I told him I felt its aura of sanctity as well.

He smiled sadly. "As God is my witness in this sacred place," he said, "I meant every word I said the other day."

My eyes filled with tears. He said he didn't want to offend me but he thought of me as his very own darling. Would I make him the happiest man in the world by agreeing at least to consider his proposal of a private marriage? He went on to say that of course as soon as he was a free man, we could be married in the eyes of the world as well as of God.

"I'm not as young as I was," he said in a voice that shook with emotion. "I feel I must take my happiness when I can. It won't wait for me." He looked meaningfully at me and said that of course we had both learned that from experience.

I knew that he was referring to Vernon, my lost love. Isn't it odd? I hardly think of him now. At the back of *my mind was the thought that, as I'm older than Joseph, I have even less time than he does.*

There and then, in this sacred and beautiful place, he went down on one knee and took from his pocket a small maroon box. He held it out and opened it. Three diamonds sparkled on a gold hoop. It was the most beautiful ring I had ever seen.

He spoke these very words: "Will you—dare I hope that you will consent one day to be my wife?"

I could hardly breathe. I let him take my hand, my left hand, and gently remove the glove. He slipped the ring onto my finger. It fit perfectly. He bent his great, grizzled head and kissed the hand. I was trembling violently. With my right hand, I stroked his hair, so surprisingly vigorous for a man of his age. I heard him give a sob.

I can write no more this evening. My heart is too full. Joseph, my own dear one.

The ring and the chapel, that beastly little dog and all those sickly sweet nothings—didn't she understand what was happening? Joseph Serridge was asking a respectable spinster several years his senior to come and live in sin with him. Did she really think he loved her? Did she really think that her money had nothing to do with it?

On Thursday morning Rory went to the library in Charleston Street to fight his way through the crowd and consult the Situations Vacant columns on the noticeboards. Living at Bleeding Heart Square was more expensive than boarding at Mrs. Rutter's, mainly because he had to find all his own meals. I must economize, he thought, perhaps learn to cook. It can't be that difficult.

Hopelessness threatened to overwhelm him. Employers wanted reliable gardeners and experienced parlormen, not reporters or copywriters. In any case, you probably needed to buy the newspapers when they reached the streets at six in the morning, rather than wait until the library opened. Even if he found a suitable job advertised, it might well be gone by now.

His eyes strayed toward the shelves of reference books in search of distraction. He caught sight of a familiar red spine: *Who's Who.* He fetched the portly red volume and turned to the letter C. *Cassington* leaped out at him, giving him a jolt of recognition tinged with dismay.

George Rupert Cassington, second Baron Cassington of Flaxern, born 1874, educated Rugby and St. John's College, Oxford. And so on. He had two sons by his first wife, who had died in 1904, and a daughter, Pamela, by his second wife, Elinor, whom he had married in 1908. There were three addresses—21 Upper Mount Street in Mayfair, Monkshill Park near Lydmouth, and Drumloch Lodge, Inverness-shire.

Rory closed the book. He had learned a little but not enough. The fever was upon him. Not a fever, exactly—more a malign hunger: as a child he had stolen a box of chocolates from his eldest sister, carried it to a hiding place at the bottom of the garden and gobbled the contents in a furtive haste that had little to do with pleasure; even as he ate, he knew he would soon be sick, he knew his theft would lead to punishment.

He took down *Debrett's Peerage, Baronetage, Knightage and Companionage.* There were the Cassingtons again, and this time there was more information about the peer's second wife. She had previously married Captain William Ingleby-Lewis, whom she had divorced in 1907 and by whom she had had a daughter, Lydia Elizabeth. He looked up the Langstones, and there she was again, wife of Marcus John Scott Langstone. She had been born in 1905. So she was twenty-nine; she looked younger. Marcus was older. No children, as yet. They lived at 9 Frogmore Place, Lancaster Gate, when they were in London—not as grand an address as the Cassingtons, Rory thought—and at Longhope House in Gloucestershire. Langstone had been at Marlborough.

Rory swore under his breath, and a slumbering tramp sitting across the table from him opened one eye. He and Lydia Langstone might at present live under the same roof but they belonged to different worlds. Not that it mattered, since she was married and besides he still considered himself engaged to Fenella, whatever Fenella might say. What galled him was the disparity between them. He was forced to live somewhere like Bleeding Heart Square because he was poor and getting poorer. But, given her background, Lydia must be playing with poverty. The French had a phrase for it as they had a phrase for everything: she was living *en bon socialiste*, toying with being poor, being ordinary, and it was a damned patronizing insult to those who were really poor and really ordinary.

Just like that fellow Dawlish that Fenella is so fond of.

Was that the real reason he was angry—simple, unjustifiable jealousy? Rory closed the book with a bang. The tramp opened both eyes.

As Rory stood up, Lydia Langstone herself came into the reference room. For an instant he felt like a guilty schoolboy caught in the act of something dreadful and clutched the book to his chest as if to hide it from her. She caught his eye, nodded to him and turned away to select a magazine, *The Lady*, from a rack by the window. He put the book back on the shelf, seized his hat and went out. She didn't look up.

A gray pall of rain hung over the city. It suited his mood. He walked aimlessly down to Holborn and allowed the flow of pedestrians to draw him steadily westward. So why the devil was Lydia Langstone living in Bleeding Heart Square when she could have been living in comfort in Bayswater? It was quite a puzzle, and if nothing else a distraction from his inability to work out what to do with his own life.

By the time he reached Regent Street, the rain was petering out.
He crossed the road and drifted into Mayfair. A taxi jolted in and
out of a pothole, spraying water that soaked the bottoms of his
only respectable trousers. He swore aloud. The spurt of anger
shifted the direction of his thoughts. Suddenly he was curious
to see where Lydia Langstone had lived, to glimpse the sort of
world she had turned her back on.

Upper Mount Street was lined with Georgian houses that might
have started life looking more or less the same as each other but
had long since diversified according to the wealth and whims of
individual proprietors. Number twenty-one had a bow window on
the first floor, a Daimler parked outside and a purple door whose
brass furniture gave off a soft, moneyed gleam. Tubbed and perfectly symmetrical bay trees stood like sentries on either side of
the doorway. The Daimler had pale blue curtains on the rear windows. A uniformed chauffeur was buffing the windscreen.

Rory strolled along the opposite pavement to the end of the
street. Like a character in a detective story, he pretended to post a
letter in the pillar box to disarm the suspicions of anyone who
might be watching. He crossed over the road and paused to light a
cigarette. As he was flicking the match into the gutter, the door of
number twenty-one opened and two men came out.

The first was small and elderly, with a deeply lined face. He was
wearing a top hat and a dark overcoat. The second was taller and
much younger—blond-haired, with broad shoulders, a florid complexion and large blue eyes that glanced carelessly at Rory and away.

The chauffeur opened the rear door. There was a delay as a maid
rushed out of the house, holding an attaché case which she gave to
the younger man.

"You're always forgetting something," his companion said to
him with a bray of laughter. "I tell Ellie that your memory is worse
than mine."

Rory turned the corner. Lord Cassington, he thought, and Marcus John Scott Langstone, the husband of Lydia? How odd to be

[141]

able to put probable faces on names that an hour or so ago had been no more than words in a reference book, abstractions and nothing more. Ellie must be Elinor, Lady Cassington. He had heard of none of them a few days ago—none of them knew him, none of them had harmed him—but still he felt a blind aggression that made him clench his fists inside his coat pockets.

Perhaps Sergeant Narton and Fenella's Bolshie friends had the right idea after all. Hang the bastards from the lampposts. But perhaps spare a few of those already living *en bon socialiste*?

Lydia drank her tea, which was sweet, strong and apparently flavored with boot polish, smoked a cigarette and then continued with the task that Mr. Shires had given her that morning. Her job was to work her way down a list of unpaid accounts, telephoning each client to inquire whether they had received Shires and Trimble's invoice. Whether or not they claimed they hadn't, Lydia was to tell them that another was on its way and that Shires and Trimble would be obliged to have the matter settled without delay.

"Then we give them another fortnight to stew in their own juice before we threaten legal proceedings," Mr. Shires had told her, a peppermint bulging like an unpleasant swelling in his left cheek. "It's a tiresome business, Mrs. Langstone, I don't mind telling you. It's not the law that's the problem. It's the damned clients, excuse my French. Off you go now, and I want the list back at lunchtime. Mark on it how you get on with each one. Half of them will say the check's in the post. Must think we were born yesterday, eh?"

Lydia stubbed out her cigarette and picked up the telephone. It was connected to the little switchboard in the outer office, which also served the partners' line from the private office. The connections were erratic and she heard Mr. Shires' voice in her ear. There was a crossed line.

". . . one can't rule out the possibility," Mr. Shires was saying.

"Why not?" Lydia recognized the voice as Serridge's.

"Sorry," Lydia said and put the receiver down.

The door of the private office opened.

"Mrs. Langstone? In here a moment, please."

She followed Mr. Shires into the room.

"Close the door." He sat down at his desk and waited until she had obeyed. "How are you settling in?"

"All right, I think." Lydia tried a smile. "I'm probably not the best judge."

"So far so good on that front, I understand. Early days yet, of course." He looked at her and blinked his watery eyes. "I assume it was you on the telephone then."

"Yes." She paused, and added, "Sir."

"We must get an engineer to deal with it. Ask Mr. Smethwick to get on to it right away." Shires gave her a wintry smile. "By the way, I was having a confidential conversation. Did you overhear anything?"

"No, sir. As soon as I realized you were on the phone, I broke the connection."

His eyes held hers. She fought the temptation to shift guiltily from one foot to another and stared back at him. He seemed to approve of what he saw because he nodded and gave her a smile.

"Very well, Mrs. Langstone. You had better get back to your work. Be sure to pass on my message to Mr. Smethwick."

She left the room, wondering whether he had believed her. She relayed the instruction to Mr. Smethwick.

"Righty ho." He looked at her not unkindly and said, "Did he tear a strip off you? He nearly murdered Lorna here when she had a crossed line."

Miss Tuffley simpered with quiet pride.

"It could have been worse," Lydia said.

"Old Shires can be perfectly foul when he wants to," Miss Tuffley whispered. "You wouldn't think of it to look at him but he's got a mean streak a mile wide."

"Hush," commanded Mr. Reynolds, the chief clerk, peering down at them over his tortoiseshell spectacles.

Miss Tuffley actually winked at Lydia before bending her shining head over her machine.

At half past twelve Mr. Shires went out to lunch, carefully locking the door of the private office. Lydia was left in solitary charge of the general office between one o'clock and one thirty, which was, she supposed, a mark of approval.

Mr. Reynolds had been working on the accounts, and he had left the clients' ledger on his high desk. Mainly to relieve her boredom, Lydia opened the heavy book. Mr. Serridge must have talked to Mr. Shires about employing her. This morning she had overheard the two men talking on the phone. Presumably Serridge was a client of the firm, perhaps in connection with his purchase of 7 Bleeding Heart Square. It should be easy enough to find out.

Over three quarters of the pages had been used, and the invoices went back to the end of 1927. The chief clerk wrote a beautiful hand, upright, elegant and easy to read. Lydia skimmed through the pages, working backward. Her eyes ran up and down the column that contained the clients' names. She moved through the years, faster and faster as she grew more accustomed to the task, until she reached the first entry in December 1927.

Afterward she closed the heavy book with a sigh and stretched to relieve her aching shoulders. There had been no mention of Mr. Serridge. Nor, come to that, of Miss Penhow, the lady who had owned the house, the lady who had gone away.

When Rory arrived, he found Fenella washing up in the kitchen. She wore an overlarge pinafore apron and looked like a child playing at being grown-up. He took a tea towel and dried a knife.

"Have you eaten yet?" he asked.

"There hasn't been time."

"Perhaps we can have something together, later."

She put a saucepan down on the wooden draining board with unnecessary violence and didn't reply.

"What's up?" Rory said.

"Just a gas bill. It's rather more than I'd budgeted for."

"If you let me, I'll help."

She threw him a smile. "I knew you'd say that. You're very kind."

"That sounds like an epitaph," Rory said. "May I?"

"No."

He knew she was refusing more than money. "Where does the cutlery go?"

"Still the same place. Left-hand drawer of the dresser. What have you been up to?"

Rory ignored the fact that he had spent the morning traipsing across London, looking at the former home of Lydia Langstone and feeling angry with wealthy people flirting with poverty. "Looking for a job. Nothing new's come up but I've got a couple of irons in the fire."

"It's not much fun, is it?"

"What isn't?"

"All this grubbing for money." Fenella threw the mop into the sudsy water. "I hate being poor. I need a fairy godmother."

As though in an answer to prayer, there came the ring of a bell.

"Perhaps that's her," Rory said. "I'll go." He gave her a wry smile, trying to turn the whole thing into a joke. "Are you at home?"

"I'm always at home," she said.

Rory went into the hall and opened the door. A man was standing on the doorstep with his hat in his hand. He smiled at Rory with the easy charm of someone used to being liked. It was that fellow Dawlish. Rory pretended not to recognize him.

"Good evening. Is Miss Kensley in?"

"Yes. Would you like to come in? I'll fetch her. Who shall I say it is?"

"Julian Dawlish. Thanks."

Rory showed him into the drawing room and left him standing on the hearthrug in front of the dying fire. He was not the sort of chap you would take into the kitchen.

Fenella blushed when he told her who was waiting for her. She pulled off the apron and asked Rory to tell Dawlish that she would be with them in a moment.

In the drawing room he and Dawlish talked about the weather and skirted rather uneasily around the subject of the Spanish strikes and Catalonia's abortive attempt to declare its independence from the rest of the country. Fenella's footsteps hurried to and fro across her bedroom overhead. At last she came in and the men sprang to their feet. She had changed her dress and combed her hair. Rory thought she had probably done something to her face as well.

Dawlish loped toward her, flannel trousers flapping around his legs. "I hope I haven't called at an inconvenient time, Miss Kensley," he said in his soft, expensive drawl. "You were kind enough to say I could drop in if I were passing but casual callers can be a frightful nuisance, can't they?"

She gave him her hand and smiled. "Not in this case. I hope Mr. Wentwood's been looking after you."

Dawlish smiled benevolently at the space between Fenella and Rory. "Absolutely," he murmured.

They sat down and lit cigarettes from Mr. Dawlish's case.

"What have you been up to?" he asked Fenella.

"I re-papered most of the lodger's bedroom today."

"I just don't know how you do it all." Dawlish looked admiringly at her. "Running this place and so on. She's never idle, is she, Wentwood?"

Rory muttered in agreement.

"Have you eaten, by the way?" Dawlish went on, his eyes on Fenella. "I haven't had anything since breakfast in fact, and I'm starving. I wonder whether you'd like a bite to eat. There's quite a pleasant little Italian place in Hampstead." He hesitated, only for a fraction of a second but it was enough. "We could all go, of course," he added, turning to Rory.

"I've eaten already, thanks," Rory said.

"Oh. Never mind."

"It would be lovely," Fenella said. "But are you sure that—"

"Of course I'm sure. I wanted to ask your advice in any case, so we can mix business with pleasure."

"Advice?" Fenella asked. "What about?"

"I'm writing a pamphlet. Actually, it might even be a talk on the wireless. I know a chap at the BBC. It's about the role of women—how they can make a difference in the class struggle and so on. Whether women are naturally against Fascism."

"Are they?" Rory said, determined to be contrary.

Dawlish grinned at him, refusing to take umbrage. "That's what we want to find out. But I'm sure Miss Kensley has a better idea of how to do it than I do."

It had been neatly contrived, Rory thought bitterly, as he walked back to Bleeding Heart Square. There had been no reason for him to stay, since he claimed to have eaten already, which he hadn't. Dawlish, ever the perfect little gent, had offered him a lift to the nearest Tube station, which Rory equally politely had declined. He walked partly to save money and partly because it fed a masochistic appetite within himself to feel even more miserable than he already was.

There was, he accepted, no one he could reasonably blame for this state of affairs except himself. Fenella had given him fair warning that their engagement was suspended, probably over: she was quite within her rights to change her mind and prefer someone else to him. He himself was hardly much of a catch. But Fenella had been a central feature of his emotional landscape for so long that her absence from it was hard to envisage.

He plodded home. In a side street off the Clerkenwell Road he stopped for a pint in a pub that sold only beer. The place chimed perfectly with his mood. It had grimy sawdust on the floor and smelled of cats' urine. Surly men played shove-ha'penny and dominoes, and stared at him with surreptitious hostility until he left.

The shops of Hatton Garden were dark and shuttered. In Charleston Street the windows of the Crozier were blazing with light. Someone was thumping the keys of a piano inside the saloon bar and producing a sound that was just recognizable as "The

Teddy Bears' Picnic." He turned into the alley leading to the square and hesitated. He wanted whisky, he thought, he wanted a whole bloody bottle of the stuff.

The music from the pub was gathering in volume, and people were singing. He didn't want to get drunk among all that cheerfulness. Besides, Ingleby-Lewis would probably be there, and perhaps Fimberry or even Serridge. He still had nearly half a bottle of gin in his flat. Drinking alone was far more appealing than that dreadful jollity inside the pub. It would be cheaper too.

He left the alley and passed into the relative gloom of Bleeding Heart Square. It was very quiet after the din of the pub. Suddenly the silence was broken by running footsteps. He had time to register that they were behind him, that they belonged to more than one person, and that they were coming toward him. He turned toward the sound.

But he was much too late. A heavy blow landed on his upper left arm, just below the shoulder. In a tiny instant of lucidity he realized that if he hadn't started to turn, it would have been his collarbone. Someone cannoned into him, sending him sprawling across wet cobbles, jarring his body with the violence of the fall.

He writhed on the ground, struggling to get up, and grabbed a man's arm, as unyielding as an iron bar. Heavy breathing filled his ears. He sensed shadowy figures surrounding him.

A boot hammered into his ribs. He cried out. He grabbed the man's wrist and pulled, trying to haul himself up. His nose exploded in pain and his head jerked back. He fell back on the cobbles. The boot went into his ribs again. He was lying on his back now with someone holding his shoulders down and somebody else trying to pull apart his legs. He twisted away but they were too strong for him.

Someone punched the inside of his thigh. *Christ, they're going for my balls.* He lost his grip on the wrist. His hands curled into fists. He lashed out and was rewarded with a grunt. Then a blow—a kick?—landed in his crotch and he screamed, a high, inhuman sound.

"Listen to me, you bastard," a voice snarled very close to his ear, penetrating the white curtain of pain. "I'll say this only once. And if you don't take notice I'm going to cut your prick off and shove it down your mouth."

A door opened somewhere. The music was suddenly louder as if the teddy bears were pouring into Bleeding Heart Square itself. Rory's shoulders and legs were free. He rolled onto his side, curling into a protective huddle. He heard voices and running footsteps.

"Hey, I say!" a slurred male voice said. "Mind where you're going, old man. What's the rush?"

The footsteps receded. Now there were other footsteps, much slower and less regular.

"I say," the voice said again. "You all right, old chap? Bit squiffy, eh?"

Another door opened, and another wedge of light spilled into the square. Rory forced open his eyes but the pain made it hard to focus. He recognized the voice rather than the dark shape looming over him. He tried to speak but there was blood on his face and some of it had got inside his mouth and made him cough.

"I don't think those fellows liked the cut of your jib," Captain Ingleby-Lewis continued.

There were more footsteps, lighter and faster than the others.

"Father, what's happening?"

"Hello, my dear. I think someone's had a bit of an accident."

Rory struggled into a sitting position. Lydia Langstone was on one side of him and her father was on the other.

"Mr. Wentwood—what on earth is going on?"

"Someone . . ." He stopped trying to get up as a twinge of pain made him groan. "Someone attacked me."

"Can you stand?" Lydia asked.

"It's a damned disgrace," Captain Ingleby-Lewis said. "This wouldn't have happened before the war, you know."

"What—what wouldn't?" Rory asked.

"This sort of barefaced robbery. What can you expect with these

Bolsheviks everywhere? It makes Jack think he's as good as his master. I'd hang the lot of them if I had my way. It's the only answer."

Rory groggily maneuvered himself onto his hands and knees.

"Father," Lydia said, "help Mr. Wentwood up."

"Eh? Oh yes. Of course."

Ingleby-Lewis hooked an arm under Rory's, the one that had taken the blow, and pulled. Rory squealed with pain. Ingleby-Lewis started back and nearly sat down.

"Let me help," Lydia said.

Together they pulled Rory to his feet. He stood swaying for a moment, supported by Lydia and Ingleby-Lewis on either side. "The Teddy Bears' Picnic" tinkled and thumped across the square. He had not realized before how damned sinister the tune was.

"Damn," he said. "I hope I'm not bleeding on you."

"Don't worry," Lydia said. "We'd better get you back to the house. Can you walk?"

"I think so."

"We need to find a policeman. What did they steal?"

"I don't think they stole anything."

"I arrived just in time," said Ingleby-Lewis with a note of congratulation in his voice. "They're yellow at heart, you know, scum like that."

"How many were there?"

"Two," Ingleby-Lewis said. "Or was it three? Great big chaps, in any case. Cowardly devils. As soon as they saw me, they—"

"Let's take Mr. Wentwood back to the house. Then perhaps you could find a police officer."

"Not much point, my dear."

"But Mr. Wentwood has been attacked."

"It does happen, I'm afraid. Especially around here. Friday night and all that. Nothing was stolen. I'm not sure the police would be very sympathetic and frankly it's a waste of time. They're not going to catch the blackguards, after all. Much better to get Mr. Wentwood cleaned up."

Lydia stooped and picked up something that glinted in the light. "Is this yours?"

Rory blinked at her.

"This cufflink," she said with a touch of impatience.

"I don't know." It was hard enough to stand, let alone talk. "Probably."

She held it out to him. Rory swayed, wondering if he would be sick. She pushed the cufflink into the pocket of his raincoat and took his arm. "Hold up," she said. "We'll get you inside."

The first step made him howl with agony, but as the three of them moved slowly toward the door of the house, the pain receded a little. Captain Ingleby-Lewis was less than steady on his feet. Rory wasn't sure who was supporting whom. Once they reached the hallway, Rory let go of Lydia's arm and took firm hold of the newel post.

"Can you manage the stairs?" she asked.

"I think so. I'm sorry to be such a bore."

"It's not your fault. Come up to our flat and I'll get some hot water."

"Brandy," Ingleby-Lewis said behind them with the air of a man who says *Eureka!* "That's what one needs in a situation like this. I'll see if the Crozier can provide some, shall I?"

Lydia took Rory into the sitting room she shared with her father, and made him sit down at the table. Ingleby-Lewis set off to the Crozier on his errand of mercy. Lydia went away for a moment.

Rory thought that the room seemed tidier and cleaner than before. Indeed, it looked almost cheerful. There was a book lying open with its spine upward, as though Lydia had put it down in a hurry on the table when she heard the commotion outside. He craned to see the title, and the movement made him wince. Virginia Woolf's *A Room of One's Own*. How odd. He would have expected an Agatha Christie novel or even a well-thumbed copy of *Horse & Hound*. A snapshot protruded from the pages, a marker no doubt. He made out the top half of a rather pretty girl in a bathing costume, surrounded by several grinning young men with little moustaches. He heard footsteps and turned away.

Lydia came into the room with a basin of hot water, a towel and a cloth. She soaked the cloth in the water, wrung it out and advised him to wipe his face. He obeyed her. Afterward he looked up at her.

"How do I look?"

"Not too bad. The nosebleed's stopped. Are your teeth all right?"

He ran his tongue over them. "I think they're all there. One of them's chipped."

"What about the rest of you?"

"A few aches and pains." He tried to ignore the agony below, to pretend it belonged to someone else. "I don't think anything's actually broken."

A silence grew between them, awkward and unwanted.

"Thank you," Rory said.

Simultaneously Lydia said, "Shouldn't I try to find a doctor? Or you could go to the Outpatients at Barts. Surely someone should have a look at you?"

"I'm all right, thanks." He felt as though he were temporarily disconnected from the world around him. He wanted desperately to be alone. "I really must go."

There were footsteps on the stairs. The door opened and Captain Ingleby-Lewis came in with a bottle of brandy in a brown paper bag. He set it carefully on the table with an air of triumph.

"There," he said. "That'll set you right. Lydia, my dear, would you bring us some glasses?"

"Not for me, thank you." Supporting himself on the table, Rory struggled to his feet. "I—I won't take up any more of your time. I'm sure I can get upstairs under my own steam."

Ingleby-Lewis protested, though not very hard, and Lydia said nothing at all. Rory thanked them both again and slowly walked out of the room, trying to hold himself very straight. The stairs stretched up from the first-floor landing, flight after flight, their summit as unattainable as Mount Everest's. But he wanted the silence of his own flat, the privacy, and the security of a locked door.

His mind was moving slowly and seemed to be full of fog. But he remembered there was something odd about Ingleby-Lewis, and as he struggled up the first flight, he remembered what it was. Ingleby-Lewis had sold Morthams Farm to Miss Penhow and Serridge. Yet here he was, living in Serridge's house, living as Serridge's tenant. Except it wasn't Serridge's house, or it used not to be. It used to belong to Miss Penhow.

After the second-floor landing, he abandoned dignity, dropped to his knees and crawled.

If only I didn't feel anything. Not a bad old stick, Ingleby-Lewis. And the girl, of course. Where did I put the bloody gin?

Finally, swearing continuously under his breath, he ascended the narrow stairs to the attic. As he searched for his key, he glanced over his shoulder, down the stairs. Serridge was standing on the second-floor landing watching him. He was in his shirtsleeves, and his face was as unreadable as the face of the Red Indian outside the tobacconist's in Charleston Street. Rory tried to say something but at that moment pain shafted through him, making him double up and screw his eyes shut. When he opened his eyes again, Serridge had gone. Perhaps the man had been a hallucination.

His sitting room was very cold. Rory locked the door behind him, lit the gas fire at the fourth attempt, and tracked down the gin to the bottom of the chest of drawers. He slumped into the armchair in front of the fire with the bottle at his elbow. He uncorked the gin and swallowed a mouthful of neat spirit. His mouth and throat burned. He coughed so hard he almost dropped the bottle. He swallowed some more. He was still wearing his raincoat and he stuffed his hands into the pockets to keep warm. The fingers of his left hand touched a small metallic object. He took it out and let it rest in the palm of his hand. A cufflink. He frowned at it.

The cufflink had an enamel design—a red circle on a blue background; and superimposed on the circle was a golden symbol he didn't recognize.

Cinderella's slipper? Find the other one, and perhaps I find who attacked me.

The words churned through his mind as the gin worked its way down to his stomach, tumbling from side to side, numbing some of the pain in his body. The words twisted and turned like dead leaves dancing in the heat haze above his father's bonfire in the garden of the house in Hereford. More gin, less pain. Mrs. Langstone had been jolly decent this evening. He must remember to thank her properly.

II

PHILIPPA PENHOW decides she is married to Joseph Serridge in the eyes of God. Joseph Serridge decides to buy them a home in the country (with Philippa Penhow's money). Then, hey presto, he produces the perfect place like a rabbit out of a conjurer's hat. It would have made anyone suspicious, you'd think, anyone but a fool in love.

Friday, 28 February 1930

Joseph and I went down to the country today to visit the farm he thinks might suit us. It's near a village called Rawling on the Essex—Hertfordshire border and surprisingly close to London (though we had to change twice between Liverpool Street and Mavering, the nearest station to the village). We took a taxi from Mavering to the farm. It's called Morthams.

Joseph said that if we do decide to purchase the property we might consider buying a little motor car. It would be so much more convenient for running up to town and might even save money in the long run. This started me thinking! I should so like to give him a present he would really enjoy and I think a motor car might be just the ticket.

The property consists of a farmhouse (most picturesque!), with a farmyard to one side and about 120 acres of good land. We drove up to the house by a muddy lane and parked between the farmyard (rather smelly!) and the house. It's a nice old place with some good-sized rooms and plenty of space for all the furniture I have in store. It would need some work on it, Joseph says, but nothing that should be too expensive. I must confess it seemed rather cold and damp to me but Joseph explained that that was because no one had been living there over the winter, since the last tenant had moved away. On the side away from the farmyard is the sweetest little cottage garden, though sadly overgrown.

As we walked in the garden, Joseph pressed my arm and murmured that it was such a romantic spot, and at last we could be alone together. I asked whether Morthams was perhaps rather lonely, a little far from the shops. But he pointed out that we should soon get used to that, and in any case we could make regular trips into Saffron Walden and even London for shopping.

The owner's solicitors had sent a clerk to open up the house for us and answer any questions we might have. Joseph had quite a chat with the man, who said he thought the owner was in a hurry to sell and might accept an offer substantially below the asking price, which is £2,100.

I was still in the garden when Joseph came to tell me this. The clouds had parted, and the sun was streaming down. Out of the wind, it was almost warm. I imagined the garden coming to life around us in a few weeks' time with crocuses, cowslips and daffodils. He asked me what I thought and I replied that perhaps we should go back to London and consider what best to do. Joseph said in that case we might lose the property because several other people were coming to see it today and tomorrow. He thinks it would be perfect for us and suggested we make an offer of £1,700. It will mean selling about a quarter of my investments, but as Joseph pointed out, the farm itself would be a far better investment than any stocks and shares and besides it would give us a home of our own, so we should save money on rent. Even if we were to sell it right away, we should make a profit.

The clerk showed us over the rest of the place. Joseph made much of the neglected state of it, but murmured privately to me that in fact the land was in very good shape underneath. Then we made our offer! I dare say we shall have to wait a day or two before we hear the owner's reply. I'm on tenterhooks!

On the train home, Joseph said that he thought it might be best to ask his own solicitor to handle the purchase. I wondered whether we should ask Mr. Orburn but Joseph said it would only add unnecessary cost and besides his man specializes in conveyancing and will do a better, faster job. I agreed. (I don't want to give Joseph the impression I distrust his judgment and of course men know more about this sort of thing than women!)

I nearly forgot to mention: Joseph asked me to wear a gold band on my ring finger, just for the look of the thing, *in case I needed to remove my gloves. He introduced me to the clerk as "Mrs. Serridge." It gave me quite a thrill!!*

How cleverly Serridge arranged it all. Morthams Farm was conveniently near London yet unusually remote from everywhere. Philippa Penhow had lived almost all her life in cities. She had no idea what the country is like. The muddy paths, the absence of neighbors, the great brooding skies and the silence. The darkness at night. The fact that there may be no one to hear you.

The office boy was still confined to bed with what his mother now claimed was German measles. Mr. Reynolds remarked that it was most inconvenient. Mr. Smethwick said the young shaver was a little beast and Miss Tuffley, as befitted a member of the gentler sex, said he was a poor lamb. One consequence of the boy's absence was that Lydia was obliged to work on Saturday morning.

As she made herself ready, she heard her father snoring in his room. In the sitting room the empty brandy bottle lay on its side in the hearth. Pulling on her gloves, she went down to the hall.

Among the small pile of post on the table was a letter addressed to her in her sister's handwriting. There was also a parcel, slightly larger than a tennis ball, wrapped in brown paper and tied with string, for *J. SERRIDGE, ESQ.*

Footsteps came slowly down the stairs. Letter in hand, she moved away from the table, reluctant to be caught spying. It was Rory Wentwood, walking slowly and a little stiffly.

"Good morning," he said. "I'm so glad it's you. I wanted to say thank you."

"It was nothing. How are you feeling?"

"Rather better than I thought I would." His dark eyebrows wrinkled into a frown and he winced, giving the lie to his words.

"Most of the time, at any rate. I know I'd be feeling a lot worse if you hadn't turned up when you did."

"It was just luck. I still think you should see a doctor."

He shook his head. "I'm all right."

"Who do you think attacked you?"

He shrugged. "Friday-night toughs, I suppose. Had a few drinks and decided to go on the rampage. I imagine they were after my wallet."

"Well, I'm glad it's no worse." Lydia moved toward the front door.

"I say—Mrs. Langstone? I'd like to thank you properly for being so sporting about this. Would you let me buy you lunch?"

She turned back. "That's very kind of you, Mr. Wentwood, but—"

"You'd be doing me a favor. Otherwise I'll feel guilty for ruining your evening." His long face grew longer and even more melancholy than before. "You could think of it as an act of charity."

She found herself smiling at him. "Very well. When?"

"What about today?"

"All right."

"Thanks awfully."

He arranged to meet her outside the office. On her way to work, Lydia opened her sister's letter. It enclosed an invitation to a private view at a gallery in Cork Street on Tuesday evening. Pammy had scribbled a few lines in violet ink.

> *Do come if you can, darling—everyone will be there. Or if you don't feel like doing the polite to all & sundry, would you like to meet for lunch at Café des Voyageurs on Wednesday? They say the new chef is divine. Let me know. With best love, Pammy.*

Lydia stuffed the envelope into her handbag and pushed open the street door of 48 Rosington Place. She missed her sister but she wouldn't go to the opening or to the Café des Voyageurs. She had finished with that sort of thing. A working woman, she marched up to the second floor.

The prospect of being taken out to lunch buoyed her up during the morning. In any case Saturday was not like other days at Shires and Trimble. It was only a half-day, and most of the time was spent on dealing with the post and tidying up loose ends from the previous week. Everyone was in a mood which if not exactly festive was at least cheerful, as though the temporary liberation of the weekend offered a glimpse of the happier world outside Rosington Place.

At half past twelve Lydia went downstairs with Miss Tuffley, who was going up west to have lunch with a friend and then on to the pictures. Mr. Wentwood was waiting for her outside the door. Miss Tuffley looked at him with interest and, Lydia suspected, would have been happy to be introduced if Lydia had given her the slightest encouragement. As it was, she said goodbye and clattered down the pavement toward the Tube station.

"Where would you like to go?" Rory asked. "I don't know anywhere around here except the Blue Dahlia."

"Let's go there then," Lydia said, thinking that at least it was cheap but wishing in a dark and shameful corner of her mind that it was the Café des Voyageurs. "Better the devil you know."

The café was less crowded than it usually was at lunchtimes, since most of the clientele had gone home for the weekend. The fat lady behind the counter greeted them with a nod. They sat down at a corner table and studied the menu.

Rory glanced at the blackboard behind the counter. "I'll have the special. Liver and onions."

Lydia thought of the parcel on the hall table at Bleeding Heart Square. Liver was offal and so was heart. "I think I'll have the shepherd's pie."

They ordered their lunch and sat smoking while they waited.

"How are you feeling now?"

Rory touched the faintly discolored skin on his cheekbone, and winced. "Still in one piece." He went on in the same tone, "I've not been altogether honest with you, I'm afraid."

It took a moment for his words to seep in. *Was he married or something?* "What do you mean?"

His face was even gloomier than usual. "About my reason for moving into Bleeding Heart Square."

"I thought you were looking for a job and needed to be near the City."

"That's true as far as it goes." He flicked ash from his cigarette. "But there's another reason. You remember the girl I was with on Sunday? In Trafalgar Square? She has an aunt, a lady called Philippa Penhow."

Lydia crumbled her bread and watched Rory. He was smoking very fast.

"They haven't been in touch for more than four years," he said, speaking quickly as if trying to get the words out before he changed his mind. "In fact Miss Penhow doesn't seem to have been in touch with anyone. Fenella—Miss Kensley—is rather worried."

So that's who she is, Lydia thought—Fenella Kensley. She supposed that some people would think the name was rather pretty.

"The thing is, just before Miss Penhow disappeared, she met Mr. Serridge. In fact he was one of her tenants at Bleeding Heart Square. She told Fenella that they were going to get married. A whirlwind courtship, I gather. They moved out of London in the spring of 1930 and bought a place in Essex, near a village called Rawling. Morthams Farm."

Lydia ground out her cigarette. "What happened then?"

He shrugged. "She left. Mr. Serridge said she met an old friend and went off with him." He paused, sowing doubt with a silence. "Anyway, a few weeks later she simply wasn't there."

"Surely people asked questions?"

"There weren't that many people who noticed she had gone. She and Serridge had only just moved to Rawling. Before that, Miss Penhow lived in a private hotel in South Ken. She hadn't any friends there, not real ones. And before that, she'd lived with an old aunt in Manchester or somewhere, but the old lady died. The only other relations she had were Fenella and her parents, but they weren't close."

Lydia wondered: then why the interest now?

"Anyway, the Kensleys had a lot on their minds," Rory continued. "Fenella's father was very ill for a year or two before he died. Afterward her mother had to take in a lodger to make ends meet, and then she herself died last summer."

"So there's been no sign of Miss Penhow since 1930, and Mr. Serridge seems to have acquired the house?"

"That's about the size of it. And don't forget the farm. That seems to be his as well."

"Has anyone talked to the police?"

"They were notified of her disappearance. But there was no sign a crime had been committed, and no reason to doubt Serridge's story about an old boyfriend. Fenella said there really was a man, years and years ago—she remembered her parents talking about it. A sailor, apparently. Miss Penhow wanted to marry him but her family wouldn't let her. And then there was a letter that seemed to confirm it. Miss Penhow wrote to the Vicar of Rawling from New York asking him to apologize to Serridge on her behalf for going away so suddenly. The police think the letter's genuine."

Penhow, Lydia thought, P. M. Penhow. The woman herself wasn't here but her name was everywhere. Her father came into her mind, bringing with him as he usually did a faint sense of anxiety.

"Liver and onions," said a loud voice just above her head. "Shepherd's pie."

The liver landed in front of Lydia, the shepherd's pie in front of Rory.

"It's the other way round," Lydia said.

"Suit yourself," said the manageress. "You've got hands, haven't you, love? You give him his, and I'm sure he'll give you yours."

Rory grinned up at her. "And that's the way the world goes round, eh?"

The fat woman roared with laughter and told him he was a caution. She waddled away from their table. Lydia and Rory exchanged plates.

"She likes you," Lydia said in a low voice. "She barely toler-ates me."

Rory looked uncomfortable. "It's because I'm a man."

Lydia shook her head. "It's more than that." Talking with a silver spoon in your mouth, she realized, could be more of a curse than a blessing. As far as most of the population was concerned, it made you a social leper and also almost unemployable because ladies weren't supposed to work. That wouldn't have mattered perhaps, if you actually owned the silver spoon and everything that went with it. But if you didn't, you had the worst of both worlds.

She and Rory were both hungry, and at first they ate in silence. Then Rory laid down his fork and looked at her.

"What is it?" she asked.

"May I ask you something?"

"Fire away."

"How long have you known Mr. Serridge?"

"I'd never even heard of him until I moved into Bleeding Heart Square."

"And your father?"

She put down her own fork. "I believe they knew each other in the army. I'll say this for Mr. Serridge—he's been very kind to him."

Rory sat back. "Did you know that Morthams Farm used to be-long to your father?"

"What?"

"The farm that Mr. Serridge and Miss Penhow bought. Your father sold it to them. Did you know?"

"Of course I didn't." She was surprised to hear her voice was calm and level. "I had no idea. Look here, I—"

"Have you ever heard him mention Rawling?"

Lydia pushed her plate away. "I don't like this. I don't see why I should answer questions about my father. And I don't really un-derstand why you feel you should ask them."

He spread his hands out, palms up. "I'm so sorry. Unforgivable of me." He gave her a rueful smile; he was rather good at those. "You know how it is—one gets carried away."

Despite herself, she smiled back. They continued with their meal. Rory diverted the conversation to neutral subjects. He made her laugh with the story of Hitler's oranges. There had been an item in today's paper, he said, about a hundred thousand Spanish oranges which had been withdrawn from auction at Spitalfields yesterday because they had been wrapped in paper with a portrait of Hitler on it.

"All one hundred thousand of them?" Lydia asked.

"So I understand. Individually wrapped. It caused a lot of excitement when they tried to sell them. There were cries of 'Heil Hitler.' In the end the auctioneer decided to withdraw them. They say the consignment was meant to go to Germany. Though personally I would have thought that an orange is an orange is an orange."

"Not if it's wrapped in a picture of Hitler," Lydia said. "It's a political statement."

"I don't know." He sat back in his chair, reaching for his cigarettes. "People make such a lot of fuss about politics. What would you like for pudding? I wouldn't recommend the trifle but the apple pie is relatively harmless."

Afterward he asked for the bill. Lydia offered half-heartedly to pay her share and was relieved when he wouldn't let her. He pulled a handful of change from his trouser pocket. There was a solitary cufflink among the silver and coppers.

"Is that yours?" she asked.

"What? Oh—you mean the cufflink." He counted out four shillings and sixpence and added a small tip. "No. A souvenir of last night."

"Cinderella."

"That's exactly what I thought." He helped her into her coat.

"Find the other one, and perhaps I find one of the men who attacked me. Perhaps."

"May I see it a moment?"

He fished it out of his trouser pocket and dropped it into the outstretched palm of her gloved hand. While she looked at it, he put on his own coat and hat.

"Ring any bells?" he said. "Looks like some sort of badge."

"I'm surprised you don't recognize it. That gold thing in the middle is a fasces. Or is it fascis? Anyway, it's the symbol of the British Union of Fascists."

He frowned. "So it is. That's the problem with having been in India for five years. I'm not quite at home here anymore. I didn't feel at home in India either. Odd, isn't it? The British Union of Fascists didn't even exist when I was last in London." He gave a little laugh as if trying to suggest that what he had said was halfway to being a joke, though it clearly wasn't. "What are you doing now?"

She wondered why he had avoided the obvious implication. "Going back to the flat."

"I'll walk with you."

He held the door open for her. Lydia thought that she didn't belong anywhere either. Bleeding Heart Square wasn't home. But neither was Frogmore Place or Upper Mount Street, let alone those tumbledown mausoleums in the country that her stepfather and Marcus were so attached to. But there was no point in worrying about it. At least she knew what she wanted now. Virginia Woolf had been right all along. One needed a room of one's own and a minimum of £500 a year. And something to do with one's life.

As they were waiting for a gap in the traffic in Hatton Garden, Rory said casually, "Serridge isn't involved with those Fascists, is he?"

So he had come to that conclusion after all. Lydia said, equally casually, "Not as far as I know."

"You see, if the cufflink belonged to one of the toughs last night, it puts rather a different complexion on things."

"Even if the man was wearing a BUF cufflink, it doesn't neces- sarily mean you were attacked by Fascists. Anyway, someone else might have lost the cufflink."

A baker's van slowed to allow them to cross the road. Rory took Lydia's arm and they jogged across to the opposite pavement.

"I take your point," he said as they were passing Mr. Goldman's shop where Lydia had sold her great-aunt's brooch. "On the other hand, these chaps knew exactly what they were doing. What's the word? They were *disciplined*. They didn't smell of drink. I should have thought of that before. I'm not even sure they wanted to rob me. I think they just wanted to give me a thrashing. Or worse. I'm pretty sure if you hadn't come along when you did, the police would have had to scrape me off the cobbles with a shovel."

She winced. "Don't."

"Sorry. But it really doesn't make sense. There's no reason why the British Union of Fascists should know of my existence. I haven't the slightest interest in politics. Whichever way you look at it, it's damned odd." He glanced at her. "Has anything else odd happened? Or was this just an isolated incident?"

There were several answers to that question, Lydia thought, and some of them involved her father and some of them involved Marcus. There was no avoiding the fact that the only people she knew with Fascist connections were Marcus, her own family and their friends. In the end she mentioned the one thing that could have nothing to do with them, partly because it was also the one thing that worried her most of all.

"Someone's been sending Mr. Serridge parcels," she said.

"Oh yes?"

"There was one on the day I arrived. It had been hanging around for a few days and it filled the house with a horrible smell." She stopped beside the Crozier, reluctant to turn into Bleeding Heart Square. "In the end we had to open it. There was a piece of rotting meat inside. Nothing else. No letter or anything. Mrs. Renton said it was a heart, a lamb's, perhaps, or a ewe's. It—it had dried blood on it. I've never smelled anything quite as foul."

"But what was the point?"

"I don't know. Some sort of message?"

"Saying what?" Rory asked.

Lydia looked into his long, ugly face and wondered whether he knew more about this than he was letting on. "Perhaps it was a way of reminding everyone of the name. Reminding us all that we live in Bleeding Heart Square. And then there was another one on the doorstep a few days ago. Mrs. Renton cooked it. It smelled rather nice, actually." She tried to smile at him to show that she was ironically amused by the whole business, that it didn't make her skin crawl, especially when she was alone at night. "There was another parcel for Mr. Serridge this morning, as a matter of fact. That's why I didn't have the liver and onions."

It was a raw, cold afternoon and Lydia spent most of it huddled in front of the fire with *A Room of One's Own*, waiting for her father to come back. A little after five o'clock, she heard his slow, dragging footsteps on the stairs. He came into the sitting room and grunted when he saw her. He wasn't drunk, she thought, but he looked pale and ill. Still in his overcoat, he sat down at the table and patted his pockets for cigarettes.

"What are you giving us for supper?" he asked.

"I hadn't thought. I ate quite well at lunchtime. There's bread and margarine if you're hungry."

"Damn it," he muttered. "A chap can't live on bread and margarine."

"I expect they'll do you a sandwich at the Crozier."

He looked up, alerted by her tone. "What's biting you?"

"I heard something today. That you sold a farm a few years ago to Mr. Serridge and the lady who used to own this house."

"What do you know about her?" he barked. "Sorry—didn't mean

to shout—you rather took me by surprise, that's all. Who told you that?"

She ignored the question. "Is it true?"

He stared at her, frowning, and said, "Anyway, I sold it to Serridge."

"Not Miss Penhow?"

He found his cigarettes and lit one. "I told you—I sold Morthams Farm to Serridge just before I went to America. My aunt left it me in her will. Nice old girl, Aunt Connie. She was my godmother too. But I didn't make a great deal of money out of the sale, because the farm was mortgaged up to the hilt and the damned tenant had let it go to pot. Still, it was a nice thought."

"But you knew Miss Penhow?"

"I met her. Must have been years ago. Serridge introduced us. Shy little thing." Ingleby-Lewis opened his bloodshot eyes very wide, the picture of slightly debauched innocence. "Someone said she moved out and married some fellow she used to know." He consulted his watch. "Good God, I hadn't realized it was so late. There's a chap I've got to see."

He struggled out of the chair. Lydia followed him onto the landing.

"Did you ever go to Morthams?"

"As a matter of fact, yes." He was halfway down the stairs now. He glanced back over his shoulder. "Not much of a place."

"What was it like?"

"There was a house. And a bit of land."

The front door slammed behind him. Lydia was about to go back to the flat when she heard footsteps in the part of the hall below that was out of sight. Mrs. Renton appeared at the foot of the stairs.

"Hello," Lydia said.

"You were asking about Morthams Farm?"

"Yes." Lydia stared at the wrinkled face upturned to hers. "Why?"

Mrs. Renton frowned as though trying to work something out. Then she said, "It's Mr. Serridge's other house."

"Yes, I know."

Mrs. Renton stared at Lydia with cloudy brown eyes. She seemed on the verge of saying something but then a car drew up outside and she rubbed her forearms, first one and then the other. The door opened and Serridge came in, his bulk blocking the light from the doorway and making the hall seem crowded. He was carrying a large cardboard suitcase and had a tweed overcoat over his arm.

"Evening," he said, advancing toward them. "That parcel for me?"

"Yes, sir," Mrs. Renton said, and her body twitched in a vestigial curtsy.

This time they met in a tea shop opposite the forecourt of the British Museum. Its window was crowded with aspidistras, a barrier of green spikes separating the interior from the vulgarity of the outside world.

The proprietress swooped on Narton as soon as he pushed open the door, setting a bell jingling above his head. With a wave of a be-ringed hand, she tried to herd him toward a table in the gloom at the back of the tea shop. He was having none of that—you couldn't be a police officer for as long as he had and allow people to push you around willy-nilly—and took up a position at the table by the aspidistras, which gave him a good view of the street outside.

The woman clucked her disapproval but recognized superior force when she encountered it. He suffered a further dose of her disapproval when he insisted he only wanted a cup of tea. Then Rory Wentwood came in, and the proprietress mellowed because he was a nicer class of customer and besides he wanted poached eggs on toast.

"You've been in the wars," Narton said.

Wentwood brushed a crumb from the tablecloth. "A couple of men attacked me yesterday evening."

"Where?"

"Bleeding Heart Square. It was about nine o'clock—I was coming back to the flat."

"After your wallet?"

Wentwood fell silent as the proprietress brought his tea. She fussed over him, making sure his knife and fork were straight, showing him unnecessarily where to find the sugar, which in any case he didn't want. After she had left, he said, "I don't think they were after money. They wanted to hurt me. To frighten me."

"Serridge," Narton said. "Ten to one he heard about you going to Rawling."

"He watched me crawling upstairs afterward. Didn't say anything. Didn't help. Just watched."

"There you are then."

Wentwood hooked a finger into his waistcoat pocket, took out something that glittered and tossed it on the tablecloth beside the cruet. "It's possible one of them left that behind."

Narton picked it up and held it to the light.

"Wearing cufflinks, you see," Wentwood went on in a voice not perfectly steady. "A nice class of footpad, eh?"

"You recognize the design?"

"Mrs. Langstone did."

Narton grunted. "So where do you stand when it comes to politics? Bit of a Bolshevik?"

"I haven't got any politics. All I want's a quiet life."

"That's what we all need, Mr. Wentwood. Maybe not what we all want." Narton tapped the cufflink with his fingernail. "What about the folk you mix with?"

"No, they're—" Wentwood broke off. "Well, actually, Miss Kensley's interested in that sort of thing. She has a—a friend who's some sort of communist, I believe."

"So someone who'd seen you together might just think you thought the same way?"

"It's possible. But it doesn't seem much of a motive for a gang of Fascist thugs to follow me home and beat me up."

Narton rubbed his eyes. He felt very weary. "It's surprising what people will do where politics is concerned. Did you hear about the big British Union rally at Earls Court in June? Things got very nasty."

They fell silent as Rory's eggs arrived.

When they were alone again, Narton lowered his voice. "Have you reported this to the local boys?"

"No. I thought I'd better have a word with you first."

Under the table, Narton wiped damp palms on his trousers. "Quite right. The last thing we want is for Serridge to get the wind up."

"If it was Serridge."

"The point is, he's not going to feel comfortable with coppers around. We wouldn't want that." Narton sipped his tea. "Trust me." He watched the other man over the rim of his cup.

"I don't know what would have happened if Ingleby-Lewis and Mrs. Langstone hadn't turned up." Wentwood jabbed an egg with his fork. "I might not have been in a fit state to talk to you."

Narton thought it very likely. "No real harm done, that's the main thing, eh?"

"I'm having second thoughts. Miss Kensley thinks I'm wasting my time. I'm beginning to think she's right."

"You're not wasting your time, I promise you that," Narton said sharply. "Not while Serridge is around. If he asks you about the attack, tell him you think you fell foul of a couple of drunks."

Wentwood pushed aside his plate, wasting perfectly good food. You could tell he'd never been poor, Narton thought, not really poor.

"Have a word with Miss Kensley at least." Narton touched the cufflink. "Ask if she has had any problems with these chaps. No harm in that, is there?"

"All right."

"Good man."

"But there is something queer going on in that house," Wentwood burst out. "Have you heard about the heart?"

Narton looked blankly at him and waited.

"Or rather the hearts. Mrs. Langstone told me about them today. It seems that somebody's been sending Mr. Serridge a parcel every now and then. Each one contains a heart, a lamb's, or a ewe's." Wentwood licked his lips. "An uncooked heart. No letter. No nothing. Just the heart."

"I know," Narton said.

"How?"

"Because I went through the dustbins."

When Rory reached Cornwallis Grove, Julian Dawlish answered the door.

"Ah, Wentwood," he said. "Splendid. We need a strong pair of arms. I say, you look a bit the worse for wear, if you don't mind my saying so."

"I had a bit of an argument with a couple of drunks last night."

"My dear chap, are you—"

Rory cut in, "It looks worse than it is. I'm fine."

Dawlish shot him a swift, intelligent glance. "Come and sit down. I'll call Miss Kensley." He shouted upstairs, "It's Mr. Wentwood."

Rory followed Dawlish into the drawing room. "What's happening?"

"Miss Kensley wanted to clear out her father's room, and I promised to give her a hand."

For the first time Rory could remember since his return from India, the drawing room felt warm. The curtains were drawn and a substantial fire was burning in the grate.

"Is she all right?" he asked.

"Absolutely."

Dawlish attacked the fire with a poker and the flames licked up the chimney. The door opened and Fenella came in. Her face was flushed and her eyes were bright. Her hair was covered with a scarf, and she was wearing slacks.

"Hello, Rory." She stopped. "What have you been doing to yourself?"

He repeated what he had told Dawlish.

"I was just saying to Julian we could do with your help," she went on, once she had established that he wasn't seriously hurt.

Julian? He was Mr. Dawlish yesterday evening.

"We're clearing out Daddy's room—his workshop upstairs. There's an awful lot of rubbish, and some of it's quite heavy."

"Unfinished oil paintings?" Rory said. "Broken armchairs? Disembowelled clocks?"

"And a half-built wardrobe," Fenella replied. "A case of so-called geological specimens. Lots of stuffed birds. Three crystal receivers—wireless was the big thing just before his last illness. He used to listen to the Savoy Orpheans on his headphones, tapping his feet and whistling along. It drove Mother mad. Before that it was going to be reupholstering antique armchairs and selling them to any American millionaires who happened to be passing." She smiled at Dawlish. "Daddy changed his hobby about once every three months. They were all going to make him rich. He spent a fortune on them. Some of it must be worth a few bob still."

She sat down on the sofa and the men followed suit in the chairs on either side of her. She held out her hands to the blaze.

"I hope you don't mind," Dawlish said. "I put a bit more coal on. It felt a bit chilly."

"Of course I don't mind."

Rory looked at the fire, which had probably consumed an evening's supply of fuel in the last half-hour. "Why are you clearing the room now? Will you use it for another lodger? Or can you sell some of the stuff?"

"We should find buyers for some of it, and the rag-and-bone man will take what's left. But no more lodgers, I hope. Julian's had an idea."

"Some friends and I are setting up a small organization," Dawlish explained. "Fenella has very kindly agreed to act as our secretary."

"What sort of organization?"

Dawlish gave no sign that he had heard the rudeness in Rory's voice. "The Alliance of Socialists Against Fascism. That's our provisional title. ASAF for short."

"Sounds a worthy cause," Rory said bitterly.

"We think there's room for it," Dawlish said. "A need, even. We want to provide a place where left-wingers of various persuasions can meet and discuss things. Joint action is the key, you see. United we stand and divided we fall. I know someone who's just inherited a house in Mecklenburgh Square, and we can have it for a pepper-corn rent as the headquarters. The members will help with the running expenses. And one of those, of course, will be the salary of the secretary."

"You must be very pleased," Rory said to Fenella.

"I am."

"I thought of Fenella right away," Dawlish went on. "She has shorthand and typing. And running a little organization like ours will be peanuts compared with running this place and dealing with lodgers."

Rory said nothing.

"It's early days yet of course." Apparently oblivious of any awkwardness, Dawlish beamed like Father bloody Christmas. "We'll have to see how things work out."

Rory turned to Fenella. "But what will you do when the lease runs out here? You'll have to find somewhere to live."

Dawlish cleared his throat. "It might be useful to have the secretary living on the premises. There's an old housekeeper's flat.

All it needs is a lick of paint and a few sticks of furniture. So there's no reason why Fenella shouldn't let this place and move in whenever she wants."

How ripping, Rory thought, how absolutely bloody topping with knobs on.

12

THE WOMAN'S stupidity makes you scream. But you put your hands over your mouth so no one but you will hear.

Monday, 3 March 1930

If all goes well, Joseph says there's no reason why we shouldn't move within a few weeks. He has sent off for some seed catalogues. He is planning to set up a market garden. Spring in the country! I can hardly believe it. And Jacko will love it too. I saw him today on our way to Mr. Shires' office. I'm sure Mr. Howlett is a kind man and looks after him very well but I can't help feeling that there was a very sad look in Jacko's eyes when I left him.

Mr. Shires is the lawyer, and his office is in Rosington Place, almost opposite the chapel which will always be so very special to us. He seems a very pleasant man, rather plump and shy. Joseph tells me he is very good at his job and not expensive.

We transacted a great deal of business in about half an hour. It's such a relief to have Joseph looking after my interests. He and Mr. Shires went through my papers and explained which shares I needed to sell and which to keep. I seem to have been poorly advised before—some of the shares are losing value, and the best thing to do is sell them while we can. I was a little worried, I must admit—I thought that if I sell some of my shares I shall have less income to live on. But Joseph pointed out I should have his income too, and anyway everything is much cheaper in the country. Between us we shall live very comfortably even before the market garden begins making a profit.

Mr. Shires had also prepared a letter for me to send to Mr. Orburn, withdrawing my legal business from him and asking him to send my file to Mr. Shires. I felt a little unhappy about this but Joseph said it was purely a matter of professional etiquette, and Mr. Orburn would not be offended. In any case he and his father have earned a handsome amount from us over the years.

Joseph and I had a long chat about how we should purchase the farm. The problem is that, even though it will be my farm (or rather ours), if we put it legally in my name then everyone will know that Joseph and I are not yet married—in the eyes of the law, that is. Joseph said there would be all sorts of difficulties if I call myself Mrs. Serridge in a legal document before I am entitled to do so. (He squeezed my hands and said that as far as he was concerned the time couldn't come too soon.) So I suggested that the best thing might be to put the farm in his name at least for the moment. The dear man objected, saying that it might not be fair to me, but in the end I managed to persuade him. That way our little deception need never come to light.

Afterward we had lunch with Joseph's friend, Captain

Ingleby-Lewis, who seems rather fond of his wine. Nevertheless anyone with half an eye can see that he's a gentleman. The Captain told me confidentially that all the fellows in his Regiment thought very highly of Major Serridge. He said that he (Joseph) is the salt of the earth. He didn't need to tell me!

Five minutes after persuading her to buy the farm, he's got her selling her shares to pay for it, cutting herself off from the one person she can trust and practically begging him to put the farm in his name.

The cufflink lingered like a bad smell in Lydia Langstone's mind. It was there when she went to bed on Saturday evening, and it was still there when she woke up on Sunday morning. It was part of the reason she decided to go to Frogmore Place.

Not to move back in, not to return to the life she had left behind less than a fortnight earlier. One couldn't go backward, she was beginning to learn, however much one thought one could. Life was like a motor car with only forward gears, rushing faster and faster into the future.

This would be a flying visit. She had not realized how cold a place like Bleeding Heart Square could be. She needed more clothes, and much warmer ones. She had also remembered the pearl necklace, once her grandmother's and now hers. It was kept in the safe behind the boring painting of a horse that hung above the fireplace in Marcus's study. There was a sporting chance that Marcus had forgotten to take it to the bank. It was insured for over a thousand pounds. She had already been obliged to pay a second call on Mr. Goldman in Hatton Garden in order to dispose of a gold charm bracelet.

As for the cufflink, she knew that probably hundreds of men were wearing identical BUF cufflinks in London alone. Nor was there reason to believe that the attack on Rory Wentwood on Friday night had anything to do with herself. But the fact remained that Marcus had recently joined the British Union of Fascists, and he was the sort of man who takes a childish pleasure in proclaiming his membership of masculine associations; his wardrobe was full of striped ties, coded sartorial statements to those in the know.

He was jealous by nature too, and capable of violence. Lydia thought this wasn't because he loved her but simply because he disliked it when anyone tried to take his possessions away—again like a child, this time with his toys. During their engagement, at a hunt ball at a neighbor's house, a drunken subaltern had maneuvered her into the morning room and tried to kiss her. Marcus, almost equally drunk, had followed them in, given the silly boy a bloody nose and thrown him out of the house, much to the delight of the servants.

It was a long step between a drunken fight at a hunt ball in Gloucestershire and what had happened on Friday in Bleeding Heart Square. But it was at least possible that Marcus or somebody watching on his behalf had seen her with Mr. Wentwood and drawn quite the wrong conclusions. Marcus was good at getting things wrong. And if he had had something to do with the attack, she might be able to find a hint of it at the house, perhaps a letter from one of his like-minded friends or even an orphaned cufflink. If nothing else, looking for a clue and failing to find it was better than doing nothing but wonder and worry.

Sunday morning was the best time to visit Frogmore Place. The house was shut up, Marcus had told her, and he was living at his club. The servants would have gone back to Longhope; the Langstones did not maintain two separate staffs. There was a caretaker, Mrs. Eggling, but she was religious, and on Sunday went to church twice a day, morning and evening.

Lydia was still, in theory at least, the mistress of 9 Frogmore

Place, and she still had her latchkey in her handbag. She was perfectly entitled to march up the steps to the front door, let herself in and take away any or all of her own possessions and also those in her charge for those hypothetical future generations of little Langstones. She would be within her rights if she commandeered the services of Mrs. Eggling to help her. But she didn't want to advertise her presence, partly because of wanting to snoop among Marcus's possessions but more because she had broken with that part of her life. If she had to revisit her past, she preferred there to be no witnesses, no accusing glances, no one to ask questions, no one to try to persuade her to stay, and above all no danger of bumping into Marcus.

A bus took her as far as Marble Arch. She walked the rest of the way. Marcus's car was not in Frogmore Place or in the mews at the back. At the house the blinds were drawn over the windows. She ran up the steps to the front door, inserted her key and let herself into the hall.

Inside, the air was cold and slightly damp. The grandfather clock still ticked and a collection of cards lay on the salver on the pier table at the foot of the stairs. Next to the salver was the crystal vase, lacking its usual flowers but still with an inch of brown water in the bottom. Mrs. Eggling was growing slack.

All the doors were closed. The inner doors to the principal rooms were locked when the house was unoccupied. She walked slowly up the hall to the cupboard under the stairs. Inside, concealed in a recess, was a row of hooks holding the spare keys. Lydia took the one for her own bedroom and climbed the stairs through the silent house. It was only after she had passed the first-floor landing that she remembered the pearls. She would need the study key for that. No matter—she would fetch the clothes first.

She unlocked her bedroom door and let herself into the familiar space beyond. The blind was down and the curtains were half drawn. The dressing table had been cleared of its usual litter of silver-backed brushes, mirrors and little pots. Why had she once needed so many expensive objects to make herself presentable to the world? No one had yet put dustsheets over the furniture. Perhaps Marcus thought that covering the furniture would lend an unwanted impression of permanence to his wife's departure. One had to think of the servants, Marcus was always saying, which made life so complicated. One had to think about what they would think and what they might say to other servants.

Lydia did not remove her hat and gloves. She lifted the empty suitcase onto the bed and opened it. From the wardrobe she selected a gray knitted frock with clear, pale blue buttons and a heavy coat, a dark navy blue that was almost black. She turned to the chest of drawers and dug out three pairs of woollen combinations and a knitted camisole. She needed stockings too, and stays. She studied the jumpers available, debating the merits of fawn cashmere or a tawny yellow silk, but decided in the end to squeeze in both of them. It was a struggle to close the lid of the suitcase.

She smoothed the coverlet where the suitcase had been and left the bedroom, locking the door behind her. It was possible that no one would know she had been here, not unless her maid went through her clothes. Lydia's mind ran ahead to what she would do next: leave the suitcase in the cupboard under the stairs; collect the key to the study; look for the necklace and search Marcus's desk in case there was anything that linked him to the attack on Mr. Wentwood.

On the final flight of stairs to the hall, just as she was deciding that she should also look in Marcus's bedroom, she heard the familiar sound of a key turning in the front door and the faint screech as the tumblers turned and the bolt withdrew into the lock.

There was no time to think. Burdened with the suitcase, she ran back to the first-floor landing. She staggered past the doors to the study and the drawing room to the lavatory at the end. This door was never locked when the house was empty. She put down the suitcase and slid the bolt across as quietly as she could. A familiar thud came from downstairs. Someone had closed the front door.

Lydia pressed her ear against the lavatory door and listened. All she heard was the uneven rhythm of her own breathing. The window was small and barred. Nothing much larger than a monkey could climb out of it. She was safe in the short term—unless somebody tried the door—but she was trapped.

Her mind jumped from one possibility to another: it was unlikely to be Mrs. Eggling—she used the basement door; even less likely to be a burglar, by broad daylight and at the front door; so that meant it was almost certainly Marcus. On the whole she would have preferred it to be a burglar.

Time passed—less than twenty minutes according to her watch but far longer by any other standard. She was forced to use the lavatory, and the flow of urine into the pan seemed as deafening as a waterfall. She dared not pull the chain.

Then, somewhere beneath her, she heard another muffled thump.

Relief poured over her. The front door again—so whoever it was had gone. But her confidence had been badly shaken. She waited for another five minutes, just to make sure, and eased back the bolt. When the lavatory door was open, she waited, listening, for thirty seconds. The house around her was silent.

She picked up the suitcase and walked slowly toward the stairs, making sure she kept to the carpets rather than the bare boards on either side. The hallway widened at the head of the stairs. She tiptoed across the carpet. Suddenly she stopped. The door of Marcus's study was now ajar.

Her brain refused to acknowledge what her eyes saw. She stared through the gap between door and jamb. Something was moving very quietly in the room beyond. It sounded for all the world as though someone were eating a sandwich with a good deal of relish and no regard for table manners.

Fear held her in a trance. She inclined her body gradually to the left so she could see more of the room. Details reached her in fragments, like pieces of a jigsaw puzzle scattered on a tray, their meaning temporarily lost. A pair of man's shoes, black and well polished. A pair of lady's shoes, maroon suede, with peep-toes: very pretty, though impractical and perhaps a little fast—and definitely not suitable for church. Dark blue trousers. A rather daring pink day dress with a very tight skirt split up the side revealing nude stockings.

Lydia raised her eyes and suddenly most of the pieces in the jigsaw rearranged themselves on the tray and there was an almost complete picture, as plain and easy to understand as anything could be. Marcus was standing, but leaning against the back of an armchair. He was wearing his Old Marlburian tie and his dark blue suit. He was breathing through his mouth, which hung inelegantly open in an O. His head was thrown back and he was staring down his nose straight at Lydia in the doorway; or he would have been staring if his eyes had been open.

Oh you bastard, Lydia thought, oh you damned brute.

Kneeling in front of him with her back to the door was a woman, thin and graceful in the pink dress. Her dark head with its carefully set curls was bent. The head bobbed up and down with tiny movements like a bird pecking at a tasty morsel. Marcus's hands rested on her shoulders.

The head stopped moving.

Still with his eyes closed and still with his blind face turned toward the door, Marcus whispered hoarsely, "Don't stop. For Christ's sake, don't stop now."

At that moment the last piece of the jigsaw dropped into place and there was no room for any ambiguity or misunderstanding, much as Lydia would have liked there to be. At that moment she snapped out of her trance. She ran down the stairs and along to the dusty hall. The suitcase banged against her leg. Her arm caught the vase and sent it flying against a radiator, whereupon it shattered into a shower of crystal. She wrenched open the

front door and tumbled into the stuccoed respectability of Frogmore Place.

On Sunday morning Herbert Narton left the room he rented in
Lambeth, locking the door behind him. He walked over the
Thames and across London to Liverpool Street, where he bought a
return ticket to Mavering. The journey took even longer on a Sunday afternoon than during the week. It was gone half past three
before he reached the little station.

Nobody else left the train. He took the footpath by the church
and plodded toward Rawling. At the fork he paused. He chose the
right-hand path, though it was the longer way to the cottage. Outside the village he glanced incuriously at the Hall. Going to rack
and ruin now the Alfordes were no longer there. His wife said the
new people were a bunch of loonies— Theosophists or something,
whatever that might mean, all physical jerks and higher thoughts—
but she didn't think they'd stay, which was just as well because
their morals were no better than they should be.

The village itself came in sight. He wandered into the churchyard. It was horribly cold and no one was around. There were lights
downstairs in the Vicarage and smoke curling up from its chimneys. Most of the inhabitants of Rawling, from the Vicar to Robbie
Proctor, who was the next best thing to the village idiot, were having cups of tea in front of the fire.

Narton lingered at the lych gate. Ahead of him a flagged path
stretched to the south door of the church. He had been married
inside that church and come out of it with Margaret on his arm
and his colleagues in their best blue uniforms lined up to greet
them. It had been spring and he remembered vividly the fresh
green leaves on the pleached limes on either side of the path. Now
the limes were leafless, and their intertwined branches and twigs
showed black against the gray tones of the grass, the stone walls
and the sky. The trees were like opposing ranks of ghostly dancers

about to sweep him into their midst and bear him away to a sinister end he could not begin to perceive.

Something nudged his memory—a conversation overheard between Malcolm Fimberry and Father Bertram at the chapel—something about a party in Bleeding Heart Square and a woman who danced with the devil. Narton had no truck with these old wives' tales, but he knew who and where the devil was. The devil was alive and well and dividing his time between Morthams Farm and 7 Bleeding Heart Square. And now, according to young Wentwood, just to complicate matters that were already unbearably complicated, someone was sending parcels to him.

Bleeding hearts to the devil?

Narton left the path and zigzagged among the gravestones. The grass was long and wet and the damp seeped through his trousers. At the bottom of the churchyard was the area reserved for newer graves. He hesitated. Amy's stone was near the yew in the corner. *Goodnight, my dear.* He cast one look back at the dancing limes and then hurried out of the churchyard by the lower entrance.

It was bloody raining now, and the light was failing fast. Narton walked faster and faster, trying to put the cold and damp behind him, though God knew there was nothing at the other end worth hurrying to. Morthams Farm was half a mile to the left, screened by a ragged belt of trees, including three tall pines. He passed the opening of the rutted track up to the house and yard. The mailbox stood askew like a drunken sentinel on the corner. Aping the gentry, Serridge called the track a drive.

The road swung to the right. Around the bend was the dark oblong of his own house, with a light in the kitchen window. The cottage had two rooms upstairs and two rooms down, plus a scullery tacked on to the end. Narton's father-in-law had spent all his working life on the Hall's home farm, and the cottage had come with the job. After he retired, the Alfordes had let him stay there. His daughter Margaret worked at the Hall, and they had let her keep the cottage after she handed in her notice to marry Herbert Narton.

Pretty young thing. Couldn't believe my luck.

The Alfordes had had their heads in the clouds, Narton considered, more money than sense, an easy touch for anyone with a sob story—which was why of course they didn't have much money left now. When they had sold up the estate, they had offered the Nartons the freehold of the cottage for not much more than the price of a decent dinner. He had been delighted at the time. He had seen himself growing old there, growing sweet peas and marrows, maybe asparagus if he could manage it; and Amy's kiddies helping him pot seedlings.

Now the garden was a dripping wilderness crowded with the remains of last summer's weeds. He glanced through the kitchen window as he passed it. Margaret, wearing coat, hat and gloves, was sitting at the table reading the Bible. Her lips moved and her finger crept along the line of text. When he let himself in at the back door, she did not look up.

Not so pretty now.

He knew better than to interrupt her. While she sat there reading, he removed his coat, riddled the kitchen range and added kindling and a thin layer of coke to the glowing embers that remained. He set a kettle on to boil and washed his hands.

Margaret came to the end of the chapter and looked up. "Nothing to eat," she said. "I didn't know you were coming today."

"It's all right. I'm not hungry."

Her eyes went back to the Bible. It was easier when she didn't talk. He investigated what was available. The leaves in the teapot could be used again. In the larder the milk jug had been left uncovered but in any case the milk had turned sour and a dead fly floated on its surface. There was however a little sugar left, and also half a loaf of stale white bread and a cup of beef dripping. He no longer had much interest in food and drink but he knew he needed them.

"Where's the key?" Margaret said suddenly.

He stood in the larder doorway and looked at her. "What key?"

"The one for the parlor cupboard."

"I've got it here." He patted his waistcoat pocket. "It's quite safe."

"I want it."

"You can't have it."

"You should burn those things you've got in there. All of them."

He sighed. "Don't be stupid. They might be important. We've talked about this over and over again. Don't you listen to a word I say?"

She stared up at him, pushing out her lower lip like a thwarted child. Her fingertip was still touching the page in front of her and moving slowly and erratically toward the right-hand margin. She had been not just pretty but beautiful, he thought, and elegant with it, like a lady; not that it mattered. He brought the bread and dripping from the larder and put them down on the table. Muttering under his breath, he picked up her left hand, the one with the thin gold wedding band.

"You're freezing," he snapped. "You silly woman. What do you think you're trying to do? Die of pneumonia?"

She stared at him, withdrew her hand but said nothing. He fetched a blanket from the unmade bed and draped it over her shoulders. She neither helped nor hindered him. He had seen mannequins with more life in them.

He touched the range with his fingers. "It's getting warmer. That's what you need, warmth. You'll be better when you've had some tea."

She looked up without smiling. Then at last she held out her hand to him.

"We're a fine pair of crocks," Narton said furiously, and took it.

He pulled out the chair beside hers. They sat there, hand in hand, staring at the kettle and waiting for the water to boil.

On Sunday afternoon Rory walked north from Bleeding Heart Square, at first in a straight line and later in a long north-westerly arc that took him through Regent's Park and over Primrose Hill.

Fenella was not expecting him. He reached Cornwallis Grove a little before half past three. Fenella answered the door. He fancied a look of disappointment passed over her face when she saw it was him. Instantly he supplied the reason for it. That was the trouble with jealousy. It created a ferocious appetite that was capable of nourishing itself just as effectively on speculation as on fact.

The hall was full of broken chairs, tins of paint, canvases stacked against the wall and an entire aviary of stuffed birds.

"Come into the kitchen," she said. "It's warmer."

On the way he tripped over a canvas bag of tools and grazed his hand on a half-built bookcase.

"I'm beginning to think I'll never be free of the old monster," Fenella said over her shoulder. "All that clutter is like having Dad around again."

"Will you miss it?"

"Why should I? Quite the reverse."

"No," he said. "I mean the house and everything. It's your home."

"It doesn't feel like it since Mother died. The only thing I really miss is the car. A car gives you freedom—you can drive anywhere you like, at any time." She smiled at him. "You can always escape."

She turned aside to fill the kettle. Rory thought she looked almost incandescent with excitement. He hadn't seen her in such a good mood since he had come back from India. It was either the job or that chap Dawlish, or more probably both.

"Listen, there was something that I forgot to ask you yesterday," he said. "It's about those men who attacked me on Friday."

Suddenly she was all attention. "The drunks? What about them?"

He chose his words with care: "There was a cufflink on the ground which might have come from one of the men who attacked me. It had the badge of the British Union of Fascists on it."

"It wouldn't surprise me in the least. Everybody knows they're brutes. Why, Julian says—"

"The point is," he interrupted, "do you think it's possible they might have attacked me because of you?"

She frowned. "Why?"

Now he had said the words aloud to her, the possibility seemed even less likely than it had before. "It's just that you go to these socialist meetings and—and a lot of your friends are that way in-clined, or more so, like that chap Dawlish. And now your new job with— what's it called?"

"ASAF. The Alliance of Socialists Against Fascism. You make it sound like some—some deviation."

"I don't mean to. It's just that I wondered whether someone might have seen you and me together and assumed I was a com-munist or something too. In other words, they attacked me for political reasons. After all, if the chap was wearing cufflinks, you'd think that he was at least halfway respectable."

"Respectable? And he goes around beating up strangers on Friday nights?"

"Not on the breadline, then."

Fenella shook her head. "I can't see it. Those Fascists are capa-ble of almost anything, but the idea of them lying in wait for you in Bleeding Heart Square and then beating you up—well, it's too ri-diculous. You came to that meeting in Albion Lane, I know, but you didn't exactly play an active part in the proceedings."

"But I know you. And I've met Dawlish."

She shook her head. "If the target were Julian or me, they would just chuck a stone through my window or perhaps beat him up. Anyway, from what you say you can't even be sure that the cufflink came from them." She paused and added in quite a different voice, "Rory?"

"What?"

"Are you all right? I know this isn't easy for you."

The gentleness in her voice took him by surprise. "I'm fine. It will be better when I find a job, of course."

"You're not going to waste any more time on this business about Aunt Philippa, are you?"

"You think it's a wild-goose chase."

"It's a distraction," Fenella said. "But you should be concentrating on finding a job, not chasing shadows."

"But I thought—"

"Even if you found her, it wouldn't be any use. Aunt Philippa went to the States to make a fresh start. Why should she give me any money? She owes me absolutely nothing."

"I want to help. That's all. You won't let me in any other way."

"I can help myself, thank you."

"You mean that fellow Dawlish can."

Fenella shook her head briskly. "It's not like that."

"Of course it is. I've seen how he looks at you."

"I'm not saying he doesn't like me. But it's not reciprocated, or not in that way. The thing is, we think the same about things and this job is a splendid opportunity. It's perfect."

Rory thought it was perfect for Dawlish because it would give him unlimited access to Fenella. He said, "It really is over, isn't it?"

"What is?"

"You and me."

She stood up. "Look, we talked about this. We were very young when we got engaged, especially me. Then you went off to India for years and years. We can't expect to just take things up where we left off. People change. I know I have. And I think you have too. Now you're just in love with a sort of idea of me, something you dreamed up while we were apart. As far as you're concerned I'm like a bad habit. You need to give me up and then you'll be fine."

"So that's it?"

"Of course it's not. We can be friends. I hope we always shall be. And who knows what might happen?"

"I'm a bloody fool," Rory said.

"No you're not. You're a dear good man. And I'm truly grateful for all you've done. Now, while the tea's brewing, will you help me

clear a space in the hall? There's so much rubbish I can't get into
the dining room."

Rory took the Tube back to Holborn. He smoked two cigarettes on
the way and glowered at anyone who he thought might be looking
at him. Until now, despite the evidence to the contrary, he had
taken it for granted that he and Fenella were destined eventually
to spend most of their lives together. His assumptions about the
future had been based on that proposition. He scowled at his reflection in the window on the other side of the carriage. All that
wasted time and emotion. Narton be damned. If Fenella didn't
care what had happened to Miss Penhow, why should he? What
was the point? What was the point of anything?

When he left the Tube, it was almost dark. The thick, heavy air
tasted of coal dust and chemicals; fog was on its way again. He hurried along the north side of Holborn. As he was passing the long,
dark facade of the Prudential building, he drew level with a woman
walking more slowly in the same direction. He glanced at her face.
In the same moment she turned her head toward him.

He touched his hat. "Mrs. Langstone. Good afternoon."

She frowned as though she had been accosted by a stranger.
Then she recognized him. "Oh hello."

"Beastly weather." He peered through the gloom at her. "I say,
you feeling all right?"

"Yes—no. I mean, I think I might be going down with something. A chill, perhaps."

They fell into step and returned to the square by way of Rosington Place. A furious yapping came from the lodge. Howlett's face
appeared at the little window. He raised his hand in a half salute.
Faster and faster, as though someone were pursuing them, they
walked toward the chapel and the gates at the end.

"Are you enjoying the job?" Rory asked as they passed Shires
and Trimble's office.

"Not particularly." She did not look at him. "But then that's not really the point, is it?"

They reached the gates that led to the square. He opened the wicket and stood to one side so that she could precede him.

She hesitated, and looked suddenly up at him. "Have you ever felt you'd be better off dead, Mr. Wentwood?"

"I imagine most of us have." In fact the thought had crossed his mind not twenty minutes earlier. "But think of the mess it would make."

Her blue-gray eyes stared up at him. There wasn't an answering smile on her face. "Life's messy enough anyway. What's a little more here or there?"

"What's wrong?" There was nothing like misery for making one blunt. "Is there anything I can do?"

"It's very kind of you, but no. I shouldn't have said anything. I'm sorry."

She stepped into Bleeding Heart Square. He followed, closing the wicket. She stopped suddenly, so sharply that he almost cannoned into her. He heard her mutter something under her breath.

Serridge was walking from the direction of the garage toward the house. His loud check overcoat was open and flapped on either side of him like the wings of a brash and enormous bird. One hand was in his trouser pocket, and the other held a cigar. He caught sight of them at the gate and waved.

"Mrs. Langstone. Good afternoon." He added, clearly as an afterthought, "Mr. Wentwood. Have you been out for a walk?"

He was looking at Lydia but she didn't answer, so Rory said, "No, we met by chance in Holborn."

Lydia moved toward the house and the two men followed.

"I don't suppose you're putting the kettle on, Mrs. Langstone?" Serridge said.

"No. I'm not feeling well." She pushed her latchkey into the lock.

Serridge joined her on the doorstep. "You do look a bit under the weather if you don't mind my saying so. A cold or something?"

"Something like that." She got the door open at last and almost ran into the house. She murmured goodbye and set off up the stairs.

"Let me know if there's anything you need, eh?" Serridge called after her.

"Thank you," she said without turning her head.

Serridge stood in the hall and watched her on the stairs. Rory was surprised to see an expression of what might have been tenderness on the other man's face, as incongruous as an oasis in a desert. For the first time, he was struck by the absolutely revolting possibility that Serridge was sweet on Lydia Langstone.

13

Saturday, 8 March 1930

Well, I've done it! I took Joseph to meet John and Agnes. It was fortunate that Fenella was there, which made things a little easier than they might have been, but it was pretty ghastly. I must admit I'd been dreading this, and I was right. It's one thing Joseph coming to the Rushmere, where frankly anyone in trousers is likely to be lionized, but it's quite another to take him to Cornwallis Grove. My brother is such an awful snob! Not that he's got very much to be snobbish about, if the truth were known. And I've always felt that he begrudged Aunt's money coming to me, though heaven knows there was no reason why any of it should have gone to him. She was MY father's sister, not his. He wasn't even related to her.

Agnes wrote and asked me to tea, which was the first I had heard from them since Christmas. I know one shouldn't think badly of people but I can't help suspecting that John put her up to writing to me for mercenary reasons. (Even as a little boy, he was very greedy.) I asked if I might bring a friend, and you should have seen their faces when they opened the door and realized that I meant a man friend!

I had warned Joseph they might be a little stuffy, which turned out to be just as well. They had got out the silver tea service and the Crown Derby. Old Mary, who has never been more than a maid of all work and not a very good one at that, had been forced to come in on Saturday afternoon and drilled so hard in the duties of a parlormaid that she didn't know whether she was coming or going. John took one look at Joseph, and clearly decided that he wasn't enough of a gentleman for him, though anyone can see that Joseph's more of a man than John could ever be.

Anyway, John, who can talk the hind leg off a donkey, went on and on about this and that, trying to make Joseph look small. At one point he asked him what he thought of young John Gielgud's Hamlet and later he pretended to be very surprised when he learned that Joseph had not been to a public school. I was never so ashamed of my relations in my life, but dear Joseph rose above it splendidly. He spent a lot of time talking very nicely to Agnes about her work with the Girl Guides and to dear little Fenella, asking her about her studies and so forth and what she plans to do with her life. She's such a sweet little thing—she takes after my side of the family. I told her I had been using the diary she gave me at Christmas.

And then we had the row!! Beforehand, I had thought about telling John and Agnes about our engagement while we were there—not the full story, of course, because that concerns only Joseph and me—but decided it might be better to break the news when we next met. But John was *so beastly I changed my mind. I slipped out of the room, put on my engagement ring and went back and said, cool as can be, "By the way, Joseph and I have some news."*

Well, you should have seen their faces drop. John began to splutter—he was so angry and surprised he could hardly get his words out. If looks could kill!! At least Agnes and Fenella managed to congratulate us. I couldn't wait to get away. I made our excuses as soon as I decently could.

We walked to the Tube station. I was still seething with indignation on Joseph's behalf. But he said that it was quite all right and he understood why they had been like that.

"I know I'm a bit rough round the edges, my darling," he said. "But the heart's as true as oak, I promise you that. And you were so brave in there. Like a lioness."

I suppose that was what made me do it—not John and Agnes's despicable behavior but Joseph's truly manly generosity and the loving tone of his voice to me despite the insults he had received. I told him that I felt we were now married in the eyes of God. I was trembling in every limb. "I want to be your wife in every way, dearest." I repeated it: "In <u>every</u> way, Joseph. Do you understand?"

Philippa Penhow saw a chance of happiness and she took it. She gave more than she took. You have to admire that, don't you?

His wife had taken to sleeping in the kitchen. At bedtime Narton watched her pulling the mattress out from the scullery and unrolling it in the corner by the range, which had been banked up for the night. Margaret lived in the kitchen, which made sense in this weather because it was the warmest room. If you were going to spend your days there, Narton supposed, you might as well spend your nights there too.

Margaret had once been house-proud to the point of mania. She had kept the floor so clean you could eat off it, and she used to give the Vicar tea with newly baked scones in the parlor. On more than one occasion, Mrs. Alforde herself had come with him.

Without looking at him, Margaret made the bed with blankets from the dresser drawer. Narton wondered whether he should stay with her in the kitchen, but only for a second. Anyway it was only a little single mattress of lumpy horsehair. It had gone on the bed they had given Amy when she was ten years old. All in all, he preferred to lie upstairs in the big double bedstead that sagged in the middle, turning restlessly to and fro between the dirty sheets, weighed down by too many memories and a mound of frowsty bedding.

He drifted into unconsciousness at about five o'clock in the morning. The bang of the back door roused him abruptly from a deep sleep at a quarter past seven. His limbs were aching and his mind was as misty and full of foulness as a London fog. Margaret had gone to work. He rolled slowly out of bed and painfully forced his body back to life. It was still almost dark outside. He had slept in shirt and underclothes. He urinated in the pot and pulled on his trousers and socks, noticing without much interest that the hole in one of the sock heels seemed to have grown larger overnight. He stumbled down the narrow stairs into the kitchen. As he had feared, the range was out. Margaret would get a cup of tea and perhaps a slice of toast at the Hall. She worked there for the loonies, whose souls were far above such mundane matters as keeping the kitchen clean.

It took him well over an hour to light the range, boil a kettle, shave and make tea. Afterward he put on his overcoat and walked into the village. It was a gray morning, raining slightly, and he met no one until he was nearing the shop by the church. Robbie Proctor was standing under the lych gate, with his mouth open as usual and his nose in need of wiping. Had a screw loose, that one. When the boy saw Narton, he turned tail and ran off among the gravestones.

Things weren't much more welcoming in the village shop. Rebecca, the Vicarage parlormaid, was there, and a couple of laborers' wives from Home Farm. They nodded a greeting but sidled away from him, re-forming in a whispering huddle on the other side of the shop. What were they afraid of? That he'd contaminate them like a cloud of poison gas?

He bought five gaspers and a loaf of bread. No one wished him goodbye. He knew that as soon as the door closed behind him the conversation would begin again. Margaret told him that everyone in the village thought he was mad. Perhaps they weren't so far wrong.

At the cottage, he put the kettle on again and ate some of the bread. Afterward he lit one of the cigarettes and wandered from room to room. It already had the feeling of an abandoned house. He came to a halt at last in the parlor, where he studied the cupboard beside the fireplace. He threw the butt of the cigarette into the empty grate and fished out a key from his waistcoat pocket. The door creaked as he opened it. There were three shelves. The upper two held toys, one or two books, some clothes. On the bottom one was a flat, soft parcel loosely wrapped in brown paper. Narton took articles at random from the top two shelves—a copy of *Alice's Adventures in Wonderland*, a woolly hat with a bobble on the top, a tiny china pony that he had won for Amy with an air rifle at a fairground stall in Saffron Walden.

There was a hammering on the back door. Narton closed the cupboard, locked it and went unhurriedly back to the kitchen. The knocking continued. He opened the door and found Joseph Serridge standing outside and leaning on a stick. He wore a heavy raincoat and galoshes thick with mud.

"I reckon it's about time you and I had a man-to-man chat," Serridge said in a flat voice.

"I thought you were in London."

"You going to let me in?"

"No point. You won't be here long."

Serridge came a few inches closer. He towered over Narton, even though the latter was standing on the doorstep. "Suit yourself. I think this fun and games has gone on a bit too long. Don't you?"

"Fun and games? Is that what you call it?"

"You can call it whatever you want," Serridge said. "But it's going to stop. You are making a laughing stock of yourself. And I'm getting tired of having you hanging around."

Narton said nothing.

"I could write to the Chief Constable. Or I could try something more straightforward."

Serridge's right hand shot out and caught Narton by the throat. Narton's head slammed into the doorpost. Serridge tightened the grip round Narton's neck. Narton tried to pull Serridge's arm away. Serridge was too strong. He tried to kick Serridge's shins. He couldn't reach them. When Narton realized there was nothing he could do, he did nothing. He stared at Serridge, and Serridge stared back.

"So," Serridge said at last, as though the silence had been filled with a conversation and he were now summing up its conclusion. "You're too much of a fool even to be frightened. I wonder if your wife feels the same."

Narton tried to speak but Serridge's hand over his throat wouldn't let him.

"Yes," Serridge said thoughtfully. "Your dear lady wife, Margaret. Skivvying up at the Hall. Works all hours, I'm told. No choice, eh? This time of year, she must be walking there and back in the dark. Not like London here, is it? Night really means something. Easy to trip over something in the dark, you know. Might have a nasty fall one day if she's not careful. Or she might bump into some tramp or other. There's a lot of funny customers around, you know—you know that better than I do. Too lazy to get a job. Work-shy. Call themselves ex-servicemen but if you ask me most of them are blackguards who'd cut their grandmothers' throats for sixpence. Or maybe there might be a fire while you're up in the Smoke making a bloody ass of yourself. Easy to knock over a candle, ain't it? An old place like this would burn like a torch." The hand tightened, and Narton gargled deep in his throat. "Yes, old man. If I were you I'd be worried about your Margaret."

Serridge's hand released its grip. Narton stayed where he was, rubbing his neck. Serridge took a step back and smiled.

"No one knows I'm here," he went on. "That's the beauty of a motor car. You're free as air, aren't you? I parked up a lane the other side of Mavering and walked over the fields. So it's just you and me, old man."

"You can bugger off. That's what you can do."

Serridge didn't move. "How's Margaret, by the way? Still like to ride on top? Used to be quite a goer in the old days. And the way she squeals, eh? Like a stuck pig, she was. Had to cover her mouth. But maybe she's a bit quieter now."

Narton said nothing.

"Been nice to have a chat," Serridge said. "But all good things must end." He was still smiling.

There was another parcel for Mr. Serridge in the afternoon post. But this one was different. It was oblong in shape and about the size of a shoebox. It was wrapped as usual in brown paper and fastened with string. The name and address were printed.

When Lydia came back from work, she found Mrs. Renton examining the parcel.

"It's bigger." Frowning, she picked it up and shook it gently. "But lighter."

"Do you think it's from the same person?" Lydia asked in not much more than a whisper.

"How do I know?" She put it down on the hall table. "You look like you need a tonic. Are you eating properly?"

"Yes. It's this beastly weather. It's enough to make anyone feel a little blue round the edges."

Mrs. Renton sniffed. "Your father's upstairs. Mr. Fimberry's with him. They were in the Crozier at dinnertime."

"I didn't think that was really Mr. Fimberry's sort of thing."

Mrs. Renton lowered her voice. "He can be sly, that one."

"What do you mean?"

"Ask me no questions, dear, and I'll tell you no lies." The old woman shuffled down the hallway to the door of her own room. "Men, eh? You watch out."

Lydia went upstairs to her bedroom, where she took off her hat and coat. If only it were Rory Wentwood with her father, not Malcolm Fimberry. In the sitting room she found the two men sitting by the fire. Her father was sprawling like a discarded rug over the sofa, snoring quietly. Glass in hand, Fimberry leaped out of his chair as soon as he saw her, his pince-nez tumbling from his nose. Drops of beer spattered the arm of his chair. A smile like a nervous twitch cut his pink face in two.

Oh dear God, Lydia thought, I do believe the blasted man's in love with me.

"Mrs. Langstone!" he exclaimed. "I just popped in. I remembered your father saying that you found the nights a little cold. I—I have a spare hot-water bottle, and I wondered whether you might find it useful." He gestured toward the table where six empty pale ale bottles stood in a row. Beside them was a hot-water bottle made of stoneware. "Old-fashioned, I know. But so much safer than rubber."

"I'm sure it is. But I couldn't possibly—"

"It's no trouble, really. As I said, I've got two."

"In that case, thank you, Mr. Fimberry. I had one of those when I was a child. My nurse used to call it a stone pig."

"Stone as in stoneware, of course," he said eagerly. "Pig in the sense of an oblong mass of something, I suppose. It's a difficult word to get hold of."

"Do sit down, Mr. Fimberry." She wondered how much beer he had managed to consume.

He smiled at her again, and dabbed his face with a handkerchief. "Don't mind me, Mrs. Langstone."

"Actually, there are one or two things I need to do."

He sat down rather suddenly in his chair. "You carry on. I'll be perfectly all right. I just need to catch my breath if you don't mind."

"Would you like some tea?"

"Eh? No, thank you."

Fimberry was still there, still nursing his beer, when Lydia returned a quarter of an hour later with a cup of tea. He started up again like a jack-in-the-box when he saw her. She told him to sit down. No sooner had she herself sat down at the table, than he leaped up again to offer her a cigarette. Meanwhile Captain Ingleby-Lewis continued to doze, his snoring modulating to a noisy breathing with a squeak in it that reminded Lydia of the creaking stable weathervane at Monkshill.

Without much enthusiasm, she tried to turn her mind toward the subject of what she should cook for supper. Her mind, on the other hand, seemed to have a will of its own: it wanted to think about that hateful scene at Frogmore Place yesterday or, failing that, to wonder whether Rory Wentwood was upstairs and to speculate about what he had been doing during the day. She heard Mr. Fimberry laboriously clearing his throat.

"I—I did enjoy our conversation the other day, Mrs. Langstone, about the old legends. You remember? The ambassador's dance and all those Catholics who are secretly buried here. Of course that story about the devil must be a folk tale of some sort. But it got me thinking about where the name might have come from. Bleeding Heart Square, I mean. I've done a little research. There was a story in the last century that the square took its name from the bishop's slaughterhouse on this site."

"It doesn't sound very romantic."

"No. But there are other possibilities. In the old days there were a number of public houses called the Bleeding Heart. So is the name a medieval survival? Perhaps it was originally attached to pilgrim stories, and the heart in question was the bleeding heart of Jesus."

"Or I suppose they might have got the spelling wrong," Lydia said. "They weren't very good at spelling in the old days, were they? Even Shakespeare couldn't spell his own name."

Fimberry blinked but a moment later he followed her train of thought. "Yes. I see what you mean. Hart meaning a stag." He frowned. "A hart is an immature stag, I fancy, to be absolutely precise. Let me see—a hart of grease meant a fat hart and a hart royal of course signified a hart that had been chased by a king. So perhaps a bleeding hart would be a hart that had been run down by the hounds, and torn apart." He leaned forward, his face pinker than ever, and the muscles of his mouth working as though endowed with independent life. "And perhaps the heart of the hart was bleeding, if you see what I mean . . . It all comes back to the bleeding heart, Mrs. Langstone. I saw a bleeding heart once." He stared blankly at Lydia. "Did you know that?"

"Really?" Lydia kept her voice calm and quiet, sensing that the conversation had shifted abruptly into another direction.

"A man's heart, that is."

"How interesting, Mr. Fimberry. And where was that?"

"In France," he said, as though stating the obvious.

"In the army?"

He nodded. "I still dream about it, you know. Not just the heart, all of it." His eyes were imploring, asking for something that it was not in anyone's power to give. "I was only out there for three months. Passchendaele. They sent me home after that. Invalided out. My nerves have never been quite right since then."

Lydia said that she was sorry to hear that too. It was a shockingly inadequate thing to say but it seemed to satisfy Mr. Fimberry, who nodded and smiled greedily at her, which made her feel even worse. It was almost with relief that she heard a car drawing up outside the house.

"I wonder if that's Mr. Serridge," she said.

"I shouldn't be surprised," Fimberry said in a normal tone of voice as though nothing had happened. "He spends a lot of time driving about, doesn't he?"

Neither of them spoke. They listened to the sighing and whistling of Ingleby-Lewis's breathing, to the slam of the front door and to movements in the house below. Lydia finished her tea.

There were heavy footsteps on the stairs. Serridge came into the room without knocking. He was still wearing his hat and overcoat, and he had the parcel under his arm.

"When did this come?" he demanded.

"Mrs. Renton said it was this afternoon," Lydia said.

He grunted and swept off his hat. "Sorry to barge in, Mrs. Langstone. I'm just wondering if this is another of those damned pranks. Somebody's idea of a practical joke."

Ingleby-Lewis sneezed. His eyes opened and focused on Serridge. "Ah—there you are, old man. Got your parcel, I see."

"I've a good mind to throw it in the dustbin."

"Can't be sure it's one of those," Ingleby-Lewis pointed out. "No reason why it should be."

"I'll take it away." Serridge glanced at Lydia. "In case it's something not fit for a lady's eyes."

"Lydia won't mind," Ingleby-Lewis said. "Will you, my dear?"

She smiled at him. "If you say so."

"Chip off the old block, eh? Tough as old boots."

Serridge said, "If you're sure, Mrs. Langstone," and put the parcel on the table. He took out a pocket knife and cut the tightly knotted string. He tugged the paper impatiently and it glided away to the floor. Lydia, who was sitting across the table from Serridge, saw that the parcel contained a cardboard box marked *City Superfine Laundries Ltd.* He eased off the lid, revealing yellowing newspaper roughly crumpled into balls. She leaned forward. There was something white beneath the yellow. Serridge poked it gently with his forefinger.

"Christ," he muttered. "Sorry, Mrs. Langstone."

"What have you got there?" Ingleby-Lewis said, his hand groping blindly for the glass on the table beside the sofa.

"It looks like bone," Lydia said.

Serridge's hand plunged into the box. "It's a bloody goat," he said in a flat voice. "Pardon me, Mrs. Langstone. An old billy goat by the look of it. Look at that forehead. Must have been a real bruiser in its prime."

Lydia stared at the long skull with its curving horns. The lower jaw was missing. It wasn't like the head of an animal, she thought, more like a weapon. She heard the creak of Fimberry's chair and his uncertain footsteps coming toward the table.

"A goat's skull," he said. "A billy goat. Yes, most interesting. I suppose it fits perfectly, doesn't it?"

Serridge said in a very gentle voice, "What does it fit, Mr. Fimberry? Come on, tell us."

Fimberry gave a nervous little laugh. "With Bleeding Heart Square, Mr. Serridge. With the legend of the lady dancing away with the devil. The goat is a symbol of Satan."

On Tuesday morning Rory walked to Southampton Row, where a former colleague on the *South Madras Times* now had a position as a copywriter with the marketing department of a firm manufacturing sanitaryware. The colleague was unfortunately too busy to see him. Rory returned to Bleeding Heart Square, making a detour via Farringdon Road to buy tobacco.

His route took him past Howlett's lodge at the bottom of Rosington Place. The Beadle was in the act of opening the gate to let in a large silver-gray car, a Derby Bentley sports saloon with a uniformed chauffeur at the wheel. The nearside window at the back of the car glided down. A man threw out a cigarette end. He had a smooth, pale face with rounded features; he was clean-shaven except for a small moustache, and his black hair was swept back from his forehead, exposing a neat little widow's peak at the center.

Rory had never seen him before. But he recognized the man sitting beyond him on the other side of the car. He had only a glimpse of the profile but it was enough. It was the younger of the two men he had seen coming out of Lord Cassington's house in Upper Mount Street. In other words, it was almost certainly Marcus Langstone.

In the few seconds that Rory was waiting on the pavement, he had time to notice that Howlett was all smiles. He actually saluted as the car slid past him into Rosington Place. The impression of a loyal retainer welcoming the young masters home was only spoiled by Nipper's behavior. The dog had been shut inside the lodge but he had scrambled up to the window ledge and was making his feelings felt with a piercing yapping.

Something to do with Lydia Langstone, Rory supposed—perhaps they were going to call on her at Shires and Trimble. The poor kid. Her family wouldn't leave her alone. Not that she was a kid, of course. She was as old as he was, and a married woman.

On Tuesday Lydia had a day off. She had only learned about it the previous evening. Mr. Shires was proving infuriatingly vague about when he wanted her at the office, which made it difficult to plan anything.

After breakfast she tidied away and made the beds, her father's as well as her own. He had gone out, and she was alone in the flat. She found the brown paper from Mr. Serridge's parcel under the table. She smoothed it out, folded it up and put it in the kitchen drawer. Waste not, want not, as Nanny used to say. These days she had no choice in the matter.

As she was sweeping the hearth, she heard a car drawing up outside the house. The doorbell rang. Mrs. Renton's footsteps dragged along the hall.

"Mrs. Langstone?" she called upstairs a moment later. "A visitor for you."

Lydia ripped off her apron, glanced at her reflection in the mirror by the door and went to the head of the stairs. It might be Marcus or possibly her mother, and in either case she was ready for a fight. There was no going back now in any sense, not after what she'd seen on Sunday at Frogmore Place.

"Lydia! Darling!"

Standing in the hall was her sister Pamela. As soon as she saw Lydia, she ran upstairs with her arms outstretched.

"Sweetie! So this is where you've been hiding yourself. It's lovely to see you." She flung her arms around Lydia and enfolded her in an embrace that drove the breath out of her. Pamela drew back and looked at her. "Darling—you feel so thin. Have you been on a diet?"

"No—well, yes, in a way."

"And your hands! When did you last have them manicured?"

Mrs. Renton was still looking up at them. There were voices outside, growing nearer, and one of them was Serridge's.

"You'd better come in," Lydia said, opening the door to the sitting room of the flat.

Pamela followed her in. For a moment she stood in the doorway, looking around. Her eyes lingered on the ruined armchair in the corner. "Good Lord. I say, this is jolly. So . . . so Bohemian."

"No, it's not," Lydia said. "There's no need to be tactful. But it'll do for the time being."

Pamela's eyes widened as they lingered on the pipe in the ashtray on the table. "Is it—is it all yours?"

"Hasn't Mother told you? This is my father's flat."

Pamela blinked. "Your father? But I thought he lived abroad."

"Not now. He came back."

"I see." Pamela smiled. "Anyway, I'm glad I'm here at last. It's been horrible without you."

Lydia turned aside to pick up yesterday's evening paper from the sofa. "Won't you sit down?"

Her sister fluttered onto the sofa, where she perched like an expensive bird. She opened her handbag and took out a cigarette case with a diamanté clasp, rather dressy for a morning call.

"I'm afraid I can't offer you coffee," Lydia said. "Would you like tea instead?"

"Not for me, darling." She held out the cigarette case.

Lydia shook her head. "How did you get the address?"

"I asked Mother." Pamela lit a cigarette. "I do think you're a beast not to write."

"Sorry," Lydia said.

"Did you get my note with the invitation?"

Lydia nodded.

"I wish you'd sent me a postcard or something. Or rung me up. I've been worried about you. Why did you do a bunk?"

"Marcus and I haven't been getting on very well."

Pamela pursed her lips. "Are you sure it's not just one of those things that marriages go through? You know, one of those things they warn you about in the instruction manuals: for better or worse, richer or poorer, all that sort of thing."

Lydia shook her head.

"He's always been as nice as pie to me."

"You're not married to him, Pammy."

Her sister exhaled slowly, squinting at her through the smoke. "You've changed. I don't know, you're . . . You seem harder. I know it must be nice to see your father after all these years"—her tone suggested the opposite—"but it can't be much fun living like this. I mean, how do you manage with things like cooking and washing?"

"With difficulty," Lydia said. "Like most people, I suppose."

"Mother says you've got a job."

"I work in a solicitor's office."

"How amusing."

"I'm one down from the office boy. Part-time. Ten bob a day."

"But that's frightful. Do you actually need some money? It never occurred to me. But I've got—" She broke off and reached for her handbag.

"No," Lydia said. "Thank you, but no. It's very kind of you, but I'm managing very well."

Pamela subsided. She stubbed out her cigarette and leaned forward. "Actually, it was Mother who suggested I come and see you."

Lydia said warily, "What does she want you to do?"

"Just to see if you're all right. She is awfully upset, you know."

Lydia nodded. There had never been much wrong with Lady Cassington's intelligence. Their mother had calculated not only that Lydia might refuse to see her but that she would want to see Pammy; and also that, for Pammy's sake, Lydia would keep quiet about what she had seen on Sunday morning. That, of course, assumed that Lady Cassington had realized that Lydia had seen her in flagrante with Lydia's husband.

Marcus is being very patient. But he's a man, you know, and men have needs.

"Anyway," Pamela went on, "I must tell you my news. Rex Fisher has asked me to marry him."

"Mother thought he might. Are you pleased?"

"Of course I am. I mean, it's always nice to be asked."

"And what did you say?"

"I said I needed to think about it. And talk it over with Fin and Mother, of course. It doesn't do to seem too eager, you know."

Lydia thought that her sister had a point. She herself had worn her devotion to Marcus on her sleeve. When he had asked her to marry him, he hadn't even waited for her answer. He had taken it for granted she would say yes, and so had she and everyone else.

"But I will say yes, of course. I know he's dreadfully old. I looked him up—he'll be forty-one next birthday. On the other hand, he's very well preserved, apart from the slightly gammy leg, but that's just a war wound. All his own teeth, and he doesn't look silly in a bathing suit. And on the practical side there's the money and the title. I know some people say the Fishers are trade, but that's all nonsense nowadays. It's only snobs who say that. Nobody else cares." She took out another cigarette. "He gave me this case, actually. Isn't it pretty?"

"Charming. Is it silver and enamel?"

"Platinum, darling. Did you know that Rex's almost certainly going to stand for Parliament? I do like a man who *does* something, don't you? Fin says he'll probably end up in the Cabinet. I say, wouldn't it be fun if he and Marcus were in the House together? It's perfectly possible if Mosley decides to field a few candidates in the next election. They're just the sort of men he'd want. They won't frighten the left-wingers or spit in the Lobby. And above all they're not *decrepit*." She flashed a smile at Lydia. "Anyway, it's all the more reason for you to go back to Marcus, darling. Then we can be political wives together. We can start a salon and invite lions every Tuesday evening. Think what fun we can have."

She began to giggle, and Lydia found herself first smiling and then laughing.

"That's better," Pamela said. "You've been looking ever so solemn. And hardly any make-up, either."

"Do you love him?"

"Rex? I suppose so. I like him, and he makes me laugh. He makes me feel safe too. I'm sure everything else will come naturally after we're married."

"Wouldn't it be better if you were in love with him now?"

"As you were with Marcus?"

"That wasn't love. That was idolatry. And it's all over now."

Pamela stretched out her hand and took Lydia's. "Look, Lydia. I'm twenty-one. I've been out for *years*. The only people who've wanted to marry me have been quite unsuitable. Either they hadn't got a bean or they were perfectly loathsome. And now here's Rex. He may not be absolutely perfect but he's streets ahead of the competition. The odds are, I'm not going to get a better offer. One has to face facts."

Lydia said nothing but she returned the pressure of her sister's hand.

"Incidentally, if you'd rather not bump into Marcus, I shouldn't go out this morning."

"Why? Is he outside?"

"No. Not exactly—and he's not coming here as far as I know. But he and Rex are visiting a BUF branch in Clerkenwell this morning. And Rex said they were going to call at Rosington Place because he needs to see someone who lives opposite where you work."

"Not many people live in Rosington Place. It's mainly offices now. Including mine."

"Well, that's what Rex said. They were calling on someone who lives there."

"Anyway, there isn't a house opposite our office. It's an old chapel."

"There we are then," Pamela said with another giggle. "I expect Rex and Marcus are calling on God."

14

Tuesday, 11 March 1930

Men are such BRUTES. My hand trembles so badly I can hardly hold the pen. I am writing this by candlelight in our room at the Alforde Arms. Yes, OUR room. Joseph is in the bar downstairs talking to some men of the village.

He didn't mean us to spend the night here. The plan was that we would come down to Morthams Farm for the day and make a list of what we needed to buy, and discuss what would have to be done to make the house ready for us to move in. The trouble began on the train from Liverpool Street. There was a young woman in the compartment—I really cannot call her a lady—wearing a great deal of lipstick, black satin high-heeled shoes, a vulgar little cloche hat and a very short skirt. She pretended to have trouble lifting her case onto the rack, and Joseph sprang to his feet and helped her. It was the way he did it. And the way she responded. I doubt if the horrid girl was more than eighteen—a mere child, which made it worse.

During the journey he kept ogling her, and once or twice I noticed her looking at him in a very sly way. Then he asked if she would like to borrow his newspaper. Of course she did. Soon they were chatting away like old friends and completely ignoring me. I felt so mortified. We weren't alone in the carriage, either—there was a very nice elderly couple as well. I couldn't say anything in front of everyone so the only thing I could do was stay calm and stare out of the window and hope my agitation wasn't obvious to everyone.

Fortunately, when we changed on to the branch line to Mavering, we were by ourselves again. Joseph was suddenly all courtesy and consideration. I said I'd noticed him making eyes at that girl and he denied it all and grew quite angry. I decided to let it go. Like all men, Joseph has something of the brute in him. He has his animal instincts. One can hardly blame him for that. So he was easy prey for a designing girl. It occurred to me that there was a simple solution to the problem. All I needed was a little courage.

I waited until we had nearly finished at the farm—where Joseph could hardly have been more attentive to my little wants and needs. I said, as we were standing in what will be my drawing room, that I hadn't forgotten what I had said the other day after our visit to my brother John's. We were already married in spirit, I reminded him, and it was high time we were married in the other way. He seized me in a great bear hug and covered my face in kisses. I could hardly breathe.

He pointed out that everyone in Rawling already knew

us as Mr. and Mrs. Serridge, so here would be the perfect place, and of course it would signify the beginning of our new life together, etc., etc. Obviously we couldn't stay at the farm, because nothing was ready, but he had noticed the village inn was a most respectable-looking establishment and a sign in the window there said that there were rooms to let. I was beginning to have second thoughts so I said there were things I needed to purchase, which was true. He swept away my objections, and later that afternoon we took a taxi into Saffron Walden so we could buy what we needed for the night.

And then—and then—it all went horribly wrong. We dined at the inn—on dreadful, fatty mutton—and Joseph ordered a bottle of Burgundy, most of which he drank himself. We retired to bed early. It was not even nine o'clock. I'm sure the landlady suspected something.

I cannot bear even to think of what happened next, let alone describe it. It was horrible. Dirty. Painful. Disgusting. We didn't even change into our nightclothes. He pushed me on the bed and ATTACKED me.

The whole business can't have taken much more than a minute though it seemed to me that every second lasted an hour. I felt I was being smothered, though that was the least of my troubles. I had not expected him to be so rough. I had not expected it to hurt so much. Is this what it all means, what it all comes down to?

At least, I thought while he was doing it to me, he will never leave me now. He will be mine for ever. When he had finished, however, there were no signs of tenderness. He just patted my shoulder and said I was a good girl. Then he *got out of bed, pulled on his trousers and walked up and down smoking a cigarette. I turned away and pretended to sleep. After a while, I actually heard him relieve himself in the pot. Then he whispered loudly to me that he was going down for a nightcap. I didn't reply.*

So here I am, writing by the dying fire. I don't want to see anybody so I won't ring for more coals. They are still talking downstairs, and I think he's laughing at something. Laughing. I know it's a sin, dear Jesus, but sometimes I wish I were dead.

When you finish reading this entry, you want to forget it at once and forever. But instead you read it again. And again. That's what hell means, perhaps, being compelled not just to live but to re-live.

Rory might have ignored the smell for another day if it hadn't been for the letter, which was from the editor of a small-circulation trade magazine specializing in hosiery. Through the medium of his secretary, the editor regretted to inform Rory that the post of junior feature writer had just been filled by another candidate so his, Rory's, presence at an interview that afternoon would not after all be required. The editor regretted any inconvenience caused and wished Rory every success in his career.

Rory flung the letter in the waste-paper basket. Thursday now stretched in front of him, unattractively empty. He hadn't had much hope of being offered the job, but at least going for an interview for it would have given him something to do other than combing the Situations Vacant in the library.

Since he had nothing better to do, he decided to investigate the smell. This had been puzzling him for the last thirty-six hours, during which time it had been growing steadily stronger and more unpleasant. It did not take him long to trace it to a tin of Argentinian corned beef, opened at the weekend, half-eaten and subsequently forgotten in the cupboard of the chiffonier under the window. He wrapped the tin in yesterday's newspaper and stuffed it in the enamelled bucket used for kitchen rubbish. Leaving his windows wide open, he carried the bucket downstairs and into the little yard at the back of the house.

The sun never shone on this small rectangle of cracked and blackened flagstones, and probably never would. The yard smelled, and so did the contents of the dustbins that lined the walls. Tall buildings reared up on every side, and the inhabitants of all of them left their rubbish here. A narrow passageway running between number seven and the house next door provided shared access to the square.

Rory opened the nearest of the bins. It was three-quarters full—plenty of room for the contents of the bucket. He was about to upend the pail into the dustbin when a name caught his eye.

He looked into the bin. *Narton*. The name was on a newspaper wrapped around some rubbish. At least a third of the bundle was saturated with moisture, and the paper was dark and disintegrating, revealing wet tea leaves, fragments of tobacco, a cigar butt. When he tried to pick up the newspaper, the bundle fell apart completely. Fragments of newspaper came away in his hand. Rubbish spilled out. He glimpsed something underneath that made him cry out, something white and nightmarish.

Sanity took hold again. Yes, it was a skull, with the rakish horns of a goat. Rory lifted it gingerly from the bin. The horns were bleached and fissured like driftwood. Between them was a V-shaped ridge of bone, bisected vertically with an indentation like a frown. Much of the nose had collapsed, leaving a prow of sharp white spikes sheltering rolls of finer bone, perforated like lace. The eye sockets were vacant, seeing nothing, wanting nothing. He let the skull drop from his hand and back onto its bed of rubbish.

He pulled the remains of the newspaper from the dustbin. Narton's name had caught his eye in a stop-press item at the bottom of a page.

RAWLING MAN DIES

On Monday evening, police were called to a house in Rawling following an unexpected fatality. The dead man is believed to be Herbert Narton, the house's owner.

Rory unfolded what was left of the newspaper on the flagstones. The masthead was still intact: *The Mavering Advertiser & Weekly Herald*. Serridge must have brought it back after his last visit to Rawling.

He sat back on his heels and whistled. Narton dead? It didn't seem possible. The poor devil had seemed well enough on Saturday in that tea shop near the British Museum. He tore out the stop-press item and dumped the rest of the newspaper in the bin.

The poor bloody chap. He was sorry that Narton was dead, even though he hadn't much liked the man. It must have been very sudden. A heart attack, perhaps. What would happen now? Would one of Narton's colleagues get in touch?

It was then that the idea came into Rory's mind. He emptied the contents of his own pail into the bin and went back up to his flat. He smoked a cigarette and thought about the idea and its implications.

Why not? What else had he got to do?

By the time he reached the fork in the path, it was nearly lunchtime and Rory was growing hungry. Instead of turning right, as he had before, he turned left onto the path that would bring him more quickly to the village and the Alforde Arms. The fields on either side were three or four feet above the level of the path and bordered with lank hedgerows. After a few hundred yards, he glimpsed roofs through a gap in the right-hand hedge. He stopped to look. A field sloped gently up to a huddle of trees. On their right was a group of farm buildings. The chimneys of a house were visible above the trees.

Morthams Farm?

Movement caught his eyes. He was just in time to see a boy running along the hedge bordering the field. How long had the boy been there? Was someone watching the watcher?

Unsettled, Rory continued along the path and came eventually to a narrow road with large, muddy fields on either side. He turned right, in the direction of the village. Almost immediately he saw the cottage, which stood by itself in an overgrown garden; the gate from the road had fallen from its hinges and was lying on the verge, and the roof of a small lean-to building at the end had lost many of its slates. But a trickle of smoke rose from somewhere behind the house.

He paused by the gateway. Behind the strip of garden was a neglected orchard. A tall, gaunt woman was standing with her back to him among the trees, tending a bonfire. Despite the cold, she was wearing only a long, thin cotton dress with a faded floral print, covered with a stained apron.

"Good morning," he called.

For a moment he thought the woman hadn't heard him. He was about to repeat the greeting when she turned away from the fire. In her hand was a stick she had been using as a poker. She stared at Rory, who raised his hat.

"Good morning. I'm looking for Mrs. Narton."

"That's me." The voice was harsh and low like a man's.

"I knew Sergeant Narton. Am I right in thinking he was your husband?"

She nodded.

"I was so sorry to hear of your loss."

"He wasn't a sergeant, though."

"I beg your pardon?"

"He wasn't a sergeant," the woman repeated. "Not when he died."

"I don't understand."

"They took that away from him," Mrs. Narton said. "Three and a half years ago. That and everything else. Cheated him out of his pension too." Stick in hand, she advanced through the ruined garden toward Rory, the skirts of her dress trailing through the long, wet grass. "Them devils at headquarters as good as killed him. I'd like to see them hang, every man jack of them. I know it's a sin, but I would."

"But I thought he was in the police. Now, I mean. He said he was. That's why I've come. I was going to—"

"More fool you for believing him."

"Look, I'm terribly sorry about his death. How did it happen?"

She pointed the stick at the lean-to beside the cottage. "He was cleaning the shotgun." Her eyes focused on Rory's face.

"So it was an accident?"

The muscles around her mouth twitched. "What were you up to with him, mister?"

"Have you heard of a lady called Miss Penhow?"

"Of course I have. Mrs. Serridge. So-called."

"Like your husband, I wanted to find out what had happened to her."

"Why?"

"Her niece is a friend of mine. It was on her behalf."

"After the money, are you?" It was not really a question.

"No. I—" Rory broke off and started again. "We want to be sure she's all right."

"I can't help you."

For a moment they stood there separated by a couple of yards of nettles and long grass. Mrs. Narton was so pale that she looked like a ghost, not a person of flesh and blood.

"I'm so sorry," Rory said again. "If there's anything I can do to help, will you let me know?"

She stared at him, saying nothing, and he realized the futility of what he had said. Nevertheless he opened his coat and took out a propelling pencil and his notebook. He wrote *R. Wentwood, 7 Bleeding Heart Square, London EC1.* He tore out the page and held it to her. She didn't move. He took a step closer to her. She stared at something behind him. He dropped the piece of paper in the pocket of her apron.

A thought occurred to him. "What happened to his notebook?"

"I don't know."

"It wasn't found?"

"Go away," she said. "Just go away."

He nodded. As he was leaving, he glanced at the bonfire. There was a child's book on it, he noticed, the remains of a pink eiderdown and what looked like a doll. There was also a fragment of charred cardboard that might have come from the cover of a small, black notebook.

It was after one o'clock by the time Rory reached the gates of the Vicarage. Mr. Gladwyn's Ford 8 was standing outside the front door. He would be at lunch now. Narton had said you could set your watch by Mr. Gladwyn.

Rory didn't mind the delay. He wanted time to think. If Narton had no longer been a police officer, then what the hell had he been doing? The only answer that seemed to make sense was that he had been pursuing a vendetta against Serridge.

He went into the saloon bar of the Alforde Arms and ordered beer, ham and eggs. Narton had not mentioned that he lived so near Morthams Farm, claiming that he had not considered it relevant. But if some sort of private feud, not an official investigation, was the reason behind his interest in Serridge, that might have been another reason to keep quiet about where he lived, in case it suggested to Rory the possibility of a personal connection between the two men.

It was almost two o'clock by the time he finished his meal and paid the bill. Outside, a small, untidy boy with a flabby mouth was sitting on the edge of the horse trough in the yard. He glanced at Rory and then away, continuing to whittle a stick with a penknife. He seemed faintly familiar. Was it the boy he had glimpsed near Morthams Farm? But the world was full of small boys.

It still seemed a little early to call on the Vicar. Rory spent ten minutes in the church, which was small and dark. It had been carefully restored by yet another Alforde in 1876–8 and made even gloomier than it need have been with pitch-pine panelling and pews. He worked his way round the walls, reading the memorial tablets. The Alfordes went back to the middle of the eighteenth century. The most recent in the sequence was Constance Mary Alforde, widow of Henry Locksley Alforde. She had died a few months after her husband, in 1929. "The Lord is my shepherd."

He walked slowly through the churchyard, glancing at the graves on either side, in the direction of the Vicarage. This brought him to the section where the newer graves were. For the second time that day the name Narton caught his eye. It was on a neat new stone marker beside a yew tree. For an instant his mind grappled with the impossible: surely Narton wasn't dead and buried already? Then his mind caught up with what he was seeing, with the smooth green mound and the rest of the inscription on the marker:

Amy Constance
Beloved daughter of Margaret and
Herbert Narton
1915–1931
"Whom the Lord loveth He chasteneth."

Thanks to Pammy's warning the other day, it did not come as a complete shock to see Marcus in Rosington Place. That did not make him any the more welcome. It was just after lunch, and Lydia had returned to work at Shires and Trimble. She was alone with Miss Tuffley—Mr. Reynolds was in conference with Mr. Shires, and Mr. Smethwick had gone to see a client.

Lydia was watering the dusty plants that wilted quietly on the windowsills of the general office. The windows overlooked the chapel on the other side of the road. A large car drew up outside. A chauffeur emerged and opened the nearside rear door. Two men got out. One of them was Marcus and the other was Sir Rex Fisher.

Automatically she drew back from the window. Miss Tuffley, whose typewriter stood on a table by the other window, was less bashful.

"Oh—now that's what I call a proper car. They was here the other day. That chauffeur is a big chap, isn't he? And look at the two gents. You can tell they had silk-lined cradles. First class all the way, eh? I wouldn't mind being whisked off my feet by one of them, the tall one, especially."

"What are they doing here?"

"Not coming to see me. No such luck. Yes, I thought so—they're ringing the bell of the Presbytery House. They want Father Bertram. A lot of the toffs are Romans, you know. Funny, that." A thought struck her. "You're not one of them, are you?"

"What?"

"A Roman. You know—a papist."

"No." Lydia pulled out a drawer of the filing cabinet with such force that it collided painfully with her knee and laddered her stocking.

Miss Tuffley continued her commentary. "What's that chauffeur doing? Golly! Look at those flowers! Roses in November! Must have cost a fortune!" She gasped. "He's crossing the road."

Lydia could bear it no longer. She muttered something about powdering her nose and locked herself in the lavatory for five minutes. When she came back, she found two dozen red roses on her desk. Miss Tuffley was staring at them with covetousness and curiosity.

"There's no card with them—I've looked," she hissed. "The chauffeur just gave them to the caretaker's boy downstairs, along with sixpence for his trouble. Sixpence for running up and down the stairs! But the boy said they were for you. Mrs. Langstone, care of Shires and Trimble. There can't be any mistake."

Lydia looked out of the window. The car was still there. She had never had much time for roses. They needed too much attention and they had too many thorns. Even when somebody else did the work and removed the thorns, as now, they looked lifeless and artificial and smelled overpowering.

"You know those men down there, don't you?" Miss Tuffley said, chewing on the problem like a dog with a bone. "And you never let on. Which one sent the roses?"

Lydia ignored her. Marcus thought women were like children: you could woo them with toys. But he didn't even trouble to find out what toys they liked.

"You can have the blasted things," she said abruptly.

"What?" Miss Tuffley said in an unladylike squawk.

"You can have the roses. I don't want them."

"But why ever not? They're lovely."

"I'd like you to have them," Lydia said doggedly. "Otherwise I'll throw them away."

"All right. If you're sure. Thanks ever so."

"But there's one condition." Lydia lowered her voice. "If either of those men ever comes to the office asking for me, or if that chauffeur does, say I'm not here."

Miss Tuffley's eyes were large and round. "But why?"

"Because I don't want to talk to them," Lydia said. "That's why."

At the Vicarage he recognized the maid who opened the door, and she recognized him. When he asked if he might see Mr. Gladwyn, she led him into the house and left him staring at the engraving of

Rawling Hall. A few minutes later, she ushered him into the study.

"I'm not sure I can be of any further use to you, Mr. Wentwood," Mr. Gladwyn said after they had shaken hands.

"I imagine you knew Herbert Narton, sir?"

The Vicar stared at him. "So that's the way the land lies. What's this about? Have you been pulling the wool over my eyes, young man? Are you one of these reporters?"

"I promise I've nothing to do with any newspaper," Rory said carefully. "And it's perfectly true what I told you about Miss Kensley. I saw her only a few days ago and . . . and she's much easier in her mind about her aunt now. But I owe you an apology—I wasn't entirely frank with you when I last called."

Gladwyn frowned. He had not asked Rory to sit down. "Then you'd better explain yourself."

"A week or two ago, I was approached in town by someone who knew of my friendship with Miss Kensley." It was a slight perversion of the truth, but it would serve. "Herbert Narton."

"Bless my soul. What was the man up to?"

"He led me to believe he was a police officer, a plain-clothes man engaged in an undercover investigation."

"Into Miss Penhow's disappearance?"

Rory nodded. "And into Serridge. I'm renting rooms in Serridge's house in Bleeding Heart Square. The house that used to belong to Miss Penhow."

"So you actually know Mr. Serridge? You really have pulled the wool over my eyes."

"I'm sorry, sir. But you must remember that I believed that Narton was a police officer and that I was helping him in his investigation. I only found out the truth this morning. I saw Mrs. Narton."

"Poor woman. She's taken this very hard. It is not to be wondered at."

"She was acting very strangely, sir. She was having a bonfire."

"Yes. The contents of that cupboard, no doubt."

"What?"

"It was a bone of contention between them, Mr. Wentwood." Gladwyn opened his tobacco pouch. "You'd better sit down. Perhaps you deserve some sort of explanation."

He waved Rory to an armchair and began to fill his pipe. "It's perfectly true that Herbert Narton was a police officer. He was a detective too, in the latter part of his career. He married a local girl, Margaret—he was a Saffron Walden man himself—and came to live in Rawling. It must be said they weren't particularly well liked—they were a self-contained couple, kept themselves to themselves, and he never let anyone forget he was a police officer. They had one child, Amy."

"I saw her gravestone on my way here."

Mr. Gladwyn picked up his matches. "A silly girl, I'm afraid. Head full of fancies. Not very bright, either. Still, there was no real harm in her. Miss Penhow hired her to work at Morthams Farm soon after they moved here. They were doing the girl a favor, really. She was barely literate, and she hadn't any training in domestic service. And morally—well, I hate to speak ill of the dead, but I suspect she was sadly free with her favors. Some of our village girls are little better than animals in that respect. Well, in due course the inevitable happened and she found herself pregnant. She refused to say who the father was. Her parents were very upset, and it didn't do much for Narton's career, either. But they didn't throw her out. I think they were going to make the best of it. Put the child up for adoption, perhaps, or bring it up as their own. Unfortunately it never came to that. There were complications in childbirth. The baby was stillborn and the girl herself died. It shook the parents very badly. Narton was never the same."

"I suppose his death was suicide?"

"Eh? It's not for me to say. There will have to be an inquest of course, but I understand that the verdict will probably be accidental death. After all, there's nothing to show it wasn't an accident. The shotgun had belonged to his late father-in-law, I'm told—it hadn't been used for years. No one will want to make this harder for Mrs. Narton than it need be. Our thoughts and prayers must go out to her at this sad time."

"But why did he do it?" Rory asked.

"As I said, let us assume it was an accident."

"Not his death. I mean why did he pretend he was still in the police?"

"The short answer is that his mind was unhinged, Mr. Wentwood. He was a fantasist. I believe the doctors call it persecution mania nowadays. He was convinced that Mr. Serridge was responsible for all his woes just because Amy had once worked at Morthams Farm. She was there for a few months. She wasn't even a live-in servant, either. But none of this mattered to Herbert Narton. The baby's father could have been any one of our many local scoundrels. But he decided it must have been Mr. Serridge. That's why he wanted to reopen the Penhow investigation. He wanted to embarrass Mr. Serridge as much as possible. I've no doubt that what he would really have liked was to see Mr. Serridge in the dock for the murder of Miss Penhow." Mr. Gladwyn at last struck a match. He stared fixedly at Rory. "In his strange, twisted mind Narton no doubt thought that was the only way he could avenge what he thought of as the murder of his own daughter."

For the rest of the afternoon, Miss Tuffley glanced regularly out of the window. She kept up a running commentary when Father Bertram ushered Marcus and Sir Rex out of the Presbytery House and into their car.

The worrying thing about it all, Lydia thought, was that Marcus might be back, particularly if he and Rex Fisher had been arranging with Father Bertram to hire the undercroft for another British Union meeting. She knew that the undercroft had been used for the purpose before but she wouldn't put it past Marcus to have suggested it again simply because it was close to her refuge in Bleeding Heart Square.

She left the office a little after six o'clock. Miss Tuffley walked downstairs with her, sniffing the roses as she went.

"You know what I need?" she said cheerfully. "A nice gentleman admirer who knows how to treat a lady."

Lydia smiled at her. "We could all do with one of those."

Miss Tuffley turned left toward Holborn, and Lydia turned right toward Bleeding Heart Square. There was a letter waiting for her on the hall table. She took it upstairs to the sitting room. She didn't recognize the writing, though the white envelope was good quality. She tore it open.

10 Alvanley Mansions
Lower Sloane Street
London SW1
Telephone: Sloane 1410

November 21st

My dear Lydia

Your godfather reminded me that I have been most remiss in not writing for so long. I don't think we have seen you since your wedding. Your godfather's health has not improved, sadly, and we are unable to get about as much as we should like. But I wonder if I might prevail on you to have tea with us? The weekend would suit us best—Saturday or Sunday.

Do let me know—this weekend if you like. Your godfather sends his affectionate good wishes, as of course do I.

Yours very sincerely,
Hermione Alforde

My godfather, Lydia thought, just what Miss Tuffley ordered? A gentleman admirer who knows how to treat a lady?

There was a knock on the door. When she opened it, she found Mr. Serridge standing on the landing and looking intently at her.

15

HEARTS. This is all about hearts, restless or yearning, broken or bleeding.

Saturday, 15 March 1930

Such a busy time. I bought some material yesterday and arranged for the woman Joseph found for me to run up a summer dress suitable for the country. I have given my notice at the Rushmere and made arrangements for Aunt's furniture to come out of store and be taken to Morthams. Not just furniture, of course—there's the china, the cutlery, the pictures and heaven knows what. I can hardly remember! We shall be at sixes and sevens for weeks, if not months, while we sort everything out.

I explained the suddenness of my marriage by saying that Major Serridge may have to go abroad at very short notice, and naturally I should want to go with him. Cards, good wishes, etc. from all and sundry. Old Miss Beale said: "Good for you, my dear. Get out while you can. Otherwise the shades of the prison house will close in around you." But then she cackled in a very unsettling way.

I must be honest and say it's been an unsettling time altogether. What happened at the Alforde Arms on Tuesday made it worse. I know Joseph was all contrition in the morning, but still it hurt. But I suppose we women have always had that cross to bear. The simple fact is that men are different from us. But at least I know that now. Really know. Just to show that everything is all right between us I have ordered a car for him. We chose it together. He was so pleased, just like a little boy! It is a second-hand Austin 7, a nice shade of blue that goes with his eyes. We shall look very smart as we motor through the countryside in our own car.

I broke down in floods of tears again when he telephoned this evening. There I was in the little booth in the hall, hoping against hope that no one would notice me crying my head off. He was so gentle and loving. Tuesday night has had the strange effect of making me love him even more. How mysterious are the ways of Love! I should tear out my heart and bring it to him if it brought him a moment's happiness. My heart is yours, my darling, how I wish you could keep it in your pocket, fluttering and beating like a bird beside yours, and my heart would warm itself with your love for ever and ever. I wish I could send you my heart in the post and you could keep it safe beside you for always. How silly I am. Sometimes he makes me feel seventeen again.

Hearts by post. There's an idea.

A voice at his elbow said, "Mister? Mister?"

Startled, Rory looked round and down. His eyes met those of a small boy standing in the angle between the Vicarage gatepost and the garden wall. It was the one who had been whittling a stick outside the Alforde Arms, and perhaps the one in the field near Morthams Farm. He wore a jacket which was too small for him and buttoned up to the chin. His cap was squashed down over his hair, which was ragged and curly. His shorts reached below the knees. There was something slimy on the lower half of his face. As Rory watched, the boy wiped the back of his jacket sleeve under his nose. His eyes were large, brown and long-lashed, as beautiful as a cow's. It looked as though his tongue was too big for his mouth, despite those big, slack lips.

Rory fumbled for a penny. "What is it?"

The boy thrust out his hand. In it was a dirty piece of paper, much folded. Rory took it and gave the penny to the boy, who spat on the coin and frowned. He waited while Rory unfolded the piece of paper. It was a note written in pencil.

MR. WENTWOOD, Could I have a word with you before you go. The boy will bring you. Something most particular to say. Sorry to write but its better that Vicar dont see us.

There was a signature underneath but it was illegible. Rory looked up the drive. Mr. Gladwyn's round head was bent over his desk in the window of the study.

"Who gave you this?" he asked.

The boy muttered something unintelligible. He pointed a grubby finger down the lane.

"Mrs. Narton?"

The boy shook his head. The finger moved toward the left.

"Somebody at Morthams Farm? Not Mr. Serridge?"

The boy shook his head more violently than before. Rory fancied there was panic in the lad's face. He muttered a monosyllable twice and finally it made some sort of sense. *Barn. Barn.* The finger was pointing toward a sagging roof visible perhaps a couple of hundred yards away beyond the boundary hedge along the lane. The boy took Rory's arm and tugged gently.

Rory set out with him. There seemed no harm in following the lad and trying to find out what this was all about. He pulled at Rory's arm again, urging him to go faster. He might be mentally or physically deficient in some way but he seemed to have a very clear idea of what he wanted. He led the way over the stile and along the line of the hedgerow. The barn stood at the top of a newly ploughed field on the far side of another hedge.

Close to, the building proved to be not so much a barn as a tumbledown shed of brick and timber. Its roof had lost its tiles at one end and been patched with corrugated iron. The big double doors were held in place by a heavy bar secured to the wall with a padlock. The boy darted through a gap in the hedge beside the building and beckoned. Rory hung back. The boy vanished round the corner of the barn.

Rory scrambled reluctantly through the hedge and followed. Set in the wall opposite the double doors was another, much smaller door, and it was ajar. Beside it stood a woman wearing a headscarf and a long brown raincoat. She was smoking a cigarette with quick, impatient movements. She stared without smiling at Rory. The boy ran up to her and nuzzled against her. She patted his head as though he were a dog.

For a moment Rory didn't recognize her. She threw away the cigarette.

"Rebecca, sir," she said. "Rebecca Proctor. Mr. Gladwyn's parlourmaid at the Vicarage."

"Of course. Hello."

Without her uniform, she looked completely different—tough and competent, entirely at home with herself.

"Thank you for coming. I had to send our Robbie. He's my sister's boy. Not quite, you know." One hand was still resting on the boy's head. With the other she tapped the side of her own head. "He's a good lad, aren't you, Robbie?"

He gave her a gap-toothed smile, responding as much to the tone as to the words.

Rory said, "What's all this about? Why couldn't you have said something at the Vicarage if you wanted to see me?"

"Mr. Gladwyn said we weren't to talk to you. More than my place is worth if he sees me with you. He's a good master too, not like some, but he's that strict, you wouldn't believe. I can't afford to lose my job because if I do, this one and his ma won't be able to live. Won't be able to eat, won't have a roof over their heads. And if that happens they won't be together anymore because they'll put the boy in a home and my sister in a loony bin." The woman stared at Rory. "I'm sorry to go on, sir, but it's better you know where I stand. I don't want it coming out that you've talked to me."

"All right."

"We'll go inside," she said. "Otherwise somebody passing might see us or hear us, and if that happens it will be all over the village before you can say knife."

Robbie pushed the door fully open and led his aunt inside. Rory followed. There was more light than he expected, some from the doorway, some from holes in the roof and some from two window openings, one in each gable wall, which had been roughly boarded over. There was an earth floor under their feet, quite dry, and a pile of straw in the corner. The place smelled of must and stale tobacco.

"This is on Mr. Serridge's farm," Rebecca Proctor said. "Morthams. Did you know that?"

Rory shook his head.

"Don't worry. Serridge won't come here. No one comes here any more. That's why Robbie comes, see—it's safe. They bully him something terrible in the village. Bleeding kids." As she spoke, her voice was becoming rougher, more countrified, as if she had abandoned the smooth, respectful tones of her profession along with its uniform. "Anyhow, I wanted you to see this place. It's where it happened, you see."

"Where what happened?" Rory said with a touch of irritation because he disliked the idea that the woman had thought him frightened of Serridge.

"Where that poor girl died. That's why nobody comes here. They're a superstitious lot. They think her ghost walks. Anyhow they're scared of Serridge. Not that he wants to come here either. You wouldn't think it to look at him but I reckon he's scared."

"Of what?"

"Ghosts. Like the rest of them."

Robbie tugged at his aunt's arm and pointed up into the shadows.

"Do give over," she said. "You can show the gentleman later if there's time."

"What does he want?" Rory asked.

"To show you his bones. Nasty dirty things."

"Who died here?"

"Why, Amy Narton, of course. In those last months, when she was living at home, she used to spend most of her time just walking around. She didn't like being in the house. Her parents were angry because of the baby on the way. She wouldn't say who'd got her into trouble. That made it worse. And nobody else wanted to give her the time of day." She glanced down at Robbie. "They can be like that round here. Anyhow, Amy was like a dog with a litter of puppies inside her. She wanted to find somewhere quiet and private and dark when her time came. So she came here. But she didn't tell no one. So nobody missed her at first, not for hours, because she was always going off, like I told you. And when they found her at last, it was too late, for her and the baby. They were over there." Rebecca nodded toward the straw. "It was Serridge, of course."

"Who found her?"

"No." Rebecca stared at him, silently reproving his stupidity. "Who put her in the family way."

"Are you sure?"

"Amy's not the first maid he's got into trouble and she won't be the last." Rebecca opened her handbag and took out a small, creased photograph, which she gave to Rory. "Robbie found it in the straw. Afterwards. After they took her away. Look at it in the light."

Rory took the photograph to the doorway and studied it in the daylight. It was a small sepia-toned snapshot of a girl astride a bicycle. Behind her, a field sloped up to some trees and the chimneys of a house. A scrappy little dog was sitting on the grass beside her and scratching its ear. The girl was smiling broadly and proudly at the camera. She looked very young, fifteen or sixteen perhaps. There was nothing strange about the photograph except that it was a man's bicycle and the girl was wearing no clothes.

"That's Amy," Rebecca said.

"She's in the meadow between the footpath and Morthams Farm, isn't she?"

"Yes. The way you came this morning. He's taught two or three girls how to ride a bicycle there."

"Without any clothes on?"

"Serridge could make them think black was white if he set his mind to it. He tells them it's how all the smart ladies up in London are taught to ride. He tells them it's healthier. More hygienic."

Rory gave her the photograph. "And Miss Penhow?"

"She was a nice lady."

"Not a young one, though."

"Serridge just wanted her money, and that was clear enough to anyone except her, poor thing. And she wanted a husband so badly that she'd do anything for him. I used to work for them, you see. Not for long, just a few weeks. When they moved into Morthams Farm, they took me on as a maid of all work, living in and all found. They hired Amy to help me. The idea was I'd train her up. That was a laugh. The only person who gave her any training was Joe Serridge."

"So he was actually carrying on with her while Miss Penhow was living at the farm?"

Rebecca hesitated. "Yes and no. I saw him touching her, accidentally on purpose. And I think he kissed her in the larder once because she came out all pink and giggling and then he came out with a smirk a mile wide on his face. But it didn't get serious till after I went."

"When was that?"

"A few days before Miss Penhow left. Couldn't stand it any longer. He was a surly brute most of the time, and he made Miss Penhow's life a misery. It was worse when he was at the brandy, and after she'd gone he drank even more."

"And that was when he and Amy . . . ?"

"Yes. He had someone else before that, I think—not a local girl. Used to go off to see her and come back the next day looking like the cat who'd got the cream. Amy said she came to the farm once, when Miss Penhow was here—the girl, I mean. Just a girl, Amy said, no better than she should be. Reckon Amy was jealous."

Robbie tugged Rebecca's arm like a bell pull and said, quite distinctly, "Golgotha."

"For heaven's sake," his aunt said, shaking him off.

"Golgotha?" Rory asked.

"It's in the Bible. Place of the skull, where Our Lord was crucified. Robbie got it at Sunday school. It doesn't matter. Anyway, I left the farm. Didn't even work out my notice. But poor Amy stayed. Not live-in, but who cares? Serridge didn't. She was fifteen. He always liked them young, mind, the younger the better. He tried to get his hand up my skirt once, and me not a day over thirteen."

"Now one moment. You knew Serridge when you were thirteen?" He tried to guess Rebecca's age. At least forty, if not more. "Where was this?"

"Here in Rawling."

"So are you telling me that Serridge used to come here before the war?"

Rebecca snorted. "That's what I said, didn't I? He came to the Hall once or twice when the Alfordes were there. They had lots of big parties with people down from London. I'd just gone to work there, that's how I met him. And when Serridge didn't get anywhere with me, he tried it on with someone else."

"Ah—Mrs. Langstone," Serridge said, smiling at her and bobbing his big head in what was almost a bow. "I thought I heard you come in."

"Hello, Mr. Serridge." Lydia slipped Mrs. Alforde's letter into her handbag. She forced a smile. "What can I do for you?"

"I wanted to see how you're settling in. Must all be a bit strange for you, eh? Not what you're used to." He was no longer smiling. "Job all right?"

"Yes, thanks."

"If you need any advice, you'll have a word with me, I hope? I know the Captain's not always the most practical of men."

"Thank you, Mr. Serridge." Lydia forced another smile. "I'll bear that in mind. Now would you excuse me? I've just got back from the office, and I really must—"

"Of course, my dear, of course."

He bobbed his head again, sketched a vague salute and crossed the landing to his own rooms. Lydia closed the sitting-room door, put down her handbag and peeled off her gloves. The brief interview had unsettled her. She felt uncomfortable as the object of Serridge's concern.

There was a faint tapping, almost a scratching, at the door. Not Serridge, probably—there had been nothing faint about his knock. Lydia was tempted to pretend she was not here. But whoever it was must be able to see the light under the door.

She took a deep breath and turned the handle. Mr. Fimberry was waiting on the landing, smoothing back his hair with his fingers.

"And how are *you*, Mrs. Langstone?"

"All right, thanks. Is there something you want?"

Mr. Fimberry ignored the question. "I've had a most interesting day," he said. "I thought you'd like to know that I've found fragments of medieval encaustic tiles embedded in the wall of the Ossuary."

"The what?"

He settled the pince-nez more firmly on his nose. "It's a small chamber beside the main crypt in the undercroft. Didn't I mention it the other evening? The theory is that in the Middle Ages it was used for holy relics, for bones. That's one explanation. But it's also been suggested that the bodies of Catholics who died in the seventeenth century lay there before they were secretly buried beneath the chapel, all piled together in their shrouds. Or that their bones were put there before they were reinterred." He came a step closer as though trying to insinuate himself into the room, but Lydia did not give ground. "Of course the theories aren't necessarily incompatible. There's a good deal of discussion about the subject but very little hard evidence, I'm afraid. On the other hand, the wall is hard enough." He laughed. Then, recollecting himself, he went on, "But you must let me show you the Ossuary some time. It's generally kept locked. Of course, if you come to the meeting, you'll probably be able to see it then."

"What meeting?"

"Father Bertram tells me that the British Union have hired the undercroft for a meeting on Saturday week. It's at lunchtime, and they are laying on bread and cheese. It's for the business people in Rosington Place. They want to explain how their economic ideas will work in practice. I gather Howlett will be putting up notices. I'm sure they'll soon know all about it at Shires and Trimble."

"Excuse me," Lydia said bluntly, unable to bear it any longer. "I have to go."

She shut the door in his face, lit a cigarette and went to stand by the window. She felt both furious and unsettled. This was all she needed. It was as if Marcus were pursuing her, even here. The problem was, she could see no way out of Bleeding Heart Square. She couldn't go back to Frogmore Place. But if she left this flat and her father, where else could she go? She had too little money to rent a room of her own. It had already been made painfully clear to her that she had no marketable qualifications. And her job at Shires and Trimble, such as it was, depended on her being here.

Unless, of course, Colonel Alforde would help her. She took Mrs. Alforde's letter from her handbag and reread it. The Colonel was her godfather, and perhaps that might count for something. She was uncomfortably aware of how cynical she was becoming. But cynicism went hand in hand with poverty.

She had never heard of the Alfordes having any children. Lydia couldn't recall meeting them when she was a child. Lady Cassington had added their names to the list of wedding invitations. Why had he been chosen as her godfather?

She heard familiar footsteps on the stairs. The door opened and collided with a chair. Her father walked slowly and carefully into the room. He waved at Lydia and, without saying anything or removing his overcoat, sat down very carefully and slowly.

"Father? I had a letter from Mrs. Alforde today."

Ingleby-Lewis frowned. "Who?" Then his face cleared. "You mean old Gerry Alforde's wife? Is he dead yet?"

"Apparently not. He is living in Lower Sloane Street. He's my godfather, you know."

"Oh yes. I used to see a lot of him at one time."

"Was he related to the lady who left you Morthams Farm?"

"Aunt Connie? Yes, indeed. As a matter of fact, she was his aunt too—by marriage, though. Gerry's father was the second son, you see." A gleam of interest came into his eye. "I suppose if there was anything left after they sold up it would have come to Gerry. Harry and Connie didn't have any kids so he must have been the next in line."

"Mrs. Alforde asked me to tea. I wonder why."

Ingleby-Lewis stretched out his long legs and patted his pockets in search of cigarettes. "It's up to you, of course, but I shouldn't go if I were you. Gerry was always a bit eccentric, and he had a bad war, poor chap. Last time I saw him—must have been ten or twelve years ago at least—he was babbling utter nonsense. You couldn't believe a word he said."

Lydia nodded, without committing herself either way. Her father was looking at her with an intent expression on his face. She glimpsed the ghost of a younger, harder man behind the bloodshot eyes and the blotched and wrinkled skin. She shivered.

"Growing chilly, isn't it?" her father said. "You'd better light the fire."

Robbie was growing restless. He ran his fingers along the wall of the barn, muttering "Golgotha, Golgotha" over and over again in a squeaky little sing-song voice that might have belonged to a much younger child.

"What was Serridge doing down in Rawling?" Rory said, picking his way through the possibilities. "Was he someone's servant?"

Rebecca shook her head. "Not exactly. The Alfordes used to have shooting parties before the war—they did all sorts of entertaining. Had royalty once, the Duke of Connaught. They'd sometimes take on extra staff."

"So he worked as a servant?"

Robbie snuffled moistly and tried to pull her by the arm.

"Stop it, dear. No, not as such. He was something outdoors like a loader or a beater. They put him up with one of the gamekeepers. He didn't stay at the house. I think the first time he came, Captain Ingleby-Lewis had something to do with arranging it. Maybe he'd been the Captain's batman in the army. I know he used to be a soldier." She glanced at the boy, who was now looking for something on the shelf where the top of the wall met the slope of the rafters. "Of course Serridge looked very different. Thin as a rake. Big moustache. But he always fancied himself."

Rory said, "Did he recognize you when he came back to Rawling?"

She laughed. "I looked very different then too. Anyway, I doubt he really looked at me. Not properly."

"But you didn't mind going to work for him at Morthams Farm?"

"Didn't have much choice, did I? A job's a job. I hadn't had a steady position since the Alfordes sold up. I could have found something in London easy enough, but I didn't want to move, because of Robbie and my sister. Besides, Miss Penhow was there. She was meant to be the mistress. I thought I'd be working for her, not him."

"What was she like?"

"She was kind. A bit soft, maybe. He wore her down, you know, even in the time that I knew her. Got so bad that she'd jump at her own shadow. He didn't let her talk to anyone except when he was around. I think he kept her letters from her too. He used to collect the post every morning, you see, from the mailbox on the lane. I remember her saying to me once how strange it was that no one had written to her since she moved here."

"She wrote letters herself?"

"Oh yes, and she gave them to Mr. Serridge to post." Rebecca paused, allowing time for the implication to sink in. "She didn't walk much because it was so mucky underfoot. Town-bred, you see, wasn't used to mud. So if she wanted to go anywhere she had to go in the car, and that meant Serridge drove her. She never really got away from him."

"You make it sound as if he was planning something right from the start."

"I don't make it sound like anything, Mr. Wentwood. I'm just telling you what happened."

"Did she talk to anyone else much?"

"Besides me and Serridge and Amy? No. She met one or two tradesmen, I suppose, and Mr. Gladwyn, and the farm workers. But she didn't talk to them. Not really talk, I mean. If you want to know what was in her head, you'd have to find her diary. She was always scribbling in there."

"She must have taken it when she went away."

Rebecca was watching Robbie. "What? Maybe she did. I don't know what happened to it. Mark you, she didn't take much when she went."

"What happened to her clothes? Her furniture. Everything."

"Some of it's still up at the farm. But Mr. Serridge packed up a lot of her things. All the clothes and knick-knacks. He went funny after she went away. Turned the place upside down, inside out."

"Looking for something?" Rory suggested. "The diary?"

"God," Robbie said. "Where's God?"

"He's gone, lovey," Rebecca said. "You know that."

"I want God."

Rory looked at the boy's pale, vacant face. He was on the verge of tears.

"You can't have him," Rebecca said.

"God?" Rory asked. "He's looking for *God*?"

Rebecca turned back to Rory. "Not God, sir: goat. He's lost his goat."

Robbie pulled at Rory's sleeve, dragging him toward the wall.

"There now," Rebecca said comfortably. "He must have taken quite a fancy to you. He wants to show you his Golgotha bones."

The boy reached up and very carefully lifted down a small skull, not much larger than a lemon. Its lower jaw was still attached, and along the top of it ran a high, vertical ridge of bone like the crest of a Roman helmet.

"It's his badger," Rebecca explained. "It's his favorite now the goat's gone."

"God," Robbie said. He lifted the badger very carefully back onto the wall and pointed to the space beside it.

"That's where it was," Rebecca said. "You've got lots of others though, Robbie, haven't you? Show Mr. Wentwood your sheep."

Robbie lifted down two skulls, one a ram's with sawn-off horns and the other much smaller, a lamb's. There were cats too, and birds, most of which Rebecca could identify. "That's a magpie, that's a pigeon, that's a starling." Finally there was a frog, this one a full skeleton with brown, leathery tatters of skin attached to it, its long, graceful rear legs trailing into the air.

"He collects them?"

"Yes. I got one or two for him from the keepers up in the Hall woods, but most of them he finds himself. He had this great big skull of a billy goat. Lost it the other week, and he won't stop going on about it." She patted the boy's head. "Nasty-looking thing, mind you."

"God," said Robbie, spraying spittle over the frog.

"No, dear. Goat. And if you ask me it looked more like the devil."

16

YOU LIKE TO THINK that in those days Philippa Penhow had moments of happiness.

Saturday, 5 April 1930

Here I am, sitting at my desk in the window of my own morning room looking out at my own garden! For the first time in my life, I am the mistress of my own establishment. How strange and delightful—I have always lived in other people's houses—the first with Mother and Father, then with Aunt, and then at the Rushmere.

We moved in only yesterday, in a great rush, and my heart sinks when I think of everything there is to do. This room and our bedroom are reasonably habitable, but everywhere else needs redecorating. I have two maids to keep in order—Rebecca, a nice sensible sort of woman who once worked at Rawling Hall and knows how things ought to be done, and Amy, a rather flighty young thing—I can see already that she will need a good deal of instruction and supervision. When I was giving my orders to Rebecca after breakfast, Amy came running into the kitchen like an excited child. She was holding a dripping skull in her hand! A goat's skull! One of the farm workers had been clearing a ditch and he had found it in the water. He left it on a tree stump in the orchard. These simple country folk have a very strange sense of humor, I must say.

The sun is out, I'm in my new home, my spirits are high. But I must confess that yesterday evening I felt a little low. Joseph was very preoccupied. He spent much of the day driving our new car up and down the drive, practicing the gears, etc.

I had expected that he would share my excitement at being here. I must sound very foolish but I had hoped for a loving word or a gentle touch. I'm sure my Joseph is as happy as I am, but men find it hard to show their feelings. And of course he has a lot to worry about. I thought he drank rather a lot of brandy after supper. I went up to bed, expecting him to join me. He did not, however. This morning, at breakfast, he said he had not wanted to disturb me, as he had stayed up late with the accounts, and so he dozed on the sofa in front of the fire. He said that old soldiers can sleep anywhere.

He may have to go up to London on Monday on business. I thought perhaps he might invite me to come with him but as yet he has not. I expect it has not occurred to him that I might like to come. Perhaps I shall mention it.

On Saturday Lydia caught a tram down from Theobald's Road to the Embankment and walked along the river. It was a fine, cold afternoon and the water swayed and sparkled like shot silk.

Here at least was a sense of space. Lately, as the city became increasingly oppressive, closing round her like one of its own fogs, she had begun to dream about the countryside. She wanted trees, rivers, muddy fields and broad, empty skies. Rory Wentwood had gone down to Hereford for the weekend, and she envied him.

The walk took longer than she had expected, and she was footsore by the time she turned up from the river toward Sloane Square. Alvanley Mansions was a large block of flats perhaps thirty years old. It was a solid, dull place of red brick, with gleaming brass letter boxes and scrubbed steps. She enquired for the Alfordes at the desk, and the porter directed her to the lift.

A middle-aged maid showed her into a drawing room at the front of the flat. The room was so full of things that for a moment Lydia failed to notice the people. You could hardly see the wallpaper because there were so many pictures, hung seemingly at random in order to squeeze as many as possible onto the wall. Then Mrs. Alforde rose from a desk tucked into the corner beside an immense glass-fronted display cabinet crammed with china. And Colonel Alforde tottered out from the shelter of a high-backed sofa, his left arm outstretched, and his right arm hanging awkwardly by his side.

"My dear Lydia. Very glad you could come." His left hand shook her right.

Mrs. Alforde was short and plump, whereas her husband was long and thin. She shook hands vigorously, as though operating a pump handle. "You've got quite a color in your cheeks, dear," she said in a tone which made it hard to distinguish whether it was intended as a compliment or a criticism.

"I walked up from the Embankment."

"A nice afternoon for it." Colonel Alforde settled her in a chair. "Hermione tells me you're staying at Bleeding Heart Square. Can't say I can place it. Where is it precisely?"

"Near Holborn."

"I don't think I've ever known anybody who actually lives in that part of the world." Alforde chewed the ends of his long, gray moustache. "Still, it must be very . . . very central. And your father? How's he keeping?"

"Very well, thank you," Lydia said, and added another lie: "He sends his regards, of course."

Both Alfordes looked disconcerted by this news. "Not seen him for a while," the Colonel said at last. "Used to run into each other a good deal before the war." The muscles around his mouth trembled. "Things were different then. Everything was very different."

The maid brought the tea. Alforde's good hand trembled so much that he spilled his over his waistcoat. Mrs. Alforde dabbed at him with a napkin; her passionless efficiency suggested that this was a regular occurrence. He ate nothing, but pressed cake on Lydia as though she were a hungry child.

"And how's that husband of yours?" he asked. "Nice young fellow."

"He's very well, I believe."

"I hear he's joined the Fascists. They seem a pretty sound outfit. A lot of ex-servicemen so they understand discipline. And they realize the importance of avoiding another war and the importance of the Empire. This Mosley chap has the right idea. Of course he knows first hand what war was like. I met him once in France, you know. Quite a young firebrand in those days, a little too reckless, but he's settled down since then. No more war, that's the important thing. No more war." He began to speak more slowly, like a clockwork motor running down. "No more war."

Mrs. Alforde patted his shoulder. "There, there, dear. It's all right. Nobody is going to be silly enough to have another war."

He looked at his wife with wide, panic-stricken eyes. "You can't be sure of that. And the next time nowhere will be safe. They'll bomb all our cities."

"Of course they won't, dear. Now, isn't it time you had your medicine and a little lie-down? I'm sure Lydia will excuse you."

Mrs. Alforde rang the bell. She and the maid helped the old man out of the room. When Mrs. Alforde came back alone, Lydia was on her feet.

"I think perhaps I ought to be going. Thank you so much for asking me."

"Do sit down, and in a moment we'll ring for more tea. I'm sorry you had to see Gerry like that."

"Is he all right?"

"Not really. He was too long in France. They kept sending him back to the front, and he felt so responsible for his men. He can keep up appearances for a little but you can never quite tell what's going to set him off. Sometimes it's a motorbike backfiring on the street. Or seeing a soldier in uniform. Or a headline in the paper. Even the mention of war can do it."

"I'm so sorry."

"Yes, well we have to make the best of it." Mrs. Alforde folded her hands on her lap and looked at Lydia with bright little eyes. "We all have our crosses to bear." She went on, without any change of tone: "I had lunch with your mother on Tuesday."

Lydia said nothing.

"She is very worried about you, you know. I gather you and Marcus have been having a difficult time."

"That's one way of describing it."

"You mustn't mind my talking about it, dear," Mrs. Alforde said. "After all, Gerry's your godfather, and if his health permitted, I'm sure he would be saying exactly the same things as I am."

"My mother asked you to talk to me, I suppose."

"Yes."

"I don't want to go back to Marcus."

"That's as may be, dear. But it doesn't follow that it's suitable for you to be with your father."

Lydia frowned. "I don't understand. I know he's not well off but at least he is my father."

"I'm not disputing that. But I don't think you fully understand about his little weaknesses. Your mother has always tried to spare you. She thinks now however that you ought to know. And she asked me to talk to you because she wasn't sure you'd believe her." Mrs. Alforde looked sternly at Lydia over the top of her glasses. "Which is in itself a very sad state of affairs."

Lydia looked around the overcrowded room. She heard movement elsewhere in the flat, a door closing, raised voices. Was the maid some sort of nurse as well? She wondered what it was like to live with someone poised on the brink of a mental breakdown, someone who occasionally fell over the brink. She said, "If you want to tell me something about him, you'd better go ahead and get it over with."

Mrs. Alforde nodded. "Very wise. It's always more sensible to know these things. Now, let me see: you were born in 1905, weren't you? It all came to a head the previous winter. Gerry and I had been married in July and it was our first Christmas together. We were down at his uncle's place. Rawling Hall, near Saffron Walden. Your father was there too. He was Aunt Connie's nephew. Gerry knew him quite well—he'd met him out in India once or twice when his battalion was there. But your father had resigned his commission since then. It had all been rather sudden, I'm afraid, and in the circumstances Gerry was quite surprised to see him at Rawling." Mrs. Alforde paused. "To be perfectly frank, my dear, he left the army under a cloud. In fact, if his CO hadn't wanted to avoid the scandal, he would have been cashiered."

"What had he done?"

"Forged several checks, falsified the accounts and embezzled the mess funds," Mrs. Alforde said crisply, abandoning finesse. "No doubt about it. One of the NCOs was involved as well, a mess sergeant. I believe the sergeant went to jail. And there was your father, as bold as brass, at Rawling Hall. But Aunt Connie always had a soft spot for him. She'd given him a little job to do—he was making pen-and-ink sketches of the chimney pieces that Gerry's uncle had put in the drawing room and the library. Can't think why—horrible pseudo-Jacobean things; best forgotten. The maids hated dusting them."

"I'm glad someone had a soft spot for him."

Mrs. Alforde glanced at her. "I'm sorry to have to say that he was cold-shouldered by the men down there and by most of the women too. And then he seduced your mother under our very noses. Do you know, she was only just sixteen? She wasn't even out. He was after her money, of course. Not that she wasn't very lovely too. And the very final straw was that he didn't even trouble to take precautions. He made the poor girl pregnant. With you, in fact. Of course she had no choice but to marry him. We all rallied round, for your mother's sake. But no one was surprised that the marriage didn't last."

"You make him sound very ruthless," Lydia said quietly. "Very calculating."

"My dear, he was. Of course he ran through the money in a year or two. I gather he's a sad case now. Even so, he's not to be trusted. So that's why I think you're better off without him."

Lydia sat staring straight ahead and said nothing.

"All marriages have their ups and downs," Mrs. Alforde went on. "Gerry and I—well, I won't go into details but it hasn't always been easy. But one soldiers on. I'm sure you and Marcus will soon be rubbing along together perfectly well again. And it would make your mother so happy."

Lydia looked at her hostess. Mrs. Alforde was a nice woman, she thought, and doing her best. It wasn't her fault that her best had nothing to do with what Lydia wanted, and nothing to do with what was actually happening.

"Now promise me, dear—you will at least think about it."

Lydia shook her head. "I'm sorry, I'm not going back to Marcus. I wasn't before and I'm certainly not now, when I've seen him and my mother behaving like farmyard animals together."

She sat back and watched the blood leave Mrs. Alforde's face. All the vitality drained out of the older woman. She looked small, pale and frightened.

By the middle of Tuesday morning Rory had already smoked the third of the three cigarettes which were, in theory, his ration for that day. He was typing yet another letter of application on the Royal Portable and trying to resist the temptation to light a fourth.

He had spent the weekend in Hereford with his parents and his sisters. Here the familiar rituals of his childhood continued to be observed, except all the participants were older than they had been. Despite the comforts of home—despite the freshly laundered sheets, the excellent leg of lamb for Sunday lunch, his father's Navy Cut cigarettes—there had been something unreal, even stultifying, about the weekend. He had been glad to get away, even though it was only to return to the uncertainties of an independent life with a failed engagement, dwindling savings and no prospect of ever earning a decent income.

He heard the muffled sound of the postman's knock, and movement in the house below. Then came footsteps on his own stairs and a tap on his door. When he opened it, Lydia Langstone was waiting outside on the landing. She was carrying a parcel and her face was slightly flushed from the exertion of climbing the stairs.

She held out the parcel. "It was for you. I thought I might as well bring it up."

"Thank you."

She turned to go, and then looked back at him. "Do you remember when you showed me that cufflink the other day? When we had lunch."

He nodded. "Of course."

"I happened to hear at the weekend that the Fascists have hired the chapel undercroft for another meeting."

"Really? When?"

"Saturday week. The first of December, I think. Apparently it's part of a big push to attract businessmen to the movement."

"By telling them the Fascists will shoot all the reds under the beds and make sure there will always be a market for British goods?"

"Something like that. Do you think it was Fascists who attacked you?"

He shrugged. "I don't know. I couldn't find anything else that supported the idea. The most likely explanation is that somebody just happened to lose a cufflink there and it had nothing to do with me whatsoever."

He thanked her again and said goodbye. He stood for a moment watching her as she clattered down the stairs. A strange, nervy woman, he thought, all bones and breeding like a racehorse. He went back into his sitting room, pushed the typewriter aside and put the parcel on the table. It was addressed to him at Bleeding Heart Square but he didn't recognize the writing. He cut the string with his penknife and pulled the brown paper apart. The paper was creased and with jagged edges, part of a larger sheet that had been used before.

There was another layer of darker brown paper underneath. The second layer wasn't secured in any way. He saw material inside, some sort of tweed. He pulled it from its wrapping and held it up.

It was a skirt made of blue-green Irish tweed, rather worn in places. Part of the hem had come down. A sheet of lined paper fluttered from the folds of the skirt and down to the floor. He picked it up. The enclosure looked as if it had been torn from an exercise book. It was a letter, without date or address at the head, written in round, unformed writing.

Dear Sir,

This was in Narton's cupboard. I reckon it belongs to Miss Penhow.
I don't know how to find her or the lady it's addressed to, so
maybe her niece had better have it for her. It's no good to me. I
don't want it.

Yours faithfully,
M. Narton

Rory dropped the note on the table and picked up the inner packaging. Nothing was written on it apart from Mrs. Renton's name in neat, familiar handwriting.

Mrs. Renton?

Something blue protruded from the waistband of the skirt, an unsealed envelope also with Mrs. Renton's name on it in the same handwriting. Rory removed the single sheet of notepaper it contained.

Morthams Farm
Rawling
Saffron Walden
Essex

April 22nd 1930

Dear Mrs. Renton,

As we arranged, I enclose my winter skirt for alteration. I think it
has at least another year in it, perhaps two. Please take in the
waist by three quarters of an inch. Would you redo the hem as
well—as you will see, it is coming down. If the blouses are ready,
please put them in with the skirt and give them to my husband
when you see him.

Yours sincerely,
P. M. Serridge (Mrs.)

Rory took out his writing case and compared the letter with the sample of Miss Penhow's handwriting that he had found in the chest of drawers. There was no reason to doubt that they had been written by the same person.

He sat down at the table and lit a fourth and unlicensed cigarette. Mrs. Renton—what on earth had she to do with this? Leaving that aside, nothing in the letter suggested that Miss Penhow was planning to leave Morthams Farm and Serridge. Nothing suggested that there was any strain between the two of them, either. On the other hand, if Miss Penhow had been devious, the letter might have been designed to throw Serridge off the scent. Rory's mind followed the tortuous logic of this: but perhaps that implied that Miss Penhow expected Serridge to read the letter, and the further implication of that was that she had reason to believe that Serridge no longer trusted her. And then there was the question of how Narton had come to have the parcel. Rory could only assume that it had been taken as evidence when the police were investigating the disappearance of Miss Penhow, and that Narton had removed it for his own purposes after he had lost his job.

He smoked the rest of the cigarette. He folded the skirt and its accompanying letter in the brown paper and carried it downstairs to the first floor, where he knocked on the door of Ingleby-Lewis's sitting room. Lydia opened the door.

"Sorry to disturb you, but I wonder if you could advise me about this parcel." He shifted his position in order to get a better view, trying to establish whether or not Ingleby-Lewis was inside. "That is, if you've got a moment."

"Yes, of course." She stood back, holding the door open.

To Rory's relief, there was no one else in the room. It looked as if Lydia had been writing a letter. "Are you busy?"

"Nothing that can't wait." She moved swiftly past him, slipped her letter under the blotter and capped her fountain pen.

"What is it?" she said, looking at the parcel.

"It's a skirt. It's all rather odd." At that moment it occurred to him that he and Lydia had not talked properly for days and even then, at their lunch at the Blue Dahlia, he had said nothing about Narton. Lydia was looking at him with close attention, as if she found what she saw very interesting. He went on in a rush, "When we had lunch the other week, I told you something about Miss Penhow."

"I remember."

Still standing, they faced each other across the table.

"I didn't tell you everything." He paused, and wished that she would say something. "In particular, I didn't mention that I had been approached by a man called Narton, who's been watching this house for some time. He said he was a plain-clothes police officer and he wanted my help. Like me, he was interested in the Penhow case. He said the police hadn't been able to find any evidence that Serridge had done away with her, but they weren't satisfied."

"A little man, middle-aged, in an old tweed coat and a hard collar?"

"How did you know that?"

"I saw you together once in the Blue Dahlia."

"You're observant. You think there's any chance that Serridge might have seen us too?"

Lydia shrugged. "Not that I know of. Anyway, what happened?"

"He persuaded me to go to Rawling and talk to the Vicar. He said he couldn't go himself, or one of his colleagues, because the Vicar was a chum of Serridge's, and he didn't want to run the risk of Serridge finding out that the police were still interested. But then I happened to discover that Narton himself lived in Rawling, which was something he hadn't seen fit to tell me. The next thing was that I found a copy of the local newspaper in the dustbin downstairs when I was throwing out my rubbish." He wondered whether to mention the goat's skull but decided to leave that until later. "It must have been Serridge's. There was a stop-press item about a man who had died at a cottage in Rawling at the beginning of the week. It was Narton."

The silence in the big, cold room lay heavily over everything. He watched Lydia swallow. He wished he hadn't been such a fool as to mention this. She would blurt it all out to her father, who would tell Serridge. Or she would even tell Serridge herself, Serridge who might well be sweet on her.

"I think we'd better sit down," Lydia said. "Don't you?"

She sat down and waved him to the seat opposite hers. He laid the parcel on the table, dislodging the blotter in the process. Rory felt the muscles in his shoulders relax. He had been tense for a long time, he realized, though he had not been aware of it. The reason for the slackening of tension arrived in his mind a split second afterward: it was a relief to have told someone about Narton at last, even Lydia Langstone, a woman whom he didn't really know.

Shifting the blotter had exposed part of the letter that Lydia had been writing. Rory had just time to read the address, the date and the salutation of the letter: *Dear Mrs. Alforde.* Lydia pushed the blotter to the other side of the table, covering the letter as she did so.

Once again his muscles tensed. He hadn't been open with her, so why should he expect her to be open with him?

She was looking at him, her lips slightly parted. "How did he die?"

"While cleaning a shotgun."

"Which means it was probably suicide?"

"Yes. And there was something else," Rory went on. "Mrs. Narton said that her husband had been forced to leave the police force three years ago."

"Then why was he still so interested in Serridge?"

"I'm coming to that. I thought I'd go and see the Vicar again, see if he could help. It was lunchtime so I had to kick my heels for a

time. I was in the churchyard and I saw a gravestone for Amy Narton, who died in 1931. She was the daughter. Then I talked to the
Vicar, who more or less came out and said that Narton had been
unbalanced by his daughter's death. She died in childbirth and
nobody knew who the baby's father was. She had worked at
Morthams Farm, but the Vicar saw no reason to believe that it was
Serridge. But later I talked to the maid, and she told a rather different story. She had no doubt Serridge was responsible." He hesitated and then plunged on. "She'd found a photograph of Amy in
the nude on a bicycle. Apparently that was part of his courting
technique."

Lydia snorted with laughter. "Surely that's a joke? Please tell
me it is."

"I don't think so. Serridge persuaded the village maidens that it
was how smart ladies up in London learned to ride their bikes."

"Imagine it. Hyde Park on a Sunday afternoon."

He smiled at her. "Rebecca thought he was keeping Miss Penhow a virtual prisoner at the farm, and that he had another mistress in London as well. A strange girl was seen at the farm just
before Miss Penhow disappeared. And there were two other things
which were even stranger. The first was that Serridge used to come
to Rawling Hall—that's the big house near the village—before the
war. So he knew the place already. And the second thing was even
stranger, and I don't pretend to understand it. There were—some
skulls, the skulls of animals, in the place where the maid was
talking to me. Her nephew was with us, and they were his pride
and joy. And it seemed one of them had gone missing. The skull of
a billy goat."

Lydia stiffened. "With very long horns? Sort of swept back?"

"So you saw it too?"

"Yes. Or something very like it. It came in the post for Mr. Serridge. He opened it in here." She caught up with the implication of
the word *too*. "But when did you see it? And where?"

"Last week. It was in one of the dustbins downstairs. Along with the Mavering newspaper that mentioned Narton's death."

"None of it makes sense, does it? Not if you try to put it all together. What will you do?"

Rory ran his fingers through his hair. "I don't know."

"And now Mrs. Renton? How does she come into it?"

"No idea. Have a look at the parcel. I suppose I should give it to Miss Kensley."

He watched Lydia reading the letters and examining the skirt. She looked at him.

"Why don't you show this to Mrs. Renton first? After all, it's addressed to her. See what she says—it can't do any harm. So when you give it to Miss Kensley, you can say you've done everything that you possibly could."

"All right. I'll ask her now. Thanks awfully. You've been very helpful."

She glanced sideways at him. "Not at all."

He picked up the skirt and the letters and went downstairs, leaving her folding the wrapping paper at the table. He knocked on the door of Mrs. Renton's room. There was no answer. He knocked again with the same result. He went back upstairs. As he reached the first-floor landing, Lydia came out from the little kitchen.

"No luck?" she said.

"She's not in." Rory's mind ran ahead to the rest of the day: he himself would have to go out, back to combing through the Situations Vacant boards in the public library. "It will have to wait. I need to go out."

"Would you like me to ask her about it?" Lydia said. "As it happens, I'll be in for most of the day."

"Would you? That's very decent. If you're sure it's no trouble?"

"Not at all. I want to see Mrs. Renton about some mending."

Rory handed over the parcel and Miss Penhow's letter. He

continued upstairs, with Mrs. Narton's note in his hand. Lydia Langstone was really quite a good sort, he thought, despite the airs and graces and the cut-glass accent. Almost pretty too. She had, he thought, a trustworthy face. But perhaps that was wishful thinking, and what the devil was her connection with Mrs. Alforde?

17

READING THIS NOW, it's obvious to you that even then Serridge was desperate to get away from Philippa May Penhow. Be honest. She probably revolted him.

Tuesday, 8 April 1930

I tried to keep myself busy while Joseph was in London. He drove to Bishop's Stortford all by himself, and took the train from there.

Of the two maids, Rebecca will, I think, prove a tower of strength. She is a little slow and sullen, as these country folk are apt to be, but she is a sensible woman and knows what she is about. I am less certain about young Amy, who seems rather sly and surly. She broke one of the Royal Doulton teacups as she was unpacking—how furious Aunt would have been!—and then tried to pretend it wasn't her fault. Rebecca tells me that Amy's mother used to work at the Hall too, but unfortunately she seems not to have passed on what she learned to her daughter!

All the while today I was listening out for the sound

of the car on the drive. But Joseph didn't come back until after teatime. He swept in, in a very jolly mood, apologizing for his lateness, saying the train had been delayed. When he embraced me, I thought I smelled an unfamiliar perfume on his collar. And there was a long, fine hair on his jacket. I pointed this out to him and he became quite heated. He said there had been two little girls in the compartment of his train and the hair must have been one of theirs, and probably the perfume was on one of the cushions.

I am afraid I allowed my wretched jealousy to run away with me and burst into angry tears. After a while, Joseph pulled me onto his knee and soothed me as if I were a child. That made me weep all the more at first but soon all was smiles again!

While this was going on, poor Jacko had no idea what was happening and was running to and fro and getting underneath our feet and barking and whining. He was much happier when he saw that his master and mistress were the best of friends again.

Later, as we were waiting for Rebecca to bring in our supper—I hesitate to call it dinner—Joseph produced two little packages, one for me and one for Jacko. Mine was a beautiful silk scarf from Liberty's with a Japanese design on it. As for Jacko, he is now the proud owner of a smart new green leather collar with a brass buckle and seven shiny brass stars on it. Joseph said the collar made him look like a ferocious guard dog. How we laughed!

How you laugh too. He fooled everyone. Even Jacko.

Finding Mrs. Renton was harder than Lydia had expected. She wasn't in her room all day. That in itself was not unusual because she often visited her clients, who were scattered across London, and sometimes would work in their homes. Mrs. Renton returned to Bleeding Heart Square at some point in the evening but it was too late to call on her.

The following day, Wednesday, Lydia was at Shires and Trimble. The job was becoming less of an ordeal than it had been. Mr. Reynolds had decided that Lydia was quite useful for a woman. She had what he called a refined telephone manner and was also capable of understanding his filing system.

As for the others, Marcus's roses had effected a decisive shift in the balance of power in the general office. Miss Tuffley confided to Lydia that Smethwick could be "an awfully vulgar little tyke" and that he had had too much cider and been a bit fresh with her on the firm's summer outing in July, which frankly was a bit thick. She also volunteered the opinion that "Us girls should stick together." It wasn't just the roses that had done it. It was also the realization that Lydia had some sort of a connection with godlike males who were ferried around in silver Bentleys driven by uniformed chauffeurs.

Mr. Shires came in at nine thirty. He greeted everyone and walked rapidly into the private office. Lydia gave him ten minutes and then picked up her notepad and tapped on his door. He was standing at the big desk with the waste-paper basket beside him, working his way through the morning's post.

"May I have a word, sir?"

He glanced at his wristwatch. "Very well. I can only spare you a moment, though."

Lydia closed the door behind her. "I wanted to ask your advice on a personal matter."

He frowned. "That's a little unusual." He walked round the desk to his chair. "You'd better sit down." He pulled a small white paper bag toward him and helped himself to a peppermint.

"I want a divorce," Lydia said.

"I beg your pardon?"

"A divorce."

"Bless my soul. Mrs. Langstone, have you any idea what that would entail?"

"That's one reason I've come to see you, sir. So I can find out." She paused but Shires said nothing. "I'm living with my father because I have left my husband. I left him because he hit me."

"Dear me. I'm sorry to hear that. Were there any witnesses?"

Lydia shook her head. "However, he has also committed adultery."

Shires leaned back. "Oh dear. On the surface that would certainly be grounds for divorce. But you would have to prove it." He sucked on his mint, and Lydia heard a faint squelching sound. "Are you able to do that, Mrs. Langstone? And, if you are, are you prepared for your private life, as well as that of your husband, to be discussed in court? There's no such thing as a quiet divorce, you know, even if you could persuade your husband to—ah—cooperate. There tends to be an unhealthy interest in these matters, particularly if the principals have any connection with the peerage. The publicity would be distressing."

Lydia noted the fact that somebody had told Shires about her family. Serridge or her father? She said, "And the cost?"

"It would not be cheap. Going to the law is always an expensive business." He smiled complacently at her. "Fortunately for us lawyers."

"If I could raise the money, however, and if I could get the evidence, there's no reason why I shouldn't go ahead with the divorce?"

"These are big conditions. Yes, though. All things being equal. Since the most recent Matrimonial Causes Act, a woman is entitled to petition for divorce on the grounds of the husband's adultery. Until then a woman could only sue for divorce on those grounds if it were aggravated by the man's desertion or his cruelty to her. But in your case there might be another complication. If I understand matters aright, it is not he who has deserted you, but you who have deserted him."

"Because he attacked me."

"So you say. We come back to the question of proof. Or of your husband's willingness to admit guilt."

Lydia drew a little gallows on the notepad and adorned it with a stick figure of a man. "But if I were able to find the money and the evidence, would you be able to help me deal with this?"

Shires stared coldly across the desk. "It is not the sort of work we usually undertake, Mrs. Langstone. Nor do I feel happy about the prospect of one of my employees appearing in a divorce court. I have this firm's reputation to consider. And there's still the matter of the money and the evidence you would need. These are not matters to be taken lightly."

Lydia stood up. "Then I take it you are not willing to help?"

Mr. Shires sighed. "I wish you young people wouldn't leap to conclusions. I haven't said I will help you, and I haven't said I won't. All I have done is point out some of the problems that you will need to resolve if you decide to go ahead with the matter, including the fact that it may affect your position with this firm. What I will say is this: I will consider what you have said and let you know my decision in due course. Now would you be so good as to ask Mr. Reynolds to spare me a moment?"

At Cornwallis Grove events began to move fast, as if an invisible brake had been removed. Almost overnight Fenella became full of energy and decision. Rory was afraid that the reason for this was the arrival in her life of Julian Dawlish.

If you had to design an elegant single solution to all of Fenella's problems, you could hardly have done better than copy the man, inch by inch, atom by atom. He was rich, politically congenial and a gentleman. Like a fairy godfather, he produced flats and jobs at the click of his manicured fingers. To add insult to injury, Rory found himself rather liking the man.

It had been Dawlish who had pointed out that, now the lodger was no more than an unhappy memory and some curious stains on the carpet in her room, there was no longer any need for Fenella to remain at Cornwallis Grove, unless of course she wanted to, which she did not. The Alliance of Socialists Against Fascism was anxious to get itself up and running as soon as possible. The house in Mecklenburgh Square was standing empty. The flat in the basement could be made ready whenever she wanted it. Dawlish had visited an estate agent in Hampstead Village who was convinced that he would have no trouble in letting the Kensleys' maisonette in Belsize Park for the remainder of the lease; in fact he already had a prospective tenant in mind.

Suddenly, it seemed, there was no reason for Fenella to stay and every reason for her to go. On Tuesday evening, Rory received a postcard from her, asking if he could spare the time to help with the clearing out; the Kensleys had been storing some of his belongings while he was in India, and she would be grateful if he could remove them.

Early on Wednesday afternoon, he took a tram in the Hampstead direction and was at Cornwallis Grove a little after two o'clock. Fenella was alone in the house. She was wearing overalls and her hair was bound up in a headscarf. The hall was still cluttered with the mortal remains of Mr. Kensley's ill-fated hobbies.

"Work first," she said. "Tea later."

As he followed her toward the stairs he stumbled again over the bag of tools and narrowly avoided treading on a crystal receiver.

"Careful," she said over her shoulder. "I'm sorry to hurry you, but I've got the estate agent coming round next week and I want the place to look as clear as possible."

She took him up to the box room, a former dressing room on the first floor where the Kensleys had deposited anything they didn't want but could not bear to throw away. Rory found himself looking at two suitcases, much scuffed and dented, adorned with faded labels recording long-forgotten railway journeys. He had left them with the Kensleys just before going to India in what seemed another lifetime, and one that had belonged to someone else. He carried the cases out to the landing and rummaged half-heartedly through their contents. As well as clothes and bed linen, he found a tobacco jar, books he could not remember reading, chipped crockery, a stack of lecture notes and an embarrassing attempt at an extended poetic analysis of the discontents of civilization written in the style of *The Waste Land*.

"I'm not going to want much of this," he said.

Fenella wiped a grimy hand across her forehead and grinned at him. "Nor am I. Why don't you sort through it and chuck out what you can?"

He spent the next fifteen minutes picking through the contents of the cases. Moths had got into one of them. In the other, however, he found a heavy suit which still had some wear in it. The jacket fit and the trousers would probably do if he asked Mrs. Renton to alter them. By the time he closed the lid of the second suitcase, his hands were filthy and he had had more than enough of the detritus of his own past.

He poked his head back into the box room. "I've gone as far as I can go. One suitcase can go on the rag-and-bone pile. I'll keep the other. I can give you a hand in here, if you like."

"Thanks. Could you lift down the box from the top of the wardrobe?"

The cardboard box brought a shower of dust with it. He put it on the floor and pulled open the flaps. It was full of dusty papers, letters and photographs.

"How will you get the suitcase back to your flat?" she asked.

"Carry it to the bus stop, I suppose. Less walking than the Tube."

"No, don't bother. Julian's coming round later in his car. I'm sure he won't mind dropping it off."

"Oh. That would be very kind."

Fenella dug her hands into the box and deposited its contents on the carpet. A little photograph slipped to one side. Rory picked it up. It showed a woman on a park bench with a little dog at her feet.

"Who's this?" he asked casually.

Fenella took the photograph from him. The good humor left her face. "It's Aunt Philippa."

"She looks rather pretty," Rory said, surprised. "And I thought she'd be much older."

"It's not a very good likeness," Fenella said, dropping the photograph in the open box.

"In what way?"

Fenella turned away and opened the wardrobe door. "She made herself up as if she was ten or twenty years younger than she was. But if you got close to her, you could see the cracks. Literally. She plastered on the make-up. Father used to say Aunt Philippa made herself look ridiculous, mutton dressed as lamb."

Late in the morning, Mr. Smethwick tripped over the caretaker's bucket and dropped three box files outside the general office. The contents of the files related to some of the late Mr. Trimble's pre-war clients. Pieces of paper floated over the landing and into the stairwell. Some reached the landing below, and two letters fluttered all the way down to the hall. Mr. Reynolds rushed out of the office and gazed in anguish at the cascade of yellowing paper, rusting paper clips and pink ribbons.

"Smethwick! What were you thinking of? Mrs. Langstone! Come here at once!"

Lydia had never seen him so agitated. She and Smethwick gathered up the papers. Then it became her task to restore them to order, and Mr. Reynolds would not let her take her lunch break until she had finished.

It was after two o'clock before she was able to escape. On her way to the Blue Dahlia she called into Mr. Goldman's shop in Hatton Garden. He was hunched over a necklace, peering at it through a jeweler's glass. He looked up when the door bell pinged and uncoiled his long body.

"Good afternoon, madam."

"Hello, Mr. Goldman. I don't want to sell today but I wanted an idea of what you'd give me for something."

He inclined his head but said nothing. Lydia put her bag on the counter and took out a box containing a diamond and sapphire ring. It was the third and last of Lydia's pieces of her great-aunt's jewelry. Goldman opened the box and eased the hoop from its velvet setting. He screwed the glass back into his eye and examined it, breathing heavily through his nose.

"I know it's old-fashioned," Lydia said, hating the hint of desperation she heard in her voice. "But the stones alone must be worth a good deal."

He ignored her and continued his examination. She turned aside and pretended to look at one of the displays. Beans on toast, she thought, her mind running over the Blue Dahlia's limited menu, and a cup of tea: I can afford that. Push the boat out and have an egg as well?

"It's a handsome ring," Mr. Goldman said at last. He rubbed it gently. "Forty or fifty years old. The sapphires are particularly fine."

"What would it be worth?"

"What were you hoping for?"

"I've no idea. A hundred, perhaps? A hundred and fifty?"

He shook his head. "There would be a case for reusing the stones. I might manage forty pounds. Forty-five, even." He saw the expression on Lydia's face. "You might be able to get more elsewhere. Or you might decide to pawn it instead, although of course that would not raise as much."

She thanked him and went to lunch. Food made her feel a little more cheerful. After all, she had a roof over her head, a meal inside her and clothes on her back. She also had a job of sorts to go to. It all depended on one's perspective: she had more than most people on this crowded planet. And because she had taken a late lunch, at least it would be a short afternoon.

Three hours later, as Lydia was putting on her hat before leaving the office, Miss Tuffley's bright face loomed behind her in the mirror.

"Hard luck," she whispered, nudging Lydia's shoulder. "His nibs wants you in his room." She rubbed some of the condensation from the window next to the mirror. "Ugh. The fog's getting fouler and fouler."

Lydia went through to the private office where she found Mr. Shires standing at his desk and putting files in his briefcase.

"Ah, Mrs. Langstone. Shut the door, please." He strapped up the briefcase. "I've considered your request this morning, and I'm inclined to look favorably on it."

"Thank you, sir," Lydia said, surprised.

"Mind you, I'm not saying we are prepared to act for you in this. But I shall take it a stage further. See how the land lies with Mr. Langstone, hmm?"

"As to the cost, I—"

Mr. Shires held up a small pink hand. "We shall leave that to one side for the moment. We like to help our employees where possible, and in the circumstances there's a chance we may be able to oblige Mr. Langstone to meet our costs. But we shall see, eh? Let's not cross our bridges before we come to them. Leave it with me for the time being. Let me see, you're not coming in tomorrow, are you, but we're expecting you on Friday? If I've time, we'll have a word about it then."

He dismissed her for the evening. The outer office was now empty. Lydia ran down the stairs feeling more light-hearted than she had for some time. She had clearly misjudged Shires. He wasn't such a bad old stick after all.

Outside the pavements gleamed with rain and the gathering fog reduced the street lamps to fuzzy globes of moisture. She found her way to Bleeding Heart Square as much by touch as by sight. As she let herself into the house, she heard the whirr and clack of Mrs. Renton's sewing machine in the room by the front door.

There was a letter for her on the hall table. She picked it up and went upstairs, ripping open the envelope on the way. It was from Mrs. Alforde. She had replied to Lydia's letter almost by return of post.

Captain Ingleby-Lewis was not in the sitting room. Lydia put down her handbag and scanned the contents of the letter, which was dated that morning.

My dear Lydia,

Thank you for your note. It's sweet and generous of you to apologize but the more I think about it, the more I think it was foolish of me to take what your mother said entirely at face value—I should have known better. The truth is, I'm a meddlesome old woman with too much time on my hands.

Will you do me the great kindness of letting me make a fresh start? My time is rather taken up with your poor dear godfather—he often becomes agitated if I am not around—but tomorrow is Thursday, and therefore his day for Sergeant Stokes. Stokes was with him for most of the war. For some reason—it seems perverse to me—Gerry finds his company soothing.

As it happens I have to run down to Rawling for a funeral tomorrow morning but I hope to be back by teatime or a little later, and I could pick you up if you are free. (I have a little motor car now, which has transformed my life!) Alternatively, if you would like a day in the country you could come with me, and we could talk on the way. I could drop you in Bishop's Stortford or Saffron Walden and show you where to find a decent lunch. But of course this may not be convenient, or you may feel enough is enough! Whatever you decide, I shall quite understand.

I hope to hear from you—perhaps telephone me this evening if you would like an excursion tomorrow?

With affectionate good wishes from us both,

Yours sincerely,

Hermione Alforde

Lydia put the letter away and went into her bedroom, where she took off her hat and coat. She picked up Miss Penhow's skirt and the accompanying letter from the bottom of her chest of drawers and took them downstairs. She knocked on Mrs. Renton's door. The old woman's wrinkled face brightened when she saw Lydia.

"Hello, dear. I was just going to make some tea. Would you like a cup?"

Once the kettle was on, Lydia said, "I've something I want to show you."

Mrs. Renton eyed the skirt. "A bit of sewing?"

"In a way."

"I'm afraid I'm rather busy at present."

Lydia laid it on Mrs. Renton's table. "It's not for me, though."

Mrs. Renton lifted up the skirt, feeling the material, running her fingers along the seams. She frowned.

"Do you recognize it?" Lydia asked.

"I'm sure I've seen that tweed before." She turned a bewildered face to Lydia. "It's not Miss Penhow's, is it?"

"Yes."

"She showed it me just before she went away to the country. She wanted it altered. But she decided to wait until the weather was warmer."

"There's a letter with it." Lydia handed the note to her.

Mrs. Renton read it, and when she had finished she dabbed her eyes with her apron. "For a moment I thought she must be back. Miss Penhow, I mean. But this letter's years old, isn't it? Poor woman."

"I didn't realize you knew her," Lydia said.

Mrs. Renton glanced at the door as if to confirm it was shut. "Mr. Serridge introduced us. I did some sewing for her while she lived in Kensington. Made her a nice little silk tea gown too. And then she married and moved away, and I didn't hear from her again. Where did that skirt come from?"

"Someone found it at Rawling. That was where she moved to."

"Does Mr. Serridge know?"

Lydia shook her head.

"It might be better not to mention it. They say she left him. You wouldn't want to open old wounds."

"You must have wondered what had happened to her."

"None of my business," Mrs. Renton said. "That kettle must be boiling."

18

THE TONE of the diary is darkening now, three days after Serridge came back from London. But Philippa Penhow soldiers on like a little hero in the battle of life.

Friday, 11 April 1930

The Vicar called this morning. He is a Mr. Gladwyn, a clergyman of the old school. I must confess I have been rather worried about church. I don't feel I can take Communion at present. After all, in a sense Joseph and I are living a lie, though of course God knows the truth and understands. Still, I felt a little awkward with Mr. Gladwyn. Not that I had a great deal to do with him. He and Joseph got on very well. They talked mainly about cars—Mr. Gladwyn plans to buy one soon and wanted to pick Joseph's brains about them. Joseph took him for a spin in our Austin 7.

Now the weather is better, I have begun to explore the farm. I have been finding the house rather claustrophobic of late. It's partly because we see so few people, but mainly (I expect) because I'm used to towns and lots of comings and goings. Here there is so much silence. Sometimes I see countryfolk in the distance and once or twice have ex-changed waves. I have not had any conversations with them yet.

This afternoon, I brought my diary with me. Sometimes I feel a little self-conscious about writing my diary in the house—Joseph is always asking what I'm doing. So today I am writing this al fresco, as the Italians say.

It's very odd that I have had no letters since we moved. I wish I knew what it was best to do. I feel stupidly worried a lot of the time and I don't quite know why. I tell myself not to be silly. But the worry is there when I wake up, sitting like a weight in my stomach, and it's there when I go to sleep. Sometimes I don't sleep very well either. My heart is heavy. I wish I could stop feeling. If only I could tear my heart from my breast and take away the pain forever.

You want to tap her on the shoulder and say it's always wiser to be cowardly than heroic. Not that she would have listened if anyone had. But let's not anticipate.

"Good morning!" Mrs. Alforde said when Lydia came to the door, already drawing on her gloves. "Glad you're punctual. I can't bear unpunctuality."

Once they were in the little car, a gray Morris Minor with scratched and dented wings, Mrs. Alforde nosed her way up to the Clerkenwell Road and then turned east toward Shoreditch and Hackney. She drove badly but with the sort of panache Lydia as-sociated with the hunting field. She kept up a running commentary which needed no response from Lydia and was actually rather restful, unlike the driving itself.

"The blithering idiot, can't he see it's my right of way? Are you deaf or something? Look at those houses over there, aren't they dreary? They get worse and worse. Really, how the government can look itself in the eye I just do not know. Ha! That will teach you!"

Lydia luxuriated in the absence of responsibility. From Dalston they went to Leyton. From Leyton they went to Walthamstow. Now they were on the A1 and almost in real country. She stared hungrily at trees and grass. Even Mrs. Alforde seemed to feel their soothing effect because she settled down to drive far more calmly and now seemed disposed for conversation.

"Now what would you like to do? Poor Mr. Narton's funeral's at a quarter to twelve. I can drop you off at Bishop's Stortford if you like—I can show you where to get quite reasonable coffee and a bite to eat—or if you want to see Rawling itself you could come with me. You needn't feel you have to come to the funeral, of course, but the Vicar will give us lunch. I should warn you, though, there's not much one can do in Rawling."

"I think I'd like to come with you," Lydia said.

"It's entirely up to you. You could always have a walk, I suppose—at least it's not raining and I see you're wearing sensible shoes." While speaking, Mrs. Alforde glanced down at the shoes, causing the car to swerve and almost collide with an oncoming lorry. "Blast the man—you'd think he'd realize that he's not the only person on this road. Yes, or you could wait at the Vicarage if you prefer—I'm sure Mr. Gladwyn wouldn't mind. I imagine the funeral itself wouldn't be your cup of tea."

"I'm not really dressed for it."

"Don't let that put you off, my dear. I doubt there will be many people there so there won't be anyone to notice. Anyway, you'd be with me."

"That would make it all right?" Lydia asked, amused.

"Well, yes—I'm sure it would. Old habits die hard, especially among the older villagers. I remember when I was first married, going for a drive with my father-in-law, and the women would come out of the cottages and curtsy as the carriage went by. It was really rather touching."

Lydia laughed.

Mrs. Alforde glanced again at Lydia, and the car gave another reciprocal swerve in the other direction. "You're looking much better than you were on Saturday, if you don't mind my saying so."

"It must be the country air," Lydia said.

They drove on for another mile in silence. With a grating of gears, Mrs. Alforde pulled out to pass a cyclist who was wobbling in the middle of the road.

"Silly ass," Mrs. Alforde said. "He'll get himself killed if he's not careful." She added, without any change of tone, "Sorry about the other day."

"That's all right."

"I'm afraid I rather got the wrong end of the stick. Your mother can be very persuasive."

"I know," Lydia said. After a pause she went on, "I think Mother tried to warn me. She said something about men having their needs. She plays fair after her own fashion."

"There's no malice in her," Mrs. Alforde said. "I give her that."

"But she thinks rules are for other people," Lydia burst out, the anger unexpectedly erupting.

"She was always like that. She was an only child and your grandfather spoiled her. And remember, in those days the only thing that really mattered was appearances. You could do whatever you liked as long as you knew the right form. Though I must admit the business with your father took everyone by surprise. They had been very discreet about it. And she was so very young—a schoolgirl. Even so, she was enchanting. Men liked her."

"They still do," Lydia said. "What actually happened when my parents met? Nobody would ever tell me. Only bits and pieces. Did they know each other before?"

"No—your mother wasn't even out. She had just left school and she was there for Christmas with her friend Mary, who was a god-daughter or something of Aunt Connie's. That was why your mother had been invited—to keep Mary company, and then Mary spent most of her time in bed, laid up with a feverish cold. It was obvious that some of the young men were eyeing her over but I didn't realize your father was interested. He seemed much older, and of course he had that cloud hanging over him." Mrs. Alforde smiled fondly. "Poor Willy. He was rather dashing in those days, despite everything. He didn't shoot, and nor did your mother of course, so perhaps that's what threw them together."

"Long country walks when everyone else was busy?"

"Very likely. It would have been noticed if they had spent much time together in the house. Anyway, the party broke up and we thought no more about it until the following Easter. That was when it all came out. Your grandfather wrote to Gerry's Uncle Henry—a real stinker of a letter, it was—and more or less accused him of letting his only daughter get pregnant while she was under his roof. He knew your father was responsible—your mother must have told him. Unfortunately he also knew your father by reputation, so he wasn't pleased about that, either. Still, after a lot of discussion, everyone decided that the only thing to do was make the best of it. Your parents were married very quietly in some provincial register office where no one knew them. And a few months later you were born. Then one didn't hear very much."

"Where did they live?" Lydia asked.

"I don't think they lived together after the wedding—your grandfather saw to that. Your mother must have stayed at home, and I believe your father was abroad for a lot of the time. Then your grandfather died and your parents divorced. And Fin Cassington was already on the horizon."

They drove in silence for another few minutes. Lydia stared at the twisted gray ribbon of the road. She wasn't sure what she had hoped to hear—perhaps that, against all the odds, she had been the child of a grand passion, at least conceived in love. That her parents had been happy in the early days of their marriage. That they had wanted her. Instead, the only emotions that seemed to come out of their story were lust and greed, regulated only by a desire to observe the proprieties.

Mrs. Alforde cleared her throat. "I'm sure they're both fond of you. In their way. Nothing turns out quite as we'd like, after all. Gerry and I would have liked children, for example, but it wasn't to be. Would you light me a cigarette, dear? You'll find some in the glove compartment. Have one yourself."

"I'm sorry," Lydia said, alerted not by Mrs. Alforde's words but by an infinitesimal alteration in her tone.

"Why?"

"Because I've been feeling so sorry for myself I've not been thinking of anyone else." She lit two cigarettes and passed one to Mrs. Alforde. "You must think I'm a selfish little beast."

"Not at all. We all have a right to feel miserable sometimes."

"It must have been perfectly foul for you. The war and everything."

"The only thing I really mind about is what happened to Gerry. I don't mind about not having children, or not now. One gets used to it. And as for having to sell Rawling that's neither here nor there. Owning land is an awful burden nowadays, and I never really liked the house. But Gerry's another matter. I should be grateful that he came home in one piece when so many others didn't, but he doesn't deserve to be as he is. So fragile. It's such a waste. He dreams about bombers almost every night."

"Over London?"

"Yes. He came through France with hardly a scratch, though he must have seen the most ghastly things. Probably did them too. But he was there in Southampton Row, on leave, when they dropped the bomb on the Bedford Hotel. It was the big one in '17—a lot of people were killed, and he was one of the injured. That's why he can't use his arm. And now he can't get the idea out of his head:

swarms of bombers like rooks and the bombs falling like hail. Civilians dying in droves. Nowhere to hide. Nothing one can say can reason him out of it."

"I suppose it's the next best thing to impossible," Lydia said. "Arguing him out of it, I mean."

The car swerved again. Mrs. Alforde said, "I don't follow. Why?"

"Because he could well be right."

There was something about Julian Dawlish that made people want to trust him. If he had been a dog, he would have been a St. Bernard patrolling the Alpine passes with a keg of brandy attached to his collar and panting to offer a warming drink to any benighted traveler he might encounter. His face and perhaps his behavior seemed to promise an inner philanthropy. Even Mrs. Renton, not the most trusting of human beings, wasn't proof against his peculiar form of charm. That was why she let him into the house and allowed him unescorted upstairs. That was why, when Rory opened his flat door, he found Dawlish standing outside with a smile on his face and Rory's suitcase in his hand. And that was why Rory smiled back with a pleasure that was both unforced and unexpected.

"Hello, Wentwood. The lady who let me in said I could come up. Hope it's not a bad time."

"Of course not." Rory opened the door more widely, aware that his unexpected visitor had a good view of the unmade bed through the open door of the bedroom; in the sitting room he would soon be passing within eighteen inches of the remains of Rory's breakfast on the crumb- and ash-strewn table. "This is very kind of you."

Dawlish put down the suitcase. "Phew."

"Everything all right?" Rory said suddenly.

"Absolutely. If you mean at Cornwallis Grove, that is. Though in point of fact Fenella's not there at present. She's in Mecklenburgh Square."

Rory swept a pile of papers from the seat of the one comfortable armchair. "Do sit down."

"Thanks, but no. I've left Fenella measuring up for curtains. I was only in the way so I thought I'd run your things over. But I promised I wouldn't be long."

The two men went downstairs. Rory was relieved to get Dawlish out of the flat. He himself had grown accustomed to the place, after a fashion; but having Dawlish there made him see it abruptly and cruelly through Dawlish's eyes. A squalid little place, he thought, dirty and utterly depressing. And it was costing him more than he could afford. Ahead of him his life stretched as a vista of ever more unpleasant homes.

"You and Fenella will almost be neighbors," Dawlish said. "Which reminds me: would you like to pop over there for lunch today? Just a scratch meal, she said."

Rory thought there was pity in Dawlish's eyes. Damn the man. "Thank you," he said. "But I'm not sure I can."

"Shame. But if circumstances alter, do come along. It's number fifty-three, the basement entrance. One o'clockish."

They passed the first-floor landing. Rory half-hoped Lydia would be there. He wouldn't have minded Dawlish meeting her—she came from the same social drawer as Dawlish, if not the one above. But she had gone out for the day, according to Mrs. Renton, with a lady who had called for her in a car. Judging by the snores, Captain Ingleby-Lewis was still asleep, which was just as well. Serridge was out. That left Mrs. Renton, who had returned to her sewing machine, and Malcolm Fimberry, who was unfortunately standing in the hall, pince-nez askew on his nose, his hair carefully arranged so that it looked like a heap of buttered curls, and his flies undone.

"Hello, Wentwood. I wonder if you could lend me a pinch of tea? I've run out and I don't want to ask Mrs. Renton again."

He peered at Julian Dawlish, so Rory had to introduce them. The three of them went outside. A large maroon Lagonda was standing outside the front door. Two small boys were examining it with careful nonchalance.

"That's a fine car," Fimberry said, bestowing a cautious pat on the nearside front mudguard.

"Not mine, actually," Dawlish said, looking as close to embarrassed as Rory had seen him. "It's my brother's bus. Mine's in for a service." He glanced around him, clearly trying to distance himself from the magnificent vehicle. "Interesting place—I've never been here before. What's that chapel over there?"

The question loosened Fimberry's tongue in much the same way that brandy in its early stages loosened Ingleby-Lewis's. Soon he was describing the vanished palace of the bishops.

Dawlish plunged into the flow. "That chapel, Mr. Fimberry—is that where they're having the meeting on Saturday? I've seen a poster for it."

"On my window, perhaps," Fimberry said. "Yes—in the undercroft."

"It's a public meeting, is it?"

"As far as I know. They're particularly interested in attracting the businessmen in the area. That's why they're having it at Saturday lunchtime. I'm sure you'd be most welcome if you wanted to come." He gave a high, nervous laugh like a horse's whinny. "The more the merrier, that's what the organizer said to me." He smiled and brought his face uncomfortably close to Dawlish's. "He's called Sir Rex Fisher. I don't know if you know him?"

Dawlish shook his head. "We've never met. I know of him, though." He turned to Rory. "I must push off. We'll run into each other at Cornwallis Grove, I expect. But do come to lunch if you can manage it."

"And of course if you come to the meeting," Fimberry went on, "you'll be able to see round the chapel. If you're lucky you'll see the Ossuary as well."

"We brought nothing into this world," said Mr. Gladwyn, "and it is certain we can carry nothing out. The Lord gave, and the Lord hath taken away; blessed be the Name of the Lord."

It was cold in the dark little church, and Lydia's hands burrowed deep in the pockets of her coat. She was beside Mrs. Alforde in one of the pews at the front. A sparrow had found its way into the church and every now and then it launched itself into flight, fluttering in vain around the pitch-pine beams, searching for the sky.

The plain coffin was resting on trestles in the chancel. There were no flowers. Someone was crying quietly.

"I held my tongue," Mr. Gladwyn was saying, "and spake nothing: I kept silence, yea, even from good words; but it was pain and grief to me."

In the other front pew was a tall woman in a long, dark, shabby coat, with her face hidden by a veil. There were two other women, both old, one on either side of her. The undertaker's men and the sexton were behind them.

"Thou turnest man to destruction: again thou sayest, Come again, ye children of men."

Mrs. Alforde stood, sat and knelt, and Lydia followed suit. There was no singing. The Vicar had pared the service down, and its brief, stark finality was terrible. When the time came, the little congregation trooped out after the coffin to the open grave at the bottom of the churchyard. They watched the undertaker's men lowering the coffin into the raw earth. The sun came out from behind a cloud and suddenly the churchyard was bright and full of color, inappropriately festive.

"He cometh up, and is cut down, like a flower; he fleeth as it were a shadow, and never continueth in one stay."

It was then that Lydia noticed the neighboring grave. Amy Narton's. She glanced at the veiled woman on the other side of the coffin and wondered what on earth she must be feeling. Her husband and her daughter were lying side by side.

Earth pattered on the coffin. The undertaker's men looked straight ahead, their faces full of sombre boredom. The last prayers were said, and then the collect, and then at last it was over. Lydia wished she had not come: idle curiosity had made her a tourist in someone else's grief. There was no excuse for that.

Afterward, as the knot of people around the grave disintegrated, Mrs. Alforde went up to the woman with the veiled face. Lydia watched them talking. Then Mrs. Alforde said something to one of the elderly women beside her and rejoined Lydia, who had waited several yards away on the path.

"Poor woman," Mrs. Alforde said. "I hope you don't mind; I've promised to go and see her after lunch. It shouldn't delay us too much."

"No, of course not."

She fell into step beside Mrs. Alforde and they went through the gate into the grounds of the Vicarage. Lydia glanced back at the women near the grave. Mrs. Narton had raised her veil and was staring after them. As soon as she saw Lydia had turned, she let the veil drop.

"A very poor turnout," Mrs. Alforde murmured. "Narton wasn't much liked. And even though his death was officially an accident while cleaning a gun, everybody knows it must have been suicide. They don't like suicides here. It's felt that they bring shame on everybody."

"You've no objection to pork, I hope," Mr. Gladwyn said, shaking out his napkin.

"I like it very much," Lydia said.

"Good, good." He sharpened the carving knife on the steel. "And I can particularly recommend the broccoli. I always find that being outside in this raw weather gives one an appetite."

There were only the three of them at lunch, the Vicar, Mrs. Alforde and Lydia. The meal was served by a middle-aged maid who bobbed a curtsy to Mrs. Alforde.

"It was good of you to come down today," Mr. Gladwyn said after he had taken the fine edge off his hunger. "I'm sure it was a comfort to poor Mrs. Narton."

"I said I'd look in and see her this afternoon," Mrs. Alforde replied. "At least she has the cottage."

"Only in a manner of speaking, I'm afraid. I'm told that Narton took out a mortgage on it."

"Because he lost his job?"

"Not just that. No, the problem was that Narton became quite obsessed with one of his neighbors, a man called Serridge. Quite a decent sort of fellow—perhaps you've met him?"

"I don't think I have."

"He bought Morthams Farm a few years ago. He was very helpful when I took the plunge and purchased a motor car. When he moved in, he brought a lady with him whom he introduced as his wife. She left rather suddenly a few weeks afterward and it transpired that they weren't married after all. No one knew where she had gone." Gladwyn frowned as he concentrated on trimming the fat from his meat. "You can imagine the gossip it caused. People are always willing to believe the worst. Indeed they want to, in some cases. In the end it turned out that she was alive and well and living with an old friend in America. But Narton was still convinced that Mr. Serridge was responsible for some sort of skulduggery. What really drove him was the death of his daughter. Do you remember?"

"Yes, poor Amy." Mrs. Alforde helped herself to another sprout. "A dreadful shame."

"She'd worked briefly at Morthams, and Narton was convinced that it was Serridge—" Gladwyn coughed, glanced at Lydia, deposited the fat on the side of his plate and then continued "—that it was Serridge who was responsible for her plight, and therefore indirectly for her death. He became so obsessed with pursuing the poor man, against all reason, that he lost his job. But that didn't stop him—he's been harassing the man ever since. Poor Mrs. Narton, how she's suffered. First the shame of what happened to her daughter, then Amy's death, then her husband's increasingly bizarre behavior, and finally his death too. Between ourselves, whatever the coroner decided, I've little doubt that Narton finally snapped under the strain and took the easy way out." Gladwyn sighed gustily and wiped gravy from his chin with his napkin. "Still, who are we to judge?" He turned to Lydia. "I'm so sorry. Here we are, Mrs. Alforde and I, chattering on about old acquaintances and quite forgetting how tedious this must be for you."

"Not at all. It sounds a sad story."

"And Mr. Serridge?" Mrs Alforde put in. "Is he completely blameless in this, do you think?"

"There's little doubt that his relationship with the woman was unorthodox," Gladwyn said weightily, with another glance at Lydia. "He has in fact subsequently talked to me about it at some length. He says he was sadly misled by her, and he's heartily sorry for what happened. He hoped they would marry but she left him in the lurch. There's no doubt about that, incidentally—she actually wrote to me and explained the circumstances. No, Serridge spent a lot of time in the colonies, and to be frank he's not the sort of man you would expect to meet in a lady's drawing room. But he's very straight, if I'm any judge of character."

The maid returned to take out the plates. Mrs. Alforde smiled up at her and asked how her sister and nephew were.

"They're doing quite well, thank you, ma'am. And how's the Colonel keeping?"

"As well as can be expected, thank you, Rebecca. I know he would have liked to have come today, but he's not in the best of health."

In the lull between courses, Lydia excused herself and left the room. She went to the lavatory that opened off the hall. She wanted time to think. There were too many apparent coincidences. There had to be an underlying pattern. Her father had inherited Morthams Farm from old Mrs. Alforde. He had sold it to Serridge, who had used Miss Penhow's money to buy it and had moved in with her. Miss Penhow had gone. Her father had gone away too, but now he was living at Bleeding Heart Square, in the house apparently owned by Mr. Serridge but which had formerly belonged to Miss Penhow.

But there was another layer of connections that added further complications. Her own parents had met at Rawling Hall, and she herself had presumably been conceived there. And now here she was, nearly thirty years later, brought here by the current Mrs. Alforde, who had originally approached her at the instigation of Lydia's mother.

She flushed the lavatory, washed her hands and went back to the hall, where she met Rebecca bringing in the pudding. In the dining room the Vicar was mourning the good old days.

"Nonsense," Mrs. Alforde said, breaking into a lament for Christmas Past. "The Hall was impossible in the winter. There is a great deal to be said for central heating."

Mr. Gladwyn shook his head slowly. "The old order changeth, yielding place to new."

"Dear Lord Tennyson," said Mrs. Alforde tartly. "Not a man with much sense of humor and not an optimist either. By the way, talking of people without much sense of humor, what are we going to do about Margaret Narton?"

There was a low rumbling from Mr. Gladwyn which Lydia at first took for flatulence but a moment later realized was laughter. "I have a feeling you're going to tell me."

"From what you say, her only source of income must be her wages from those dreadful people up at the Hall—all high thinking and low living, I understand, and not very good at paying their bills."

Gladwyn grunted. "She's not in the best state of health, either."

"She's not old. She can't be much more than forty-five. Such a shame: she was rather attractive when she was younger."

"She's very devout." Mr. Gladwyn frowned. "Almost worryingly so."

"Dear me," Mrs. Alforde said. "Anyway, I shall make enquiries. Gerry feels very strongly about not abandoning former servants in their hour of need. What I should really like is to find a more suitable position for her, and possibly lighter work too. Tell me, is Mr. Gregory still the caretaker of the village school?"

"Yes, yes he is."

"He must be nearing eighty by now. Perhaps retirement is indicated. Gerry is chairman of the trustees, as you know, and with your support it should be quite straightforward."

"We've never had a woman as the caretaker of the village school."

"The old order changes, Vicar. No reason why we shouldn't. Old Gregory does nothing more arduous than lock up and occasionally sweep the leaves. And Mrs. Narton would be able to help with the indoor cleaning too, which is something Gregory would never dream of doing."

"It's certainly an idea," conceded Mr. Gladwyn. "If you think she'd be up to it."

Mrs. Alforde turned to Lydia. "If you don't mind, I shall go and see Mrs. Narton after coffee. What would you like to do?"

"I might go for a walk," Lydia said. "Look, the sun's come out. It's an omen."

"I'm not sure Mr. Gladwyn approves of omens," Mrs. Alforde said.

The sun was still shining when Lydia and Mrs. Alforde left the Vicarage. They parted at the gate, Mrs. Alforde turning right toward the Nartons' cottage, and Lydia turning left, which took her past the pub and the church.

Walking on, she caught sight of the Hall on the low ridge that raised it above the farmland and village. The park looked unkempt and one of the lodge gates had parted company with its hinges and was lying on its side in the ditch. She turned and retraced her steps through the village. She had felt a certain delicacy about mentioning to Mrs. Alforde where she really wanted to go.

The roof of a small barn appeared in the distance, on the far side of a field. She glanced up and down the lane. No one was in sight. She went through the field gate and followed the line of the boundary hedge.

The barn was exactly as Rory had described, with the boarded windows, the heavily guarded double doors at the front, and the single door standing ajar at the back. Once she was inside, her enthusiasm for what she was doing abruptly dwindled. A girl and her baby had died in this place, alone and probably in pain. She told herself not to be foolish and lit a cigarette to drive away the ghosts. Then she stripped off her gloves, stood on tiptoe and felt along the top of the wall until her hand touched something smooth and hard. She wrapped her fingers around it and lifted it down. It was the skull of a lamb, an exhibit in Robbie Proctor's private Golgotha, his personal ossuary. She put the skull back and continued to run her hand along the wall, palpating with her fingertips, feeling the outlines of skulls small and large.

At the end of the ledge, tucked in the corner where it ran into the gable wall, she came to another shape and a different texture—something which had rectangular corners, and which felt both warmer and smoother to the touch than the skulls had done. She ran her fingers over and around it. A small box. She lifted it down and discovered that it was very light and that something shifted inside when she moved it. The box was gray with dust and old cobwebs. She brushed away the worst of the dirt with a handful of straw. It had once held cigars and there was still a label attached to it.

Lydia took the box to the window opening in the nearest gable wall and held it in the light that streamed between two of the planks. She turned it upside down, and something rattled inside. She read the label and the stamp on the bottom. The box had once contained Jamaican cigars from Temple Hall, which proudly proclaimed itself "the original Cuban settlement." According to another label on the side, the cigars had been bought at the Army and Navy Stores. She flicked up the lid and parted the leaves of the paper lining inside. The interior was empty apart from a broken pencil about three inches long.

She frowned at it, a sense of anticlimax washing over her. For an instant she had thought there would be something inside that would miraculously resolve the whole messy business: something she could show to Rory with the words, "There—I've done it."

A broken pencil?

Lifting the box, its lid still open, she sniffed it. Faint but unmistakable, the aroma of ghostly cigars touched her sense of smell, unlocking a tangled mass of memories: of Fin after dinner in the library at Monkshill; of Marcus at their wedding breakfast, swooping down to kiss her, his moustache as bristly as a toothbrush; and of other cigars in other places at other times, down the long and misty perspectives of childhood.

At that moment the small door behind her slammed into its frame and she heard a scraping and thumping on the other side of it. She dropped the cigar box, ran to the door and tried to push it open. It didn't move.

19

SHE'S ACTING like a prisoner now, isn't she? It's not just Serridge who's keeping her there, it's herself, her sense of shame—she's terrified that people will find out not just what a fool she's been but that she, Miss Philippa Penhow, has fornicated with a man who is not her husband.

Sunday, 13 April 1930

I am walking about the farm much more. I am trying to become hardier, and more used to walking on mud, etc. The country is such a very uncomfortable place. There are sometimes cows in the fields, and a horse tried to attack me the other day. Joseph said it was just being friendly.

I wonder if I could walk as far as Mavering.

I'm sure Joseph has been looking at Amy more than he should. I have heard them giggling together once. It is so DEMEANING. I actually said something to him about it but he told me not to be a fool, and was really quite rude.

Worst of all, Rebecca has handed in her notice. She said the farm is too lonely for her and she needs to be nearer her family. I think she senses that something is wrong here.

I have found a safe place to keep my diary. I daren't leave it in the house. I'm sure Joseph is going through my things. Two of my rings have vanished. It might have been one of the maids but I think it's him.

And there's another reason why she stays: mad though it is, in some part of herself she's still hoping, against all the evidence, that there will be a happy ending.

Hunger is one of the most powerful arguments in the world. That was the main reason why Rory found himself walking up Doughty Street to Mecklenburgh Square at five to one. He had already spent his allowance for the week. Any sort of lunch would be better than none, and pride was a luxury reserved for those with full stomachs.

Number fifty-three was on the north side of the square, one of a terrace of tall, stately Georgian houses which had seen better days. Rory opened the gate in the railings, went down the area steps and knocked on the basement door. It was opened by Julian Dawlish, who was holding a cigarette in one hand and a glass of whisky in the other.

"Glad you could come, Wentwood." He stood back to allow Rory into the house. "Fenella is hacking things up in the kitchen, and I'm in charge of liquid refreshment. It's going to be a sort of indoor picnic in the primitive style. Can't manage cocktails yet but do you fancy a spot of whisky? There's gin if you prefer, and I think there's some beer somewhere."

"Thanks. Whisky, please."

Fenella appeared in a doorway at the end of the hallway. She was wearing a long apron stained with what looked like blood. "Rory, how lovely." She held up her cheek to be kissed. "I opened a tin of soup and it sort of exploded. Give him a drink, Julian, while I lay the table."

They were acting just like a bloody married couple already, Rory thought savagely, as he followed Julian Dawlish into a sparsely furnished sitting room at the front of the house. Dawlish splashed whisky into another glass and handed it to Rory.

"I know what you're thinking," he said. "What a hole. Help yourself to soda."

"Not at all," Rory said stiffly. He squirted soda into his glass. "Cheers."

"Cheerio." After they had drunk, Dawlish went on, "It will look very different once it's properly decorated and the curtains are up. Fenella is going to move some of her own stuff in. It will be very snug, I think." He snapped open his cigarette case and held it out. "Smoke?"

They lit cigarettes and sat down opposite each other on hard chairs. They both drank more whisky. Rory was nervous and he drank faster than usual. Before he knew what was happening, Dawlish had topped up his glass again.

"How's the job-hunting going?" Dawlish asked.

"So-so," he said, feeling a warm glow suffusing itself through his stomach.

"Do you do any freelancing?"

"I've not had much time to look into that. One needs the contacts, you see. And having been in India . . ."

"Yes, of course. And it's damned hard these days, I imagine, finding the openings. But would you be interested, in principle?"

The second whisky was rapidly joining the first. "I'd go for it like a shot."

"Because I might be able to put you on to something. If you're interested, that is." Dawlish smiled apologetically—he had to a fine art that knack of making it seem that you were doing him a

favor by allowing him to do you a favor. "Pal of mine edits a magazine. A weekly. I know he's always looking for good stuff. Every
time I see him he goes on about how hard it is to find reliable con-
tributors."

"What's it called?"

"Berkeley's."

"I know it." Of course he knew of *Berkeley's*, a magazine that
specialized in political analysis and cultural reviews. Lord Byron
had probably read it. So had Gladstone. So did everyone who was
anyone except for dyed-in-the-wool Tories, whose reading was
confined to the *Morning Post.*

"Interested?" Dawlish said.

"Very much so. But I'm not sure what I can offer."

"Ah," Dawlish said. "I think you underestimate yourself. Look,
it's easier if I put my cards on the table. This could do you a good
turn, but it could do me a good turn too."

"I don't follow."

"I know the editor is interested in how the Fascists work in this
country. Their recruiting, their propaganda and so on. As you
know the magazine, you'll appreciate they're—well, let's say skep-
tical about Fascism and all its works. There's the meeting coming
up in Rosington Place at the end of the week. Now that's interesting, because it shows that Mosley is trying to target the business
community in particular. He's not a fool—he realizes he's not going to get anywhere without financial backers, without substantial support from the City—not just the big guns but the little
fellows too. And a lot of his sponsors were put off by the violence
in Earls Court in June. The iron fist was a little too obvious, if you
follow me. So if you were to write a piece of say a thousand or fifteen hundred words about the meeting, showing how they're trying to recruit support, I think that could be interesting. And if
there's anything I can do to help, just ask."

He leaned forward with the whisky bottle. Rory held out his glass.

"You're assuming I would take a critical slant?"

Dawlish smiled. "I'm assuming you'd report what you saw and heard in an accurate and interesting way. Fenella showed me some of your cuttings. She's got a scrapbook, you know."

Rory tried to remember what he had sent her. There must have been the usual drivel he wrote for the *South Madras Times*—pieces on receptions and cricket matches, court cases and anecdotes. Samples of the jobbing work of a provincial journalist.

"What particularly interested me were the ones on the Congress Party. There was one on the consequences of the Gandhi–Irwin Pact, I remember, and another on Gandhi's work with the untouchables. It's a shame there weren't more like that."

"They didn't go down well with all our readers," Rory said. "Nor with the editor. I only got some of the pieces through because he was on leave. But they weren't political in stance. I was only reporting what was actually happening."

"I don't think *Berkeley's* would mind that sort of reporting. In fact I think they'd rather like it. It's a fresh eye, the outsider's perspective. Have you got a typewriter, by the way?"

"Yes, of course."

There were footsteps outside. "Lunch is served," Fenella said. "Bring your glasses."

Fear smothered her like black treacle, making it hard to breathe and impossible to think. She tried the door again. It wouldn't move. She ran to the window and peered through a gap between the planks. All she could see were dying nettles and a stretch of ragged hedgerow. She opened her mouth to call for help and then closed it.

There were two possibilities: either a sudden gust of wind had improbably blown the door shut and somehow wedged it, or somebody had closed it deliberately with the intention of making her a prisoner. If she called out, the only person likely to hear would be her captor—assuming there was a captor.

Lydia had been standing with her back to the doorway looking at the cigar box. Nobody could have closed the door without seeing her inside. Why shut her in? She tried to think it through but there was not an obvious answer.

Sooner or later, she told herself firmly, she would be missed. She had been seen in the village. She had little doubt that Mrs. Alforde would organize a search party, and little doubt that Mrs. Alforde would find her. It was tiresome—not least because it was growing colder—but surely nothing to worry about.

In the depths of her mind, however, more malign possibilities were stirring. A mother and baby had died in this nasty little barn. It was a place that aroused strong emotions. As the minutes passed, she found it harder and harder to be entirely rational. The light was fading, and she thought she heard rustlings in the straw and saw minute movements on the very edge of her range of vision.

And were there rats too?

"Help! Is there anyone there? Help!" She waited by the window, and then tried again, crying out the same words that were flat and useless because there was nobody to hear them.

Lydia's throat was growing sore. There were half a dozen smoke-blackened bricks in one corner of the barn, perhaps a make-shift hearth for a tramp or even Amy Narton. She lifted one of them. Holding it in both hands, she banged it against the planks of the door. And again, and again, and again. The door didn't budge and showed only the smallest indentations under the rain of blows.

The rough surface of the brick was chafing her hands. She put on her gloves again and kept hammering as rapidly as she could. The brick grew heavier, her arms more tired and her hands more pain-ful. Each time she hit the wood, she gasped; and she had the strange, uncomfortable thought that Amy Narton must have made similar rhythmic sounds in the last desperate hours of her short life.

Finally, her strength gave out. She took a step back and dropped the brick, which fell with a dull thud to the earth floor. Her arms were trembling. The blood pounded in her veins and her throat was dry. She was slightly deaf. The brick had ruined the gloves, in places cutting through the kid leather and digging into her skin beneath. She held up her hands to the light from the window. There were smears of grime and blood on the pale leather. At least she was warmer. She would rest her arms for five minutes, she decided, and then try again.

It was then that she heard somebody rattling the door. The emotion that surged through her was panic, not relief—suppose it was her captor coming back? She bent down and seized the brick. Light flooded into the barn, making her blink. It must be earlier in the afternoon than she had thought. The doorway was almost filled by a large, bear-like silhouette.

She raised the brick. "You? It was you?"

There was a deep chuckle. "Mrs. Langstone," Joseph Serridge said. "I don't think you'll be needing that."

She lowered the brick. For the first time she sensed the nature of the man's charm, a blind force like magnetism or a seismic tremor. Except it wasn't really charm but a sort of hypnotic spell, an impression of overwhelming power. For the first time she also understood what had happened to Miss Penhow and Amy Narton.

"Thank you. I wasn't quite sure—"

"What happened?" Serridge said, his voice hardening. "Are you all right?"

"Yes." Lydia dropped the brick on the pile in the corner. "I am now, at any rate."

"What's been going on?" Serridge advanced into the barn, forcing her to step back. He glanced around quickly. "You're the last person I expected to see." He swung round and towered over her. "What are you doing here?"

"I came for a walk," Lydia said sharply, feeling rattled. "I knew the farm my father used to own was over this way, and I thought I'd have a look at it. He told me he sold Morthams Farm to you."

"But what are you doing in Rawling? You didn't come all this way just to look at Morthams."

"No, of course not," Lydia snapped. "I came with Mrs. Alforde."

"I didn't realize you knew her."

"Colonel Alforde is my godfather," Lydia said.

"The devil he is. Well, I'm damned." Serridge began to smile, but then his face changed again. "So why is Mrs. Alforde here today, and why has she brought you?"

"Look here, Mr. Serridge, I know I'm probably trespassing, and I apologize for that. But I don't see why you should interrogate me like this. I'm having a day out of London with Mrs. Alforde. We've just had lunch with the Vicar."

"Oh, I see. Narton's funeral, I suppose. Mrs. Narton's an old servant, isn't she, and her dad worked on the estate."

"And now I'd better be getting back to the Vicarage," Lydia said, moving toward the door. "Mrs. Alforde and Mr. Gladwyn will be wondering where I am."

"Of course. But somebody shut you in. Who?"

Lydia was outside now. On the ground was a length of iron piping about five feet long.

"I don't like people going in here," Serridge said. "The structure's unsafe. I'm going to have it pulled down. It's not used for anything now."

Lydia pointed at the pipe. "Is that what was keeping the door shut?"

He nodded. "It had been wedged against it. Used to be the downpipe from the guttering on the corner."

A long, rounded indentation marked where the pipe had lain, imprinting its outline on the smooth, clay-streaked mud beneath. Lydia noticed a small footprint at one end.

"You didn't see anyone?" Serridge asked. "Hear anyone?"

Lydia turned back to him, smudging the footprint with the heel of her own shoe as she did so. "No, I had my back to the door. There was an almighty bang. Somebody's idea of a practical joke, I suppose."

Serridge scowled, his face a dark red. "If I catch whoever did it, they'll be sorry. I promise you that, Mrs. Langstone. Now, do you want to come up to the farm? I've got the car up there—I can run you back to the Vicarage."

"Thank you, but no. They'll probably be worrying about me. It won't take me ten minutes to get back."

He hesitated, and she thought he would try to persuade her to come to Morthams Farm with him. She didn't want to go, for reasons she could only half acknowledge.

"All right. I'll walk you back to the road."

Lydia tried to protest that there was no need but he insisted. Serridge made her walk on the tussocky but relatively firm ground beside the hedge while he lumbered through the raw, recently ploughed earth of the field itself. At last they came to the gate. On the other side lay the lane, with the lights of the Vicarage already glimmering a hundred yards away.

Serridge paused, with his hand on the iron latch. "You'll be making plans soon, I reckon."

"What do you mean?"

"About what you do with your life."

Lydia looked coldly at him and said with all the haughtiness she could muster, "I'm afraid Mrs. Alforde will be getting worried, Mr. Serridge. I wonder if you could open the gate?"

He looked down at her, his forehead corrugated with lines, his heavy brows huddled together. He looked so woebegone that for a second she almost felt sorry for him. Then it struck her that it was almost as if he knew about the divorce, or at least that a longer separation was likely. Had her father told him? But even her father didn't yet know about her conversations with Mr. Shires.

Serridge unhooked the gate and pulled it open, standing aside to allow her through. "I'll say good afternoon, Mrs. Langstone." He touched the brim of his hat with a forefinger. "Mind how you go."

Rory was still a little drunk by the time he returned to Bleeding Heart Square. He wasn't so far gone that he was incapacitated, either mentally or physically, but he was saturated with the fuzzy self-confidence that whisky brings, and as yet had little trace of the hangover that might follow. It wasn't just the whisky that was affecting him. It was also the possibility of work, real work. A connection with a magazine like *Berkeley's* could make all the difference. It might even be possible, using that as a springboard, eventually to make a living as a freelance, which was his real ambition. At this moment even Julian Dawlish seemed not such a bad fellow. After all, the chap could hardly be blamed for falling in love with Fenella, if that was in fact what had happened. They had arranged to meet on Friday evening to confirm the details for Saturday.

At the corner, Rory paused. There were people drinking in the Crozier. He heard a loud yapping at knee level and looked down. Nipper had been attached to the old pump with a piece of string. Howlett was visible through the window of the lounge bar, and his top hat was resting on the window ledge.

Rory bent down and scratched Nipper behind the ears, which seemed to please him. He rubbed the dog's neck, pushing his fingers under the collar. It was rather a handsome collar, or at least it had been, with a tarnished brass buckle and little brass stars set into the strap. There were footsteps behind him. He gave the dog a last pat and straightened up. Mrs. Renton, laden with a shopping basket, was coming up the alley from Charleston Street.

"Good afternoon," Rory said, cheerfully. "Let me carry that."

"Thank you." She held out the basket and he took it from her.

Nipper strained toward her, his tail wagging and his yapping intensifying.

"Oh stop it, do," Mrs. Renton said and backed away from him.

She made a semicircular detour around the pump, keeping her distance. "Nasty thing."

"He's all right," Rory said. "I think he's pretty harmless, really."

Mrs. Renton shook her head. "I can't abide dogs. You can't trust them, not really. They'll go with anyone who feeds them."

She set off toward the house. Nipper backed away, squatted, and scratched vigorously behind his left ear with a hind leg. Fleas, probably, Rory thought. Behind him there was the ring of a bicycle bell and one of the mechanics at the workshop at the end of the square cycled past. It was the conjunction of those two factors, the bicycle and the dog scratching its ear, that collided with a third item that was lying like an unexploded bomb in his memory.

Mrs. Renton was unlocking the door of the house. "Are you coming, Mr. Wentwood?" she called. "I haven't got all day, you know."

"Oh dear. Oh dear me. A fall? How very unfortunate."

Lydia stripped off her ruined gloves. "No bones broken. It was all my fault. Luckily Mr. Serridge came to my rescue."

Cheerfulness broke like sunshine across Mr. Gladwyn's round, red face. "Serridge—yes. One of nature's gentlemen. Rebecca, take Mrs. Langstone upstairs and see what you can do to help."

Lydia held up her arms as Rebecca helped her out of her coat. "Is Mrs. Alforde back?"

"No—she's still at Mrs. Narton's, I presume." Mr. Gladwyn gnawed his lower lip. "She wouldn't want us to wait for her, I'm sure, especially in the circumstances. You'll need something to sustain you, Mrs. Langstone. As soon as you are ready, we shall have tea." He glided into his study to wait for it.

"This way, madam." Rebecca led Lydia toward the stairs. "I'll see what I can do with the coat while you're having your tea."

"Thank you."

"But I'm not sure there's much we can do with the gloves," Rebecca said as they climbed the stairs.

"Throw them away." Lydia wondered how long she would have

to work at Shires and Trimble to earn enough for another pair of
gloves like that.

Rebecca showed her into a guest bedroom with its own washbasin. Lydia removed her hat and stared at her pale face in the
mirror above the taps. How on earth had that smear of mud arrived on her nose? Rebecca brought towels and a flannel. She
murmured that the WC and bathroom were next door.

Lydia turned on the hot tap and picked up the flannel. "Rebecca?"

"Yes, madam?"

"I went to the little barn." She watched the maid's face in the
mirror. "The one you can see from the lane. Where Amy Narton
died."

Rebecca's face remained blank and faintly disapproving, the
face of a well-trained servant.

"I didn't fall over," Lydia went on, turning off the tap. "Someone shut me in. They wedged the door closed with a bit of piping.
That's how I ruined the gloves, by picking up a brick and hammering on the door."

"Oh, madam," Rebecca said. "Shall I ask Mr. Gladwyn to call
the police?"

"That depends. I think I know who did it, you see." Lydia rubbed
at a smear of mud that had unaccountably appeared on her cheek.
"There was a fresh footprint in the mud underneath where the
piping was lying. Someone with small feet. A child, probably." She
rinsed the flannel and wrung it out. "So that means it was almost
certainly Robbie."

The color slipped away from Rebecca's face. But most of all Lydia
noticed her eyes, the way they moved to and fro, looking for something that couldn't be found. It was a miserable business, bullying
someone, which was what this came down to.

"What—what do you know about Robbie, madam? You do mean
my nephew?"

"Yes. I know that you're fond of him. And I know that the barn is a special place because no one else normally goes there, even Mr. Serridge. Perhaps especially Mr. Serridge."

"Did Mrs. Alforde tell you, madam?"

"Not about Robbie. Mr. Wentwood did. As it happens, he's a friend of mine."

Rebecca let out her breath but said nothing.

Lydia picked up the towel and turned to face her. "It's all right. I don't want to make life difficult for Robbie. Or for you. But I thought you should know what happened. And there's something else: Mr. Serridge said the barn was dangerous. He's going to have it pulled down."

"I'm so sorry, madam. I just don't know what to say. If Mr. Gladwyn hears that—"

"There's no reason why he should," Lydia interrupted.

"You see, he's so funny about that barn and the skulls. Robbie, I mean. They're . . . they're special."

"His private Golgotha?"

For the first time Rebecca smiled, as one woman to another. "Yes. Mr. Wentwood told you about that."

Lydia turned back to the basin and buried her face in the flannel again. Afterward she said, "You'd better warn Robbie. He'll want to move his skulls."

"There's no harm in them," Rebecca said, as though Lydia had said something quite different. "It's just that they're like toys to him. Or even friends. He was that upset when one of them went. I don't know what he'd do if they all did."

"When he lost the goat's skull?"

The maid nodded. "He thinks it was old Narton."

"Hold on." Lydia dried her face again and sat down at the dressing table. "Sergeant Narton? When?"

"I'm not sure. Robbie's not very good with time. Must have been only a few days before he died."

"Are you sure he meant Narton?"

"Yes. He saw him coming out early one morning. He didn't dare go up to him. Narton hit him once."

Lydia picked up the hairbrush. "Robbie told you all this?"

The maid hovered at Lydia's shoulder. "He can speak more than you'd think, madam. It's just that he doesn't like doing it with strangers and it takes a bit of practice to understand what he's saying." She bent closer. "Are you really not going to do anything?"

"About Robbie this afternoon? Of course not." For a moment she thought the maid was about to burst into tears. "It didn't matter."

"Thank you. He was a bit funny today, you know, a bit overwrought. That must have been why he shut you in. He probably thought you were after the other skulls."

It occurred to Lydia that at no point had Rebecca questioned Lydia's accusation: she had assumed that it was perfectly likely, even probable, that Robbie had shut her in the barn.

"I'll take the coat down to the kitchen, shall I, and dry it by the fire. That mud will soon brush off."

"Thank you. Tell me, what was she like? Miss Penhow, I mean."

"I called her Mrs. Serridge, of course. She was all right, quite a nice little thing. I was only with her for a week or two, but we got on fine. She gave herself airs sometimes but there was no harm in it. And you couldn't help feeling sorry for her. She was so unhappy."

"Was that obvious?"

Rebecca nodded. "She wanted to follow him around like a spaniel but he wasn't having any of it. She spent a lot of time crying. Or sulking, or trying to coax him round. She thought—she thought she was, well, attractive to him. That she could win him round that way. But then she found she couldn't."

"Was she pretty?"

Rebecca shrugged. "She could make herself look well enough. She needed an hour in the morning to get ready. I used to help her sometimes, and she was so fussy. But she dressed quite well, I'll say that for her. And she wasn't bad-looking, either, not when she had her teeth in and she'd had her hair tinted. She was a lady who needed her rouge and powder. Even so, you could see just by looking at them together that he was a good ten or fifteen years younger. And then if you saw her when she wasn't ready for company, you saw how old she really was. I dare say she felt younger than she was."

"We all feel that."

"Anyone with half an eye could see it was pointless."

"What do you mean?"

Rebecca drew herself up and stood primly, her hands clasped together in front of her. "He likes the younger ones, madam. Girls."

Lydia stood up, leaving the towel draped on the end of the bed and the flannel on the edge of the basin. Rebecca folded the coat neatly over her arm and opened the door. It was odd, Lydia thought, and rather unsettling, how quickly one became used to servants again. Or rather to not noticing all the little things they did for you.

"Rebecca? I found something else in the barn."

The maid stopped, her hand on the door handle and her face anxious.

"Nothing to worry about. Something on the ledge with the skulls, right at the end in the corner. An old cigar box. Do you know anything about it?"

"It was Mrs. Serridge's—Miss Penhow's, I mean. I remember Robbie showing it to me."

Lydia blinked. "She smoked cigars?"

Rebecca's face creased into a grin. "Oh no, madam. It must have been Mr. Serridge's once, I suppose. She used it for her diary. She was always writing in it."

"Why on earth did she keep it there?"

"Maybe so it wasn't obvious if Mr. Serridge went looking for it. I caught him looking through her writing desk once when she was having a bath."

"It can't have been very big."

"It wasn't. Just a little green book with hard covers."

That explained the pencil. Lydia said, "Do you know what happened to it?"

"Not seen hide nor hair of it since I left the farm. He'll have got his hands on it after she went, if she didn't take it with her."

Lydia nodded to Rebecca to open the door. As they crossed the landing and went downstairs, normality reasserted itself, and the maid, one step behind Lydia, kept her head modestly lowered and her hands clasped round the coat. The distance between them seemed ridiculous, given the nature of the conversation they had just had in the bedroom.

In the hall, Lydia turned to Rebecca and said in a low voice, partly because things had changed between them and partly because she wanted to show that she had no desire for them to return to their old formal footing, "You'll have to find another Golgotha, I suppose."

Rebecca looked at her and opened her mouth as if about to speak. Then her face changed as if a cloth had been wiped over it.

"Ah," Mr. Gladwyn said, emerging from the drawing room. "There you are, Mrs. Langstone. Fully restored, I hope?"

Lydia turned to him and smiled. "Yes, thank you. Rebecca's been looking after me very well."

"Good, good. Now come and get warm, and Rebecca will bring us our tea." He stood aside to allow her to enter the room. "What was that about Golgotha?"

"No—taffeta," Lydia said swiftly as she passed him in the doorway. "I was asking her advice about how to clean a dress."

Mrs. Alforde was sitting smoking by the fire. She said hello but hardly looked at Lydia. She looked tired and also older, as though she had lived too much time too quickly since lunch.

"Sorry I've kept you both waiting," Lydia said.

"Not at all," Mr. Gladwyn said earnestly. "Tea won't be a jiffy now, I'm sure."

"You've been in the wars, I gather," Mrs. Alforde said, tapping ash into the fire.

"No lasting damage except to my gloves. How was Mrs. Narton?"

Mrs. Alforde looked away. "As well as could be expected."

"I shall tell Cook to send her some soup," Mr. Gladwyn announced. "Ah, here is tea."

His ears had caught the rattle of the tea things in the hall. Rebecca shouldered open the door and wheeled in a trolley. It was a generous tea, with hot buttered crumpets, two sorts of cake and two sorts of sandwiches, as well as bread and butter. Mrs. Alforde poured and Mr. Gladwyn handed round the cups, the sandwiches and a little later the cake. At first there was not a great deal of conversation. Mrs. Alforde concentrated on eating, and so did Mr. Gladwyn. Lydia picked at a sandwich and drank two cups of tea.

By the time he had reached his third cup of tea, Mr. Gladwyn had time for his conversational duties as a host. "Yes, Golgotha," he said. "A foolish mistake of mine—though I suppose it's natural that a clergyman should hear Golgotha rather than taffeta. Curiously enough—" here he leaned back in his chair and stretched out his legs "—it reminds me of rather a good story that went the rounds when I was up at Cambridge. There was a gallery in the university church, you know, which was where the heads of houses sat. And we undergraduates always called it Golgotha because it was the place of the skulls or heads." He paused and beamed at them, preparing them for the climax. "And of course we young wags used to say that Golgotha was the place of empty skulls."

He glanced from one face to another, clearly expecting a suitable response. Lydia managed a smile, and hoped that her expression implied that she was suppressing with difficulty an almost overwhelming desire to laugh immoderately.

Mrs. Alforde merely set down her cup on the table and reached for her cigarettes again. Lydia realized that she had not been listening to a word that Mr. Gladwyn was saying.

Neither of them spoke much on the drive back to London. Lydia was glad of this for several reasons, not least because it was dark and both Mrs. Alforde's driving and her temper had become even more erratic. They reached Bleeding Heart Square a little after seven o'clock. Mrs. Alforde stopped the car outside the house.

"Would you like to come in for a drink?" Lydia asked, glancing up at the facade of the house, at the lighted windows on the first floor; the top-floor windows were dark. "It looks as if Father's in."

"No, no, thank you," Mrs. Alforde said, too baldly for politeness. "I must get back to Gerry."

Lydia was relieved, partly because she wasn't sure what state either her father or the flat would be in, and of course finding something to drink might be difficult. She thanked Mrs. Alforde, who in turn thanked Lydia for keeping her company and hoped that she had not found Rawling too dreary. She murmured something about getting in touch soon and drove off rather quickly.

That night Lydia slept badly, skimming on the surface of unconsciousness, moving in and out of dreams which never made sense enough to be frightening but which left her profoundly uneasy. There was too much to think about. Sometimes she thought she heard dance music, and at other times a woman crying and the sound of Mr. Gladwyn's measured voice as the mourners clustered around Narton's open grave. And what had happened to Mrs. Alforde? She had seemed almost hostile on the way home. She badly needed to talk to Rory. If only he had been at home. And that in itself was a thought that made her restless because it took very little to imagine him with Fenella Kensley instead.

By half past five, she had given up trying to sleep. She lay in a huddle, to conserve warmth, while her mind roved among the events of yesterday. Everything has an explanation, she told her-self, and somewhere in the world is the one that fits all this.

At half past six, cold and thirst drove her out of bed. It was still dark. She washed sketchily in cold water from the jug, dressed, put on the kettle and went into the sitting room. The curtains were still drawn from the previous evening. She pulled them aside because the room caught the best of the morning light when at last it came. She lit the gas fire and went back to make the tea.

When she returned, the room was warmer. The sky was very slightly lighter toward the east now. She lingered at the window, warming her fingers on the cup. A heavy bird fluttered past and glided toward the old pump on the corner by the Crozier. There were other birds there already, perching awkwardly on the pump handle and pecking at something. When the new arrival joined them, there was a great flurry of wings as though the newcomer were not a welcome guest.

Lydia huddled over the fire, drank her tea and smoked the first cigarette of the day. What on earth were the birds doing? She had never seen them there before. When she had finished the tea, she went back to the window. The birds were still outside by the pump.

She put on her coat and hat, went downstairs and opened the front door. As she approached the pump, the birds scrambled into the air. They were big, black crows and not in a hurry to leave. She glanced over her shoulder at the house behind her. All the win-dows except her own were still in darkness. But she thought she caught a movement at Mrs. Renton's window on the right of the front door, the merest glimpse of gray smudge behind the glass, a possible face.

She drew nearer the pump. A rusty nail protruded from one of the supports of its dilapidated wooden canopy. Hanging from it was a long and slightly twisted metal meat skewer with a ring at one end. The skewer had been driven through a lump of matter the size of a misshapen tennis ball. Or an overripe orange from

Covent Garden with Hitler's picture on the label, or a russet from one of the old trees in the Monkshill orchard, or a very large egg from a bird or reptile.

The ring had been looped over the head of the nail, and tied to it was a brown luggage label. Lydia touched the label gently with her finger. There was only one word on it and, as the nausea rose in her throat, she knew what it would be before she made out the letters: *Serridge*.

20

YOU NOTICE that the entries near the end look different from those near the beginning. All the London ones are written in ink, as are the first few entries at Morthams Farm. And the very first ones are much more neatly written than those that come later. At the start, Philippa May Penhow is writing to impress an invisible posterity. Then she writes for herself, because she wants to. These last entries are in pencil and the handwriting wobbles all over the place. Those were the ones she wrote after she moved the diary from the house.

Finally, at the end, where in places the words are almost impossible to make out, she writes in a rapid, almost illegible scrawl because she has no one else to talk to, and she's desperate.

Monday, 14 April 1930

> *Last night was a full moon & it kept me awake. Joseph didn't come up. As the sun rose, I slept & did not wake till after nine o'clock. When I came downstairs Joseph had left the house. Rebecca said that he had told them to wait until I was down before clearing away the breakfast things. On the table was a bunch of daffodils in a vase, and*

*on my plate a little envelope with my name on it in my
darling's hand. "My sweet love, forgive your little boysie
for upsetting you. I tiptoed out of the house this morning so
as not to wake you. Your loving Joey."*

Oh how could I have doubted him?

*He came back for lunch with little Jacko at his heels
& two dead rabbits. He had shot them himself this
morning. Jacko was smelly and dirty after his morning's
fun, and I told him he could not come into the house
until Amy had washed him under the tap in the
scullery!*

A bunch of daffodils and a snatch of baby talk—and she comes running back into his arms again. But not long now. You are counting the days.

"Now look here, Byrne. What's it to you?"

Mr. Byrne, who had been sweeping sawdust, propped his broom against the wall of the Crozier and put his hands on his hips. He scowled at Serridge. "It's next to my pub. That's what it's got to do with me."

"It's not there now."

"But it was. And having that bloody disgusting thing hardly a yard from the door is hardly going to encourage trade, is it?"

Rory waited on the doorstep of number seven.

"I shouldn't think it would have much effect one way or the other," Serridge said coldly. "It's not your pump. It belongs to the freeholders."

"I'm a ratepayer, aren't I?" Mr. Byrne had leaned forward, unmistakably hostile. His bald head was like a blunt instrument. "My old woman nearly had a fit when she saw what them birds were pecking at."

"Don't see why. She hangs out bacon rind for the bloody blue tits."

"That's not the same—anyone can see that. Look, someone round here is off his head. And the label had your name on it, Mr. Serridge—you remember that."

Serridge stood there, not giving an inch either literally or metaphorically. His overcoat was open and his hands were deep in his trouser pockets; he had a cigar in the corner of his mouth and his hat on the back of his head. He looked like a farmer confronting an irritable porker.

"None of your bloody business," he said with an air of finality. "You're just the brewery's tenant."

At the sound of Rory's footsteps, the other men glanced toward him.

But the porker wasn't so easily put off. "You've been having quite a little problem with these hearts, I'm told," Byrne said to Serridge, and as he spoke he came half a pace closer. "Parcels in the post from what I hear."

"Who told you that?" Serridge snapped.

"The Captain."

"And you believed him? I thought you had more sense."

"I believed him because he was telling the truth, Mr. Serridge. And what interests me is why haven't you been to the police about it? I mean, somebody's making a nuisance of themselves. And maybe somebody's trying to tell you something."

"Nonsense."

Rory had reached the corner now and was skirting the two men by the pump. He was on his way to the Central Library, where they had a back file of *Berkeley's*. Later, in the afternoon, he wanted to practice his shorthand skills. He wouldn't have much time in the evening because he was meeting Dawlish for a drink.

"Hey, there—Mr. Wentwood. You know about these hearts, don't you?"

"Which hearts?"

"The ones that Mr. Serridge here has been getting in the post."

Serridge turned toward Rory, towering over him, his face impassive. He didn't need to say anything.

"I'm afraid I can't help you, Mr. Byrne," Rory said. "I don't look at Mr. Serridge's post. Only my own."

"Because he knows it's none of his business," Serridge said, turning back to Byrne. "He's not a fool, unlike some I could mention."

There was a crack as the latch rose on the gate from Rosington Place. The wicket opened and Nipper scampered into Bleeding Heart Square, followed by Howlett.

"Morning, gents. I thought I heard your voices."

"Mr. Howlett," Byrne began. "It's got to stop."

"What has?"

"We've got someone with a nasty mind playing pranks around here. It's not nice. If my little girl had seen what was left on the pump this morning, it would have given her nightmares."

"Good morning, Mr. Howlett," Serridge said. "How do?"

Howlett touched his hat. "All right, sir."

"Suppose Byrne here tells you what's on his mind. Once he's got it off his chest, maybe he'll feel better."

"Bloody disgusting," Byrne said. "That's what it is. Jesus Mother of God, someone needs their head examined."

Howlett listened gravely while the landlord explained what had been left on the pump and what Captain Ingleby-Lewis had told him about Serridge's parcels. Nipper cocked his leg against the corner of the pump and squirted urine over the side of the stone basin. Rory tried to slip away but Serridge wrapped a hand around his arm. He squeezed it so firmly that Rory winced.

"Mr. Wentwood lives in my house, Howlett—if you want to ask him, he'll soon tell you this business about parcels is nonsense."

"You let me know if it happens again, Mr. Byrne," Howlett said at last when Byrne had finished. "And I'll keep my eyes open, don't you worry about that. If you ask me it's some boy's prank. If I catch him at it, I'll take a strap to him and then I'll hang him up there to rot instead."

Sitting at her desk by the window, Lydia Langstone glanced down into Rosington Place and saw Rory Wentwood standing outside the chapel and looking up at the great east window. In the background, Miss Tuffley's voice rose and fell, swooped and dived, just as it had done all afternoon and did every afternoon unless Mr. Reynolds stopped her. She was talking about films at present, comparing Robert Donat in *The Count of Monte Cristo* with Leslie Howard in *The Scarlet Pimpernel*. Miss Tuffley wasn't stupid. She concentrated her romantic urges on men who could be trusted to remain safely two-dimensional.

Lydia wished she wasn't mooning over Rory Wentwood. She wasn't in love with him, of course. She simply liked looking at him and talking to him and being with him. There was nothing wrong in that. The other silly symptoms were the accidental side effects of her leaving Marcus and turning her life upside down. All these emotions were flying around inside her like a swarm of bees and they had simply settled for the time being on Rory Wentwood, who was entirely unsuitable and in any case in love with someone else. Perhaps that was part of his charm. Still, he did look sweet in that cap of his, like an outsized little boy. She hoped he would be in that evening. They needed to talk. Also, it would be nice to see him again.

Rory glanced up at the windows opposite the chapel. Automatically Lydia pulled back a little. She wasn't that far gone. It was one thing to watch him but quite another for him to know about it. He set off in the direction of Bleeding Heart Square.

"I mean, if you were marking their smiles out of ten," Miss Tuffley was saying, "I think I would have to give Robert an eight and

Leslie only a five, or perhaps a six. Leslie always makes me feel a bit sad, if you know what I mean. He's much more *spiritual.* I think you could have a really, really deep conversation with him, don't you?"

The door of the private office opened. "Mrs. Langstone?" said Mr. Shires. "Will you bring in the letter file? I shall be leaving early this afternoon."

Lydia gathered up the folder containing the day's letters waiting for signature.

"You can wait while I sign them," he said. "Shut the door, will you—there's a draught."

He flipped open the folder, uncapped his fountain pen and began to sign the letters, his eyes running swiftly over the contents of each. Lydia waited, standing by the door.

"Do sit down, Mrs. Langstone. I wanted a word with you." He scrawled his signature, blotted it and moved on to the next letter. "With reference to our earlier conversation, I intend to write to Mr. Langstone over the weekend, according to your instructions." He looked up, peering at her with watery eyes. "After due consideration, I think it would be better for all concerned if it were not generally known that I am acting for you, particularly in this office. One wouldn't want to encourage tittle-tattle during office hours, or to bring undesirable attention to the firm. But I have a small private practice which I run from home. Of course, some publicity will be inevitable in the long run, if the affair proceeds to its conclusion. But we need not anticipate it unnecessarily."

"I'm still rather concerned about the cost, sir."

He nodded. "I'm glad to hear of it. Money matters, Mrs. Langstone, as I'm sure you've noticed. We shall move cautiously. As we were saying earlier, since you're the injured party, I see no reason why Mr. Langstone shouldn't pay any costs incurred. On top of that, we shall ask him to settle an annuity on you. We shall also need to take into account anything of material value that you've brought into the marriage."

"He spent all that long ago," Lydia said, and was surprised to hear the bitterness in her voice.

"It would be very helpful if you would let me have a note of the details as far as you are able. Let me have it tomorrow morning. If there was any formal arrangement, I imagine a solicitor was involved—perhaps Lord Cassington's family solicitor? It would be helpful to know. Copies of any documents relating to the settlement would be invaluable. In the meantime, I shall write to Mr. Langstone. You must give me his address tomorrow as well. He should receive the letter on Monday."

"Thank you."

Mr. Shires sighed. "Don't get your hopes too high, Mrs. Langstone. We have a long way to go."

Lydia spent the rest of the afternoon in a daze. At last it seemed possible that there might one day be an end to all this uncertainty—and to the poverty too. It was reassuring that she had an ally in the shape of Mr. Shires. She didn't much like the man but she had no reason to doubt his professional competence. His personal probity was another matter—she remembered that odd snatch of telephone conversation she had overheard between him and Serridge. There was nothing to show that either Serridge or Miss Penhow had ever been a client of Shires and Trimble. But they might be Mr. Shires' private clients, and in that case their names would not feature in Mr. Reynolds' files.

At the end of the day Lydia and Miss Tuffley went downstairs together. Miss Tuffley paused in the hall to light a cigarette before venturing outside. Lydia asked if she had any plans for the weekend.

"Not really. I'll probably go to the pictures on Saturday afternoon. Do you ever go to the pictures?"

"Occasionally."

"You can tag along sometimes if you want." Miss Tuffley lowered her head over the match. "It's not much fun going by yourself, is it? Just let me know."

"Yes, thank you."

Miss Tuffley opened the front door and led the way down the steps. It had started to rain. Rory Wentwood was waiting outside under an umbrella. He raised his cap when he saw them.

"Good afternoon, Mrs. Langstone," he said.

Miss Tuffley nudged Lydia. "You lucky thing. They're all after you, aren't they? It's not fair. Can't you spare one for me?"

She squealed with laughter and waved to them both. She set off along the pavement toward Holborn, swaying on her high heels and leaving behind her a sweetly entangled smell of Woodbines and cheap scent.

"There's so much we need to talk about," Lydia said quietly to Rory as they were walking toward the gate to Bleeding Heart Square.

"I know. And I've got a favor to ask. Are you busy this evening?"

"Not particularly. Why?"

"Because I wondered if you'd be kind enough to—" He broke off as the wicket gate opened, revealing Malcolm Fimberry framed in the doorway between Rosington Place and Bleeding Heart Square.

"Mrs. Langstone! Good evening." Fimberry beamed at her and then added with less enthusiasm, "Hello, Wentwood."

Rory nodded to him.

Fimberry stayed where he was, blocking their way. "I promised to show you something of the chapel, Mrs. Langstone. If you've got five minutes to spare, I can promise you won't regret it."

"Some other time, perhaps—I have one or two things to do."

"Just for a couple of minutes? You see, because of the meeting tomorrow, Father Bertram has entrusted me with the key of the Ossuary. He can't be there tomorrow himself, you see—there's a diocesan committee at Westminster, so he's asked me to liaise with Sir Rex in his place." He took off his rain-flecked pince-nez and polished them on his tie. "It's a very good opportunity to see the encaustic tiles. I probably won't have a chance to show you tomorrow—these meetings can be a little hectic, and I shall have to be on hand to help."

"It's very kind of you, Mr. Fimberry, but I'm—"

"We'd love to," Rory interrupted. "Thank you so much."

"Oh," said Fimberry, disconcerted. He added gloomily, "Well, yes, I suppose the more the merrier."

Lydia glanced at Rory's face. She felt his touch on her arm and wondered why this was important to him. "All right. If it really won't take long."

"Follow me."

He set off toward the chapel. Rory mouthed "Thank you" to Lydia. Fimberry held open the door in the little forecourt in front of the east wall of the chapel. It led into a flagged corridor running the length of the building and sparsely lit with electric wall lights.

"This way," Fimberry said. "This is all that remains of the cloister, by the way. Sadly altered, of course."

On the left was a row of windows looking out into darkness; on the right was the south wall of the chapel, a patchwork of masonry studded with blocked openings. The place smelled damp. Lydia watched Fimberry's shadow flickering first in front and then behind him, along the wall and along the floor, but never in one place for long and never quite where you expected it to be. In the gloom at the end of the corridor a flight of stone steps rose up to the entrance of St. Tumwulf's Chapel.

Fimberry glanced back at them. "We'll save the chapel itself for another day, Mrs. Langstone. There is so much to see, and so little time!"

"Sorry about this," Rory murmured behind her. "I'll explain."

"This is the undercroft," Fimberry said, waving to a door set three steps down from the floor level of the cloister.

"May we see in there too?" Rory said, darting down the steps and trying the latch. The latch lifted and the door opened.

"Very well. But mind the steps, Mrs. Langstone, they can be treacherous. Just a moment—I'll turn on the lights."

A line of bare light bulbs came to life, revealing the stark outlines of a long, low whitewashed room bisected on its east–west axis by a row of wooden posts.

"Victorian," Fimberry said dismissively. "The interior had to be almost entirely refurbished when the Church bought St. Tumwulf's in the eighteen seventies."

Lydia looked around. Rows of chairs and benches had been set out. Near the door were tables holding crockery and urns. At the east end, five high-backed chairs stood behind a table on a low platform.

"It looks as if the Inquisition will soon be in session," Rory said.

"Sir Rex and his people made the arrangements. Well, there's not much to see here. Shall we move on to the Ossuary?"

"Does Father Bertram let the undercroft to anyone who asks?"

"Oh no." Fimberry looked shocked. "That wouldn't be appropriate. One couldn't have atheists here, for example, or communists or people of that sort."

"But Fascists are all right?"

"Father Bertram was actually presented to Signor Mussolini when he last visited Rome. He was most impressed. One can't deny Il Duce gets results."

"I thought the Pope didn't like him much," Rory said. "Mussolini, I mean, not Father Bertram." Lydia punched him lightly on the arm in an attempt to shut him up.

"Father Bertram says that the Holy Father and the Italian government have had one or two differences but they will soon be sorted out. After all, Mussolini's a son of the Church."

Fimberry shooed them back to the cloister and led them to another, much smaller sunken doorway set in the wall just before the flight of steps leading up to the chapel itself. He took out a bunch of keys from his raincoat pocket, unlocked the door and pulled it open. He switched on another light.

"Here we are. Come and stand by me, Mrs. Langstone, and you'll be able to see properly. This is a good time to come because the chairs are usually stored in here. We're directly under the ante-chapel."

The high, windowless room was long and thin. It smelled mysteriously of cats. In the far corner was a heavy table with bulbous legs.

"They say that this is where the bodies of the faithful lay before they were secretly interred beneath the undercroft. Do look at the ceiling: the rib vaulting is original."

"How nice," Lydia said, feeling she should contribute something to the conversation. "Is it very old?"

"Late fourteenth century at a guess." Fimberry squeezed past the table and stabbed an index finger at the far wall. "Now you see the tiles? They were covered with layers of whitewash but I scraped it off. No doubt they were used to patch the mortar by some long-forgotten builder. Almost certainly they came originally from the floor. This tile's nearly complete—look, it's the arms of the See of Rosington. That one is probably a scallop shell, the pilgrim badge of the shrine of St. James of Compostela. Isn't it interesting?" He turned back to Rory and Lydia in the doorway of the Ossuary. "The past seems so close to us here, so close that one can actually touch it. Quite literally in this case." Smiling, he leaned across the little room and ran the middle finger of his right hand over the putative scallop shell. "Don't you feel it sometimes, Mrs. Langstone? The touch of the past?"

"Mr. Fimberry," Lydia said suddenly. "What's that in the corner?"

"What?"

"Down there." She pointed. "On the floor between the table and the wall."

The shadow of a table leg ran across something pale and jagged half-covered by a rag. *A trick of the light*, Lydia thought; *it can't be anything else.* Rory stirred beside her. She heard him sucking in his breath.

A trick of the light?

21

SOMETIMES you think it's a game to him. He has luck on his side too. Even Jacko was his ally in the end. You can't trust anyone.

Friday, 18 April 1930

Jacko bit his mistress last night when I tried to make him jump down from the sofa. Not hard, but even so I was VERY cross. I shut him in the scullery. Unfortunately he howled so much that Joseph let him out.

I did not come down for breakfast today but stayed in my room. At lunch, Joseph said he had talked to Rebecca this morning and she had told him that there was another reason why she needed to hand in her notice. Her sister has been very ill with influenza, and so has her little boy, Rebecca's nephew, and Rebecca wants to be able to spend more time looking after them during their convalescence. They live on the other side of the village, quite a distance from here.

Joseph has decided not to insist on her working out her month's notice. He has told her she may leave after supper

tomorrow, and he will run her over to her sister's in the car.
He thought it would be kinder to her and her family, and
also better for us in the long run because servants are never
very satisfactory when they are working out their notice,
and it will be better for us to find her successor sooner
rather than later. He will pay her up to the end of the week.
I put the best face on it I could. I was tempted to
remind him that it is usually the mistress of the house who
has the management of the indoor servants. But it didn't
seem quite the right moment. What is done is done.

After this, you know there will be no more daffodils from her
sweet Joey. All that's over and done with now. Rebecca will soon be
gone. Poor, foolish Amy doesn't count.

"You don't mind, do you?"

"The thing is, there's a lot we need to talk about."

"Yes, yes." Rory closed the cover of the typewriter. "I know. But I
haven't much time. I have to go out in three quarters of an hour."

"Why do you suddenly want to practice your shorthand?"

"Julian Dawlish—Fenella's friend—he knows the editor of
Berkeley's."

"The weekly?"

"I'm doing a piece on spec for them about tomorrow's meeting."

"That's marvelous."

"If they use it." He rubbed his eyes. "I can't stop thinking about
it. Damn it, it could make all the difference. It's the first sniff of
real work I've had, work that could lead somewhere, since I came
back to England. That's why I was keen to see the undercroft, to
get an idea of the layout."

"Of course. Poor Mr. Fimberry."

A trick of the light.

"Beggars belief, doesn't it? I couldn't believe my eyes when I saw that goat's skull under the table in the Ossuary. Why didn't he just leave it in the dustbin? Why put it in the Ossuary? And why did he want to show it to Father Bertram?"

"Because he thinks it might be the devil," Lydia said. "That's my theory. So it's safer on consecrated ground until Father Bertram can see it. There's a sort of logic to it."

"Mad as a hatter, in my opinion."

"He's ill," Lydia said, thinking of Colonel Alforde. *No more war.* "You can't blame him for that."

Rory glanced at his wristwatch. "Would you mind if we start? I promised to meet Dawlish for a drink, and I haven't used my shorthand for months, not properly. And it's like speaking a language, you see. If you don't use it for a while you have to get your ear in again."

"Does it matter what I talk about?"

He shook his head. "I've got it all worked out. I think it will be best to start with something completely unseen, completely unexpected. And then try something political from the paper—something with the same sort of vocabulary as they're likely to be using tomorrow. Afterward I'll try and read it back to you." He smiled at her. "Are you sure you don't mind? I know it's an awful lot to ask."

"It's all right. We've had supper—there's nothing else I need to do." That was untrue. If you didn't have servants, Lydia had discovered, there was always something you needed to do. "I'll just talk away, then. Are you ready?"

He picked up his newly sharpened pencil and turned over a page in his shorthand pad. "Fire away, Lydia—oh damn. Sorry. Mrs. Langstone, I mean."

"It doesn't matter. You can call me Lydia if you want."

"As long as you call me Rory. Right, Lydia. I'm as ready as I ever will be."

"I talked to Mrs. Renton," Lydia began, her cheeks a little pinker than before. "I showed her the skirt and the note. She used to do sewing for Miss Penhow. Mr. Serridge introduced them. She even made some clothes for her." Lydia watched Rory's pencil traveling across the paper. "Then Miss Penhow moved to the country, and she lost touch." She paused again. "As a matter of fact I went to Rawling yesterday."

The point of the pencil snapped. "What were you doing in Rawling, for God's sake?"

"My godfather used to live there. His wife had to go down for a funeral. I went with her."

Rory pushed the pad away from him, abandoning the shorthand. "I don't understand. I don't even begin to understand."

She smiled at him. "It's much less complicated than it seems."

"Just a whacking great big coincidence. Yet another."

"Not really. Serridge only bought Morthams Farm because my father sold it to him. My father only owned it because he was left it by old Mrs. Alforde. My godfather is another Alforde—so he's a sort of cousin by marriage to my father. That's why he's my godfather—he and Father used to know each other long before I was on the scene. The Alfordes know my mother too—they came to my wedding, actually. My mother asked Mrs. Alforde to talk to me. To try to persuade me to go back to Marcus."

Rory looked consideringly at her. "And did she?"

"Yes and no." The color rose in her cheeks. "She tried but she didn't succeed." She rushed on, stumbling a little over her words. "My mother and father met at Rawling. In a way the Alfordes connect everything, you see. Mrs. Narton worked at the Hall when they were there. And so did Rebecca at the Vicarage."

"You met her?"

"When we had lunch with Mr. Gladwyn. It didn't end there, either. I went to have a look at that little barn you mentioned, the one with the skulls. Robbie shut me in. He thought I was trying to steal his skulls."

He whistled. "As the goat's skull was stolen?"

"According to Rebecca, he's convinced Narton took it."

"When?"

"Probably a few days before he died."

"I saw him on Saturday," Rory said. "He could have posted it then. So Robbie thought you were another skull thief? How did you get out?"

"I banged on the door. Mr. Serridge rescued me in the end."

"Serridge? What was he up to? Was he following you?"

Lydia shivered. "I'm not sure. He was very strange—in one way he was as nice as pie to me. But he was also rather terrifying. I'm sure he's up to something. And there was another thing—I found something else on the shelf with the skulls, a cigar box. Rebecca told me that when she worked at Morthams Farm, Miss Penhow kept her diary in it. She thinks Miss Penhow was hiding it from Serridge."

"When did you manage to talk to Rebecca?"

"Afterward, at the Vicarage. I felt rather sorry for her. I imagine Robbie's hers, don't you?"

"What? Why do you think that?" Rory felt, as he often did when talking to his sisters, that where relationships were concerned they were equipped with a form of perception that he lacked. "I thought he was her nephew."

"He may be, I suppose. But she dotes on him. It's far more likely he was Rebecca's little accident, and her sister unofficially adopted him."

"Anything else?" he asked with a trace of sarcasm in his voice. "Or have you pulled the last rabbit out of the hat for the time being?"

"There's the heart this morning," she said, smiling back at him.

"I know about that. Serridge and Byrne were having a row about it when I went out this morning. Howlett came and calmed them down."

"It was nasty," she said soberly.

"Sorry," he said perfunctorily. "I've got a couple of scraps of information of my own," he went on. "Nothing to compare with yours but better than nothing. I saw a photograph of Miss Penhow at Fenella's. She looked quite pretty, but Fenella said she was older than she looked."

"According to Rebecca, she spent a lot of time and effort trying to make herself look youthful. It was rather pathetic, actually—she was trying to make herself attractive to Serridge, and he only had an eye for the girls."

Rory looked at his watch again. "I'd better go. Are you coming tomorrow?"

"No," she said. "My husband will be there. Not to mention my future brother-in-law."

Rory saw her out of the flat. At the head of the stairs he said, "By the way, talking of photographs, you remember the one Rebecca showed me?" He lowered his voice. "Amy Narton in the altogether on Serridge's bike? There was a little dog in it. There was also a dog in that photograph of Miss Penhow. It could have been the same one. Yesterday I was standing outside by the pub and someone went by on a bicycle. Nipper was there. And that was when it clicked: the dog in both photos looks just like Nipper."

Fenella was a bitch. In fact, she was a bloody bitch. And if one were to be absolutely precise about it, as Virginia Woolf would no doubt wish one to be, Fenella was a bloody, calculating bitch.

Lydia huddled over the fire in the big cold sitting room of her father's flat with *A Room of One's Own* open but unread on the arm of her chair. It was a short book but was proving very hard to finish.

She was pleased for Rory—of course she was: she hadn't seen him so happy and excited since she had met him. But she couldn't help suspecting that Fenella had an ulterior motive. Perhaps she was one of those women who are constitutionally incapable of releasing old lovers: they want to retain the advantages of the relationship without the romantic drawbacks. Fenella was keeping Rory dangling and she was probably doing the same with the unfortunate but well-connected Julian Dawlish.

She had to face facts, Lydia told herself: one reason she felt unsettled was that if Rory became a regular contributor to magazines like *Berkeley's*, he would no longer have to live at Bleeding Heart Square. The only things that connected them were the accident of their being under the same roof and this disturbing business about Miss Penhow. And it was all so humiliating too—she really didn't want to be so interested in an unemployed journalist who had been to a grammar school and had holes in his socks. She wasn't in love with him—it was simply a morbid fascination that had nothing to do with Rory but everything to do with Marcus.

If she didn't soon find a more effective distraction than Virginia Woolf, she would drown in her own thoughts. There was no one to talk to—she was alone in the house; even Mrs. Renton's room was in darkness. She could hardly swagger into the saloon bar of the Crozier and order a large whisky. Without warning, she had an acute sense of her own isolation and, before she knew what was happening, she felt tears in her eyes.

But she was damned if she was going to wallow in self-pity. She looked around the room, for distraction, for anything that would take her away from her own emotions. Her eyes fell on her father's old writing box, which was still on the shelf on the left of the fireplace. Fimberry had disturbed her when she was looking at it before.

She put the box on the dining-room table and removed the lid with its broken hinges. Inside was the jumble of dried-up inks, stubs of sealing wax, rusty nibs and paper clips, broken pencils and scraps of paper. There was the sheet of foolscap with the list of names—the *same* name: P. M. Penhow, written over and over again—as if someone had been practicing it. On the smaller sheet of paper were the words *I expect you are surprised to hear*. She turned over this second sheet and discovered that there was something else on the back, written faintly in pencil at the top of the page. It was not in the same handwriting but in the clumsy, rather childish version of copperplate that they used to teach in board schools.

and so tell the padre you're sorry for all the upset, that you met an old pal, a sailor who you were going to marry, and you went off and married him, and now you're making a new life in America. We want him to break the news to all and sundry because you're ashamed. A lot depends on this, old man. You won't let me down.

There was no signature. The last page of a letter to America? She had wanted a distraction and now she had found one, she wished she hadn't. She fetched her handbag from her bedroom and emptied its contents onto the table.

An astonishing amount of rubbish had accumulated since she had left Frogmore Place. There were more paper clips, an old matchbox with no matches in it, three bus tickets, a silver three-penny piece, a partly used lipstick that she had forgotten she had owned and at least half a cigarette's worth of tobacco flakes. Finally she found, crumpled into a ball, the note that Serridge had given her with Shires' address and the time of her first appointment with him. She smoothed it out and laid it side by side with the penciled notes from the writing box.

The first was in ink and very short; the second was in pencil and not much longer. The handwriting wasn't very distinctive, in any case—hundreds of thousands of people, perhaps millions, must have been taught to write like that. All she could say with any certainty was that they might have been written by the same person. And that the person might have been Joseph Serridge.

A sense of urgency gripped her. She folded the two sheets of paper and tucked them into her handbag. She piled her own belongings on top of them, and felt happier when they were out of sight and the handbag was closed. She shoveled the rest of the items back in the box and returned it to its shelf.

But closing the handbag and putting the box away didn't obliterate what she had seen: Miss Penhow's name, written over and over again, and that fragment of—what? A letter? An instruction? *A lot depends on this, old man. You won't let me down.*

Like falling dominoes, the thoughts led from one to the next, as if they had been queuing ever since she came here, waiting for this moment. Scraps of Mrs. Alforde's conversation rose up from her memory like unwanted ghosts: "making pen-and-ink sketches of the chimney pieces that Gerry's uncle put in the drawing room and the library"; "forged several checks, falsified the accounts and embezzled the mess funds."

And then there was her father returning from America where Miss Penhow's letter had come from. Now he was living without visible means of support in Miss Penhow's house. Except it was no longer Miss Penhow's house; it was now apparently owned by Joseph Serridge.

"Damn the man," she said aloud. How could her father have been so stupid? If he had forged a letter from Miss Penhow on Serridge's behalf, that must mean one of two things: either Serridge knew that Miss Penhow was dead and he was trying to cover up the fact, or he had no idea where she was and was trying to avoid being accused of her disappearance. Either way, her father was an accessory to whatever Serridge had done, and something was very wrong.

The front door banged. Lydia's pulse began to race. There were heavy and uneven footsteps on the stairs, followed by a tap on the door. When she opened it, she was almost relieved to find Malcolm Fimberry on the landing. At least he wasn't Serridge.

"Mrs. Langstone, good evening. I'm glad to catch you in." It was a cold night but the sweat was running down his face. "I wanted to apologize."

"There's nothing to apologize for."

"Oh but there is." He came up to her and laid his hand on her arm. "I cannot forgive myself for not warning you about the skull."

"It really doesn't matter at all." Lydia brushed his hand away from her arm, casually as though it were a fly. "After all, I'd seen it before."

"Yes, but it must have been such a shock." He snuffled and swallowed noisily. "However, it was such a pleasure to see you there this afternoon. I wonder—would you allow me to show you the chapel itself?"

"Thank you. But I'm—"

"What about tomorrow afternoon? I shall still have the keys after the meeting's over, you see. That would make everything much more convenient."

"I don't think I can manage that."

"Oh, but Mrs. Langstone, it really—"

He stopped as they both heard the rattle of the front door again, followed by a confused fumbling in the hall and the sound of Serridge saying wearily, "God damn it." As soon as he heard his landlord's voice, Fimberry backed rapidly away from Lydia as though he had suddenly realized that she was the bearer of an infectious disease.

There were dragging footsteps in the hall below. Lydia came out of the room and went to the head of the stairs. Serridge was at the bottom, supporting her father.

"Evening, Mrs. Langstone," he said in a flat voice. "I'm afraid the Captain's had one over the eight." He caught sight of Fimberry behind her. "Fimberry, come down and lend a hand, will you? It'll be easier with two of us."

Lydia went into her father's bedroom and straightened the bedclothes. The two men manhandled him upstairs. He was conscious, quite cheerful and rather sleepy.

"On the bed?" Serridge said.

"Yes, please." Lydia edged away from him. "Is he all right?"

"He'll live." Serridge nudged the bedroom door fully open. "Best thing for him now is sleep. If we hold him up, would you pull his coat off?"

Ten minutes later, Lydia was alone with her father. He lay on his back, snoring loudly. She hung up his overcoat and jacket, removed his shoes and covered him with two blankets.

When she had finished, she stared down at him on the single bed beneath the unshaded bulb dangling from the ceiling. He looked very peaceful. If he had been awake and reasonably sober, she would have had to sit down with him and demand an explanation for what she had found in the box. She would have had to argue with him, cajole him, upbraid him and condemn him. Instead she inserted the wooden trees into his shoes—he was particular about maintaining their shape—and slipped them under the bed. Her father's snoring stopped. She looked down at him and saw that his eyes were open. He smiled sweetly at her, and she knew she was smiling back.

"Thank you, my dear," he said.

The eyelids slipped over the eyes like blinds over a window. He began to snore again.

His watch had stopped. But Rory knew it must be later than he had thought. The windows of the house were in darkness. There were still lights downstairs at the Crozier, although the outer door that led to the bars was closed for the night. He paused on the corner by the pump, turning his head to and fro, looking for movement in the shadows and listening for sounds. He was always cautious now when coming back to the square after dark.

Dawlish had taken him to the American Bar at the Savoy, where they had shared a bottle of champagne with a third man who had turned out to be a regular columnist on *Berkeley's*. A decent chap, Dawlish—the better he knew him, the more obvious that was. It made everything more complicated.

Rory walked slowly across the cobbles and let himself into the house. From somewhere above his head came the rhythmic drone of Captain Ingleby-Lewis's snores. He followed the stairs to his own flat. He ought to be feeling tired but he was still wide awake, buoyed up by the excitement of the day and the fact that he now had at least the possibility of a future. Before he went to bed, he would have another go at the shorthand. He pushed the Yale into his door and let himself into the flat. Just as his hand touched the sitting-room switch, he registered the fact that there was an unexpected smell in the air.

The tang of spirits.

He brushed his hand down the switch and the room filled with the harsh glare of electric light. The first thing he saw was Joseph Serridge sitting in his armchair.

"Look here," he said, stumbling over the words, "what are you doing in my flat?"

"That's a question I want to ask you, young man."

Rory glanced around the room. His books were askew. One of the drawers in the chest was half open. His writing case was on the table. Even the cover was off the typewriter.

Serridge felt in his jacket pocket and produced a hip flask. He unscrewed the cap and drank. All the while his eyes remained on Rory's face. He capped the flask and stowed it away.

"What's your dirty little game, Wentwood?"

"I don't understand what you mean."

"Of course you do. You're a reporter."

"Yes. I'm not working, though—as you know I'm looking for a job."

"Balls. Absolute balls."

"But it's not," Rory said feebly.

"Listen, Wentwood—if that's your real name—you wormed yourself into this house. You—"

"I needed somewhere to live," Rory put in. "I'm paying you rent. It's as simple as that. And I wish you'd leave now."

Serridge glared up at him. "And you've been to Rawling. Not once but twice."

"Who told you that?"

"I'm asking the questions. Who are you working for?"

"No one."

"That's not what I've heard. A little bird told me that you went down to Rawling on behalf of a third party."

It couldn't have been Narton, Rory thought feverishly, because he was dead. Mrs. Narton? Rebecca? No, it must have been Gladwyn. According to Lydia, Serridge had been in Rawling yesterday. If the Vicar had come across him, he might well have mentioned Rory's visits.

"So are you doing it for love or money?" Serridge went on. "Or both?"

Rory did not reply.

"Not Fenella Kensley, by any chance?"

Rory sighed. "You know it is. You've been through my papers. May we stop playing games?"

"Me?" Serridge pantomimed surprise. "I don't think I'm playing games. I'm not the one who's been going around under false pretenses and telling lies and making nasty accusations and insinuations."

"All I was trying to establish on behalf of Miss Kensley was where Miss Penhow is. Nothing more, nothing less."

"So you're not a journalist? Instead you're a spy?"

"It's a private matter. It's perfectly reasonable for Miss Kensley to want to know where her aunt is."

Serridge stood up. "I don't know anything about that. All you need to know is I want you out of this flat and out of this house. And I don't want you trying to talk to any of the other lodgers. For instance I don't want to see you pestering Mrs. Langstone any more. Got it? Just leave her alone or you really will regret it."

"You can't really expect me to—"

"Let's say first thing Monday morning, shall we?"

Serridge stretched out his arm and touched the top of a large gold-rimmed vase standing on the mantelpiece. He moved his finger an inch. The vase toppled over, falling to the tiled hearth. It shattered into a dozen fragments.

"Dear me, Mr. Wentwood," Serridge went on in the same level, almost monotonous tone. "Look what you've done. That was one of my mother's favorites too. Rather valuable. I'm afraid I shan't be able to return your deposit. And of course, as you're leaving without notice, that means you forfeit your month's rent in advance. Oh dear, dear."

Rory stared across the table and said nothing. Serridge stared back. He was standing directly under the electric light and the little bald patch on the back of his head gleamed pinkly.

"And a word of advice, young man: that girl of yours is clearly a bit of a nutter. If I were you I'd steer well clear of Miss Kensley. Because what's all the fuss about? Her auntie's in America. Everyone knows that. And remember what I said about Mrs. Langstone."

Serridge left the room. He closed the door gently behind him, which was worse than if he had slammed it. Rory listened to the heavy footsteps descending the stairs. His legs began to tremble. He pulled out a chair and sat at the table. He rested his head in his hands.

Nothing had happened, he told himself, only a broken vase and a few threats. The bad news was that he would have to find somewhere else to live, but that wasn't the end of the world. What was worse was the fact that Serridge had made the connection between him and Fenella. But there was no need to panic, he told himself—the thing to do was to concentrate on tomorrow. He mustn't allow this business with Serridge to distract him from the *Berkeley's* article.

He pulled his notebook toward him and flipped through the last few pages until he found the few lines of shorthand he had managed to write this evening. He stared at the dense mass of gray squiggles. For all the sense they made, they might have been written in ancient Sanskrit or they might be a mass of microscopic animals under a biologist's microscope.

There was another odd thing, Rory thought—the way Serridge

warned him away from Lydia. What did that suggest? That he had lined up Lydia as his next victim?

Rory's eyes traveled from the notebook to the typewriter. Its case was open. He distinctly remembered closing it before he went. He pulled the machine toward him. The light glinted strangely on the bars in the type basket. At least half a dozen of them had been pulled up and bent to one side or the other, so they looked like greasy spikes of hair after a man has scratched his head. He touched a key at random. Nothing happened. The machine was unusable. So how in hell's name was he going to type his piece for *Berkeley's*?

He stared at the twisted bars of metal, and suddenly understood what they represented. Serridge was a man without boundaries. What he did to a machine he would do to a person.

22

YOU HOLD the diary up to your face. Is it your imagination or does it still smell faintly of his cigars? The smell clings to everything. It reminds you of Joseph Serridge, that and the smell of brandy.

Saturday, 19 April 1930

If only dear Jacko could talk. Every morning after breakfast, Joseph lights his first cigar of the day and goes out for what he calls his constitutional. Rain or shine, he takes Jacko for a walk down to the road. Usually the postman has been by then so he collects the letters from the box at the end of the drive and walks back.

What worries me is that the letters are almost always for him. Once or twice there's been a circular or something of that nature for me but nothing from the bank manager in reply to my letter last week and nothing from John. Nothing even from Miss Beale, who I know for a fact makes a point of replying to her letters on the very day she receives them.

I never thought I would feel nostalgic for the dear old Rushmere but I do.

*I'm sure he's got somebody else—he goes up to London
so often and when he comes back, he won't even look at me.
He always sleeps downstairs now.*

*Rebecca leaves today. Oh God. Please God, dear God,
help me. Help me to know what to do.*

That's why you *smell* the diary—to remind you of why you hate the
smell of cigars, the smell of fear.

Unfortunately Lydia was working at Shires and Trimble on Saturday morning. She would have to be particularly careful not to
bump into Marcus or Rex Fisher on her way to and from the
office.

As she was crossing the square, she heard the door opening
again behind her. She looked over her shoulder. Rory was walking
rapidly toward her. He was unshaven and his hair was tousled. He
wasn't even wearing a coat.

"I'm glad I caught you," he said, breathing hard as though he
had been running. "Something happened last night."

"Are you all right?"

"Yes. At present, anyway. When I got back yesterday evening, I
found Serridge waiting in my flat. Just sitting there with the lights
off. He knows why I came here."

"About Fenella?" Lydia felt the familiar twist of an emotion
that couldn't possibly be jealousy.

"Gladwyn must have told him about my going to Rawling. I've
got my marching orders. I have to be out by Monday."

"Where will you go?"

"I haven't the faintest idea."

"Surely he has to give you more notice?"

"He's keeping my deposit, too." Rory swallowed. The cold had made the tip of his nose quite pink. "He—he broke a vase too —deliberately, I mean."

"He's trying to intimidate you."

"He's succeeded. The worst thing is, he wrecked my typewriter—bent the keys—which means I'm not going to be able to type up that piece about the meeting." Rory ran his fingers through his hair. "Still, that's my problem."

"You can't let him get away with that."

"I don't have much choice." He smiled at her. "I don't suppose you've a spare typewriter tucked away, have you? And there was something else—something that affected you. As a sort of Parthian shot, he said he didn't want me pestering you any more. Or else I really would regret it."

"He has absolutely no right to say that sort of thing."

"I don't think right had anything to do with it. Anyway, I hope I—" He broke off and glanced up at the blank windows of the house. "I'll let you get on. We'll talk about it later." He raised a hand in farewell and walked away.

Lydia watched him for a moment. "Rory?" He turned. "If I don't see you beforehand, good luck at the meeting."

"Thanks." A smile spread over his long, sad face. "Thanks, Lydia."

There was the usual Saturday atmosphere of subdued merriment at Shires and Trimble. Mr. Reynolds confided in Mr. Smethwick that he was greatly looking forward to a concert on the wireless in the evening. Mr. Smethwick reciprocated with the information that he had tickets for that new show at the Palladium. Miss Tuffley was going to the pictures as usual and then going to stay overnight with her married sister in Croydon. Everybody, it seemed, had plans except Lydia.

At a quarter to ten, Mr. Shires came in, shaking drops of water from his umbrella and complaining about the weather. "Reynolds," he said as he hung up his hat and his dripping raincoat, "I shall leave at midday today. I don't want to get caught up in the fuss over the road."

"The Fascists, sir?" Reynolds inquired.

"Yes—I dare say there'll be a lot of people milling around beforehand."

"Would you object if I go to the meeting, sir?"

"Not at all. You must tell me what that chap Fisher says." Shires fumbled in his trousers for his keys. "All I know is that whoever is in power there'll always be a need for lawyers. Good news for us, eh, Reynolds?"

"Yes, sir."

"I thought I might pop along too, sir," Smethwick said. "There's free tea and sandwiches."

"Good, good. Can't look a gift horse in the mouth, eh?" Shires bustled over to his door. "When Mr. Reynolds can spare you, Mrs. Langstone, I'd like a word, please."

Five minutes later, Lydia went into the private office. She found Mr. Shires reading *The Times*. He nodded to her to close the door.

"Well? Have you got Mr. Langstone's address for me?"

She gave him an envelope containing the note she had written last night. "He's staying at his club, I gather. I put that address first. Then there's the London house underneath and also Longhope, though I doubt he'll be going down to the country for a few weeks. Lord Cassington's solicitors are Rowsell, Kew and Whiston of Lincoln's Inn. I can't remember the name of the firm the Langstones use but I'll find out."

"They're in London?"

Lydia nodded. "By the way, he'll probably be at the meeting over the road."

"Mixed up with the Fascists, is he?" Shires leaned back in his chair and tapped his teeth with his propelling pencil. "Then I assume you're not going?"

"No."

"Good. I shouldn't advise it. The less contact you have with your husband the better. All in all, it might be wise if you were to leave with me. I'll find an errand for you." He paused for a moment and in that instant transferred her from one category of human being to another, from client to employee. "That will be all, Mrs. Langstone."

Shortly after ten o'clock, a black van with a loudspeaker mounted on the roof drove slowly up Rosington Place. "Come and meet Sir Rex Fisher, the British Union's Deputy Director of Economic Policy, at one o'clock in the Rosington Chapel undercroft hall. Find out what British Fascism offers the British businessman. Join us for a cup of tea or coffee and a sandwich. God save the King!"

At the end of Rosington Place, the van made a three-point turn at the gates and drove slowly back down to the lodge, repeating its message. It spent the morning driving around the vicinity, sometimes nearer, sometimes farther, the announcer's voice growing hoarser and hoarser. Mr. Reynolds went down to the bank on the corner of Rosington Place and returned with the news that the van's route included Clerkenwell, Farringdon Road, Holborn and beyond. He rubbed his hands together in a rare show of excitement. "They must be expecting quite a turnout."

Sitting by the window, Lydia and Miss Tuffley could hardly avoid noticing the activity outside the chapel. There was a disconcertingly domestic air about the proceedings. A plain van arrived. Lydia watched two young women, younger than Miss Tuffley, carrying plates of sandwiches into the cloister at the side of the chapel and flirting with the driver. Two men wheeled out a trolley laden with cups and saucers, but this had to be abandoned because of all the steps. The van with the loudspeaker drove up and down again with a slightly modified message. "The British economy should be for the British people. Your work deserves its reward. Let the British Union show the way at one o'clock in the Rosington Chapel undercroft hall. Free coffee, tea and sandwiches."

"Ooh," said Miss Tuffley. "There they are again. You know, the gents that came to see Father Bertram. You must come and watch. The younger one's in uniform now."

Lydia stood to one side of the window so she could see but not be seen. Fisher's big car had pulled up behind the van. Marcus was on the pavement; his black tunic and peaked cap made him look like a Ruritanian policeman. He was talking to Rex Fisher, who was dressed in a dark suit. A larger van, this one painted black, drew up behind the car. More Blackshirts emerged in an orderly file from the back.

"Why are only some in uniform?" Miss Tuffley asked. "They look much smarter than the chaps in civvies."

"The ones from the van are the Blackshirt Defense Corps," Lydia said.

"So that nice one who was here the other day, the one talking with the other gent, he's their sort of captain, is he?"

"I shouldn't be at all surprised."

Miss Tuffley looked down at the group on the pavement. Slowly the enjoyment ebbed from her face. "You know, it doesn't seem quite right, really. All those uniforms. Makes them look more official than they really are."

"I suppose that's the point. Are you tempted to go?"

Miss Tuffley shook her head. "I went to one of their meetings once. Some of the chaps look all right but they're awfully boring once they start talking."

"Like so many men."

Miss Tuffley squealed with laughter. Mr. Smethwick looked up, clearly wondering whether he was being mocked. Mr. Reynolds clicked his tongue against the roof of his mouth but said nothing.

Lydia lowered her voice. "You don't happen to know if there's a typewriter I could use over the weekend?"

"Here? They wouldn't let you into the office. Mr. Shires is ever so strict because of the files." She wrinkled her nose. "But there's my old machine in the walk-in cupboard on the landing. It's just sitting there gathering dust."

"Would they mind if I borrowed it?"

"You couldn't take it home, dear. Not by yourself. The nasty thing weighs a ton. You'd need about five of them Blackshirts to lift it."

"Could I get into the house?"

Miss Tuffley glanced at Mr. Reynolds, who was hunched over his ledger. She pulled out the drawer underneath the telephone switchboard. Among the scraps of paper and stubs of pencil was a Yale key with a pink ribbon tied to it. She looked at Lydia, making sure she had seen it.

"Perhaps you happened to be looking for a rubber or something and you saw that," she said softly. "Perhaps it happened to fit the street door." She closed the drawer. "But don't come when it's dark if you can help it because Howlett or the caretaker might see the lights, and remember the cleaners get here at seven thirty on Monday. The other offices are the same—there's usually no one here at the weekend."

"What about the cupboard?"

"There's a spare key on the ledge over the door—just run your hand along and you'll feel it. You'll either have to lift the typewriter down to the floor if you can, or stand up and use it on the shelf. Are you really sure you want to be bothered?"

"Yes, quite possibly," Lydia said. "And thank you."

Miss Tuffley put her head on one side. "Well! I must say you're full of surprises."

Mr. Shires was as good as his word. Shortly after midday, he emerged from his room with a large brown envelope in his hand. "Mrs. Langstone, would you take this to the Inner Temple for me? I want you to deliver it by hand and right away. Mr. Reynolds has given you your wages, I take it? Good. In that case you might as well leave now. I don't think there's any point in your coming back to the office afterward."

The errand was genuine, and it was nearly one o'clock by the time Lydia reached Bleeding Heart Square. She avoided Rosington Place and walked round to the Charleston Street entrance by the Crozier. The van with the loudspeaker was still doing its work. "Find out what British Fascism can do for the British businessman. God save the King!"

She let herself into the house. No one was in the hall. She looked through the little pile of letters on the table. There was one for her father. She didn't recognize the handwriting, though it looked faintly familiar, as did the envelope itself. She took it upstairs.

There were voices in the sitting room and she heard her father's hoarse, croaking laugh. The old man had extraordinary powers of recuperation. She pushed open the door. He was standing astride the hearthrug, cigarette in hand—Turkish, judging by the smell in the air—shaved, combed, wearing his one good suit and his regimental tie, and looking every inch like an elderly but well-preserved gentleman with four thousand a year to live on and not a stain on his conscience.

He looked up as Lydia came into the room. "My dear. Ah! There you are!"

"There's a letter for you, Father." She put it on the table.

He dismissed it from his mind with a lordly wave of the cigarette. "Why didn't you tell me you had such a charming sister?"

The back of the sofa had concealed Pamela. She scrambled up and fluttered toward Lydia, arms outstretched. "Darling! You look so frightfully businesslike. Your father says you've been working all morning." She swept Lydia into a soft, perfumed embrace and drew her over to the sofa to sit beside her. "Isn't this nice? Your father and I have been getting along splendidly. We were just saying how strange it is we haven't met before. After all, there's no reason not to, not nowadays, when almost everyone one knows has these complicated families. Anyway, how are you? I must say you're looking wonderfully well. Anyone would think you'd been to a health farm or something."

"And what about you?" Lydia asked. "Is everything all right? How's Mother?"

"Oh you know—much the same as ever. Life just seems to bounce off her like water off a duck's back." Pamela seized Lydia's hand. "I expect you are dying to know why I've come."

Lydia banished the unworthy hope that Pamela had come to ask her out to lunch. "I expect you're going to tell me."

"I'm engaged! Well and truly. Absolutely sign here on the dotted line and then love, honor and obey. It's going to be in the papers next week, but I wanted to tell you first."

"Oh darling," Lydia said. "I hope you'll be very happy."

"Of course we shall." Pamela smiled at Captain Ingleby-Lewis. "And it's only fair you should know before it's announced too—after all, aren't you my stepfather or something?"

He took both her hands in his and stared down at her, just as a proud and happy stepfather or something should do. "I'm sure you'll be very happy, my dear. You certainly deserve to be. And who is the lucky chap?"

"Rex Fisher. He's a friend of Marcus's, actually."

"If you ask me," Captain Ingleby-Lewis said, "this calls for a celebration."

Simultaneously Lydia said, "Rex's here today—at the meeting in Rosington Place."

Pamela glanced up, bright-eyed and as quick as a bird. "Yes, I know."

"What?" Ingleby-Lewis said. "At that Fascist affair? They've had that wretched loudhailer blaring away all morning. Woke me up."

"He's the main speaker, actually. Rex is their Deputy Director of Economic thingummy."

"I remember. Saw the name on the posters. Isn't he a bart?"

"Yes." Pamela stubbed out her cigarette. "And it's just as well he's not a viscount or something because then I'd take precedence over Mother, which would absolutely infuriate her."

"Are you going to the meeting?" Lydia asked.

"No—Tony Ruispidge is home on leave and I promised Sophie I'd have lunch with them. To be honest, it's not really my thing."

Somewhere a clock struck the half-hour.

"Good Lord," Ingleby-Lewis said. "Is that the time? I'm afraid I shall have to dash. Got an appointment."

"It's been lovely to meet you," Pamela said, holding out her hand.

"My dear, the pleasure has been all mine. And I hope I shall be able to renew the pleasure very shortly. Goodbye, Miss Cassington."

"You must call me Pammy. Everyone else does."

"Pammy then. I'm not sure what you should call me. Uncle William, perhaps." He took her hand and raised it to his lips. "Or plain, homely William, even? Until we meet again."

He swept his overcoat off its hook, seized his letter from the table, set his hat on his head at a jaunty angle, and left the room. They listened to his footsteps going downstairs. The front door slammed.

"I am so, so sorry," Lydia said.

Pamela patted her hand. "You don't need to be. He's a pet."

"No, he's not. He's an awful man. He sponges off everyone, he's an old soak, and he's my father."

"All I can say is that he was very nice to me."

"He can put on an act for five minutes but that's all it is. An act. He's probably hoping you'll persuade Mother to ask him to the wedding so he can get sozzled on Fin's champagne." Lydia was suddenly aware that tears were rolling down her cheeks. "Oh damn and blast it."

Pamela, nothing if not practical, opened her handbag and produced a freshly ironed handkerchief smelling of musk and flowers, Jean Patou's Sublime. Lydia dabbed her eyes. Pamela kept hold of Lydia with one hand and opened the platinum cigarette case with the other.

"There, that's better. Try one of these. I'm not sure I like them very much but they're meant to be frightfully good. Rex has a little man who makes them up for him."

Automatically Lydia took a cigarette. "To be fair, he's given me a home." She remembered yesterday evening, when she had settled him down for the night. "And he can be very sweet sometimes."

Pamela clicked her lighter and Lydia bent her head over the flame.

"You know Marcus is at the meeting too?"

Lydia inhaled and sat back nodding. "I saw him this morning."

"Did he see you?"

"No. Thank God."

"You're very bitter," Pamela said gently.

"There's a good reason for that. In fact there are several."

"Do you want to tell me?"

Lydia shook her head. "Another time perhaps. Are you really sure about Rex?"

"I know you don't like him, but yes, I am. We understand each other, you see. I know what he wants and he knows what I want."

"If it doesn't work out, you can always come and share my room here."

Pamela giggled. "That would be lovely. We could become chorus girls or something. And we'd have rich protectors, awfully vulgar but with hearts of gold, and they'd simply dote on us." Without warning, which was characteristic of her, she changed the subject. "So you'll have seen Marcus in his uniform? He looks frightfully dashing. I say, he's convinced you've got a boyfriend. Is it true? Do tell—I won't breathe a word. Why didn't you tell me?"

"Because it's not true."

"You're going pink on your cheekbones, darling. That always means you're lying. You're a dark horse, I must say. Anyway, I don't want to know. Or rather I do but there's no immediate hurry. The thing is, Marcus *thinks* you have. He got some of his toughs to warn him off. Did you know they call them the Biff Boys because they go around biffing people? It makes them sound like some dreadful music hall act but really it's not very nice, is it? I heard Marcus telling Rex they were interrupted and he's going to get them to finish biffing up the boyfriend if there's another chance. That's why I thought I'd better pop in. Not that I didn't want to in any case."

"So it was Marcus. I thought it probably was."

"Ah—so there *is* someone."

"No, there isn't. Anyway, what gave him the idea?"

"Apparently your father told him that somebody had been hanging round you in a rather objectionable way."

"But if anyone fits that description, it's poor Mr. Fimberry. Not—not the one who was attacked."

"So you've got two? How super."

"I haven't even got one. Mr. Fimberry's a bit tiresome but there's no harm in him. He certainly doesn't deserve to be beaten up. His nerves are all to pieces."

"That won't help him if Marcus gets hold of him. So you're saying Marcus has got the wrong one?"

"I keep telling you, there isn't one to get," Lydia snapped. "And yes, he has got the wrong one. If I did have one, I mean. Oh damn. Typical bloody Marcus."

"All I can say, darling, you'd better tip the wink to your young man who isn't your young man. If he's planning to be at the meeting, he should watch out. The Biff Boys are jolly good at keeping order, you know. When they've roughed him up to their satisfaction, they'll probably pop a knuckleduster in his waistcoat pocket and claim he's a communist agitator. But he's not going to the meeting, is he?"

"Oh yes, he is," Lydia said. "He'll probably be sitting in the front row taking notes."

"They look like Girl Guides," Fenella said. "Only bigger and blacker."

She and Julian were standing in the cloister by the doorway into the undercroft. Rory was a couple of yards behind them. They had a view of the line of trestle tables running parallel to the west wall of the undercroft. The tables had been covered with white cloths. They were laden with crockery, urns, teapots and food— sandwiches, a great vat of soup and plates of biscuits. Between the tables and the wall were half a dozen women Blackshirts repelling those members of the audience who wanted to start their lunch without delay.

"You can tell they were all very good at knots and helping Mother," Fenella said.

"I wish you'd go home," Julian said. "I'm sure Wentwood agrees. This is really no place for a woman."

"Stop fussing, Julian, and don't be so old-fashioned. Look at all those Blackshirt girls. They've come along—why shouldn't I? You're not really saying that women shouldn't get mixed up in politics, I hope?"

"Of course I'm not."

"I think Dawlish is right, actually," Rory murmured. "About your being here, I mean."

Fenella glared impartially at them. "I'm not leaving. That's flat. I think you're both being most unreasonable. Besides, you shouldn't be seen talking to us, Rory. Go away."

Dawlish opened his mouth but said nothing. For the first time in their acquaintance, Rory felt a stab of sympathy for the man. Where Fenella was concerned, the poor devil really had it bad.

"Can we meet afterward?" Rory said. "There are some things I need to tell you—not just about the meeting."

Dawlish nodded. "Shall we say the American Bar again? Five thirty, all being well?"

"Fine," Rory said, though it wasn't, because if he got there before Julian, or if Julian failed to turn up, he might have to pay for a drink, which at the Savoy's prices would probably wipe out most of his budget for December. Besides, Julian had paid for the champagne last night so really Rory couldn't get out of paying. And then there was the tip: he had no idea how much one left in a place like that.

"Good man," Dawlish said. "Good luck."

"Wait a minute," Fenella said. "Why don't we meet at the flat instead? It's nearer and more private."

Dawlish shrugged. "All right. Are you happy with that?"

Rory nodded, feeling simultaneously relieved and humiliated; he suspected that Fenella had guessed what he was thinking.

"If we're not there, the spare key's in the coal hole opposite the area door," Dawlish went on. "There's a tin of whitewash on the floor. It's underneath that."

They separated, Julian and Fenella waiting in the cloister, and Rory going down into the undercroft. A couple of uniformed Fascists were manning the door and stood aside to let him pass, their faces impassive. A very pretty girl, also in Fascist uniform, smiled at him as he passed the tables and said, "Lunch in the interval, sir. Sir Rex is going to open the proceedings first."

The undercroft was already filling up. As he walked down the center aisle beside the line of posts, Rory tried to make a rough headcount: he estimated that there were chairs and benches for at least three hundred people, as well as some standing room at the back. Perhaps two thirds of the seats had already been taken. He found a chair near the front at the end of a row.

Nobody was on the platform. A microphone had been set up on the table. A man who could throw his voice wouldn't really need a public address system here. But Rory remembered the political meetings he had attended in India, and how an amplified voice had power over those that were not amplified. You had to hand it to the Fascists—they knew how to organize a meeting.

Two tall Blackshirts marched down the center aisle holding what Rory assumed to be poles. Behind them came a third, who was even taller. It was Marcus Langstone. The three men climbed onto the stage. Not just poles, Rory thought—flagstaffs. They set up the two flags in a cast-iron stand behind the central chair. On the left was the British Union's symbol; on the right was the Union Jack.

Fimberry bustled through the crowd, rubbing his hands together and smiling at no one in particular. He caught sight of Rory. "Hello, Wentwood!" he said in a high, slightly tremulous voice. "Already taking notes, I see."

Rory nodded. Langstone turned around. His eyes swept from Fimberry to Rory at the end of his row. Rory bent his head over

his notepad and pretended to write. Sweat pricked along his hair-
line.

No time to think, which was probably just as well. Lydia came
through the wicket from Bleeding Heart Square and almost immediately turned right into the little forecourt in front of the chapel. The door to the cloister was ajar. She pushed it open.

Soft, gray light filtered through the line of windows on the
left-hand side. Two tall men were standing near the door to the
undercroft. Nobody else was in sight. She walked rapidly along
the cloister, her heels tapping on the flags.

The men straightened up. They were standing either side of the
steps leading down to the undercroft door, which was closed. Their
black tunics made them look sinister but the first thing Lydia noticed was how young they were. One of them had plump, pink
cheeks and pale, straight hair like straw. He looked as if he belonged in a ploughboy's smock. The other was smaller and darker,
with bow legs and a wizened face like a monkey's.

"Good afternoon," Lydia said. "I presume this is where the
meeting is?"

"Sorry, madam," said the smaller Blackshirt. "You can't go in at
present."

"Why ever not?"

"Sir Rex's speaking. If you care to wait for the interval—"

"I don't care to wait at all." Lydia threw back her head and
thought: *How would Mother handle this?* "Do you know who I am,
young man?"

"Madam, my orders are—"

"Mr. Langstone is my husband," Lydia said imperiously, raising her voice and hearing it resonating down the corridor, bounc-
ing off the stones. "And Sir Rex is a close personal friend. Please
open that door immediately, or I shall have to take your names."

It was the ploughboy who wilted first. Then the monkey said,

"All right, madam. But you will be as quiet as possible, won't you?"

"I don't think I need your advice on how to behave," Lydia said. "Do you?"

The smaller man lifted the latch of the door with infinite care and pushed it open. Lydia went down the steps. Rex Fisher's amplified voice swept out to meet her.

"Dozens of you men here today will have fought in the war, as did many members of the British Union. Neither we nor you have forgotten the lessons we learned in those dark days when we stood shoulder to shoulder together against the foe."

The door closed behind her. Lydia paused for a moment on the last step. The undercroft was full of people. She took in the tables on the left, the crowd standing at the back, the packed seats in the body of the undercroft and the dais at the end.

Five chairs behind the table on the platform were now occupied. Marcus was on the far left. Sir Rex was in the middle. He was on his feet, with his hands planted on the table. His eyes traveled around the hall, capturing his audience. She hoped he hadn't seen her.

"And what have we seen since the war?" he was saying. "I will tell you the sad and shameful truth. We have seen a succession of fumbling and inconsistent British governments composed of old men who learned their trade, in so far as they learned anything at all, when Queen Victoria was on the throne. Under their bungling direction, we have seen this country's influence gradually diminish in the world. We have seen great cracks opening up in our empire; and our empire should be not only our greatest glory but also our greatest safeguard, both politically and economically. It is no coincidence that at the same time Britain's economy has plunged further and further into gloom. We have seen the country paralyzed by a general strike fomented by foreign agitators. Our economy has been blighted by a depression that was entirely avoidable. Yes, I emphasize that word—avoidable."

By now Lydia had mingled with the crowd. She had turned up the collar of her coat and she wore a scarf over her head. It was a pity there were not more women here. She couldn't help but stand out.

Fisher paused. "However, one politician has been neither fumbling nor inconsistent. One politician has come forward to offer clear and effective leadership. As early as February 1930, the British Union's leader, Sir Oswald Mosley, who was then in the government as Chancellor of the Duchy of Lancaster, produced a memorandum for his colleagues. It outlined a comprehensive policy which, had the government had the guts to adopt it, would have reversed this downward trend and brought the country to unparalleled levels of prosperity. We must protect our home markets, Sir Oswald said—and the only way to do that, both then and now, is by the introduction of tariffs to regulate trade. We must control the banks to promote investment. Nor can we allow agriculture to languish, Sir Oswald pointed out, because we shall always need to feed ourselves. The government must create jobs with road-building and other projects that will in time have the further benefit of enabling our economy to function more efficiently than ever. And what of our industries? We cannot do without them. Yet they are still run on piecemeal nineteenth-century principles. The government must give a firm lead. That, after all, is what governments are for."

Lydia sheltered behind a tall man in a black overcoat and hat.

"Our great industries," Fisher continued, "because of this lack of direction, have failed to take account of the changes in science and technology so they can no longer compete effectively with the industries of countries that have modernized more quickly and more effectively. The solution is in our own hands. The British Empire is the greatest empire the world has ever seen. We have the means of production; we have the raw materials; we have the expertise; we have the dogged determination and courage—and of course we have the markets as well. This country and its empire can and should stand alone. That is where our future economic prosperity must lie."

Lydia glanced around her. Unfortunately she couldn't see Rory. But she accidentally caught the eye of Mr. Smethwick, standing near the tea urns, who immediately looked away.

"Since the war," Fisher was now saying, "one government after another has led us deeper and deeper into the mire by promoting the import of foreign goods. They have allowed the big City financiers to feather their own nests by making loans to foreign countries, thereby damaging British manufacturing and British agriculture. As Sir Oswald has said, and I quote, 'These are alien hands which too long have held their strangle grip on the life of this country and dominate not only the Conservative Party but the Socialist Party as well.' There's one thing you can trust the British Union to do when we come to power: we shall not allow aliens"—he paused, laying stress on the last word—"to dictate economic policy for selfish reasons of their own."

There was a spattering of applause among the audience. The tall man in front of Lydia muttered something under his breath and stirred as though he wanted to scratch.

"Fascism can provide the answers. Not Fascism as it flourishes in Germany or in Italy—but a truly British Fascism adapted to our native genius. A Fascist government will be a strong government. But it will be first and foremost a British government presided over by His Majesty the King."

"What about Parliament?" a voice cried somewhere near the front of the hall.

"I'm glad you mentioned that, sir," Fisher said urbanely. "All governments work with Parliament, and we shall be no exception. However, under our system government departments will consult the various economic influences, whether employers, workers or consumers, and then determine what is best suited to the country as a whole. We shall set targets for output, wages, prices and profits within each industry. It is the only way to develop a coordinated and fully efficient economy. Parliament will play an important role in this, and so of course will the monarch.

I cannot emphasize enough that Fascists are, above all, loyal subjects of the Crown."

"What about the Jews then?" somebody else shouted.

Fisher ignored this. "We were talking of the war a moment ago.
We live not only under the shadow of the last war, but under the
shadow of a future war, into which our present government may
lead us through its blundering and inadequate policies. The British Union of Fascists has a domestic program that does not depend
on preparing for war. Our foreign policy is based on the maintenance of peace."

There was more applause, this time louder and more prolonged.

"Make no mistake, with a Fascist government, this country will
be stronger and more formidable than ever on the world stage.
But we will be an international force for peace. We know too well,
as you do, the folly of war. We know too that prosperity depends on
the maintenance of peace. In the second half of this meeting I
propose to deal in more detail with how the British Union intends
to regulate the distributive trade by coordinating competition
and controlling what is sold and by whom, through a distributive
trades corporation that would issue licenses, a system that would
prevent both the growth of too many suppliers of a particular sort
of goods in any one area, and also the unhealthy dominance of
large retailers. We shall insist too, as part of the terms of the li-
censing, that retail outlets deal in British goods. Alien combines
will be closed down and their retailing operations will be redis-
tributed to private traders or cooperatives. Moreover, a coopera-
tive central buying organization would allow small shopkeepers
to take advantage of low wholesale prices through bulk purchases.
It would also provide a safety net in the event of bankruptcy."

This led to more applause and even a few scattered hurrahs. A
man at the back of the hall called out, "But what about the Jews?"

"British Fascism is the only British political party that takes a
firm, clear line on aliens," announced Fisher's calm, patrician
voice. "Britain should be for the British."

"You're just like the Nazis, are you?" shouted the tall man in front of Lydia. "Is that what you mean?"

At that moment, in the silence that followed the question, Lydia realized that the man in front of her was Mr. Goldman from Hatton Garden.

"We have no quarrel with those of Jewish blood per se," Fisher said.

"Your Mr. Joyce says, and these are his very words: 'I don't regard the Jews as a class, I regard them as a privileged misfortune.' That was in January. Your Mosley says that Fascism has accepted the challenge of Jewry. What challenge?"

"Thank you, sir. The British Union requires the Jews, as we require everyone else, to put the interests of Britain first."

"And your Mr. A. K. Chesterton said—"

"That will be all, thank you," Fisher said. "You seem to have forgotten that I am addressing this meeting, sir. It's time for you to return to Jerusalem. See the gentleman out, please."

An eddy rippled through the standing crowd as three Blackshirts pushed their way toward Mr. Goldman.

"Answer the question, sir," somebody else shouted. "What challenge do the Jews pose? Are you aware that—"

"I'm aware that another gentleman would like to leave," Fisher said. "To return to the matter in hand—"

"Do you realize that in Germany—"

The question ended in a gasp, as if someone had hit the questioner. At least a dozen people were shouting now and fighting was breaking out sporadically throughout the audience. Lydia watched in a daze as Fisher beckoned to a young man at the end of the platform and murmured something in his ear.

The Blackshirts reached Mr. Goldman. Two of them grabbed him by the arms. The third man put his head in an armlock.

Lydia snapped out of her trance. "You stop that!" she shouted, and kicked the man as hard as she could in his calf.

He looked at her, open-mouthed in astonishment. "Here," he said, not relaxing the armlock, "you can't do that."

"Why not?" Lydia asked, and kicked him in the other leg.

The Blackshirts began to drag Goldman toward the door to the cloister. Suddenly the public address system burst into life. "Pomp and Circumstance March No. 1" boomed through the undercroft. Marcus was advancing into the audience with a couple of Black-shirts behind him. He pointed to his right. Lydia followed his finger and saw Rory, notebook in hand, in the act of standing up.

Behind her, one of the urns toppled off its table and somebody shouted, "Watch out! The water's bloody boiling!" The table itself went over with a clatter, and crockery smashed on the stone floor. "Pomp and Circumstance" pursued its stately course, a serene and triumphal counterpoint to the racket.

They hauled Goldman onto the short flight of steps up to the cloister. He lost his hat and his overcoat was ripped down the back. Three respectable-looking middle-aged men, none of them in Blackshirt uniform, shouted in unison, "Jew out, Jew out." They looked like a trio of tobacconists or ironmongers on an outing, determined to extract the utmost fun from the occasion.

A large blond man in ridiculously wide Oxford bags took a swing at one of the Blackshirts manhandling Mr. Goldman. The blow missed and the Blackshirt punched his attacker in the mouth, knocking off his glasses. The man reeled back, a hand to his mouth and blood seeping through his fingers.

"Jew out, Jew out."

A small woman slipped under the blond man's arm and punched the advancing Blackshirt in the testicles. He screamed and dou-bled up. The scream was high and loud and so like an animal's that it shocked everyone except Elgar into a moment's silence.

Lydia felt a momentary but painful twinge of jealousy. The woman was Fenella Kensley.

The noise began again. Mr. Goldman's attendant Blackshirts

turned aside to deal with the blond man, Fenella and a couple of other men who had come to their support. Taking advantage of their absence, Lydia ran across to Mr. Goldman and helped him to his feet. He groaned and swayed.

"Quick," she urged. "We've got to get out."

Linked together, they staggered down the cloister. The blond man ran after them, and took Mr. Goldman's other arm. Fenella followed them. Mr. Goldman was flagging badly. At the door to the chapel forecourt, Lydia glanced back over her shoulder. Marcus had come up the steps from the undercroft. He saw her: his face was white and twisted, a stranger's.

"The house over the road," Lydia snapped. "I've got a key."

They half-dragged, half-carried Mr. Goldman between Fisher's car and the black van, both of which were empty and unguarded, over the road to the doorway of number forty-eight. Lydia dug into the pocket of her coat and pulled out the latchkey. Her hand was shaking so much that she couldn't get it in the lock at her first attempt. The second attempt succeeded. The door opened into the high, musty hallway, with the dark linoleum stretching away to the stairs.

"Quick!" Fenella said in her ear. "I can hear them running."

Lydia and the blond man, Fenella and Mr. Goldman almost tumbled into the house. Lydia closed the door behind them and rammed the top bolt home. Mr. Goldman was gasping for breath.

"Damned barbarians," the blond man said. "Are you all right, sir?"

Lydia ignored them. She knelt and opened the flap of the letter box. This gave her a narrow, rectangular view across the road to the chapel. At the far right of the rectangle was the left-hand leaf of the double gates to Bleeding Heart Square. To her horror, she saw Serridge standing in the angle between the gate and the pillar supporting it. He was smoking a cigar and staring placidly down the length of Rosington Place.

They had a witness.

Marcus burst into view, followed by three Blackshirts. They hesitated for an instant on the forecourt. Marcus walked into the road and looked up and down. He saw Serridge.

"I say!" he shouted. "You there! Which way did they go?"

Serridge unhurriedly removed his cigar. "Who are you talking about?"

"Two women and two men. You must have seen them."

Serridge pointed the cigar down Rosington Place toward Holborn Circus and the thin, fussy tower of St. Andrew's beyond.

"But we'd still see them if they'd gone that way."

"No, they went down past the lodge and turned right." Serridge turned his head to his left. "Ain't that right?"

Another man came into view—Howlett, stately in his uniform frock coat, with Nipper at his heels. He touched the brim of his top hat to Marcus. He looked every inch the loyal servant. But whose servant, Lydia wondered, and why?

"That's right, sir," Howlett said. "Went down there like bats out of hell. As if the devil himself was after them."

23

YOU ARE HAUNTED by the ghosts of what might have happened. If Philippa Penhow had had the sense to run away to the village. If she had hammered on Mr. Gladwyn's door. If she'd run into the Alforde Arms. If she'd stumbled across the muddy fields to Mavering.

Sunday, 20 April 1930

I think he's looking for this diary. He was searching my things this morning. Someone—it must have been him, unless it was one of the maids—prised open my little writing box where I used to keep the diary. They forced the lock. I didn't dare say anything.

Rebecca went away last night. Amy's getting worse. At breakfast, she was positively insolent when I asked for fresh tea. I'm sure she's wearing lipstick too. Joseph told me to stop fussing. He said I was only making the girl nervous. But she's a nasty baggage.

I said to Joseph at lunchtime that they must think us strange in the village because we hadn't gone to church. He said, not at all—he had told the Vicar I wasn't well, that

I'd had a breakdown and couldn't stand meeting people or crowds, and that was the real reason we'd come to live in the country.

So I see it all now. He's made them think I'm a madwoman. And he's made them think that he's a saint, looking after me. I wish I hadn't signed all those papers. "Another one for your autograph, my darling."

So you see she couldn't go to the village or anywhere else because of the shame of it. She believed they already thought her a lunatic. And she and Serridge weren't married. Either way she would have faced ridicule and censure, either way she would be ruined. At the back of her mind was the bitter knowledge that she didn't know what she'd signed over to him during the last few weeks.

Most of all, you believe, she stayed at Morthams because in some small and tender place in her heart there still lived a sickly hope that this was really a bad dream, and that soon her Joseph would change back to the man she knew he really was. Perhaps this was some sort of test, and all she need do was endure. Perhaps she could make him love her, as she did him. She would tear out her heart for him if it would make him happy.

The smell of cats was stronger. The cold seeped from the flagstones and oozed out of the walls. He sat on the table, his back against the rough, whitewashed wall.

It was not entirely dark. As his eyes adjusted, Rory made out a faint rectangle at the other end of the room, which must mark the door. On the other side of the door was the cloister and the fading, gray light of a winter afternoon. But very little sound penetrated the thick walls or the heavy door. It was as if he was entombed. The loudest sound was his own breathing. He was very cold—he had left his hat and his raincoat in the undercroft.

They had taken his notebook, presumably during the fracas. In his mind, he went over the sequence of events, trying to memorize them. He was damned if he was going to let them prevent him from writing this article. First, there had been an interruption to Fisher's speech—the tall old man who looked Jewish, though presumably not orthodox or else he wouldn't have been here on the Sabbath. Then the scrap, when the Blackshirts waded in to remove him. Then Lydia was mixed up with it and then Fenella and Dawlish.

Why the hell had Lydia been there? Surely she wanted to avoid her husband?

When the row started, Rory had stood up without thinking, drawn partly by a journalist's instinct to move toward trouble rather than away from it, and partly to help Lydia. But the Blackshirts were already on him.

The timing was important. It suggested they must have been told to keep an eye on him, presumably by Marcus. Told to pounce when there was trouble in the audience, told to extract him neatly and swiftly as though he were a troublesome tooth, and they were a pair of pincers. He gave them full marks for efficiency. They had frogmarched him out of the undercroft. One of them kept his hand clamped over Rory's mouth. They had been so extraordinarily polite and unemotional about the whole thing.

"Excuse me, sir, would you let us through? Gentleman needs a breath of air."

Everyone must have known that he was being ejected, Rory thought, but his escorts contrived to do it in such a way that many of the bystanders would have assumed the fault was his, not the Fascists'.

More Blackshirts had been milling around in the cloister, mainly at the far end, near the door to the street. His escorts hadn't waited for orders and they hadn't tried to turf him out. That must be significant as well. They had simply wheeled him round to the right and down into the Ossuary, where they kicked his legs from underneath him and forced him down to the floor.

Rory had forced himself not to cry out, not because he was brave but because he thought if he did he might attract more violence. Mercifully they seemed to lose interest in him: closed the door gently and turned the key in the lock. Darkness fell like a stone. The light switch was outside the door.

When they left him alone, he had stood up and swept his hands over the walls, exploring the Ossuary by sense of touch. All it contained was the table. The chairs had gone. He hooked his hands under one side and lifted. It rose a couple of inches, and then the weight was too much for him. He considered trying to wedge the door with it, but remembered that the door opened outward, toward the steps down from the cloister.

Sooner or later, he told himself, someone would come. This will end. Everything ends. He shied away from the thought that whatever replaced this might be worse. Time passed. At one point he thought he heard distant music on the edge of his range of hearing. Perhaps the meeting was over, and they were playing the National Anthem. The theory was confirmed when he heard the rumble of voices and footsteps, a whole tide of them, in the cloister. All those clerks and commercial travelers and office boys were going home to the suburbs for the weekend. He would have given anything to be one of them. He hammered on the door and shouted, trying to attract their attention.

No one came. Had Fenella and Lydia and Dawlish got away safely? It was quite possible that they didn't realize what had happened to him. It might be hours until he was missed—at the very earliest, not until he failed to turn up at Mecklenburgh Square at half past five.

Everything was now quiet outside. Time trickled slowly away. Rory's mind wandered. He saw sand dribbling through rows of hourglasses, then the hands sweeping round an infinity of dials, all the clocks and watches of London measuring out his life.

At last, the key turned in the lock, the sound jolting him painfully back into his own chilly and uncomfortable body. The door opened, and blinding light streamed into the Ossuary. In the heart of the light was a shimmering shadow.

"They've gone back inside," Lydia said.

"All of them?" said the large, untidy stranger.

"As far as I can see. Serridge and Howlett are still by the gate."

"Barbarians," Mr. Goldman muttered behind her. His face was gray and he was breathing hard.

"Are you all right?" Lydia asked.

He nodded. "Just out of breath. And angry."

"Have you far to go?"

"I have a flat over the shop."

"I say," the other man said, blinking at her. "We should introduce ourselves. My name's Dawlish, Julian Dawlish. This is Miss Kensley."

"How do you do?" Lydia said automatically. "This is Mr. Goldman, who has a shop in Hatton Garden. My name's Lydia Langstone."

"Are you related—" Dawlish began.

Simultaneously Fenella Kensley spoke for the first time: "We've met, haven't we? On Remembrance Sunday in Trafalgar Square."

"That's right. You were with Mr. Wentwood."

"Yes."

"He's in there now, you know," Lydia said. "Did you see him?" Fenella nodded.

"I think they may be after him."

"Because he's a journalist?"

"Not just that," Lydia said. "There's—there's something else as well."

"Mrs. Langstone," Dawlish said, "forgive me for asking, but it's not a common name . . ." His voice trailed away before he had actually asked anything.

"Marcus Langstone is my husband," Lydia said evenly. "I've left him."

"Oh. I'm sorry. I didn't mean to pry, but in the circumstances . . ."

"It really doesn't matter." She bent down and opened the letter box again. "I can't see anyone outside the chapel. And there's no sign of Serridge and Howlett now. If I were you I'd leave while you can."

"Yes," Dawlish said. "Mrs. Langstone, I can't thank you enough." He added, stiffly and absurdly, "We mustn't take up any more of your time."

To her surprise, Lydia realized, she felt quite calm. "We had better leave together but then split up. Perhaps Mr. Goldman and I should go through the gates to the square and you and Miss Kensley out by the lodge."

Dawlish nodded. He was peering at the noticeboard listing the house's tenants. Fenella tugged at his sleeve like a child trying to attract her parent's attention.

"Julian, come on. I don't like it here. Please."

Instantly he was all concern, inquiring solicitously about how she was feeling while blaming himself for being insensitive. Lydia looked at her more closely. Fenella was trembling slightly and her face was gray.

"The thing is," Dawlish said, "what about Wentwood?"

"There's not a lot we can do," Fenella said. "Let's face it, they can't really *hurt* him. Anyway, they don't know he's a journalist, and perhaps they'll leave him alone. You'd think they'd have chucked him out already if they were going to."

Dawlish looked from one woman to the other. "Perhaps we should—"

"Can we go? *Please*, Julian."

"The sooner we leave the better," Lydia said, turning away so neither Fenella nor Dawlish would see the anger in her face. "I'll tell Mr. Wentwood what's happened, if you like."

They slipped outside. Rosington Place was deserted. Fenella, clutching at Dawlish's arm, almost dragged him away. He turned and waved to Lydia. She and Mr. Goldman went through the wicket gate into Bleeding Heart Square.

"I can manage by myself now," he said, scowling at her. "Thank you for your help, Mrs. Langstone." He stalked off, leaving Lydia staring after him.

"Mr. Goldman?" she called. "Are you all right?"

He paused by the pump and looked at her. "No, I'm not, Mrs. Langstone. How can I be? I'm frightened."

He raised his hat in farewell and a moment later was out of sight. It was only as Lydia was letting herself into the house that she realized what he had meant. He was not frightened of the uniformed thugs in the undercroft. He was not even frightened for himself. He was frightened of what the uniformed thugs stood for. He was frightened on behalf of all those people who stood in their way. He was frightened of the future.

Slowly the light faded from the afternoon. Lydia sat at the table in her father's flat and looked down at Bleeding Heart Square, at the wicket gate to Rosington Place and at the wall of the chapel beyond. Reckless of expense, she had turned up the gas fire as far as it would go and fed the meter with shillings. Her father was still out. Among the butts in the ashtray beside her were a couple from Pamela's cigarettes. The room felt empty without her.

At last the meeting in the undercroft came to an end. Most of the audience walked down Rosington Place toward Holborn. A trickle came through the wicket into the square, among them Mr. Byrne from the Crozier and one of the mechanics from the workshop at the other end of the square. Mr. Fimberry hurried after them.

But there was no sign of Rory. Lydia didn't want to feel solicitous about him but it seemed she had no choice. *Bloody Fenella didn't give a damn about him.* Anyway, she needed to tell him about the typewriter.

Ten more minutes passed at a funereal rate. There was still no trace of him. She went downstairs and tapped on Mr. Fimberry's door. There were shuffling footsteps in the room. The door opened a crack.

"Mrs. Langstone!" The eyes blinked behind the pince-nez. "What—what can I do for you?"

"Do you know where Mr. Wentwood is?"

"No." Fimberry was in his shirtsleeves. "I've no idea, I'm afraid."

"Was he still at the meeting when you left?"

"Oh no. He left just after you did. Were you all right? I was quite worried."

"Never better, thank you. When you say Mr. Wentwood left, what do you mean exactly?"

"A couple of the Blackshirts escorted him out. I didn't see quite what was happening but I'm afraid he upset them." He peered at Lydia. "In fact I assumed you had all gone together—you and he and those other people."

"No. We got away."

"I—ah—I expect he will turn up." Fimberry swallowed. "They—they were rather rough, weren't they?"

"They behaved like animals," Lydia snapped. "Do you have your set of keys?"

"Eh? Oh—you mean for the chapel? Of course. I shall go in later and make sure everything's shipshape."

"So the Fascists were still there when you left?"

"They were tidying up. They do a very neat job, I must say, un-like some."

"Will you come over there with me?"

"Now?"

"Yes—with your keys." She spoke slowly, as though to a child. "You've a perfect right to be there. After all you're representing Father Bertram. And you need to make sure everything's safe and sound."

"But what about you, Mrs. Langstone? If your husband—"

"That's my affair, thank you."

Mr. Fimberry wilted under her gaze. To her horror, Lydia saw that the eyes behind the pince-nez were swimming with tears.

"I'm sorry," he said. The door began to close. "Really I am. But I'm not a brave man. Physically I—I suppose I'm a bit of a coward." He was trembling now. "I'm so sorry. I've seen too much. I've seen what's under the skin, you see, all the flesh and bone. It was the war, Mrs. Langstone. I was very different before the war."

Shades of dark gray became blinding white. Rory screwed up his eyes against the glare from the lightbulb dangling from the vaulted ceiling. Iron scraped on stone. He slid off the table and stood up. The door opened. Slow footsteps approached.

Three men faced him: two Blackshirts and, standing in the doorway with his back to the cloister, the dapper figure of Sir Rex Fisher.

"Good—not damaged," Fisher said to the two Blackshirts, addressing them with a certain formality as if he stood on a lecturer's podium. "Force should always be proportionate." He abandoned his lecturer's manner and approached Rory, limping slightly. Lips pursed, he stared at him. There was something both fastidious and contemplative about his gaze: he might have been at Christie's, examining a picture which had little obvious merit and which he did not want to buy. He glanced over his shoulder. "And what were your instructions exactly?"

"Mr. Langstone—"

Fisher hissed, a tiny sign of displeasure.

The man recovered swiftly. "This chap was pointed out to us before the meeting began as a likely troublemaker. Believed to be a communist agitator, sir. If there was any sort of trouble, we was to nab him and put him in here. As you see." There was a hint of truculence in the man's voice. "Nipping trouble in the bud, that's what we was told."

"Has he been searched?"

"Not yet, sir."

Fisher's neatly plucked eyebrows rose. He turned back to Rory. "And what is your name?"

"Roderick Wentwood."

"Address?"

No point in concealing it: they would find out soon enough if they searched him. But would Fisher know that Lydia Langstone was living under the same roof?

"Seven, Bleeding Heart Square."

"And why are you here, Mr. Wentwood?"

Rory rubbed his cheek where a bruise was coming up. "As an interested member of the public, Sir Rex. Finding out what British Fascism has to offer the British businessman." He leaned back against the table, hoping to conceal the fact that his legs were trembling. "I want to leave now."

Fisher's face was unsmiling but not hostile. "I'm sure. But I don't think you should leave, Mr. Wentwood. Not just yet. It might be rather amusing to find out what you had to say about us first."

"I don't understand what you mean."

"Of course you do." Fisher removed Rory's notebook from the pocket of his own overcoat. "I understand you were writing in this before you felt obliged to join the rowdy elements in the audience and try to disrupt the meeting." He flipped through the pages. "I don't read shorthand myself. But many of my colleagues do. And I see that you have thoughtfully written some words *en clair*, as it were. *Berkeley's*, for example. I wonder whether that might be the weekly magazine? Rather strange you didn't think to mention that you're a journalist."

The door leading to the cellar was open. Lydia heard Serridge's voice below, and Howlett replying to something he had said. They were moving furniture around down there. Serridge intended to sell the better pieces.

She tapped again on Mr. Fimberry's door, which he had shut in her face five minutes earlier. She heard scuffling on the other side.

"Who is it?"

She did not reply. She waited, her body tense, just outside the door. The men's voices continued in the cellar, backward and forward like a long rally in a tennis match. It was all nonsense about women being gossips, she thought—men were just as bad.

There was stealthy movement in Fimberry's room. Almost simultaneously Lydia heard the clatter of claws on the cellar stairs. Nipper appeared at the end of the hall.

The key turned in the lock. The door began to open. Nipper yapped and launched himself down the hall. Lydia flung her weight against the door and pushed her leg into the gap between it and the jamb. Fimberry's pink, sweating face appeared, only inches away from hers.

"Please go away, Mrs. Langstone."

She pushed harder. "If I scream, Mr. Serridge will hear me."

Fimberry stood back. The door swung open, banging against the edge of his washstand. Nipper shot through the gap. Lydia followed. The dog ran round the room, sniffing vigorously.

"Please, Mrs. Langstone," Fimberry whimpered, "please leave."

"Serridge and Howlett are in the cellar," Lydia said firmly. "In a moment or two, I'm going to go and see them. I'm going to tell Mr. Serridge that I saw you buying offal at Smithfield. That I saw you buying *hearts*. Do you understand what I'm saying, Mr. Fimberry? If necessary I will also say I've seen you posting them."

"But, Mrs. Langstone, I didn't. You *know* that's untrue. You know—"

"I don't care what is true or untrue," Lydia interrupted, magnificent in her ruthlessness. "The only way you can stop me is by letting me borrow the chapel keys for five minutes."

"I've already explained—"

"And I've explained what will happen if you don't let me have them. You don't have to come with me."

Nipper sniffed Fimberry's ankles. Fimberry edged away from him, his eyes still fixed on Lydia's face.

"Oh, and by the way," Lydia added, deciding that she might as well be hanged for a sheep as for a lamb, "I shall also tell Mr. Serridge that you tried to kiss me."

Fimberry backed over to the bed, sat down and put his head in his hands. For a moment she felt a terrible urge to comfort him.

"Please, Mrs. Langstone. Please."

"None of this need happen," Lydia said gently. "Not if you're sensible. Where are the keys?"

"In the top drawer. On the left."

She knew she had broken him. She felt ashamed. She opened the drawer and took out the keys. "Which is which?"

"The small modern one is the door into the cloisters from the road. The Yale keys are for the storeroom and the vestry." His voice was muffled because his head was still in his hands. "The others, the big iron ones, they fit the Ossuary, the undercroft and the chapel itself."

Lydia glanced round the room. His overcoat was on the back of the door. She lifted it off and dropped the keys in the left-hand pocket.

"I'm going to leave your overcoat on one of the hooks in the hall. Then I shall take the keys from your pocket. So if anyone asks, you're in the clear. You happened to leave your coat in the hall, and the keys happened to be in the pocket. And somebody happened to come along and take them. But nothing is going to go wrong, is it? No one's going to ask you anything."

He raised his face to her. His eyes were puffy. "Mrs. Langstone, it's already gone wrong."

Nipper followed her out of the room and ran down the hall toward the door to the cellar, toward the sound of footsteps on the stairs. Hurriedly she took out the keys, dropped them in her own pocket and hung up the overcoat. The door on the other side of the hall opened a crack. Mrs. Renton looked out.

"That dratted dog again," she said to Lydia. "I wish he wouldn't bring it in the house."

She shut the door. Serridge came into the hall, followed by Howlett.

"Ah—Mrs. Langstone." Serridge's heavy features rearranged themselves into a smile that was the next best thing to avuncular. "And how did you enjoy the meeting this afternoon?"

She stared at him. He was probably unaware that she had seen him, and therefore he did not realize that she knew he had sent Marcus and his Blackshirts on a wild-goose chase for her sake. "I found it very interesting, thank you, Mr. Serridge. But I had to leave halfway through."

"They certainly had a good turnout, ma'am," Mr. Howlett said, bending to scratch Nipper. "Mind you, I don't know how much use it all is. The world goes on turning, whatever we try and do about it."

"They get some rough types there, though," Serridge went on. "I hope you're all right."

Lydia nodded, smiling like an idiot, and said goodbye. Nipper tried to follow her outside. She shut the front door in his face, remembering as she did so the little dog Rory had seen in the photograph of a naked Amy Narton astride a bicycle. That was the reality, she thought, not this amiable old chap like Father Christmas in mufti: Serridge was a middle-aged man who had a taste for vulnerable girls without any clothes on, and preyed on elderly spinsters with more money than sense.

And if Nipper's the same dog, does Howlett know where he came from? Are we all Serridge's creatures in this house? Or his victims?

She ran across Bleeding Heart Square.

Marcus Langstone was alone, and that was something Rory had not been expecting. Langstone was cautious, though: he switched on the light, opened the door and then stood back.

Fisher and his men had left perhaps twenty minutes earlier. Langstone looked at Rory leaning against the wall near the table at the far end of the Ossuary. Rory felt sick in the pit of his stomach. But there was relief of a sort that the waiting was over.

Langstone slipped a bunch of keys into his pocket. A short rubber cosh was looped over his right wrist, swinging like a pendulum in a clock case. He was a big man, Rory thought, not just tall but surprisingly broad. His face looked so misleadingly wholesome—the pink and white complexion, the fair hair, the baby-blue eyes.

The cosh swung to and fro. Langstone didn't speak. There was an element of calculation in all this. Rory felt an extra spurt of fear which mysteriously converted itself into something like anger. The man was being so bloody childish. This was how bullies behaved in the school changing room or the corner of the playground. Standing there in his uniform he looked more than ever like a sinister Boy Scout, his emotional and intellectual development doomed to remain forever somewhere between thirteen and fourteen years old.

"I hope you've come to let me out," Rory said. "And an apology would be nice too."

Marcus actually raised an eyebrow—a single eyebrow, just as though he were a villain in an old-fashioned melodrama. He thwacked the cosh against the palm of his left hand. "I don't think so."

"You can't really think it's a good idea to go around treating members of the public like this. Surely it's bad for business?"

"You're not a member of the public. You're a dirty little journalist and a lying cheat."

"For all you know I could be a dirty little journalist who supports Fascist principles."

Langstone shrugged. The black shirt and dark trousers flattered his figure but there was a distinct thickening around his middle. "In my book, all journalists are dirty," he said. "It's not a job for a gentleman, is it? But you'd be dirty whatever you were. And that's why I'm going to teach you a lesson." He walked slowly toward Rory. "I've known about you for a long time. You live in Bleeding Heart Square. You've got the room on the ground floor on the left of the front door."

"You're mistaken," Rory said. "I—"

"You can't lie your way out of this. I've seen you there." He added with an air of triumph, "You even admitted it to my colleague."

Rory swallowed. "You've done more than see me, haven't you? The other weekend—that was you, wasn't it?"

Langstone smiled. "My people. Not me."

"Your tame Biff Boys?"

"You wouldn't have been able to get up off the ground if it had been me."

"And how are you going to explain this? You can't hope to get away with what you're doing."

"Why not?" Marcus had stopped about three feet away from Rory. "Unfortunately we've had a great deal of trouble with left-wing agitators at our meetings. Communists, Jews, foreigners, people who have the morality of the gutter. They bring all sorts of weapons and try and stir up trouble. Bicycle chains, knuckledusters, knives—you name it, they've got it."

"Whereas you go in for rubber coshes?"

"My mechanic advised me to buy one of these. Know what they call them, Mr. Wentwood? The motorist's friend."

"It's an offensive weapon."

"Defensive, please. We have to do our best to cope with this wicked violence, don't we? For the sake of the public, for the sake of democracy. We Fascists stand for free speech and free debate. We can't let you people interfere with that. It just wouldn't be right, would it? And of course you end up getting hurt. I'm about to act in self-defense, in case you were wondering, and later on there will be witnesses to confirm it. They will also confirm that you were armed." He smiled. "In point of fact I'm looking ahead: there aren't any witnesses just at present. So you can squeal as loudly as you like."

"That's the trouble with you lot," Rory said. "You start off thinking the end justifies the means. And then you don't bother justifying anything at all. You just do what you bloody want."

The last word came out like a bullet on a rush of air as Rory kicked Marcus's left kneecap. Marcus shouted and lunged forward, his face contorted, and brought the cosh down in an overarm blow. Rory ducked to the left and the cosh hit him like a brick on his right arm, just below the shoulder.

An instant later, Marcus's left fist caught him full on the mouth. Driven backward, Rory fell against the table, the corner jabbing into the soft flesh between his rib cage and thigh. Marcus lashed out with his boots, aiming for Rory's crotch.

Rory squirmed. A toe cap thudded into his leg. Cold stone grated like sandpaper against his cheek. He curled himself up and tried to roll away from the kicks. He collided with a table leg. His mouth filled with liquid. He spat, and saw a fine red spray in front of his face. His left ankle exploded with a pain like an overwhelming flash of electricity. He screamed and wriggled farther under the table, scrabbling to escape the kicks and blows. He pushed himself into the corner where the two walls met.

Stone on two sides. All that solid mahogany above. There was an instant of calm, unutterably sweet.

Langstone's breathing changed tempo. The table trembled. Rory stared between Langstone's legs, thick and as solid as an elephant's, at the half-open door to the cloister. The table grated on the floor. The bastard was trying to drag it away from the wall. Automatically Rory threw his weight against the table leg behind him.

There was a grunt. Then the side of the table nearer the door began to rise. Langstone was lifting it up. Rory's hands scrabbled for purchase.

And he touched something.

Something that wasn't made of stone or mahogany. He laid his hand over it. Something dry, angular and hard, equipped with extraordinary jagged edges, ridges, holes and protuberances. This part here, he thought, which was almost straight, was like the teeth of a saw blade.

Like teeth.

Fimberry's skull. The goat's head that had come in the post for

Mr. Serridge, which Fimberry, governed by some strange sense of propriety, had deposited in the Ossuary, the place of the bones.

The table reared up and went over on its side with a thump that seemed to shake the foundations of the chapel. As it rose, Rory uncoiled his body and launched himself like an exploding jack-in-the-box at Langstone. Langstone gave ground, lifting the cosh as he did so.

Rory rammed the goat's skull into Langstone's face. The points of the two horns dug into the sockets of his eyes, tearing into soft tissue, jarring on bone.

Langstone shouted. He reeled back, slapping his hands over his face. Rory curled his right hand round one of the horns, raised the skull again and this time brought it down in a sweeping backhand arc. The other horn snapped on impact. Jagged fragments of bone raked through the skin of Marcus's cheek and ripped into the flesh beneath. Something pattered on the flagstones, like a flurry of sleet.

Goat's teeth?

Rory ran for the door. There was no one in the cloister. The electric lights were on and the windows were black mirrors. He stumbled over the uneven floor, pain shooting up his left leg from the ankle Langstone had hit with the cosh. He was only halfway down the cloister when he heard footsteps, boot heels slamming against the stones.

He glanced back. Langstone's face was a blur of blood, with a single eye and white flashes of teeth. Rory staggered on. From behind him came a laugh.

"It's locked," Langstone said.

Rory looked over his shoulder again. Langstone was swinging the cosh, breathing hard in a series of rhythmic snarls, blood trickling down his face and bubbling beneath his nostrils.

He heard another sound: metal moving on metal, a key turning in a lock.

The door to the outside world swung open. A current of cool air flowed through the cloister. Lydia Langstone was standing on the threshold. Her eyes widened when she saw him.

Rory gaped at her, his mouth open. "Run," he whispered. "Run."

She stepped closer to him, reached up and grabbed his tie. She yanked it as if it were a lead and he a reluctant dog. He plunged through the doorway and sprawled in a huddle of bruised limbs on the forecourt. He was still holding the remains of the goat's skull.

As if from a great distance he heard the sound of the key turning in the lock of the door.

For the second time that afternoon, Lydia hurriedly unlocked the door of 48 Rosington Place and pushed it open. She retrieved Rory, who was holding on to the railing beside the door and swaying gently, and towed him into the hall. She shut the door and slipped both bolts across. She turned to look at him.

He had propped himself against the wall; his eyes were closed and he was breathing fast and noisily through his mouth. He had a split lip and perhaps he had lost a tooth or two. Blood trickled over his chin and there were drops of it drying on his tie, his collar and shirt. Just below the left eye, the cheek glowed an angry red. She wondered what had happened to his raincoat and cap.

Lydia stooped and opened the letter flap. No one was within her range of vision. There was just enough light to see that Fimberry's keys were where she had left them, in the lock of the door to the cloister, preventing Marcus from unlocking the door from the inside. Marcus would have to find another way out or somehow raise the alarm—though in that case he might face awkward questions.

She stood up and looked again at Rory. His eyes were open now. He tried to say something but his words mingled with blood and spittle and emerged as an indistinguishable mumble.

"There's a lavatory with a basin at the end of the hall," Lydia said.

He tried his weight on his left leg, and winced. "Ankle," he said.

She knelt down in front of him and rolled up the trouser cuff. He grunted as she eased down the sock and probed the ankle with her fingers. She lifted the leg and moved the foot to and fro and from side to side.

"I think it's a sprain or bruising," she said, hoping she was right. "You'll have to lean on me and sort of hop if necessary."

"Second time," he muttered.

"What?" As she spoke, she realized he was trying to smile.

"Second time you've done this."

Come to the rescue? She smiled. "We mustn't let it become a habit."

"I don't know." He paused, gathering energy. "You're rather good at it."

With her supporting him, he hobbled down the hall. He paused at the newel post to draw breath. She was surprised how heavy the weight of his arm over her shoulders became, and surprised at the racket they made in the silent house. He smelled of tobacco and faintly of mothballs, as though his clothes had been hanging too long in a wardrobe somewhere, as perhaps they had. The tweed of his sports jacket felt rough and stiff; off-the-peg stuff.

Once again they moved forward like a wounded crab, his arm still draped over her shoulders.

"Are you all right?" he said, his voice much clearer now.

"It's you I'm worried about."

"I didn't mean to—"

"Save your breath."

Rory was flagging badly. Step by step, they struggled onward. Lydia kicked open the lavatory door. She maneuvered him inside, lowered the cover over the pan, and sat him down. His breathing began to quieten. She turned on the Ascot and filled the basin with hot water. There were two damp hand towels on the rail. She used one as a flannel to bathe his face. The water in the basin turned a darker and darker shade of pink. He kept his eyes closed, and she examined the blue veins on the lids. It occurred to her

with a little jolt of surprise that this was the first time in her life
that she had ever washed anyone other than herself.

"How does your mouth feel?" she asked.

The eyes flickered open. "Like a battlefield."

"Have you lost any teeth?"

"I don't think so." He ran his tongue around the inside of his
mouth. "One's chipped."

"You're going to have some bruising on your face. I'm not sure
what to do about the ankle. Assuming it's a sprain, we take off the
shoe, bandage it up and raise it on a stool or something. The trouble is—"

"No bandage, no stool," he said. "Also, if I take the shoe off I'm
not sure I'm going to get it on again. Where are we? Is this where
you work?"

"Shires and Trimble are two floors up. I think I'm going to have to
get help. You can't walk out of here. You'll need a taxi. The problem is
we don't want to get you out while Marcus might still be around."

He nodded. "And I'd better not go back to the flat."

"The others were going to Mecklenburgh Square."

"I know," he said absently. Then he looked sharply at her. "But
you were with them, weren't you—Fenella and Dawlish? And that
old chap who stood up and started shouting."

"Mr. Goldman. He's a jeweler in Hatton Garden."

"What happened?"

"We hid in here. The Biff Boys thought we'd had time to get
away." She didn't mention Serridge, and how he and Howlett had
lied to save them. It was an odd circumstance; it needed more
thought.

"I think they planned to get me from the start," Rory said. "As
soon as the row started at the back of the hall, a couple of them
near the front made a beeline."

"I was afraid of that."

He glanced up at her, and his eyes were bright with intelligence.
"Is that why you came? To warn me?"

"My sister told me Marcus was after you."

"I thought you wanted to avoid your husband."

She tried to ignore the embarrassment she felt. Rory was fiddling with a patch of grazed skin on his knuckles; perhaps he was embarrassed too. For a moment neither of them spoke.

At last he lifted his head. "Thank you. He arranged the attack outside the house the other night too." He hesitated. "A case of mistaken identity."

"I don't understand."

"I gathered from something your husband let slip that he thought I'd been—pestering you. He thought I was Fimberry."

"Poor Mr. Fimberry," Lydia said automatically. "But why?"

"He must have seen me in Fimberry's room when I was helping Mrs. Renton with the curtains. Has he always been like that? So—so possessive?"

"Yes." Lydia thought of the shocked and bloody face of the amorous subaltern at the hunt ball and Marcus's smirk when he threw the boy out of the house in front of Lydia and the servants. Desperate to change the subject, she said, "The other reason I wanted to see you was because of the typewriter." She was talking too quickly, and he was looking puzzled. "That's why I've got the key to this house. There's a cupboard on the landing upstairs outside our office, with an old typewriter inside. If you needed to use one over the weekend for your article, I thought you could use that. I know where they keep the key."

Rory stared at her as though seeing her for the first time. "You're very kind," he said slowly. "Thank you. But listen—there's something I need to tell you. I'm worried about your husband. He attacked me with a cosh."

"You're safe here."

"No—I'm worried about *him*. I had to fight back however I could. I used the goat's skull as a weapon. What happened to it?"

"It's still outside the chapel as far as I know. You dropped it. So you actually *attacked* him with it?"

"I jabbed it in his face. I may have poked it in his eye. Possibly both eyes."

"He didn't seem too badly damaged," Lydia said. "Judging by the way he was coming after you."

"I've never gone for anyone like that. Do you understand? It was like sinking down to their level. I—I didn't feel quite human anymore."

Lydia bit back the retort that Marcus had often had that effect on her too. "If it's any consolation, I doubt Marcus is worrying about the damage he did to you. What Marcus does has to be right. That's article one of his personal code."

He was staring at her. "You're a strange mixture."

"What you're thinking is that I'm bitter," she said. "I know it's not a very endearing trait but believe me that's what living with Marcus does to you."

At that moment it struck her that this was the strangest conversation to be having at this time and place, and with a man like Rory Wentwood. But she didn't care anymore, not about that sort of thing. She felt that she had earned the right to speak her mind. She thanked Marcus for that at least.

She turned away from Rory and examined her face in the mirror over the basin. After the events of the last few hours, she was surprised how respectable she looked. A trifle pale and a trifle shabby, she thought, but you could take me almost anywhere. Aloud she said, "I'd better go and tell Mr. Dawlish and Miss Kensley where you are. What's the house number in Mecklenburgh Square?"

"Fifty-three. You'll probably have to go down to the area door."

It was a relief to be dealing with practicalities again. Lydia warned Rory about the danger of showing a light. She gave him a cigarette and left him smoking it forlornly on the lavatory.

At the front door, she knelt to look through the letter box. The street lamp on the other side of the road was already alight. The muddy golden aura around the bulb holder was streaked with rain, and the roadway glistened with moisture. No one was about.

She let herself out of the house and ran over to the wicket gate in Bleeding Heart Square. On the way, a puddle caught her unawares, soaking her shoes and ankles. In the square there were lights in the windows of her father's sitting room and of the two ground-floor rooms—Mrs. Renton's and Mr. Fimberry's. As she approached the door of number seven, Mrs. Renton's curtain twitched.

Upstairs, the sitting-room door was ajar, and she heard her father's voice. He had a visitor. *Marcus?* She slipped across the landing and into her bedroom, where she opened the wardrobe as quietly as possible. She changed her stockings and shoes, found her umbrella and tiptoed back toward the stairs.

The sitting-room door opened.

"Lydia, my dear," Captain Ingleby-Lewis said. "There's someone else to see you. We're having quite a day, aren't we?"

The heartiness in his voice made her instantly suspicious. *Marcus? Please God, not now, not ever.* Her father's articulation was clearer than it usually was at this time of day, which suggested that he hadn't had as much to drink as usual.

"Mrs. Alforde dropped in. Come along."

Reluctantly, she allowed herself to be drawn into the room. Mrs. Alforde was sitting in the armchair near the fire, bolt upright, prim and respectable, still wearing her hat.

"There you are." She held up her cheek, inviting a respectful kiss. "And how are you?"

Lydia said she was very well but unfortunately she had to go out on an urgent errand. While she was speaking, she remembered the letter for her father this morning. So that was why the envelope and the handwriting had seemed familiar: the letter had been from Mrs. Alforde. In other words, there had been nothing accidental about this visit; it was by appointment. But what reason had Mrs. Alforde to get in touch with her father?

"Now, sit down, dear," Mrs. Alforde said firmly, as though addressing a recalcitrant retriever. "I know you're in a hurry but this won't take a moment."

"I really can't stay long." The oddities were adding up in her mind: the letter to her father, the cheek offered for a kiss, Mrs. Alforde's abstracted, even unfriendly behavior on the drive back from Rawling the other afternoon.

"Captain Ingleby-Lewis has been very worried," Mrs. Alforde said serenely. "He came to see me this afternoon and we put our heads together."

"The thing is, old girl," Ingleby-Lewis began, patting Lydia's arm, "one has to think of what's right and proper, eh? A woman's reputation is above rubies. Isn't that what they say?"

Mrs. Alforde quelled him with a glance. "The point is, dear, the Captain's very worried about your staying here. He feels quite rightly that it's not a suitable neighborhood for a lady."

"I'm not going back to Marcus," Lydia said. "My solicitor will be contacting him on Monday about a divorce."

Mrs. Alforde's eyes widened. "You don't let the grass grow under your feet. Neither Captain Ingleby-Lewis nor I are saying that you should go back to your husband, even though let's not rule out the possibility that perhaps in the long run you yourself may feel—"

"If I'm sure of one thing," Lydia interrupted, "it's that I'm not going back to Marcus. Ever. I thought I'd made that clear. And why."

She stared at Mrs. Alforde until the older woman looked away.

"Seems a nice enough chap to me," her father said. "Mind you, I'm not married to him, so I suppose I can't say." He smiled approvingly at Lydia. "You must do as you please. I like a girl who paddles her own canoe."

"William," Mrs. Alforde said quietly but with unmistakable menace. "Would you mind if I finished, as we discussed?"

"Of course not. Mustn't let my tongue run away with me, eh?"

"We are agreed that your living here is simply out of the question," Mrs. Alforde went on, with a hint of regality attached to her choice of personal pronoun. "But we accept that you don't want to go back to your husband. However, there is a simple solution. You must come and stay with Gerry and me while this tiresome legal business is sorted out. There's a perfectly good spare bedroom at the flat. It would be so much more—more comfortable for you. It's not as if we're strangers. After all, Gerry is your godfather and a sort of cousin too so it's quite suitable."

"But I'm living with my father," Lydia said. "Surely that's even more suitable?"

Mrs. Alforde stared at Captain Ingleby-Lewis, who sat up sharply, as though she had prodded him with a stick.

"My dear Lydia, Hermione—Mrs. Alforde—is quite in the right of it, I'm afraid. Much as I like having you here, it's not really ideal for either of us." He ran his finger around his collar. "I'm sorry, my dear—it's all agreed: you have to go."

Lydia stood up.

"What are you doing?" Mrs. Alforde asked.

"I'm going out," Lydia said. "I'm not sure when I'll be back."

24

Now you know what it was like for Philippa Penhow. Now you know the real price that had to be paid.

Wednesday, 23 April 1930

Shakespeare's birthday. I was quite sure that today would be the day. Yet here I am, sitting on a fallen tree trunk on the footpath at the bottom of the meadow.

Scribbling & crying & it's raining.

This morning I gave Joseph a skirt for alteration to take to Mrs. Renton when he was next in Town, so he'd think everything was normal. But then a telegram came for him & he went out, saying he wasn't sure when he'd be back & leaving the skirt behind. Lunch was late, & Amy brought bread & cheese in though I had ordered lamb cutlets & I'm sure I smelled them grilling. Amy said the master had eaten them last night. I KNOW that's a lie.

After lunch she carried the mirror from the spare bedroom up the attic stairs. When I asked her what she thought she was doing, she said the master told her that she could take it. I know what she's up to. She wants to try on the finery he's given her & prance up & down in front of the mirror & admire herself.

I felt so angry I didn't need to be brave. I put on my hat & coat, put my purse into my pocket & set off without giving myself time to think. I marched down to the barn & collected this diary. I walked across the meadow (not caring about the mud) & set off on the footpath to Mavering. I know the path gets there eventually—I remember Rebecca talking about it.

But it has begun to rain, one of those violent April showers. I've a nasty blister on my left foot. I am sheltering under a tree. I took out my purse to count my money. I know I had thirty shillings in notes, as well as some change.

But the notes & the silver have gone. All that is left is a handful of coppers—certainly not enough for the rail fare. That wicked, wicked girl has pilfered my money. I shall have to . . .

You close the book. You don't want to turn the page.

The lavatory was not entirely dark because there was a light shining in the yard between number forty-eight and the house that backed on to it. Rory had found a stub of pencil in his jacket pocket and a couple of creased envelopes in his wallet. He tore an envelope apart and laid it on the windowsill. A faint, diffused light penetrated the frosted glass. He could hardly read the words he wrote.

Not that it mattered. He scribbled faster and faster. He forgot about writing for *Berkeley's*. He forgot about editors and readers and his hope of future commissions. The only thing that counted was the need to get the words on the paper.

> *I have been working in India for five years, and found myself on my return in an unfamiliar political landscape. When I went to a small British Union of Fascists meeting on Saturday afternoon, I had few preconceptions and no political axe to grind. When I left the meeting less than an hour later, dragged out by a pair of Blackshirts, the arguments against Fascism were beginning to impress me. After the Blackshirts had imprisoned me, after they had beaten me and threatened to frame me as an armed trouble-maker, the force of those arguments had become overwhelming. I suppose I should be grateful to the British Union of Fascists. I may not know much else about modern British politics but I am now able to say, with utter and absolute certainty, that I am anti-Fascist.*
>
> *Sir Rex Fisher, the British Union's Deputy Director of Economic Policy, was the principal speaker. His purpose was to—*

A key turned in the front door. There were voices in the hall. Rory pushed the envelopes into his pocket and stood up, his weight on one foot like a stork. When the hall lights snapped on, his first thought was that it must be the Biff Boys or the caretaker. But he heard Lydia calling his name and relaxed.

She had brought with her both Julian Dawlish and a taxi driver. The latter, an undersized man with an elderly bowler hat squashed on his head, ran an experienced eye over Rory and said, "Been in the wars, have we?"

"Hurry," Lydia said. "Howlett may see the lights."

The driver and Dawlish helped Rory along the hall and into the back of the taxi waiting in Rosington Place. Lydia and Dawlish squeezed in beside him. The sky had filled with the dim, un earthly radiance of a London dusk. The rain was falling steadily.

Dawlish looked out of the window toward the chapel. "There's someone over there."

"It's all right—it's Mr. Fimberry." Lydia wriggled in her seat.

Dawlish rapped on the partition with his knuckles. "Drive on," he mouthed to the cabby.

"He's picking something up," Lydia said, puzzled.

As the taxi drew away from the curb, Rory glanced out of the window at the forlorn figure of Malcolm Fimberry on the chapel forecourt. "At least he's rescued something from the wreckage."

"What is it?" Dawlish asked.

Rory was still watching Fimberry, bareheaded in the rain. He was cradling something. "It's his skull," Rory said. "What's left of it."

Fenella was waiting for them at Mecklenburgh Square. The four of them sat in the front room of the basement and drank strong, sweet tea flavored with whisky.

"I'm so sorry, Wentwood," Dawlish said. "I had no idea this would happen. I assumed they wouldn't have the slightest idea who you were."

"Somebody made a mistake," Rory said. "Nobody's fault."

"On the contrary," Lydia said. "It was my husband's mistake and his fault too. With the full support of that ghastly organization he belongs to. What on earth do they think they're playing at?"

Nobody answered.

Rory lit a cigarette. It was painful to smoke because his lips were swollen and split. "Is there a typewriter I can use?"

"I can lend you one," Dawlish said.

"Serridge wrecked mine," Rory explained. "Incidentally, he wants me out of the flat by Monday."

"Why?" Fenella asked.

"He thinks I'm a spy." He glanced at her, uncertain how she would react. "He thinks I've been ferreting around after Miss Penhow."

Dawlish frowned. "Who are these people?"

"It's a long story." Rory patted his jacket pocket. "I made a start on the article while Lydia was fetching you." He had used her Christian name without thinking, and he registered the fact that Fenella had noticed it. He didn't care. The whisky was beginning to work on him, its effect accelerated by tiredness and shock. He felt light-headed and rashly omnipotent. "I'm afraid it's going to be rather personal in tone. In fact it's one long scream of outrage."

"Where will you go when you leave your flat?" Dawlish asked.

"I don't know."

"I expect you could stay here for a week or two. While you find your feet."

Fenella sucked in her breath and said nothing.

Rory glanced at her. "That would be very kind but really I couldn't—"

"Why ever not? We've got all this space here. I don't think the attics have been used for generations."

"Won't the owner mind?" Fenella said. "Shouldn't we ask him first?"

Dawlish rubbed a coil of ash into his corduroy trousers. He had lost his glasses during the fight in the undercroft, which made him look naked and unprotected. "As a matter of fact I'm the owner."

Rory had a beguiling vision of a world where wealth made everything possible: where you had houses at your disposal, and obliging taxi drivers, and full bottles of whisky when you wanted to entertain your friends. In his half-tipsy condition, he was ready to feel jealous of Dawlish. He glanced across the room at the man and saw that he was looking at Fenella; and for a moment there was something so vulnerable and woebegone about his face that Rory stopped feeling jealous.

He said, as much to change the subject as to receive an answer, "I say, I wonder if I could ask you to read my draft when I've finished it—just to make sure I'm not wildly off the mark."

"Of course," Dawlish said. "But I shouldn't worry too much. You were there. It will work because of that." He waved the hand holding his mug of whisky and tea; Rory realized that Dawlish too was well on the way to being tipsy. "An eyewitness account. The ring of authenticity. It's not something you can fake."

There was a moment's silence. Fenella stirred, as if about to say something. But it was Lydia who spoke first.

"Yes, of course," she said slowly.

"Of course what?" Fenella asked in a rather unfriendly voice.

Lydia smiled at her. "The ring of authenticity. As Mr. Dawlish said, you can't fake it. You know, if you don't mind, I think I should go home now."

Dawlish said he would fetch a taxi. Lydia said she preferred to walk. Dawlish pointed out that it was still raining and repeated the offer; then, working out that Lydia was trying to save money, he recalled that his brother's Lagonda was parked at the back and that he had promised his brother he would turn the engine over at least once a day; so, truly, it would be doing him a favor if Lydia allowed him to run her back to Bleeding Heart Square. While he was there, he could pick up anything Rory needed for the night.

While Dawlish was bringing the Lagonda round to the front of the house, Fenella and Lydia went into the little hall where the coats hung on a row of hooks. Rory watched the two women through the open door. His tea had been replaced with a glass of whisky. He felt at peace with the world, and the sensation was all the more enjoyable because he knew it would be short-lived.

A car horn sounded outside. Lydia belted up her coat and waved to Rory. Fenella returned to the sitting room and helped herself to a cigarette from Dawlish's case, which was on the mantelpiece. She knelt in front of the electric fire which stood on the hearth. Her mood had changed again, he thought—her eyes were gleaming with excitement.

"Do you mind?" Rory asked.

"Mind what?"

"My staying here for a while."

She turned the full force of her smile on him. "Of course not, silly. Anyway, it's not my house. Even if I move in while you're here, you'll be in the attic and I'll be down here. We'll probably hardly see each other." She turned away and tapped ash from the cigarette. She confused him by adding quietly, "Though of course I hope we do."

From the doorway of number seven Lydia watched the tail-lights of the Lagonda disappearing into the narrow passage between Bleeding Heart Square and Charleston Street. The Crozier was packed because it was a Saturday night. Captain Ingleby-Lewis would be in the saloon bar.

She shut the front door. In the hall she hesitated, then she tapped on Mr. Fimberry's door.

"Who is it?"

"Mrs. Langstone."

There were no words and no movements on the other side of the door but she sensed he was standing there, very close to her, listening.

"Mr. Fimberry, I've come to apologize." She raised her voice a little. "Won't you open the door and let me do it face to face?"

"No," he said.

"I'm sorry about the keys," Lydia said, feeling foolish about talking to a door. "It was urgent or else I wouldn't have done it. One of the Fascists was trying to hurt Mr. Wentwood."

Fimberry grunted. "Looked more like the other way round to me. I saw the poor chap he attacked. Wentwood's a maniac."

"Were you able to get your keys back?"

"Yes."

"And the skull?"

"Yes. One of the horns was broken, and most of the teeth have gone."

"I'm sorry about that. Is—is everything all right now?"

"Of course it's not." Fimberry's voice grew louder as his sense of outrage swelled. "How can it be? It's a terrible world. All that blood. All that nastiness." His voice was even louder now, almost a scream. "Go away, please, Mrs. Langstone."

"Perhaps we can talk in the morning," Lydia suggested. She waited a moment but there was no reply. She wished the door goodnight.

As she turned to go upstairs, she realized that she was not alone in the hall. Mrs. Renton was standing in the doorway of her room. She could have heard the whole conversation.

"Mr. Serridge says that Mr. Wentwood is moving out," Mrs. Renton said, mumbling because her teeth were out.

"On Monday, I believe."

The little eyes considered her. "He didn't last long."

"No," Lydia agreed. "By the way, have there been any more parcels lately for Mr. Serridge?"

"Not that I know of."

"I was wondering, you see," Lydia went on. "Do you think the hearts and the skull came from the same person?"

"You'd think so, wouldn't you?"

"Yes," Lydia said. "You would. But should you?"

"What will you do with Miss Penhow's skirt?"

"I'll wrap it up and send it to Miss Kensley. Her niece."

She smiled at Mrs. Renton and went upstairs. She turned on the fire in the sitting room and drew the curtains. She had been very stupid, she thought.

She went into the bedroom and took out the skirt and the two sheets of brown paper, its inner and outer wrapping. She picked up the lighter-colored sheet of the two, the outer wrapping, and went into the kitchen. There was another piece of brown paper in the drawer. The color of the two sheets matched. In the sitting room she unfolded both of these sheets and placed them side by side on the sitting-room table. Each had three straight edges. Each had an irregular fourth edge that looked as if it had been cut by someone in a hurry with a pair of blunt scissors. She lined up the two irregular edges. They fit perfectly together.

An eyewitness account. The ring of authenticity. It's not something you can fake.

Somewhere here was the key to the whole mystery. The problem was, she didn't want to be the one to unlock it. She had enough troubles of her own already.

It was nearly midnight before she heard Captain Ingleby-Lewis's footsteps on the stairs. While she waited, she had returned to Virginia Woolf and *A Room of One's Own*. Mrs. Woolf improved on acquaintance.

Her father ambled into the room and tossed his hat onto the table. It skidded to the edge and fell to the floor.

"Hello, old girl," he said, yawning. "Thought you'd have turned in by now."

"I waited up for you."

"You shouldn't have bothered." He beamed at her. "Well, goodnight. I'm off to Bedfordshire."

"I'd like to talk to you."

Her father, who had clearly remembered the awkwardness of their last meeting, was already edging toward the door. "Better leave it until the morning. We'll be fresher then."

"This won't take a moment," Lydia said. "Have a cigarette."

Automatically he changed direction and advanced toward the packet she was holding out to him, for his responses were Pavlovian in their precision where alcohol and tobacco were concerned. He took the cigarette. She struck a match for him. He grunted with effort as he lowered his head to the flame. When the cigarette was alight, he fell backward onto the sofa.

"Are you really throwing me out, Father?"

He looked reproachfully at her. "You know it's not like that, my dear."

"That's what it seems like. Why can't we carry on as we are? I'm going to divorce Marcus, and then there will be more money coming in. Everything will be much more comfortable."

"Langstone may not make it easy. As far as I can tell, he seems pretty keen on staying married to you." The Captain was drunk but not too drunk. He added courteously, "Of course that's understandable."

"The lawyer seems to think I should be able to get a reasonable settlement. Enough to live on."

"Who have you got?"

"Mr. Shires."

"Did Serridge arrange it for you?"

"No. I arranged it myself." As she stared at her father, however, Lydia wondered whether this was in fact true. She remembered how cautious Shires had been at first when she mentioned the divorce, and how, a few hours later, he had become much more helpful, and the question of who was going to pay his bills no longer seemed to concern him so urgently.

Ingleby-Lewis shrugged. "You know your own business, I suppose. Never had much time for the fellow myself."

"Your friend Mr. Serridge seems to like him well enough," Lydia said carefully.

"Anyway, that's not the point," he went on. "The long and the short of it is that you can't stay here."

"Why are you listening to Mrs. Alforde and not to me? I want to stay here."

"It's for the best. Believe me."

"Is it because there's something going on? Something you don't want me to know about?"

He snorted. "Of course not. It's quite simple. This isn't really a suitable—"

"New York," Lydia said. "Ring any bells? Grand Central Station, New York City."

Captain Ingleby-Lewis dropped the cigarette on his lap. He leaped to his feet, swearing and patting his trousers. The cigarette fell to the carpet. Lydia picked it up and gave it to him.

"Thank you, my dear," he said, sinking back on the sofa and swiftly recovering his poise.

Lydia opened her handbag and took out the papers she had found in the writing box. "Do you know what these are?"

"Of course I don't. Not a mind-reader in a music hall, am I? Can't this wait until the morning?"

"Two pieces of paper," Lydia said, ignoring him. "There's Miss Penhow's signature on one of them, written over and over again. It looks as if someone was practicing it."

Her father stared straight ahead.

She unfolded them. "On the other bit of paper are the words 'I expect you are surprised to hear'. And there's something else on the other side." She looked up at her father but still he did not react. "It's written in pencil, in a different handwriting and rather faintly. Shall I read it to you? 'And so tell the padre you're sorry for all the upset, that you met an old pal, a sailor who you were—' "

"That's enough," Captain Ingleby-Lewis said quietly. He sat in silence while he finished the cigarette. He stubbed it out and said, "What are you going to do?"

"I don't know."

He sucked in his cheeks. "I thought you might be about to start making threats."

"So did I," Lydia said. "And perhaps I will, I don't know. Does it mean what I think it means?"

Captain Ingleby-Lewis shrugged. "That rather depends what you think it means, doesn't it?"

"I'm told that you've always been good at copying things with a pen."

He looked at her. "You mean they've told you that I forged some checks. They've told you about the mess accounts."

It was not a question so Lydia said nothing.

"I had to leave the army. I wasn't court-martialed but everyone knew the reason. The mess sergeant was involved as well. But he wasn't so lucky."

The significance hit her. "Mr. Serridge?"

Her father nodded. "He was in prison for two years. Still, all that's water under the bridge. But of course it's one reason why you shouldn't be staying with me."

Lydia folded the papers. "And what about these?"

"That silly Penhow woman, I knew she'd cause trouble. All heart, no head—that was her problem." He looked sternly at Lydia. "Running off like that without a word. Most inconsiderate."

"That's not what some people would call it."

"Oh I know. You've heard people saying that he did away with her just for her money. All those damned gossips at Rawling. I'm not saying the money wasn't the attraction as far as Serridge was concerned—but what's wrong with that? It wasn't as if she was getting nothing in return. And then she meets somebody she likes better and off she goes."

For a moment it sounded almost reasonable. Then she remembered that Serridge apparently owned the house they were living in, as well as Morthams Farm and heaven knew what else besides that had once belonged to Miss Penhow.

"What could the poor chap do?" Ingleby-Lewis asked, flinging wide his arms. "He was in an awful fix. Everyone was claiming he had done away with the poor woman and he couldn't prove he hadn't. People can be damnably malicious. Anyway, he knew I was off to try my luck in the States, and he asked if I could do something to help."

"So you faked a letter from Miss Penhow to the Vicar of Rawling?"

"Why ever not? No harm in it. I owed Joe Serridge a favor.

Besides, I'd be the first to admit that he'll cut a corner or two if he has to, but he wouldn't harm a fly. Certainly not a woman. No, I was in New York and it was simple enough for me to drop a line to get him off the hook. I couldn't see why not. Matter of common decency."

"I don't think the police would agree."

Ingleby-Lewis struggled off the sofa and stood up. "Just helping a pal out of a hole."

"As Serridge helped you? By buying the farm from you?"

"It was exactly what he and Miss Penhow were looking for. And I let him have it for a jolly good price. I could have got at least a couple of hundred more."

"And now he lets you live here. Do you actually pay rent? Or perhaps there's no longer any need to. It seems a very cozy arrangement all round."

"Don't you get on your high horse, my girl," he said, sounding both sober and angry. "It's all very well to be sitting in judgment when you've got money in the bank. You see things very differently when you haven't a couple of shillings to rub together. That's when you find out what really matters. And who your pals really are."

They looked at one another for a moment, neither giving way. But the anger drained from both of them.

"I don't want to go," she said suddenly. "I'd rather stay here."

He nodded. "I'd rather you stayed here too. Hermione Alforde is right, though. It isn't suitable. You'll be better off with them."

Swaying slightly, with stooping shoulders, he made his way toward the door. Lydia stayed in her chair, staring at the glowing tracery of the gas fire. This had started with Mrs. Alforde, she thought: something had happened to make her change her mind, something in Rawling on Thursday, 29 November.

But that made no sense at all.

The Captain's footsteps stopped behind her, and she felt a hand on her shoulder. She didn't move. His familiar aroma of dust, tobacco and stale beer enveloped her. He kissed the top of her head. She said nothing. He moved away. The door opened and closed.

It was the first time her father had kissed her.

The only bed at present in the house filled most of a small room off the kitchen in the basement—a damp cell with little natural light and a strip of wallpaper curling away from the wall like a striking snake. The large iron bedstead must have been assembled in the room because it was too large to get through the doorway. A stained mattress lay slightly askew on top of it.

Dawlish foraged on the upper floors and came back with an armful of blankets and cushions. "Will you be all right?"

"Of course I will," Rory said.

Fenella and Dawlish departed a little after nine o'clock. Rory helped himself to a nightcap from the whisky bottle. But the alcohol wasn't helping now. Quite the reverse. His body had reduced itself to a shifting, twitching network of aches and pains. Much worse than that was the fact that he was frightened, his thoughts rampaging beyond control. The violence in the Ossuary—his own as well as Marcus's—had unleashed terrors he had not known existed. What would happen if he never learned how to tidy them away into his memory, let alone how to forget them?

Without removing his clothes or bothering to wash, he collapsed on the bed and burrowed into the musty blankets. Almost instantly, sleep glided over him. He remembered nothing more until he awoke with a start, hours later. For a moment he thought he was in his old bedroom at his parents' house. He had a slight headache and his mouth tasted and felt like a used dishcloth. He lay there feeling oddly happy and full of hope, letting the memories of yesterday seep into his consciousness. He fumbled for matches and struck a light. It was only half past six but he had no desire to stay in bed.

During the morning he worked on the article, drafting and redrafting it in pencil at the kitchen table. Toward midday Dawlish turned up with a flask of coffee and a portable typewriter. Shortly afterward Fenella arrived with a basket containing their lunch, most of which came out of tins. When they had eaten, the others left him to finish the typing. He was aware of the murmur of their voices in the sitting room.

Rory finished the article and read it through. Was it finished? Was it as good as he could make it? He had read it so many times and in so many versions that he was no longer capable of judging. He went down the hallway toward the half-open door of the sitting room, intending to ask for a second opinion. His ankle was still painful but he could move quite comfortably if he leaned against the wall. But he had taken only a few steps when Fenella's voice suddenly rose in volume.

"Stop it! Just get off me. Stop mauling me, will you? You're just the same as all of them. Filthy beasts."

Careless of the pain from his ankle, Rory scuttled back into the kitchen and pushed the door to, so it was almost closed. He heard footsteps in the hall, and Dawlish saying something, his voice low and urgent. The area door slammed. The flat was silent.

Rory looked through his article again but this time his eyes would not even focus on the words. She doesn't want him, he thought, she doesn't want him. Not like *that*. He felt the beginnings of an unpleasant sense of triumph, instantly cut short by the realization that Fenella had made it quite clear that she didn't want him either. *You're just the same as all of them. Filthy beasts.* She didn't want anyone, not like *that*.

Heavy footsteps were coming slowly down the hall. Dawlish came into the kitchen.

"How's it going?"

"I think I've finished," Rory said. Instinct told him to act as if he had heard nothing of what had happened in the sitting room. He pushed the typed sheets across the table. "I'd be glad of an opinion."

Dawlish pulled out a chair. "Oh—by the way—Fenella had to go."

"I thought I heard the door," Rory said carefully.

"She was in a bit of a hurry. No time to say goodbye."

"It must be a busy time for her."

Dawlish stared vaguely at him. "I wouldn't be surprised if she's been overdoing it a bit lately."

Rory agreed. Dawlish picked up the typed sheets. Rory waited, forcing himself to stay still. Dawlish skimmed through the entire article and then turned back and read it again, this time more slowly. At last he looked up.

"This is good," he said. "Just what the doctor ordered."

"Do you think the editor will agree?"

"I'm quite sure he will." He swallowed and then went on in a rush, "I say, old man, would you mind if I asked you something?"

"Fire away."

Dawlish hesitated. "Do you think that . . ." He lost his nerve and broke off, running his fingers through his hair. He swiftly recovered. "What I mean to say is, I ought to show you over the rest of the house soon—especially the attic. See how you feel about living there for a bit. Do you think you'll be able to manage the stairs later today?"

"I hope so. I can certainly try."

"Good," said Dawlish absently. He stared at the kitchen sink, and Rory knew he was really looking at the emptiness of a world without Fenella. "Absolutely splendid."

Lydia Langstone had never traveled in a third-class railway compartment before. She discovered that, like crowded buses or bone-shaking trams, they were where you met British humanity in all its smelly, noisy variety. On that Sunday it was a slow journey punctuated with changes and delays and populated with tiresome fellow passengers. She had plenty of time to regret her decision.

Eventually and reluctantly, she reached Mavering. As she walked along the rainswept platform, she was tempted to wait for the next train that might take her in warm, safe discomfort back to London.

A porter approached her, scenting a tip. "Taxi, miss?"

Lydia shook her head and asked where the footpath to Rawling was. He looked surprised but gave her meticulous directions. She rewarded him with a sixpence and set out.

She had dressed for the weather in a waterproof coat and hat so the rain did not worry her. It was cold, however, and she forced herself to walk as quickly as possible. When the path forked, she took the left-hand turn, the one that would take her along the bottom of the meadow behind Morthams Farm. Twenty minutes later she came out on to the lane to Rawling.

The stumpy tower of Mr. Gladwyn's church was about half a mile away. No one was in sight. Less than a hundred yards from where she stood, the chimneys of a small cottage poked into a muddy gray sky. She hurried down the lane and stopped outside.

The garden gate had fallen backward from its hinges. The disintegrating corpse of a blackbird lay on the path up to the front door, and the weeds were waist high on what had once been a lawn. A wisp of smoke rose from one of the chimneys. Ignoring the front door, Lydia followed the cinder path round the side of the house. As she passed one of the windows, she glimpsed movement inside.

She tapped on the back door and waited. No one came. She was about to knock again when the door opened suddenly. A tall woman with ragged gray hair stared at Lydia. She wore a rusty black dress draped over a stick-like body. Her skin had a gray pallor, and her eyes were large, a faded blue in color. The hand gripping the side of the door had long and graceful fingers that ended with nails bitten to the quick. Lydia thought the woman had once been beautiful. She had seen her before, of course, at the graveside, but then the widow had been masked by her veil and in any case her individuality had been swamped by the occasion.

"Good afternoon," Lydia said uncertainly. "I'm Mrs. Langstone. We haven't met, Mrs. Narton, but—"

"I know who you are." The voice was low and harsh. "What do you want?"

"First I wanted to say how sorry I was about your husband."

"Why? You didn't know him."

Lydia rushed on: "I was here with Mrs. Alforde—"

"You came to the funeral," Mrs. Narton said. "I don't know why, I'm sure."

There was a long silence, during which Lydia wished more than ever that she had not come. Mrs. Narton's face remained impassive. Finally, she let go of the door and in doing so pushed it wide, revealing a low-ceilinged kitchen. She turned away and sat down at the table. She rested her hands on the table, palms down, on either side of an open Bible.

It was, Lydia decided, a sort of invitation. She went inside, closing the door behind her. She drew out a chair and sat down opposite Mrs. Narton. She waited.

When the tapping on the window started, Rory was sitting as close as he could get to the electric fire with a blanket draped like a cape over his shoulders. He was whiling away the long evening with a plump and undemanding novel by J. B. Priestley that he had found in the kitchen. At first he thought he was imagining it because the tapping was both faint and sporadic, almost as though it wasn't sure it wanted to be heard.

He put down the book, hobbled to the window and pulled aside the curtain. Lydia's face, distorted by the rain on the window, swam on the other side of the glass. He dropped the blanket on the carpet, stumbled into the hall and opened the door.

The first thing he realized was how wet she was. Her coat was streaked with mud. She didn't speak. She stood there on the doorstep and stared blankly at him until he drew her over the threshold. He helped her out of her coat and draped it with her hat on one of the pegs in the hall.

"Come and sit by the fire," he ordered.

He followed her into the sitting room. She stood in the middle of the threadbare carpet, looking around her as though wondering what she was doing here. Her skirt and stockings were filthy.

Rory touched her shoulder. "Sit down."

She sank obediently into the chair in front of the fire. He picked up the blanket and wrapped it around her shoulders. She seemed not to notice. Her teeth were chattering.

"What the hell have you been doing with yourself?"

"I—I walked from the station."

"Which station?"

"Liverpool Street."

"But that's miles away." He glanced at the mud on her shoes and stockings. "And you fell over too, by the look of it."

"That was on the footpath from Rawling."

She pulled the blanket more tightly around her. Rory limped into the kitchen and returned with Dawlish's whisky bottle and a clean wineglass. He filled the glass half full and held it out to her. She took it obediently and sipped, making a face at the taste.

"Have some more," Rory said.

"I don't like it."

"Have another sip. It's good for you."

She obeyed, wrinkling her nose like a petulant child.

"Why did you go to Rawling?"

She didn't reply. She took another mouthful of whisky. In her bedraggled state she looked much younger than she usually did.

"All right," he went on when she showed no sign of replying. "You can't sit there in your wet things. I'm going to fetch some more blankets. Then you can take your things off and hang them to dry."

He brought two more blankets from the room where he had slept. As an afterthought he added his pajamas, which Dawlish had brought back from Bleeding Heart Square the previous evening. He went back to Lydia, who was sitting where he had left her.

"You'll need to take off your shoes, your stockings and your skirt," he said firmly, as though she were one of his sisters. He laid the blankets and pajamas on the floor beside her. "The pajamas are clean. You're welcome to borrow them. I'll leave you alone for five minutes."

She looked up at him. "Thank you."

In the kitchen he put the kettle on and smoked a cigarette. When he returned to the sitting room ten minutes later, the wet clothes were drying on the chair. Lydia had changed into the pajamas and was curled up in a nest of blankets by the fire. The whisky glass at her elbow was empty. There was more color in her cheeks.

"I'm sorry," she said. "I feel an awful fool barging in like this."

"You're not."

"It's just that I didn't know where else to go." She hesitated. "The thing is, I've had a bit of a shock, and I need time to think about what to do. I don't want to go to Bleeding Heart Square."

"Has Mr. Langstone—"

She shook her head. "It's nothing to do with Marcus. If you don't mind, I—I don't want to talk about it."

"When did you last eat?"

She shrugged. "I can't remember."

"I'm going to forage in the kitchen. There is a bit of tinned ham left and some bread and one or two apples."

"I'm not hungry."

"Yes, you are, you just haven't noticed." He smiled at her. "And then we'll have some more whisky."

"I can't stay here."

"Where do you think you're going then?"

"I don't know. A hotel, I suppose."

"Don't be silly. You haven't any luggage. Besides, the weather's foul, and you can't go out dressed like that. You can have the bedroom. I'll sleep in here."

"I can't let you do that. Anyway—"

"I'm sure Dawlish wouldn't mind. You're fagged out, the weather's beastly and you've had a shock. Damn it, I won't let you go. I'll take away your shoes if you try."

She looked at him and he noticed her eyes narrowing, as they sometimes did when she was amused. "Then it looks as if I haven't got much choice."

That evening they ate an unpleasant scratch supper in front of the electric fire. They drank Dawlish's whisky and smoked Lydia's cigarettes. Lydia asked him questions. She wanted to hear about his parents and his sisters. She wanted to hear about what it was like to live in the manager's accommodation over a bank. She wanted to hear about grammar school and university and India. While he talked, she sat there, eyes half closed, glass in hand, with a dreamy expression on her face.

Had someone tried to rape her? Or robbed her?

Gradually they ran out of words. It was very quiet in the basement flat. Mecklenburgh Square had only three sides because to the west lay the children's playground, once the site of the Foundling Hospital, so Dawlish's house was effectively near the end of a cul-de-sac.

Rory felt his eyelids drooping. He wasn't used to whisky. The room was warm and stuffy. He was glad not to be alone in this big house. No, it was more than that: he was glad Lydia was here.

The next thing he knew, he was fully awake. He wasn't sure how long he had been dozing. Lydia was on her feet and folding one of the blankets. For an instant he didn't recognize her, and a shiver of lust flickered through him. She looked down at him and smiled.

"I think I'll turn in."

He yawned. "Sorry—I must have dropped off." He noticed that his article was beside the whisky bottle.

Lydia had followed the direction of his eyes. "I hope you don't mind. I read it. It's very good."

"I wondered whether it was rather personal in tone."

"Don't change a word. They deserve every last one of them."

He stood up. "Thank you. I'll show you where everything is."

She didn't move. "You've been very kind. I think I can cope now."

"What will you do tomorrow?"

She picked up her skirt and felt the hem. "The first thing I have to do is see my mother."

25

You turn over the page and read the last lines. Philippa Penhow never wrote anything else in there, and the rest of the diary is as blank as oblivion.

Wednesday, 23 April 1930 (continued)

... go back. I'll leave the diary in the barn on the way. Blast & botheration. Find some money. Try again. He can't stop me. I've made up my mind.

Car on drive. Say I was caught in rain & took shelter Jacko barking.

Oh Joseph, Joseph.

"Good morning, Fripp."

"Good morning, Miss Lydia." Fripp's eyes flickered. He opened the door wide and stood back, ushering Lydia into the hall. "Her ladyship is still upstairs, and Miss Pamela has gone out. His lordship is in the library, though."

"Thank you." Lydia allowed him to take her hat and coat. "And how are you?"

"As well as can be expected, thank you, miss." Fripp was innately conservative: in his eyes she would always be "miss," never "madam," however many husbands she acquired. "I hope you are keeping well yourself."

"Yes, thanks. Do you know where my sister went?"

"I'm afraid I can't say."

The library door opened and the little figure of Lord Cassington hurried out. He was carrying the morning's *Times* and struggling to prevent part of it slipping to the floor. His eyes fell on Lydia. "Lydia, my dear." Automatically he held up his cheek for a kiss. "Splendid—come to see your mother, eh? You'll find her in her bedroom, I believe." He looked up at her, his face a mass of wrinkles like a sun-dried sultana, and tapped the newspaper. "You've heard Pammy's news, I suppose?"

Lydia said she had. Lord Cassington said that Fisher was a splendid chap and Lydia smiled but did not reply.

"Must dash," he said. "Stay to lunch if you can."

He bustled away. He was a man of routine. For as long as Lydia could remember, he had liked to spend between ten and fifteen minutes at this time of the morning locked in the lavatory with *The Times*.

Lydia went upstairs. Her mother's bedroom was on the second floor. She tapped on the door and went in without waiting for an answer. Lady Cassington was still in bed. Her maid was doing her nails. A large notebook lay open beside her on the eiderdown, and the remains of breakfast were on a table beside the bed. Seen like this, with a scarf over her hair and her face devoid of makeup, she looked her age. When she saw Lydia, she waved her free hand and said, "Hello, darling, so there you are," as if she had been expecting Lydia to call at Upper Mount Street. Her maid was less adept at hiding her reaction: she gave a visible start and pursed her lips in a puckered circle.

"Matthews, run away now. I want to talk to Miss Lydia," Lady Cassington said. "I'll ring when I want you."

When they were alone, Lydia walked over to the window and looked down on the street below.

"Stop prowling about and come and sit on the bed where I can see you," her mother said. "Have you seen Fin?"

"Briefly." Lydia sat on the chair beside the bed, the one the maid had been using. "He seems pleased about Pammy and Rex Fisher."

"We all are. So you saw *The Times*?"

"Pammy told me about the engagement on Saturday."

Lady Cassington arched her eyebrows, which suggested, Lydia thought, that she hadn't known that Pammy had seen Lydia; that in itself was interesting. Her mother tapped the notebook. "I'm making lists. There's not a moment to lose. Pammy should be back for lunch if you want to see her. She was going to Regent Street, the Aquascutum sale, I think." She went on without any change of tone, "You will come to the wedding, won't you?"

"I don't think it's a good idea."

"But, darling, she'd be frightfully disappointed if you weren't there. You of all people."

"I mean, I don't think the wedding itself is a good idea. I don't like what I've seen of Fisher and I don't like his politics either."

"Of course there may be implications for you and Marcus. I quite understand that."

"That's partly what I came to talk about," Lydia said.

Lady Cassington helped herself to a cigarette from the box on the bedside table. She looked warily at Lydia. "I know things have been very difficult," she said cautiously. "Sometimes, though, one just has to look forward."

"That's exactly what I'm doing," Lydia said. "I want you to make sure that Marcus cooperates over the divorce."

"But darling—"

"The man hires a prostitute, doesn't he? They go to a hotel in Brighton or somewhere and register as man and wife, leaving a trail a mile wide. Isn't that how it's done?"

"I'm not sure Marcus would agree to that."

"If he doesn't manage it one way or the other, I shall go to the papers."

"Don't be childish, dear."

Lydia sat back in her chair and said very slowly and distinctly, "If he doesn't, I shall tell them what I saw you and Marcus doing in Frogmore Place the other Sunday."

Her mother sat up so abruptly that she knocked both the ash-tray and her notebook on to the floor. "Now that really is going too far. And it's nonsense too. Wicked nonsense."

"I was there. I saw you."

Neither of them spoke. Lydia listened to the clock ticking on the mantel, a car passing down the street and the barely audible sound of her mother's newly manicured nails scratching the eiderdown.

"And think of the effect on Pammy, on Fin, on—"

"I think you should have thought of the effect on them already," Lydia said. "By the way, I shall want Marcus to settle an income on me. Shall we say five hundred a year? I don't want to be greedy."

"I'm not sure he could find that sort of money."

"He can if he has to."

"He won't agree."

"He will," Lydia said. "You'll make him. I'm serious about this, Mother. I'm quite prepared to go to the papers. If necessary, I'll do everything I can to ensure that the world knows what my husband and my mother were doing together."

Lady Cassington said in a quiet, uncertain voice, "You couldn't prove anything."

"That's the point, though. I wouldn't have to prove it: I'd just have to say it."

"You wouldn't get any sympathy, you know." Her mother studied her with narrow intelligent eyes. "That's the trouble when people start throwing mud at other people. It ends up sticking to every-one. They'd think you were mad. A wicked liar."

"I'm quite happy to take that risk. Though if you can persuade Marcus to do the decent thing for once in his life there won't be any need. The point is, you and Marcus have got something to lose. I haven't. Not anymore."

Her mother picked at the eiderdown. "You've become very hard-bitten. I must say I'm surprised. And hurt."

"As somebody said to me the other day, you see things very differently when you haven't a couple of shillings to rub together."

"What have you told Fin?"

"Nothing. Yet."

"I'd hate to see him worried by something like this."

"In that case you'll make sure he isn't."

"Will you stay with your father?"

Lydia stood up, walked over to the window again and looked down at the trim self-confident street below. She turned her head and stared at her mother. She felt cruelty rising inside her, a black tide. "That rather depends on who you mean by my father."

Julian Dawlish looked as if he hadn't slept. He arrived as arranged a little after ten o'clock. He brought with him milk, tea, bread and bacon. Rory cooked them a primitive breakfast, which they ate at the kitchen table.

Afterward, Dawlish pushed aside his plate, cleared his throat and said, "Fenella rang me up this morning. It seems that she doesn't want the job after all. Or the flat." He looked like a man who has seen his own ghost.

"I'm sorry," Rory said, because he couldn't think of anything else to say.

"Of course I shall carry on with the association. It's—it's important, as I'm sure you agree after what we saw on Saturday. One has to start somewhere, doesn't one? Because otherwise everything falls to pieces and one might as well just lie down and wait for the worst to happen."

"Yes, one has to do something." Rory wasn't sure whether his host was talking about the state of his own emotions or Fascism's steady invasion of European politics. "Anything's better than nothing."

"Precisely," Dawlish said, looking even more hag-ridden than before. He took out his case and lit a cigarette. "I—I hope she's all right. Fenella, I mean. She seemed a bit—well, jumpy yesterday. I don't know whether you noticed?"

"I did notice something," Rory admitted.

There was a pause in the conversation while Dawlish stubbed out the cigarette. Then he asked Rory how he was feeling.

"Much better, thanks. I'll walk back to Bleeding Heart Square when we're done here and start packing."

"Nonsense. I'll run you over in the car. Then I'll take your piece over to *Berkeley's* and have a word with the editor."

"That's awfully kind."

Dawlish glanced at him and smiled a little awkwardly. "How long will it take you to pack your gear when you get back there?"

"I don't know—an hour or two at most, I should think."

Dawlish looked at his watch. "Suppose I pick you up after lunch. Half past two, say, will that suit?"

"Absolutely. Thank you."

"You might as well have this flat for the time being. I'll get someone in to sort out the attic."

"We must talk about rent and so on."

"Oh yes," Dawlish said. "We shall. The association won't need the whole house, after all. The ground floor and the first floor will be more than enough."

"I shouldn't be surprised if Lydia Langstone wasn't soon looking for somewhere to live."

"Women are queer fish," Dawlish went on, as if Rory had said something quite different. "That's all there is to it. Kittle-cattle, as my father used to say. Don't you agree?"

Lady Cassington sat at her dressing table, looking at Lydia's reflection in the oval mirror. She was wearing a pale green wrap with lace at the sleeves and the collar. Her feet were bare and the hand holding the hairbrush was trembling slightly. The skin at the base of her neck, Lydia saw, was puffy and wrinkled.

"I'm sure I don't know what you mean," Lady Cassington said carefully and slowly. She had just returned from a tactical retreat to her bathroom, where no doubt she had considered her possible courses of action.

"You know perfectly well," Lydia said. "If necessary, by the way, I shall make this public too."

"Lydia! Of all the wicked—"

"I shouldn't have found out if it hadn't been for you," Lydia said. "It was you who got the Alfordes to ask me to tea. Mrs. Alforde is a nice woman. She tried so hard to do the right thing. She even asked me out for a day in the country. She had to run down to Rawling, you see. There was a funeral she had to go to—a man called Narton, the husband of an old servant."

"My dear Lydia," her mother said, veering on to another tack, "on reflection, I think you're right about you and Marcus. About the divorce, I mean. Sometimes one has to draw a line under things, and make the best of a bad business. Sometimes—"

"We had lunch at the Vicarage after the funeral," Lydia interrupted. "Mrs. Alforde and the Vicar put their heads together about the best way to help Mrs. Narton. You must have seen Mrs. Narton yourself when you went to stay at Rawling Hall. She looks about seventy now, but in fact she's only forty-five. Did you know that?"

"Of course I didn't," Lady Cassington snapped. "Why on earth would I know a thing like that?"

Lydia sat down on the window seat. Her mother swiveled in her chair to keep her in sight.

"Mrs. Alforde went to see Mrs. Narton that afternoon," Lydia said. "They had a very long chat. The funny thing was, after she'd come back from seeing Mrs. Narton, Mrs. Alforde was completely different. She acted very strangely. In fact she was almost un-friendly toward me."

"I shouldn't pay too much attention to that sort of thing, dear. I expect Hermione was upset by seeing what a state Mrs. Narton was in. Or even by going back to Rawling. It was quite a comedown for the Alfordes, you know, having to give up the Hall. Gerry's uncle lived very comfortably. Hermione must have thought that one day—"

"It wasn't that," Lydia said. "I know that because on Saturday afternoon Mrs. Alforde turned up at Bleeding Heart Square. She and the Captain put their heads together and decided that I had to go and live with the Alfordes."

"I call that a very generous offer, dear," Lady Cassington said. "She has a very kind heart, I've always said that."

"But they wouldn't tell me why."

"It speaks for itself, surely."

Lydia laughed. "That depends what you think it says. It seemed to me that something must have happened. And the more I thought about it, the more I realized that it must have been something on Thursday afternoon at Rawling, when Mrs. Alforde went to see Mrs. Narton. So I went and asked her. Asked Mrs. Narton, I mean."

Her mother sighed but said nothing.

"She was in quite a state," Lydia went on. "Did I mention that they think Mr. Narton shot himself? That must have made it even worse for her, mustn't it?"

"Did he leave a note?"

"Yes, but Mrs. Narton burned it. No one else saw it."

"How very wrong of her," Lady Cassington said.

"When she was a girl, Serridge seduced her. She was very young—she had just gone into service at Rawling Hall." Lydia paused, watching her mother. "Serridge told Mr. Narton about it just before he killed himself. He didn't know, you see. Serridge told Narton that he had seduced his wife as well as his daughter. That's what the note said."

"It seems very strange Mrs. Narton should tell *you*. She's never even met you."

"She knew who I was, even so. She said she'd known who I was as soon as she saw me at the funeral. She said it was something about the eyes and the shape of the mouth. And then she asked Mrs. Alforde, just to make sure."

"Good Lord," her mother said. "I've always said you and I are quite alike from some angles. Something to do with the cheekbones, perhaps. But it's funny to think of a servant remembering me after all those years."

"Almost exactly thirty years. It was the Christmas of 1904. Serridge had been hired as a beater for the shooting. You can guess who recommended him for the job. And he was enjoying himself with Mrs. Narton, not that she was married then, of course. But then he got more interested in one of the guests at the Hall, a schoolgirl. Mrs. Narton said she was a scrap of a thing but very pretty and very keen on Serridge. That was it as far as Mrs. Narton was concerned. He just dropped her. Naturally she was jealous, and used to watch him like a hawk when she could. And the girl. So she wasn't surprised when she heard the girl was pregnant. Serve her right, she said. But of course the family covered it up. They married the girl off to Mrs. Alforde's nephew, the Captain. So that's why something about my face reminded Margaret Narton of Joseph Serridge when he was a young man."

There was silence in the big, warm bedroom with its smells of perfume, coffee and Virginia tobacco. Lydia heard Margaret Narton's voice: *That's how they do it, folk like that—they take their pleasures and they make other people pay for them. And you keep on paying, don't you? That's what I felt when Serridge came sniffing around our Amy. He broke my heart, and then he broke hers, and that broke mine all over again but far worse than the first time. Then Amy died, and the baby too.*

Lady Cassington stood up and went over to the bedside table. She took another cigarette, lit it and sat on the edge of the bed. As she blew out smoke, she asked, "Have you finished, darling?"

"Why didn't you tell me?"

"Do be sensible. It wouldn't have made it better if I had. Not for me. And certainly not for you. It was just one of those silly things that happen when one's young. And marrying Willy Ingleby-Lewis was the best way to deal with it. If you ask me, people talk too much."

"So Serridge really is my father? You admit it?"

Her mother shrugged bony shoulders. "That Narton woman's right. There is a likeness if you look for it." She ground out the cigarette in the ashtray. "He was very good-looking then, you know, and very charming when he wanted to be."

"What would you do if I told Fin?"

"Darling, now don't be so absurd. It would be too Lady Chatterley for words. Have you read the book? It's quite dreadful, of course, and really rather dull, but it would so upset Fin to have something like that in his own family. Anyway, he's never done you any harm. Quite the reverse. He's very fond of you."

Lydia stared out of the window, wondering whether she would ever again sit in this house she had known for most of her life and look down on Upper Mount Street. One shouldn't be frightened of change, she told herself, because it was going to happen anyway, whatever one felt about it.

Lady Cassington was pursuing a line of thought of her own. "Did you say the Narton woman is only forty-five? She must have been even younger than I was when—when—"

"Serridge likes them young," Lydia said coldly. She stopped, remembering Rebecca Proctor's words: *He likes the younger ones, madam.* It was a moment of illumination, as though someone had come into a dark room and flicked the switch on the wall by the door, allowing Lydia to glimpse a possibility out of the corner of her eye.

Her mother looked curiously at her. "What is it, darling?"

"Nothing," Lydia lied. "Nothing at all."

On her way out of the house, Lydia went into the library to say goodbye to Fin. He was sitting at his desk, an enormous Second

Empire piece which he claimed had once been owned by a French duke. He liked to sit there in the mornings, basking in its garish splendor, writing letters, reading the newspaper and pretending to be a man of affairs.

"I've come to say goodbye," Lydia said.

"Are you going already? I hoped you'd be staying to lunch."

"Not today, I'm afraid. Will you give my love to Pammy?"

"Of course." He screwed up his eyes and looked at her. "Are you all right?"

"Yes and no."

"Anything I can do?"

She shook her head. "I want to tell you myself: I'm divorcing Marcus."

"Your mother won't like that. I suppose there's no chance—"

"No, darling," Lydia said. "Not the slightest. It's all right, though—you needn't worry." She bent down and kissed him. "I'll be in touch."

At the door, she turned back. "By the way, I went to a Fascist meeting on Saturday."

"Really?" His face brightened at the change of subject toward the comfort of the impersonal. "Was it interesting?"

"Absolutely fascinating. What I hadn't realized is what unpleasant people the Fascists are. They're bullies, Fin. Perhaps that's why they appeal to Marcus and Rex."

He frowned. The doorbell rang. She smiled at him again and went into the hall, where Fripp was already at the door, holding it open for Marcus. He was wearing a patch over one eye and there was a dressing underneath the other. One side of his face was badly bruised. When he saw Lydia, the skin around the bruises lost its color, giving his face a mottled appearance.

"Hello," Lydia said. "I'm just going. Fripp, will you bring me my things?"

"Lydia," Marcus blurted out, careless of the fact that he was within earshot of Fripp. "I had a letter from some damn-fool solicitor this morning. He claims he's—"

"You're to leave Mr. Wentwood alone, Marcus. Do you understand?"

"You can't expect me to—"

"I don't want to talk to you, Marcus. Go and see my mother. She'll tell you what to do. And she'll also tell you what I shall do if you don't cooperate."

Fripp, his face impassive, held up her coat. She pushed her arms into the sleeves.

"Where are you going?" Marcus demanded.

"I'm going to enjoy myself," Lydia said.

It did not take Rory long to assemble his belongings. He took them downstairs and stacked them in the hall, then knocked on Mrs. Renton's door and paid what he owed for the sewing she had done.

"I'm sorry you're going, Mr. Wentwood," she said. "But if you're not happy somewhere, I always say it's wise to move on, and sooner rather than later. Mr. Fimberry's leaving too. Father Bertram has found him somewhere else to live." She looked up at him with a sudden, searching glance. "I wonder how long Mrs. Langstone will stay."

He nodded without committing himself to an opinion. "I'll leave my things out here and go and have a bite of lunch. Would you mind keeping an eye on them? I'm being collected at about half past two."

A door slammed above their heads and heavy footsteps crossed the first-floor landing. "Willy," they heard Serridge say, "I thought you'd be in the Crozier by this time. What's up with you? You've got a face like a funeral."

Rory nodded to Mrs. Renton and let himself quietly out of the house. He turned left into Charleston Street. In Hatton Garden, as he was waiting on the pavement for a break in the traffic, he glanced to his left and saw Lydia coming out of one of the shops. He walked toward her and raised his hat.

"Hello—I didn't expect to see you here." He grinned. "Idiotic thing to say, I know. You could have been anywhere."

She smiled back. "I've been to see Mr. Goldman."

"Is he all right?"

"Gloomier than ever but quite happy. I've just sold him a ring that used to belong to my great-aunt."

"I hope he gave you a good price. In the circumstances."

"He gave me what seemed to him a fair price, which is probably not the same thing. Anyway, I feel rich and I want to celebrate. Let me take you to lunch."

"I can't let you—"

"Yes, you can. Don't be gentlemanly about it. You gave me supper last night after all. How's the ankle? Can you walk as far as Fetter Passage?"

She pushed her arm through his and they crossed the road together. The Blue Dahlia was already busy. The manageress nodded when she saw them and pointed to a vacant table in the corner.

"It's liver on the menu again," Rory said.

"I'm having the hotpot."

They sat down, chose what they would have for pudding and ordered. As they waited for their lunch, the excitement drained away from Lydia, leaving her listless and silent. When he poured water into her glass, a few drops fell on the table. She made liquid circles from them on the marble top, moving her finger round and round.

"What is it?" Rory said gently.

She looked up. "I want to tell you something," she said. "Only I'm not sure I'm brave enough to do it."

"Try me."

"And it's not fair to you."

"Let me judge that."

She leaned closer to him and lowered her voice. "Do you think Serridge killed Miss Penhow?"

He nodded. "It's hard to see what else can have happened."

"And what about the others? Did they help?"

Rory ticked them off on his fingers. "Howlett will do whatever Serridge tells him, as long as he's paid. He provided the dog, and took the beastly thing back too. I'm sure there have been other things as well. He's a useful ally to have in Rosington Place and Bleeding Heart Square." He moved on to the next finger. "And then there's Shires: do you think he was in on it too?"

Lydia nodded. "I don't know how far he was implicated. But they must have had a lawyer to handle the purchase of the farm, and that was with Miss Penhow's money and in Serridge's name. And then there's the house in Bleeding Heart Square. It's hard to believe that the title deeds aren't in Serridge's name by now as well. He'd need Shires for something like that. And finally . . ."

She ran out of words and returned to making her circles on the marble.

Rory held up the third finger. "And finally there's your father. But I rather doubt he's involved, or not in an active way. I think he's just somebody who happens to be a tenant, who knows Serridge from a previous life."

Lydia shook her head. "He wrote that letter from New York. The one to Mr. Gladwyn."

He stared at her, his eyes widening. "So it wasn't from Miss Penhow? But you can't be sure of that."

"I can. I found the evidence. And he confirmed it when I asked."

"And Miss Penhow? Did he know . . . ?"

"I doubt it. I think he just looked the other way. I think that's what Howlett and Shires did too. They didn't want to see anything too unpleasant so they didn't."

"Like all those people in the audience on Saturday. The ones who just stood and watched when the Blackshirts went to work."

She rubbed the circles away with her napkin.

"Lydia," he said, "then what happened to Miss Penhow?"

"He probably buried her at the farm." She glanced up. "There must be something left of her. Something still to find."

"Not necessarily. It depends how clever he was. There was a case near Hereford when I was a boy. A chap killed his wife. He was a farmer too. There was a great heap of manure in the farmyard, and he put the body there. The police found what was left of her about six months later. I remember people saying that if it had been left in the midden for longer—three or four years, say—there would have been practically nothing left to find, except maybe a thigh bone that they couldn't identify. It's the acid, you see. It eats everything in time."

The manageress herself brought their food. She set down the hotpot in front of Rory and the liver in front of Lydia. Lydia opened her mouth and then closed it again.

"You get that inside you, ducky," the woman said sternly to Lydia. "Lot of iron in liver. And you need building up."

"Yes," said Lydia meekly.

The woman waddled away. Lydia picked up her knife and fork.

"Do you want to swap?" Rory said.

Lydia looked at him. "I wouldn't dare."

"It means you've passed some sort of test," he told her. "She's never called me ducky."

Lydia gave him a small and unconvincing smile. They ate in silence. She forced herself to try the liver and to her surprise rather enjoyed it. That was one thing she had learned in the last few weeks: food mattered.

"But who sent the hearts and the skull?" he said suddenly.

She glanced at him and said with her mouth full, "Narton, of course."

"How do you work that out?"

"Who else could it have been? Anyway I've got proof. Mrs. Narton sent you Miss Penhow's skirt. She wrapped it in brown paper. I kept the paper the skull was wrapped in. It's the same."

"The same sort?"

"Two halves of the same sheet. The join matches, Rory. And Robbie thought it was Narton who stole his skull. But of course Narton doesn't really matter here. It's Serridge that counts."

Rory laid down his knife and fork. "We can't prove anything," he murmured. "Not unless there's a miracle. He's covered his tracks too well."

Lydia did not reply. It occurred to him suddenly that she might not want a miracle: if Serridge were charged with murder, then Captain Ingleby-Lewis would almost certainly be charged as an accessory.

After another mouthful, he said, "What will you do now?"

"The Alfordes have asked me to stay. I went to see them this morning, and it's all fixed."

He concealed the disappointment he felt. "How long for? Do you know?"

She shifted listlessly on her chair. "Just for a few weeks, I hope. I saw my mother and Marcus this morning too. I don't think there will be any trouble with the divorce."

"Good. Is he all right? Mr. Langstone, I mean."

"He looks worse than you do. He's got an eyepatch like a pirate. You won't have any more problems with him, by the way."

"What will you do afterwards?"

"After the divorce? Look for somewhere of my own, I suppose, and a job."

"Dawlish mentioned this morning that he plans to let out part of the rest of the house. I—I happened to say you might be interested in a flat." He hesitated, aware he was moving into unfamiliar territory. "I hope that's all right."

Her expression was unreadable. "And Miss Kensley?"

He shook his head. "It seems that she's changed her mind."

"About the flat?"

"And the job."

She said very quietly, "You might not want me there."

"Why ever not?"

One of the Blue Dahlia's browbeaten minions arrived to collect their plates.

"Anyway, it's nothing to do with me what Dawlish decides." Rory studied Lydia's face. "I think, between ourselves, he was rather keen on Fenella."

"That had occurred to me too."

"It's strange," he said. "I thought she liked him. She—she seems to be very volatile these days. One never knows quite how she'll react. She used not to be like that, you know."

Lydia smiled. "You make it sound as if the problem is Fenella. It may just be that she doesn't like Mr. Dawlish, or not in that way. After all, there's no reason why she should."

He had an unsettling sensation that she saw the outline of a possibility he did not see. "Lydia—" he began, and put his hand on the table.

"One plum crumble with custard," said the minion, lowering a bowl with a clatter onto the table. "One apple tart, no custard."

When they were alone again, Lydia said, "I need to tell you something. You may not want to be under the same roof as me."

The possibilities chased through his mind: an old flame of Lydia's, emerging like Miss Penhow's fabled sailor from the past; or a desire to tell him that he, Rory, had served his purpose and was now surplus to requirements; or perhaps she was dying of an incurable disease or about to leave for several years on a cruise around the world; or—

"Last night," she said, "the reason that I was so upset was that I went to see Mrs. Narton. She told me something that I didn't want to hear, and my mother confirmed it this morning." She stared at her hands, palms down on either side of the apple tart, no custard; just like Mrs. Narton's, palms down on either side of her Bible. "William Ingleby-Lewis isn't my father: Serridge is."

He stared across the table at her bowed head. "Oh damn."

She didn't move. "I'm sure," she muttered doggedly. "There's no possible doubt."

He reached out and laid his right hand over her left hand, and his forefinger touched the wedding band that Marcus had given her. "It really doesn't matter," he said. "Now, would you like me to have a word with Dawlish about this flat?"

"But of course it matters. Especially if Serridge is a murderer as well as everything else."

"I don't agree. We're not our parents. If Serridge really is your father, he's nothing more than a biological accident. You can choose your own father. You can choose whoever you want. Or you can do without a father altogether."

"Something wrong with that tart?" asked the manageress, looming menacingly behind Rory.

"Not at all." Lydia obediently took up her spoon and fork. "It looks lovely."

The manageress watched her chew and swallow a mouthful. She shuffled away.

"See?" Rory said. "You're practically a daughter to her now. Next time we come here, she'll probably take the food off my plate and insist on feeding it to you."

He watched the smile breaking slowly over her face. While they ate their pudding, he told her about his hopes that the *Berkeley's* article would lead to others. Afterward she insisted on paying the bill.

Outside, he took her arm and slipped it through his. They walked back to Bleeding Heart Square together for the last time. In Charleston Street Serridge drove past in his car but he appeared not to notice them.

As they turned into the square, they saw Captain Ingleby-Lewis in front of them. He had just left the Crozier. There was a roll to his gait, as though the cobbles, puddles and cracked paving slabs were swaying this way and that on the swell of a mighty ocean. He paused by the pump, holding on to the handle to restore his balance. He heard their footsteps behind him and turned his head.

"Ah—hello, my dear." He looked first pleased to see Lydia, and then guilty; his memory was slower to respond than his emotions.

"Hello, Father," Lydia said, leaving her arm in Rory's. "I've come to say goodbye."

26

YOU MUST COME to a decision about the diary. It's a dangerous thing to keep. Besides, you have read it so many times that you know what it says: you can recite passages from memory. You are disposing of so much else, so why not this as well?

But something stops you. The diary will stay the same. You can't rely on memory to do that. Memory is a process, not something finished, complete in itself.

That is why you keep the diary. That is also why you must destroy it.

You hear the doorbell and it pulls you from a remote corner of your mind where you float between past and future. Only the standard lamp is alight, and the fire has died. The drawing room is insubstantial, full of shadows. It no longer feels like a room you have known all your life. The shabby furniture has lost its meaning, and so have the books on the shelves and the pictures on the walls. The room might just as well be a shop selling second-hand household effects.

You go into the hall and pick your way through the rubbish, your father's, your mother's and your own. You know who it will be and you do not want to have to deal with the questions. You have had enough of all this. You open the door and the shock of what you see hits you like a gust of wind. It's not Rory after all. It's not even poor Julian.

"Fenella," Joseph Serridge says. "Aren't you going to ask me in?"

"No," you say, and your voice is cold and perfectly steady.

His body almost fills the doorway, blocking out the night. He is the shadow who buys what you are and pays you with a dream that rots into nightmare.

"What the hell's going on?" he asks, with a ghost of a chuckle in his voice. "Looks like you're running a junk shop."

You hold the door to steady yourself, to keep the shadow out.

"Suit yourself," Serridge says. "We can talk on the doorstep if you want your neighbors to hear. It was you, wasn't it? Go on—admit it."

Oh it was you, all right; you never hid that from yourself. Philippa Penhow came into the barn and saw Joseph Serridge lying back on the straw and you riding on top of him with your skirt up around your armpits. His arms were clamped on your shoulders, holding you down.

Philippa Penhow couldn't have seen your face, not then, not from the doorway, but she said, "It's you, Fenella, isn't it? Oh, how could you?"

"It's you sending me all that rubbish," Joseph Serridge says. "Why now? Christ, it was years ago. What's the point?"

You tell him the truth. "Because Mother died."

"You *told* her?"

You shake your head. Because you loved Mother. Because she loved you.

Serridge stares down at you and forms his fleshy, hair-fringed lips into a silent whistle. "You're cracked, my girl. You know that?"

"I'm what you made me."

"You knew what you were doing. You wanted it—go on, admit it.

You were all over me, remember? Begging me. That's why you wired that day, that's why you came."

Oh, you remember. What you remember most of all is the absence of choice. The devil made you want him.

"All those hearts—it's like something out of a bloody fairy tale. What are you trying to do? Feed me up or something?"

You do not reply. You want to remind him what he's done, what he's made you do.

"And then that skull—you should get your head examined, my girl."

This jolts an answer out of you: "I didn't send you a skull."

"Someone did." He lunges toward you as if about to envelop you in a bear hug. You force yourself not to step back into the house. He looks down into your face and you stare back at him. The hall light shows the reddening nose and the broken veins.

"I saved your life," he says. "Remember what would have happened if I'd told them the truth. Even if they hadn't hanged you, they'd have locked you up and thrown away the key."

The truth is that you didn't mean to do it. The truth is that you were trying to save Joseph Serridge. The truth is never enough.

Philippa Penhow no longer looks like herself. Eyes and mouth gaping, arms outstretched, she drops her handbag and rushes into the barn. You scream and topple away from Joseph Serridge. He swears at Philippa Penhow, but the strangest thing of all is that he's smiling. He is enjoying this: the two women fighting over him.

Philippa Penhow has picked up a brick from the corner of the barn. She isn't fighting you: she's trying to hit Joseph Serridge with it. You didn't think she could be so strong. He's not smiling anymore. He's writhing, this way and that, encumbered by the trousers round his knees and the folds of his overcoat. She swings the brick at his face, misses, and hits his shoulder instead. He yelps with pain. She raises the brick again, in both hands. She is standing on a fold of the overcoat and her weight pins down one of his arms and prevents him from rolling away. He tries to raise the other arm to shield himself but he will be too late.

One small woman, one big man.

You throw yourself forward, knocking Philippa Penhow off balance. Her hat falls off. You struggle with her for the brick. She is stronger than she looks, stronger than she should be. You bite down on her hand and she cries out. You wrest the brick from her and raise it in your hands. She is reaching for another brick. You smash your own against the side of her head, into the wispy hair just above the ear. A corner of the brick bites into her, flinging her down onto the pile, onto another brick. You hit her again. The bricks squeeze her head like a pair of nutcrackers squeezes a walnut.

You do it to save Joseph Serridge. You do it for him.

"I saved you," he repeats. "I dealt with everything. Ever since then I've had people whispering about me behind my back." He grins at you, delighted with his own wit. "I did it all for you."

"I hate you," you say.

His smile broadens. "It's over. Live and let live, eh?"

"Where is she?"

"None of your business. By the way, why the devil didn't you leave the handbag at Waterloo? That was the plan. Then people would have thought she'd caught a train somewhere. It would have helped."

"I burned it on the range instead."

"Was her diary in it? I forgot it had a side pocket. There's just a chance it was in there. Did you look?"

"No."

For the first time he looks worried, as well he should. Because anyone who reads the diary will know who was really responsible for Philippa Penhow's death. Joseph Serridge kills without lifting a hand.

"I've looked everywhere at the farm for it." He stares at you and then shrugs. "You're sure you burned the handbag?"

You nod.

"Then there's nothing more to say. It's over, understand? No more little surprises in the post or anywhere else. If I were you I'd marry that young man of yours and go as far from London as you can."

"I don't want to marry anyone," you say. "Ever."

He shrugs again and walks away without saying goodbye. Glancing down, you see that your foot has nudged the brown canvas bag holding your father's upholstery tools. You stoop and take out the long needle, eighteen inches of steel with a champagne cork at either end for safety. Daddy never used it. You remove one of the corks.

You follow Joseph Serridge down the path. He is already climbing into his car. He hears the sound of the latch on the gate behind him and turns, half in and half out of the car.

"What is it?"

You bring the needle up in an underarm blow that catches him under the ribs. It goes in a good four or five inches. But nothing seems to happen. He stands there, frozen, neither in nor out of the car. It is too dark to see his face clearly. You pull out the needle and thrust it in again, this time harder, gripping the end with the cork in both hands. The tip jars against bone, then dives deeper. He sinks back into the car and makes a contented sound, as if he has slumped into an armchair by the fire after a long walk.

You can't leave him there. You look up and down the road. You look up at the windows of the houses on either side. You lift up the leg that is still outside the car. It bends at the knee. You push it in. You open the opposite door and try to pull him over the seats. But he's such a big man, so heavy. You haul his head and shoulders into the passenger side of the car but his legs remain on the driver's side. You take off one of his shoes and manage to get his left leg past the gear lever and over to the passenger side. There's nothing you can do about the right leg, which remains obstinately in the well below the steering wheel.

You shut the door and leave him there while you return to the house and change your slippers for rubber-soled shoes. You fetch your coat, hat, handbag and Aunt Philippa's diary. Soon the pair of you are driving down Haverstock Hill. You adjust to the unfamiliar car and its controls very quickly. The spare leg keeps getting in the way of the pedals but somehow you manage. You reach Camden Town and your sense of achievement grows. On and on you go, more or less in a straight line. You know the way because you walked here the other night, mile after mile, when you left Serridge's heart hanging from the pump by the pub.

As you turn into Holborn, a patroling policeman glances incuriously at you. You thread your way through the streets until at last you see the brightly lit windows of the Crozier. The pub is painted purple, like a slab of meat, like a bleeding heart.

You turn into the alley. When you reach the square, you drive around it, sweeping it with the headlights. No one is out, but there are lights in the two ground-floor windows of number seven.

You park by the pump and put on the handbrake. The engine stalls and the car bucks. You look at Joseph Serridge. The light from the pub reflects in one glassy eye. You get out of the car and reach into the back for your handbag. You open it and take out the diary. You have come to your decision about it. You drop the diary on the driver's seat and close the car door. You walk toward Charleston Street.

The pub door slams behind you. There are footsteps. You glance back, ready to run.

"Hello-ello," a man says. "It's my old friend Joe. Shake a leg, old boy. They're calling last orders."

The old man is very drunk. He's looking at the car. He hasn't even seen you standing behind him.

He opens the passenger door and pats Serridge's head. "Come on, old man, rise and shine. I say—you're a bit squiffy, eh?"

You walk quietly out of Bleeding Heart Square and into the gray sprawl of the city under a sky without any stars.